WISH
UPON THE
STARS

MALCOLM TENT

WISH UPON THE STARS

A Superhero Cultivation LitRPG

Book 5

MALCOLM TENT

Timeless
Wind

First published by Timeless Wind Publishing LLC 2024

First edition

Line editing by J. Massat. Proofreading by Lorne Ryburn.

Beta read by Morcant.

Cover art and typography by Richard Sashigane.

Recap of Book 4

After learning that another Wishmaster Candidate is on Callus, Shane is reeling from shock. He consults with his Uncle Zeke, who suspects that this candidate might be trying to take control of the local Wish Curse Palace (WCP) branch to undermine Shane's candidacy. If that was the case, the other candidate would likely ally with a faction within the WCP in order to exert her influence.

Shane and his team decide to investigate, visiting the Flame Riot Militia while posing as recruits. Burning Fist, the leader of the Militia, sees through their ruse but recognizes Cark's rare blue-flame pyrokinetic ability. He offers the young bounty hunter a lucrative position in exchange for information.

Cark joins the Militia, gaining access to valuable intel about the power dynamics in G-district. He reveals to Shane that an unknown force is seizing control of the territory left vacant by the death of Aiden, the leader of the Heartrippers. Investigating further, Shane and his team discover the Jerks are involved in this power grab, working to destabilize both the Cavalcade (short for Cicero Castleton's Captivating Circus Cavalcade) and the Militia.

Shane and Callie decide to help the Cavalcade, and their efforts earn them an audience with Cicero Castleton, the leader of the carnival. He reveals that a disgruntled manager, Starbreak (also known as Melissa, or Mel), is trying to overthrow him. Cicero explains how he had a falling-out with his brother Abel, who Shane knows as the sausage-selling Spruce Bunny, and that Mel wants to take revenge on Cicero for forcing his brother to leave the Cavalcade.

To regain control of his circus, Cicero tasks Shane and Callie with retrieving a crucial deed hidden in a labyrinth guarded by a phantasmal copy of his brother Abel. However, they quickly realize the challenge is incredibly dangerous, and that Cicero had deliberately sent them into a death trap.

They manage to survive the treacherous maze thanks to Callie's newly acquired Beginner Trap Mastery Skill (granted by Shane) and defeat the guardian thanks to the fact that Abel's copy has grown bored protecting the deed. As part of their deal, Cicero provides Shane and his team with F-ranked gear, though Shane no longer trusts the man due to his deceitful nature.

For the next part of their plan, Shane and his team infiltrate Starbreak's faction within the Cavalcade, the Starburst Pavilion. To be accepted into the faction, they participate in the Mirror Trial, a combat test where Pavilion hopefuls must face and defeat a reflection of themselves. They all pass, each utilizing unique strategies and skills, with Jessie claiming the Pavilion's captive F-ranked bear, Randall, as her own. From Abel's former teacher, the gravity-defying and soda-brewing Alden, they learn that Mel is collaborating with a mysterious faction.

Recognizing that they may be facing a conflict with an E-ranked faction, Shane and his team go to find backing of their own. They visit the Beast Lord Garden where they meet E-ranker Melinda and her Moondancer Weasel, Travis. Then they go to Sanctuary Hall, where Shane senses some-thing amiss with the seemingly benevolent Peace Lord. Finally, they choose to meet with Silent Dagger, led by a mysterious man known as the Nothing. The Nothing is revealed to be Callie's Uncle, Alexander Reynolds—Midknight's identical twin brother. Alexander explains that he fled Velan years ago to avoid being associated with Midknight. He offers to help Callie with Shadow Manipulation, but she declines because she wants to follow her own path.

As the conflict around the Cavalcade escalates, they realize that Sanctuary Hall is the faction working with Mel to take down the Cavalcade. When a secret meeting goes awry, Abel steps in, killing several Sanctuary Hall members to save Shane and his friends. Realizing that Sanctuary Hall will retaliate against the Cavalcade, Abel agrees to return to the circus to help.

Shane formally allies with the Beast Lord Garden, revealing his Wish ability to Melinda, the Beast Queen, in exchange for her support. He secures a contract as guest elder, guaranteeing protection and resources from the E-ranked faction.

With the Beast Lord Garden's elite G-rank forces bolstering their ranks, they prepare to defend the Cavalcade. During the ensuing battle, Sanctuary Hall unleashes the terrifying Wendigo, a former Ascendant who embraced a monstrous racial trait for power. With a combination of Shane's stored fire attacks and Randall the bear's brute strength, they defeat the creature.

Natalie, the other Wishmaster candidate, arrives and quickly realizes that fighting Shane and his friends is more trouble than it's worth. They come to an agreement—Natalie will withdraw from the Cavalcade, and in exchange Shane will offer her slots if he wins the upcoming Moonsong Glade tournament. Natalie also agrees to reserve slots for Shane and his friends—if they can defeat the rest of the Peace Lord's forces. Gaining access to the Moonsong Glade is a highly coveted prize. It offers the chance of obtaining Moonglow dew, which can grant the user an extra point of Impact.

With their agreement in place, Shane and his team rush to help their allies. They find that the Peace Lord's forces include Serenity, his daughter, and Beat and Sever, two powerful members of the Titan Twenty. Despite being outmatched, they utilize a combination of Skills, tactics, and stored attacks to gain an advantage. The fight is grueling and brutal, but they slowly whittle down their opponents and claim victory.

With Sanctuary Hall's forces routed, the Cavalcade is safe. Shane meets a second time with his cousin Natalie, securing their temporary alliance with their Wish abilities.

In the aftermath of the fight, Cicero tries to force Mel out of the Cavalcade for working with the Peace Lord, forcing Abel to make a decision between his partner and brother. However, before the conflict can escalate, Callie offers a solution. As a part of their deal with Cicero, Shane's team claims the Starburst Pavilion and its forces as their own territory. This leaves Shane, Callie, Benny, and Jessie in control of a formidable force within the WCP and poised for future challenges.

And the first challenge on their plate? Preparing for the Moonsong Glade Tournament.

Chapter One

THE WHOLE "CHECKING ON STAT GAINS" thing didn't really happen until the next day. We talked a while about the Pavilion, but eventually I caught Jessie starting to nod off and we decided to head home. She'd been life force juicing us all for most of the battle, so I wasn't really tired yet, but I knew I was going to be. Jessie's ability was damn convenient, but it wasn't infinite or free. The energy could be supplied, the life force healed you and energized you, but it didn't really fuel the actions you took with that energy, just repaired the damage from them.

It sounded like a meaningless distinction, until the charge ended, and you crashed. After just one or two boosts, it wasn't too serious, but I'd been spamming those damn heal bursts all day, and I was going to drop like a rock when we got back. Which I did. We made it back to the house just in time for me to collapse in bed and sleep for about eleven hours, thankfully completely unbothered by any outside forces as I recovered from an extremely emotionally and physically taxing day of combat.

When I woke up, I dragged myself out of my room, yawning loudly and waving to Cark and Cass, who were in the living room watching some cartoon or other. Cark waved back, looking as drained as I was, probably from constant power use. Benny was curled up on the other couch, and Jessie was sitting on the floor next to Cass, watching with her. As I headed into the kitchen, I found Callie sitting on a stool, sipping a cup of coffee and looking haggard.

I leaned down to give her a quick kiss, and she pulled back. "Gross," she groaned in annoyance. "Morning breath. Brush your teeth first." I plucked her cup of coffee from her fingers, took a sip, swished it around in my mouth, and spit it into the sink before giving her a grin. I handed it back to her, but she pushed it away. "Ew, no thanks. I'll make a fresh cup." Her eyes narrowed. "Unless you're planning to replace that one?"

"Oh, come on," I said with a laugh. "Spitting it in the sink means I didn't backwash." She glared at me venomously and I put my hands up in placation. "Sorry, sorry. I'll make you a new one. It was just a joke." I probably should have felt that out first. Some people were weird about drinking after anyone else. I made a point of putting extra effort into her coffee, giving her a huge mug with exactly the sweetener and amount of cream she preferred.

I passed it to her, and she took a long sip. "Not terrible," she intoned gravely. "I guess I can let it slide this time, but don't do it again. Your jokes aren't funny when they're at the expense of my coffee." She shooed me toward the stove. "As your final act of penance, make me an omelette. Goat cheese and fennel sausage. Five eggs."

That got a laugh from me. "Oh, I see how it is. Play up your emotional trauma so I'll be forced to be your personal chef. Fine. Since I was in the wrong, I'll play along just this once." Which was bullshit. I was always happy to cook for Callie and we both knew it; we were just bantering. I took out a full dozen eggs, deciding to make one for me as well. "So. I didn't get to ask last night, how many points did you get after the fight? I'm assuming you got some like I did?"

She grinned. "Yup. Twenty points of Creation, fifteen points of Might, ten of Perception, ten of Fantasy, and weirdly five of Vitality. I'd guess that we weren't the only ones, either. I suspect Abel and Mel were the subject of more of the stories about what happened than we were. My totals are up pretty high. I broke eight hundred points overall, which means I'm only two hundred away from F-rank." Her voice was nearly shaking with excitement at reaching the same height as our Guild Master back home, and so much earlier than she had ever imagined.

Calliope Reynolds: G-rank.

Ability: Beginner Shadow Embodiment—The ability to control and shape shadows, either molding them into

*constructs or imbuing them into specially prepared
objects to enable enhancement and control.*

Might: 198
Impact: 12
Vitality: 142
Fantasy: 85
Focus: 58
Perception: 175
Creation: 132

Pets: Wolf named Rellia

*Skills: Minor Tracking, Beginner Stealth, Beginner Trap
Mastery, Beginner Disguise, Lesser Balam Mastery,
Beginner Shadow Manipulation Mastery*

I whistled at the numbers. "Damn. Your Might has almost broken two hundred. Are you sure you want to rank up like that? From what I can tell, the result of synergizing takes into account a lot of factors, and stats are one of them. You have that Shadow Manipulation Skill to mix in, and if your Might is so high, you're going to end up with something physical and close-combat when you do it. It might be a good idea to put the rest of your upcoming points into Perception or Creation."

My girlfriend let out a sigh. "I'll consider it. Might is damn useful, and it makes fights insanely convenient, but you aren't wrong that it's not the main aspect of my combat style. Still, a more physical ability might not be as unsuited to me as you're thinking. I'll probably push Creation and Perception like you suggested, but don't be surprised if having high Might pays off in an unexpected way. I have some ideas for what I may get from the mix, and it's something I've never heard of a shadow manipulator getting, at least not around here."

I tried to pry into that statement, but she refused to say any more. I just rolled my eyes. If she wanted to keep it secret until rank up, that was her call.

"Anyway. I got a solid boost too. Thirty points to Vitality, probably from all the heal bursts, twenty-five to Might, twenty to Focus, and ten to Creation. I kind of wish I'd gotten some Fantasy, but it seems like none of my tricks really push my legend in that direction. I have other ways to pad that number, though, so it hardly matters." The stats had applied in my sleep, much like the first time I'd gained them. So I hadn't had some big dramatic stat dump.

Wishmaster Candidate Status: G-rank.

Ability: Beginner Wish—Five times a day, grant a Beginner wish in return for proper compensation. Wish must be feasibly achievable by the candidate's own efforts within a three-day period with current statistics.

Might: 122
Impact: 12
Fantasy: 21
Vitality: 101
Focus: 108
Perception: 90
Creation: 92

Pets: Wolf named Jin

Stored: 3 shadow attacks, 5 triple-strength tranq blows, 2 triple-strength density-shifted attacks, 1 spider leg attack, 2 heal bursts

Skills: Beginner Doom Sovereign Mastery, Beginner Enchanting Mastery (four charges per point of Impact), Lesser Cooking Mastery, Lesser Inventing Mastery, Lesser Stealth, Minor Piano Mastery, Minor Gymnastics Mastery, Minor Swimming Mastery, Minor Guitar Mastery, Minor Singing Mastery, Minor Poker Mastery, Minor Archery Mastery, Minor Boxing Mastery, Lesser Balam Mastery, Minor First Aid Mastery, Minor Herbalism Mastery

My stats were looking fantastic. I'd officially made it past a hundred in three of them, was only ten points from that milestone in two others, and had broken the five-hundred-point barrier on the way. I was actually at a level where I wasn't much weaker than your average G-ranker in individual stats. At least not in their unspecialized stats. Not that it would matter for long. "So," I said with a sigh as I started the omelette. "My cousin says this tournament is a big deal, and that it's aimed at the peak of G-rank."

Callie made an interested sound. "Yeah, when is it going to be? Even for us, breaking through too soon isn't going to be simple. I mean, granted, we all have some elixir capacity left, most of us a decent chunk, so we can boost stats that way. But still, Jessie and Benny are both pretty low in the G-ranks. I'm not sure if we can rank them up in time for them to be combat-viable if it's too soon. Hell, I'd say we couldn't rank ourselves up in time and still be able to put up a fight, if not for how specialized I am and your new tricks."

I sighed at that. "Two months, from what I can tell. You're right, though. I don't have the capacity to rank all of us up that quickly. Especially not with three of my wishes promised to the Beast Lord Garden." I was already kind of regretting that decision, but in the end, it didn't actually hinder me so much as force me to dedicate three of those wishes to myself daily. Plus, it left forty or so wishes for me to use to continue boosting Benny and Jessie. Not nearly enough to get them to F-rank in time for the tournament, but enough to get started.

I felt a poke in my ribs and turned to see Callie smiling up at me. "Hey, stop being such a worrier. Even if they can't participate in the tournament, we can still have them up to speed by the time we have to go to the actual dungeon, right? It's not like a tournament that size is going to be quick and painless. We'll need to deal with plenty of bullshit to get through it. That just leaves us entering as a duo. Which is fine with me. Though it's also possible Mel and Abel could be entering. Hard to say with them."

That was a good point. Abel seemed to want to be left alone, but how much of that was just trying to avoid giving his brother a chance to start trouble and drag him into it was hard to say. The man had a natural incli-nation for battle that couldn't be common even on higher-ranked planets, and a genuine love of combat. With the Pavilion severed from the circus and his own return to his former home, not to mention Mel's involvement in the place, it wasn't exactly out of the question for Apollyon and Star-breaker to return to Rajak in style.

I was reminded of my first rank up, and how I'd had to accept it. I couldn't remember hearing anything about suppressing your rank, but then again, who would bother? Maybe they'd reached F-rank a long time ago and just decided to stay where they were. It certainly fit Abel's whole foundation-building strategy. It would be convenient if nothing else. Assuming they even wanted to enter. It also opened up the possibility we would be facing other G-rankers who had done the same thing.

Either way, we had plenty of training to do before the tournament, stats to gain, combat to master, and attacks to stockpile, in my case. I had forty-eight charges per day to use for my DS Mastery now, or any Enchanting I needed to do, with the foundation to double that again sometime down the line. I still had to upgrade all my subskills in DS Mastery to reach Intermediate with it and unlock new ones too.

There were more things to do than I could possibly count, and more ways to get stronger than I could imagine. Part of me felt overwhelmed by the idea of it, and part of me was just excited. For now, I would just focus on making breakfast for Callie, and then we could check in with the others about their own gains from the big blowout. After that, I was thinking a trip up to the Academy was long overdue. We should check in with Grimmengap and invite them to the Pavilion, and collect the points from the mission we had completed. I was sure our rankings had dropped. Might as well get them back up. At the very least, I doubted we would be bored anytime soon.

Chapter Two

AFTER BREAKFAST, we went and grabbed the others. It was decided we could do the debrief on how they'd grown on the way, so we piled into the car after saying goodbye to Cass and Cark and headed for the Academy. As usual, Jessie drove because we wanted to arrive at our destination via landing and not smashing into the ground in a horrifying explosion of twisted metal. Callie was mostly used to being forbidden to operate the thing, so she hardly even pouted, though I was secretly glad she hadn't stopped completely because she had a gorgeous pout. Not that I would tell her that to her face.

Benny (being the one who wasn't driving) was the first one to catch us up, after hearing about our own growth. "Damn, that's an impressive jump for both of you. I went up twenty-five Perception, twenty Might, and twenty Creation. That last one kind of confused me, but I have to assume someone was talking about the origin of my ability being Inventing.

"Only real downside is that I guess I got Creation instead of Focus, which is what I needed, but I can always trade some attacks for more points in that." He shuddered at the idea. "Those spider leg attacks hurt a ton, but it sounds like you got some serious use from them. I might be willing to try again sometime. Anyway, this was what I ended up with."

Benicio Cortez: G-rank.

Ability: Lesser Mechanical Embodiment—Allows the integration of existing inventions into the user's body for the purposes of strengthening and enhancing them.

Might: 84
Impact: 12
Fantasy: 10
Vitality: 31
Focus: 75
Perception: 42
Creation: 30

Pet: Wolf named Rolf

Current integrated tech: 9/10.
Torso: extending rope.
Right fist: triple punch.
Left forearm: long range attack attraction.
Left fist: minor slow acting tranquilizer effect.
Right foot: density shifting to create heavier kicks and more powerful jumps.
Left foot: momentum neutralization to allow stopping instantly.
Head: slight cognitive boost to allow more thinking time.
Back: ability to grow a shell to tank damage.
Chest: pair of golden G-rank spider legs that arch up from the shoulders.

Skills: Minor Cooking Mastery, Beginner Inventing Mastery, Minor Haggling Mastery, Minor Stealth Mastery

They were solid gains. Now that I had those three mandatory wishes reserved for the Beast Lord Garden, an attack stockpile was the best way to help my friends grow from here, and I needed one badly myself. I'd burned off most of mine during the battle, but they'd been indispensable to the fight as a whole. Plus, Benny's stats were so low already that the additions to Creation and Perception provided at least a solid baseline for him to work with. No matter how specialized, it was a good idea to have at least some foundation in the other stats, especially something like Perception.

Jessie's cheerful voice rang out from the front seat. "Wow, not bad at all. I got a huge points dump into Vitality, obviously. Fifty points directly. I also got twenty-five in Focus, probably for the mental component of beast taming. Then fifteen points in Perception... most likely from using my raven to scout out Cicero's tent before we went in." I could hear the annoyance in her voice. "Once again I'm absurdly specialized without even trying. Though it's nice I at least managed to get my last two stats unlocked. It feels... strange. Hard to describe. I ended up with this, though, statwise."

Jessica Evans: G-rank.

Ability: Beginner Lifeweaving—Infuse living things with life itself and direct their actions while the user's power flows through them. Control has limited effect on sapient entities. Prolonged exposure to life energy may cause lasting effects in controlled nonsapient subjects.

Might: 52
Impact: 12
Fantasy: 28
Vitality: 191
Focus: 25
Perception: 15
Creation: 8

Pets: Wolf named Lily and bear named Randall (F-rank)

Skills: Beginner Horticulture, Beginner First Aid, Minor Herbalism, Minor Flower Arrangement, Minor Beast Taming Mastery

It was staggering how high Jessie's Vitality was, given her low total point count, but then again, her power *was* life. I couldn't think of anyone whose ability exemplified a stat so perfectly. It also explained how fast she was growing. Fifty points was a crazy amount, but it made sense. Our world tended to favor big flashy feats, and Jessie's healing had always been staggeringly effective whenever it was used. She was naturally suited to rapid growth whenever she was in battle, especially with a tamed beast like Randall.

I was honestly wondering if we should bring her with us to the tournament, but it seemed unlikely to go well. Even if Randall could keep up, she wouldn't be able to, and I had no way of raising her to F-rank fast enough to be viable. Hell, I wasn't sure *we* would be viable. We were bound to run into people just as established in the F-ranks as Abel was in the G-ranks. Could we even take someone like that? They wouldn't *be* Abel, obviously, because then we would just get crushed, but we had a long way to go, and I had a feeling I would need every advantage to make it through.

Still, we'd all made great progress from this, and it was nice to hear. I was particularly glad that Jessie and Benny had slept through their gains too. Given how large the percentage jump had been, I was guessing it wouldn't have been pleasant to experience awake. It made me wonder if letting the points slowly come in your sleep was the proper way to do things.

I decided to change topics, because we had a big one to discuss. "What are the chances there are other jobs to do with what we found? I mean, it was a pretty big conspiracy. With all that information already out, it's only a matter of time before it leaks. Might as well cash in on the points before it hits the grapevine."

"Should be decent," Callie said, contemplative. "I mean, we'll need to talk to Celine about the details, since she knows the place pretty well, but there's no way we haven't moved up the scale on what missions we can take. We might need to do some of the tests over and crank our rankings a bit. But that might be a good idea anyway. If nothing else, Jessie has a pretty amazing Vitality stat. I don't actually know what the Vitality test entails, but getting her rank up will give her some regular points that should boost her overall ranking."

I groaned a bit at the thought of all the numbers needed to calculate the rankings. There were so many factors, it really boggled the mind. The only upside to this whole mess was that the tournament was going to be far more important than the usual local one, so we didn't need to bother with ranking up to join. I was pretty sure the Moonsong Glade tournament didn't have that requirement, though I should probably learn the details soon.

All of that was a problem for future Shane. I decided to tease my best friend instead. "So, Benny. Haven't seen your girl in a while, huh? Think she's going to be mad you haven't been around? Or have you been sneaking away for long soulful phone calls every night to check in?" He had, and I knew that, which was why I said it in the most irritating way possible. In reality, I thought it was sweet, but I also remembered him constantly harassing me about Callie, and I was owed vengeance.

My best friend narrowed his eyes at me. "A joke about me being too attentive? How clever. Did you come up with that this morning while you were making your girlfriend her extravagant breakfast?" Callie smirked a bit at that, though whether it was from amusement at the barb or happiness at the memory itself, I had no idea.

I brushed off the shoulder of my coat. "Extravagant? Oh, I'm sorry, is an omelette a difficult meal for you to prepare? I'm happy to do things for Callie, but it was hardly necessary to put myself out for such a simple recipe. I think you're confusing my effort with your own incompetence." My faux-haughty tone got a legitimate laugh from my girlfriend this time. Along with an eyeroll.

"Alright, you idiots," she said through her laughter. "You're both stoic badasses who don't wear your hearts on your sleeves and remain a mystery to those around you. Can we get back on topic now? I swear, going anywhere with the two of you is like herding cats." Despite the mocking words, her tone was fond as she curled against me, and I put my arm around her as I laughed along.

Benny snickered a bit too. We both knew we were being stupid, but familiar childhood rituals were comforting. We spent the next hour or two talking about possible missions we could do to improve our rankings, provided we had enough time to squeeze them in. We wouldn't, obviously, but it was nice to just go over some of the tasks we'd first seen at the information hall, now that we were stronger than we could possibly have imagined when we first arrived at the Academy.

Part of me wanted to go challenge Fisher or one of the other heavy hitters from the scavenger hunt, just to see what they were capable of and how their growth stacked up to us. I dismissed the thought immediately. It seemed unlikely they had managed to keep up, except maybe Fisher who had been pretty terrifying in particular, with a hell of a reputation for a freshman. Maybe he would surprise us. Plus, there were always elixirs. Even then, I doubted he would have the combat ability of members of the Titan Twenty. Looking back, Beat and Sever were exponentially scarier than any of the freshman we had come across, and they were the weakest of their lineup.

When we finally arrived at the school, we headed straight for Grimmen-gap's dorm. Sarah, their cleric, answered, and beamed as soon as she saw us. She gave us each a hug. "Hey, guys! It's so good to see you. Been busy lately? We haven't heard from you in a while." She shot Benny a wink. "Celine has been extra quiet lately, and that's saying something. I don't think she's mad or anything, but she always seems happier when you're around."

My best friend's face lit up a bit at the thought that the pretty elf girl was so affected by his presence, and even I didn't have the heart to tease him about his obvious excitement. Jokes aside, I was really happy for Benny. I hoped he found with Celine what I had with Callie, and I reached down to lace my fingers with hers at the thought. She didn't look away from Sarah, but she squeezed my hand, her cheeks flushing slightly.

We headed inside to chat with the others, and I looked around with a wide smile. It felt... strange, to be back. It had been such a short time, really, but we'd changed so much. Still, it was comfortable. We hadn't spent much time in the dorm, but it had been warm and welcoming for the time we had spent.

I hoped not too long from now, our friends would feel the same way about the Pavilion.

Chapter Three

CELINE AND MARTIN were both thrilled to see us, though with Celine, it was hard to tell. Still, I had enough Perception to pick up the minute signs of her excitement at having her boyfriend back. Not that it was at all obvious from the sedate way she approached him for an admittedly warm but brief hug. Jessie all but tackled her in a hug of her own after that, then hugged Sarah for good measure because she hadn't had a chance to do so earlier, and it was hard not to smile at our shortest team member's enthusiasm.

We dropped into chairs around the room after the greetings, none of us in too big of a rush to get to the information hall. The points weren't going anywhere. I never stopped enjoying the moments of relaxation, mostly because I knew how few and far between they were. "So," I said jovially, "what have you all been up to while we were getting involved in political bullshit that was way over our heads? I get the feeling it was way more sensible than what we were doing for the last week or two."

I was curious what a "normal" few weeks of advancement looked like for an average G-ranker, as much as that term could apply to any hero. Though I supposed some of the only Job-type cultivators on the planet were a bad example of "typical."

Celine, who sat down next to Benny with graceful and remote poise (though not without slipping her hand into his surreptitiously), spoke up with a small smile. "Mostly we just did missions for the crafting hall. They aren't as lucrative as the ones at the information hall, but they're safer on the whole. Still, we haven't been lax. We've been developing quite the reputation among our classmates for efficiency and effectiveness. We've all made some decent gains from some of the feats we've accomplished. Nothing huge like the scavenger hunt, but enough small tasks add up."

"I bet," I said, interested. "I imagine that's a more stable way to progress. Don't you stop gaining points for the small tasks eventually, though? Not that I know what kind you were doing, but I know that gains are based on the spread of your legend, and when people expect something from you, your renown doesn't exactly grow. "

Celine's placid expression broke into a shark-like smile. The flash of teeth appeared and vanished too fast for most people to even notice, but none of us had trouble spotting it. "They might have expected it, except they seemed to be under the impression that we were suited to much lower-level tasks. We may have been the first-place team in the scavenger hunt, but people weren't sure how much progress we made. We started missions only slightly above the level of the last one we took, and people were shocked at how quickly we completed them."

Callie's jaw dropped open. "You sneaky bitch!" she said admiringly. "I would have never thought of sandbagging so I could put on a show of rapid growth. Shit. That would have been a great plan. I'm pissed you didn't share, not that I can blame you. Still, though, I wouldn't be too smug about it. We might not have been as clever, but we made some damn good progress during our time away. You'd barely even recognize us if you saw us in battle after all we've been through."

It was hard to read her, but I was pretty sure I saw a flash of competitive interest in Celine's normally tranquil eyes. Benny, who probably *didn't* want to deal with his girlfriend being annoyed when we unilaterally curb-stomped her team in a friendly sparring match, interrupted before things got too far. "By the way, Cel, did you guys hear about this new tournament for this special F-ranked dungeon? Apparently a ton of the strongest fighters from the whole star system are heading here to compete in it."

Whether he actually wanted to share or had told her last night on the phone and was trying to change the subject, I had no idea, but if he had, she hadn't mentioned it to the others, because Sarah looked intrigued. "Tournament? I knew there was a regular one around here, but it sounds like this one's a bit bigger. What can you tell us about it? Sounds like you guys are signing up, and if you're in, we might have a shot too." She gave us a wide grin at that last part, obviously half in jest, though also half-serious.

I picked it up from there, figuring I'd help my buddy out with his distraction. "It's aimed at peak G-rankers. Apparently the participants will be expected to break through after the winners are decided before being allowed to actually enter the dungeon. I've been thinking over the reason, and while supposedly it's to prevent the larger forces from using their foundations to bully the smaller ones, I'm pretty sure it's meant to be an equalizer of sorts. Ranks can span a wide range of stat totals. By making sure that only newly Ascended F-rankers enter, they ensure that the fighters all have around a thousand points total."

This was Callie's theory, and my girlfriend gave me a slight smirk for taking credit. I didn't care, though, I would have come up with it eventually. It wasn't my fault she was a sneaky political mastermind. Besides, she got credit for all the stuff-punching I did. We were a team, which meant we should share all of our accomplishments equally.

I paused for a second before sighing. Even I couldn't think that with a straight face. So I added, "At least, that's what Callie thinks. It sounds legit to me, though."

She gave me a look of surprise tinged with gratitude, and I was suddenly much less embarrassed to be giving up credit. I'd have given up plenty more of it to see that look on her face. I felt like I'd just passed some kind of boyfriend test that neither of us realized I was taking. But I wasn't going to question it. If I'd made her happy, that was good enough. No need to think too much about it.

Celine coughed politely, drawing my attention to the fact that we'd kind of been having a moment that excluded everyone else in public. I cocked my head inquiringly, not bothering to feel abashed or self-conscious about that. She smiled slightly. "That certainly sounds like an interesting event to participate in. Do you know any of the details of how it's going to work?"

"Sure," I said casually. "We know that much like the majority of Ascendant events, it's aimed at groups of ten. The winner gets ten slots to the Moonsong Glade. We have an agreement for slots with another group, so if we win, we'll need to give up three. You guys can sign up as well, I'm told that it's an open tournament. There's going to be G-rankers from other planets all over the system, though. I think there will be more than just people from our system entering, but I haven't had a chance to confirm that."

I made sure to point out that they could sign up, because we weren't going to be inviting them to come with us. As much as I'd have loved to bring them, there was no chance they were at a level to help us actually win. With access to powerhouses like Cark, Abel, and Mel, it would be stupid for us to team up with relative newbies like Grimmengap. Of course, I didn't say that directly, and Callie could change her mind, but I knew my girlfriend well enough to understand how pragmatic she could be.

They didn't seem to take offense, at least. They looked intrigued, and Celine looked kind of excited. I breathed an internal sigh of relief at the fact that I hadn't accidentally started a fight by excluding them. Then I flicked my eyes to Callie, mentally passing the ball now that the explanation was done, and she stood, clapping her hands once purposefully. "Well! We can look into that more on the way, but I'd love to hit the information hall. We have a mission to turn in, and I'd really love to see how high it pushes our ranking up."

Everyone stood at that, not bothered that we were done relaxing. We still weren't in a hurry, and I doubted we would run or anything, but where we all hung out didn't matter, and advancement was always at least partly on all of our minds. Besides, we could still talk on the way. Being around others would just limit the topics a bit. We headed for the information hall, and as we went, Sarah dragged Jessie ahead and started asking her all about our adventures, and catching us up on theirs.

Grimmengap had been on several interesting missions while we had been away, I had to admit. Hunting a red cap tribe, a village of goblins out in the wilderness, an actual fucking minotaur, and tracking down and capturing an Ascendant with a specialized racial trait (a Lamia) who had been poisoning search parties recently. Sarah's priest abilities allowed her to neutralize poisons pretty well (the church dealt with the Black Sorrow Cult often, and the cultists *loved* poison) which made them an ideal party to track down the G-ranked devil.

The more monstrous bearers of racial traits were lumped together as demons, while the more abstract ones were called spirits. Not that demons should be confused with Devils, which, as we had been told, were a subspecies of that overarching group and were a whole other level of scary.

The Wendigo had been a demon, and the Lamia was the same, making it really impressive that Grimmengap had managed to subdue one.

In turn, Jessie filled our friends in on us joining up with the Beast Lord Garden, and a sanitized version of our adventures in G district, minus any sensitive information. That left her more room than I'd have suspected. It always amazed me how clever Jessie could be while keeping up that same impression of cheerful obliviousness. She was sharp as a knife when she needed to be.

By the time she finished talking, she'd managed to tell most of the story without giving away any secrets, and had roused Grimmengap's interest in the Starchaser Pavilion as a whole, inspiring them to promise to come visit after we finished our business on campus. Considering how small the Pavilion currently was, it would be amazing to have them come check it out and possibly join up. Especially if word got out about the place and some of the other Academy students entered as well.

As a guest elder, I was allied with the Beast Lord Garden, but not exactly part of it, which meant the Pavilion had the unique benefit of being a new and completely separate G-ranked force with explicit E-ranked backing. We were too new to matter to the old-timers, and too powerful to be messed with by upstarts, and I looked forward to seeing what we could do with a faction like that.

In the future, after we kicked ass at the tournament, I had a feeling people would be hearing all about the Starchaser Pavilion, and I couldn't wait.

Chapter Four

THE TRIP to the information hall was a short one. We managed to find a second mission that we had accomplished by accident, which was nice, and between the points, my own ranking jumped up to 245,806. It probably would have been a bigger jump, but a week or two with no progress had caused a serious ranking drop for us, and honestly I was lucky I managed to get higher at all.

Once we got through that, we headed for the Pavilion, and once we arrived, Callie, Benny, and Jessie took Grimmengap away for introductions while I finished up the wishes for Sloane (the Beast Lord Garden's top G-ranked member) and the organization's other elites. I actually managed to get some Fantasy this time—fifteen points, bringing me up to a grand total of thirty-six. Apparently Croll, another top G-ranker, had a surplus of the stat, which crossed off one thing on my list.

Finally, I joined back up with the others, who were being introduced to Abel, Mel, and Alden. I gave a short wave. "Hey all, sorry, had to check in with our people from Beast Lord Garden. How goes the introductions? Did you show them the obstacle course yet? Because seriously, that place is pretty fantastic." I had been floored my first time seeing it, and it was amazing for training, even if it made me a bit uncomfortable when it was actually in use.

Sarah was looking around in awe, clearly the most excited of the group. "No, but that sounds interesting. This whole place is amazing. I saw funnel cake on the way in. I love funnel cake. I'm definitely going to get some as we're leaving. I can't believe I missed it when I was here before." She was practically bouncing in excitement, and I had to fight down a smile at the enthusiasm.

"Actually," I said with amusement, "I had wanted to check in with Mel and Abel about a few things." I glanced at the red-bearded man whose leg I still had to offer to regrow. "Alden, can you show our friends around? You're the only one Cicero probably isn't too annoyed at right now. I wanted to talk to you as well, but it can wait until later." I'd offer him the wish later when we had a chance to talk in private.

He just chuckled. "Aye. The boy may have irritated his brother a bit with his earlier bullying. I can show them around." He turned a welcoming smile on Sarah. "You mentioned funnel cake, little miss? I know the best stall for it, and perhaps a few other delicious treats you might enjoy." He gestured for her to follow, and Sarah trailed after, already excitedly listing some of the things she hadn't been able to try last time we were down here.

Celine and Martin trailed behind, the elf girl dragging Benny along by the hand stoically enough that if I couldn't see her gripping him, I wouldn't have thought she cared one way or the other. Jessie decided to tag along with them, leaving Callie and I alone with Mel and Abel, which had been my aim. I turned to the rabbit-masked man. "Okay, first thing. Did you hear back about the ransom for Sanctuary Hall's people yet? Is the Pavilion allowed to keep that? We did capture them in the first place, and the negotiation is through the Beast Lord Garden."

Abel laughed. "Hello to you too, Solomon. But yes to both. We made the exchange. We forced Sanctuary Hall to cough up a hundred F-ranked chits per person. They're stupidly wealthy, so I figured I'd really put the screws to them. We have the funds earmarked for faction development, but we didn't want to actually spend them before consulting you." He grimaced. "Damn, I hate being a person who says things like that now. I can't believe I have a... *boss*." He shuddered theatrically.

"You always had a boss." Mel snorted. "I just wasn't paying you for your services." Ignoring her boyfriend's mortified look, she continued. "As for the funds... I can go over options with you if you want, or I can invest them for you. I've been running this place for years. I don't have a problem with you kids taking over if it means I'm finally free of Cicero's nonsense, but that doesn't make me any less experienced at the day-to-day."

I glanced over to Callie, giving her a nod, and she shot Mel a warm smile. "Hey, we aren't stupid. We don't know anything about this place. We put you both in charge because you know what to do better than us. Invest the money how you want. Maybe talk to Sloane, though. Beast Lord Garden are allies of ours. They might be able to set you up with some tamed beasts or something." She paused. "Actually, we might be able to do that. Agria is a hell of a tamer." She waited a bit, then shook her head. "Nah, stick with the experts. I think Agria needs to be around consistently to make that arrangement."

Mel looked intrigued. "I'll ask them about it. Even if we don't go that route, I'm sure they're in touch with some useful people. In either case, thank you for trusting us. This whole thing kind of came out of left field, but I appreciate you trying to work with us on this more than you can know."

Her voice softened as her eyes turned to Abel. "It's one of the many amazing things that I can hardly believe are happening right now. My life has gone through quite a few changes, and all for the best."

Returning the smile I could hear in her tone, Abel reached out and took her hand. Knowing how long they had been apart, neither Callie nor I could bear to cut things off when there wasn't some urgent crisis coming, so we gave them their moment. It admittedly dragged on for longer than was really comfortable for us (though taking my own girlfriend's hand and squeezing tightly certainly helped, as we stared at what might be future versions of us, hopefully without the long time apart in between).

Finally Abel let Mel's hand fall. Neither of them cleared their throat uncomfortably or tried to redirect attention. They just moved on from the moment, with none of the indecision or embarrassment a less stable couple might have had.

As they refocused, I turned to Abel. "So, with that out of the way, we had something we were hoping to talk to you both about. Something we think will help with the Pavilion's reputation as well as our power as individuals. What do you know about the Moonsong Glade?"

The rabbit-masked man shrugged. "Never heard of it. Doesn't exactly sound local, but to be fair, Callus is big, so there's a nonzero chance that it could be some small faction or location no one has ever mentioned to me. Still, if it was somewhere important, I'd think I would know about it. Am I to take it this is some newly discovered spot that could be a benefit to us?"

"Not exactly," I said uncertainly. "Or maybe? I'm honestly not clear on that. I know it's a dungeon, a very important one. I know that there's a tournament that involves everyone in the system coming up. If we win, we get ten slots to enter. I doubt we'll be the only ones, but I'm not sure who else might be there. Maybe people from something bigger than the star system? Whatever that is. Point is, I don't know if Moonsong Glade is *new*, but I know it's new to us."

Abel waved a hand casually. "Same thing. Dungeons are all old as dirt, but 'recently rediscovered' is the same thing as 'new' for our purposes. It's a star cluster, by the way. Star systems are smaller portions of star clusters. There are usually ten of them in each." He paused. "I've never been sure why they divide them like that. Someone out there is really obsessed with the number ten. Anyway, that means a hundred people will be entering, if it's a cluster event. I take it you want to enter this tournament?"

I nodded. "Exactly. The place is apparently able to spawn resources that increase Impact, which is huge. It would give us a massive boost against anyone our own rank, and help bridge the gap fighting up ranks. The only issue is that while the tournament is aimed at G-rankers, the dungeon itself is F-rank exclusive. If you wanted to participate, you would need to rank up. I know how long you've been at G-rank, I wasn't sure you would be willing."

"What?" Abel asked, blinking, tone confounded. "Why would I not want to rank up?"

I blinked back. I'd been expecting to have to convince him, and had about a dozen arguments and reasons lined up to convince him that this would be a good thing for the Pavilion and him in particular.

Cocking my head, I cautiously said, "Because you spent years at G-rank, and went out of your way not to gather any extra attention or break through, presumably so you could reinforce your foundation and become stronger at your current level? Asking you to throw all that away for my own plan just seemed kind of shitty, but I'm not sure we can win without you, so I decided to give it a shot."

The gale of laughter that came out as a response to that was *not* the reply I had expected. Abel doubled over cackling at something I didn't think was that funny, but I patiently waited for him to get the laugh out of his system. "Oh, wow." He wiped away a tear of laughter. "I needed that. Thanks. But no, I'm not some kind of eternal G-ranker who wants to become skilled enough to take on the whole universe without ever Ascending. There are limits to even my hubris. I had reasons to stick to this rank, but they're pretty much all gone at this point."

Mel shrugged. "I mostly stuck around at this level because I wanted to take care of the Pavilion while he was gone. If I ranked up, I would have been leaving them under Cicero's control when I inevitably ended up heading to F district. Now that we aren't a member of his faction anymore, and our new one has ties to E district, we have a lot more leeway to control how things go down here without stepping on toes even if we rank up. I'd be down to fight in a tournament if you guys need me. It would be a nice way to break back onto the scene."

"Hell yes," Abel said excitedly. "So many people have forgotten me. Now that I'm not living in self-imposed exile, I'm itching for a fight. Plus, if we're talking foundation, early Impact advancement is the best foundation buildup you can do. No way I'd miss something like that." He looked us over. "You do realize that in order to do this, you're going to need to be at the edge of a breakthrough when we go into the tournament? You're also nowhere near tough enough to manage against most of the Titan Twenty."

With a chuckle, I said, "Yeah, that's kind of the other reason we came here. We've been training with Alden, but I'd be pretty interested in getting some lessons from you two. Especially on cooperative combat. The two of us work well together, but you guys are like magic. It'll be tough to squeeze in, since the tournament is only two months out, but we have confidence we can manage. So, what do you say, you two up to do some team training?"

Somewhere deep down, a part of me that had nearly died after all the craziness of my life whispered to me that the vicious grin Abel answered with probably boded ill for us. That was just paranoia, though, right?

Chapter Five

"Ow!" I yelped as a rock smacked into the back of my skull. The stone turned to powder on impact, having been thrown hard enough to break on my higher-ranked head.

I reached up to grip my head with a hiss of pain, spinning around to spot the person who threw it. Something I had no luck doing while wearing this gods-damned blindfold. I heard a chuckle off to one side and whirled to face that direction.

"How is this a useful training exercise?" I snarled at Abel, who was completely hidden from my sight.

His voice echoed around me. "I already told you this. When you're working with a partner, you need to be able to function as if you're two halves of a whole. It's not enough to just cover their back. You need to abandon your own defense and dedicate yourself solely to theirs. A proper partnership means you can unleash your full attack power at all times with no thought to defending yourself. Protecting your partner can be done offensively, but in order for that to work, you need absolute trust."

I whirled uselessly in circles, listening for the sound of stones flying. Not near me, but off to the side, where Callie stood. I couldn't resist pointing out the obvious though. "Yes, but there has to be a better way to do that than... *this*. This is ridiculous—"

My eyes widened behind my blindfold as I heard a whoosh. Shooting out to attack the spot, I heard the stone split the air. My fist hit nothing, and Callie yelped in pain as the sound of a rock breaking against a human skull rang dully in the air.

I winced. "Sorry, baby." I heard a groan of annoyance in response, but Callie didn't speak. Admittedly, *I had* noticed that attack, if belatedly. I groaned. "Okay. I get the basic idea, but can you explain the actual mechanics of this bullshit again? Because if you can't make it make sense, I'm going to assume you just like throwing rocks at us."

That got a snicker from our teacher. "Fine. I'll explain it one more time. When you're operating as part of a team, you are half of a whole. Concentrating on protecting yourself and working with your partner are *two* tasks. Separate tasks that detract from each other. However, when you abandon self-defense and dedicate yourself completely to cooperation, you reach a level of cohesion impossible when you're just two independent entities supporting one another."

There was another whoosh of air and a crack against my skull as I staggered under another rock blow, yelping in pain. I wasn't allowed to block his attacks on me. Only the ones aimed at Callie. I also wasn't allowed to fucking *see*. Apparently the point of this was to hone our instinctual response to danger aimed at our partner, so that it would work indistinguishably from our own survival instinct. By making it perfect reflex to defend the other person, we would have deeper integration in combat.

Being able to see the attacks coming would make this a conscious effort rather than a reflexive action. So we both got to wear fucking blindfolds and try to defend the other person in darkness based on intuition and the brief instant of noise when the rock was launched. I sighed, devoting myself to perceiving... everything. I really needed to get this down, since we apparently wouldn't be allowed to stop until we managed it.

I closed my eyes (not that it mattered with the blindfold, but it just felt right) and focused on my senses. Hearing. Smell. Taste. Touch. Literally anything that could function in a helpful way. I could have used a Skill, obviously. Seek Hidden would be perfect here. But despite my complaining, I was mildly interested to see if this would work. Already I felt I was making progress, and I didn't want to ruin my possible gains by cheating. It would defeat the whole fucking purpose of asking for Abel and Mel's help if we just ignored them.

A sigh of air split the space a few feet to my side, and I lashed out at the spot as quickly as possible. At the last second, I altered my course, aiming instead right in front of where I'd heard it. I didn't nail it, but I *did* manage to slightly graze it. The grunt I heard from Callie sounded different.

"Time out!" Mel called. "That was actually close to a proper hit. Not exactly reflexive, you're thinking too much, but it's progress, so you can have a break."

I took off my blindfold, glancing over to see Callie brushing grey dust off her shoulder. The slight graze had changed the trajectory. That wasn't bad. Still. I had to question the process. "Okay. Being able to properly predict attacks is great and all, but I don't think this is having the effect you think it is. I'm just learning to predict attacks, and there are less stupid ways to do that."

Mel snickered at that. "Do you think so? Quick question, then. If you just heard the sound of the air being disturbed and reacted, how did you know what direction it was heading? You didn't just predict where it was going, you managed to perfectly match that prediction to where your partner was standing so you could properly react to it. You showed an innate grasp of exactly where Nightstrike was positioned without needing to call out to her or bother with verbal communication."

Abel stepped into view, tossing a rock up and down casually. "She's right. You might not think you're learning anything, but your baseline awareness of each other *is* improving. It's just a slow and irritating process to go through. Trust me. We went through this training too. It's never fun." He paused, catching the rock. "Well, that's not true. It's fun actually *doing* it to someone. But experiencing the training is never fun."

"I get it," I moaned in annoyance. "I just wish I felt like we were managing this effectively instead of stumbling through it. Can we take another minute? I need more time to mentally reset."

Abel looked dubious for a second, but finally nodded, and I exhaled with relief. There was such a thing as too much training. Sometimes your brain needed to shift back to a receptive state before you could learn more.

Producing a small case from his coat, he gestured us over to the edge of the ring to sit down. We were in the Pavilion, using some sort of training setup that he'd had on hand, bracelets that partially suppressed Perception, and probably did other things I didn't notice.

When we all sat down, he opened the case and pulled out what looked like energy bars, passing one to each of us. I took mine, sniffed it experimentally, then took a bite. I was pleasantly surprised by the taste of strawberries and cream, and chewed happily.

Eventually, I swallowed and turned to Abel with a question. "Can I ask you something? It might be a little abrupt, maybe even personal depending how you look at it."

He just shrugged, seemingly uncaring, and I paused to figure out how to frame my next words.

"How do you do it?" I asked. "How do you kill people so casually? We killed a bunch of people in the siege, I killed them. I know it was necessary, that they would have killed or hurt us, but it still makes me sick just thinking about it. How do you learn to ignore the part of you that recoils at that?"

Rather than be offended, Abel just made a noise of understanding and intrigue, like I'd asked something very interesting. "I suppose to answer that, I would need to know when it happened. My case was a bit different, though. Cicero and I lost our parents young, and I think that triggered our abilities sooner than was normal. We were still children when our powers came to the forefront. We ended up down here, where Alden took us in, and we were raised for this kind of life from a very young age."

He looked at Mel wistfully. "Mel was already here when we arrived. She awakened even earlier than we did. I never asked why. Didn't seem right. I suppose none of us ever had the resistance to ending others that normal people develop and Ascendants unlearn. For other Ascendants, part of it is recursion. Cultivation is brutal, we all know it deep down. We all know that there are only so many stories to tell, and that for ours to continue, others must end, even if we fight it.

"But," he said, "if you're asking how to turn that off, how to stop caring when you take a life... don't. It's inconvenient, and messy, but caring like that makes you better. It's a little bit of humanity that other Ascendants mostly don't have. Touchstones like that are, somewhat counterintuitively, good for holding off other forms of recursion as you grow. If nurtured properly, you can use that as a foundation to build the person you are in such a way that you'll come out stronger for it." He sighed. "I'm explaining this badly, but it isn't something you can understand without a decade or two of recursion behind you. Just trust me. Don't stop caring. Not until you have to."

It was strange talking to someone at the same rank as me who was already so much further into their life as an Ascendant. Even stranger because he was so much closer to becoming a legend than I was. We had the same Impact, but it felt like he'd left behind so much more of his humanity. Was it the time? Was I somehow avoiding recursion by sprinting through the ranks? But then again, had I really? I'd changed so much since becoming an Ascendant.

Maybe it was the fact that I was a superhero. Abel wasn't exactly a villain, the WCP didn't really delineate that kind of thing, but he wasn't considered a hero even back in the day. Abel was closer to a pure cultivator than a heroic cultivator. Hell, I didn't even know if he used the Job system. That wasn't the kind of thing you asked someone who was already going out of their way to help you.

I sighed. The subject of recursion never failed to unsettle me when it came up. This shit was complicated. I finished my power bar and popped to my feet, putting the wrapper in my pocket. "Alright. I think that's enough philosophy. I believe you two still have rocks to throw at our heads. I'd like to get this training over with so we can move on. You said this is a necessary first step, right?" I was now mostly convinced it wasn't just an excuse to beat on us, but I couldn't help but ask one more time. My questions couldn't possibly be more annoying than the training itself, so I hardly had a reason to feel bad.

Abel stood up, stretching casually despite having been doing nothing but throwing rocks at us for like, two hours. "Once your awareness of each other has reached an instinctive level, we can begin combat training. I'm not going to start teaching you when you'll just develop bad habits you'll need to unlearn. This is the first step. We need to get it right so the following ones will be built on a stable foundation." He tossed a rock up and caught it, giving me a vicious grin. "Now, blindfolds back on. We have work to do."

Joy. My head was aching already.

Chapter Six

IT TOOK us the whole day to learn how to properly internalize each other's positions at an instinctual level. I was almost positive we were doing it in a way that shouldn't even be possible, though I suspected the senses we got from the Fantasy stat were playing a part. Once we managed that, we were allowed to go home, with instructions to come back the next day bright and early.

When we did return, I got my wishes out of the way first thing: another fifteen points in Fantasy to shore up my biggest weakness, and because I was starting to see how valuable that stat actually was. I'd been using all five on the crew from the Beast Lord Garden, despite being able to spare two a day, because I really needed the points. I'd be free to use those spare two wishes a day for Callie soon enough, just as long as I didn't push her past G-rank.

Today, the exercise had changed. The blindfolds were gone. In exchange, we were expected to fight against ten Pavilion fighters without using any active Skills. Balam Mastery, for example, was fine, as was Gymnastics, but DS Mastery was out.

I'd expected the training from the day before to be immensely useful for our battle, and it definitely was, but not quite as much as I had hoped. I could intuit and intercept blows aimed at Callie, but only when I could reach them, which, with so many different points of attack, wasn't all the time.

Abel, to my surprise, didn't seem even remotely disturbed by this. During one of our breaks, I asked him about it, and his response shed some light on things. "Of course you aren't keeping up," he said with exasperation. "I told you that the rock exercise was only step one. I also told you step two would involve combat. This would be that. Learning to integrate your combat style into a singular whole is about more than keeping in mind where your other half is and reacting when they're attacked.

"How to explain this?" he asked rhetorically, then stopped to gather his thoughts. "What you have right now is the beginnings of an instinct. You react when your partner is attacked, but that isn't true cohesion, it's just a learned reflex. You've spent years training yourself and being taught by experience to protect your own body first. Your instinct is to survive, and then to react after that. You still need to unlearn that. The reflex you gained yesterday is only the beginning of that process."

Abel didn't bother allowing me any more questions. As I resumed training, I considered his words. Deflecting an attack against Callie was beginning to be instinct, but that was still limited. I was reacting, but only because I was ready and waiting for a blow. This was all still a conscious effort on my part. It would take more than a few hours of training to completely abandon my survival instincts in battle and learn to rely entirely on a partner.

Even thinking about it like that felt... dangerous. So much could go wrong. That was the point, though. Trust. Absolute knowledge of and faith in your partner. I'd seen what it led to during the siege, seen what that kind of combat style could become. Mel and Abel were monsters alone, but they were a force of nature together. Granted, the instincts couldn't be completely abandoned. I knew that. Abel fought alone at times, as did Mel, and if they just threw away all survival instinct at those times, they would probably be dead.

For now, we just had to focus on being part of the whole, on knowing each other better than we knew ourselves. As we fought, that seemed to become easier and easier. The training we'd done together over the months and the awareness we had developed blended together into one cohesive whole, letting us operate on a level that was already far beyond what we'd been able to do before.

It wasn't enough. Not yet. These were Pavilion warriors, powerful and skilled combatants who focused on martial prowess above all else, and they were a unified fighting force. Not like what we were trying to become, but they knew each other well.

Our biggest advantage was in the Balam Mastery Skill, actually. Callie and I both used Balam for our combat style, and its circular nature made a shifting front much easier to manage as we moved around each other and took advantage of this new defensive sense we had.

The longer it went on, the more sense I made of what Abel had said. I was waiting for Callie to be attacked even now, but waiting was an action I was taking. The downsides to that became apparent under the barrage of attacks. After I intercepted one, my body began to relax because I'd accomplished my goal. I wasn't in danger, and I'd defended Callie like I planned, so my task was done. It left me vulnerable to follow-ups and attacks from other angles.

I had to continue to polish this instinct like he'd said, to become more in tune with danger to my partner and less in tune with danger to myself. It didn't help that my normal survival instincts were screaming at me to react to attacks on my person. Trusting Callie to protect me mentally was great, but it was harder to force my body to ignore danger, which slowed me down and interrupted my flow of battle as my muscles tensed. That might not be much normally, but against attackers this good, it was a big problem.

Which was the point: to advance by perfecting the tough skills they'd taught us.

I desperately wanted to use my overlay for this training, but I knew that having an instruction manual would actually be a liability here. I was supposed to be training my reactions, and being able to see attacks coming would make me dependent on the overlay. So I just kind of... unfocused. Let myself completely relax and just take in information.

I winced as a hammer slammed into my ribs.

"Sorry!" shouted Callie, even as I reacted to an attack aimed at her back without even seeing it. My cane whirled up to smack a metal ball at the end of a long chain before it could hit her skull. I shot Callie a thumbs-up, which she returned with a happy smile... at least until the end of a staff slammed into her eye, sending her stumbling back, cursing in pain.

I cursed alongside her, and followed after, knowing the others would attack while she was distracted. "My bad, honey. I'm having trouble sticking with this whole thing. After blocking the first attack, my instincts are just turning off." I scowled over at Abel, shouting to my mentor. "How long is it going to take before we completely convert our instincts into protective instead of survival?"

That got a laugh from the rabbit-masked man. "What? No, that isn't what we're doing. You're learning to stay in that state for the duration of the fight. Completely abandoning your survival instincts would be crazy, and it would also take literally years to learn. That shit is hard-coded into your body, it would take more than a few training sessions to get you to abandon that. Think of this more as a state of meditation you're learning to enter."

Blinking slowly, I nodded. That made much more sense. Thinking back, none of his speeches had mentioned abandoning that intuition completely. Just changing it. I probably should have figured that I'd be learning to do this for short periods of time. It made so much more sense, and it was much less daunting to think about too. I'd been worried deep down about the viability of doing something so drastic in such a short time. This seemed like a more feasible goal.

That was all the distraction I could manage before I took a blow to the side of the head. Abel laughed, calling over. "Do you really think holding a conversation right now is a good plan? You're having enough trouble with this as it is. Adding another person to take up your attention is bound to ruin the flow of battle. Not that you won't need to learn that eventually, but ignoring distractions is the next lesson. You have to walk before you can run, kid."

Letting out a growl of annoyance, I stepped closer to Callie. I couldn't defend myself, and if she didn't do it, I'd be screwed, which meant I had to defend her and stop getting diverted by Abel's nonsense. I was distracting her, too, which was just making all of this worse. My cane flashed out, knocking a pair of strikes away from her, and then whirled the other way, intercepting another blow from that damn chain ball.

I had to stop myself from freezing at that. I'd done it.

Only for a second, but I'd been so distracted I hadn't had to focus at all on ignoring my survival instinct, just losing myself in the task of protection with no interruption.

Callie's fist smashed into the hammer I'd been hit by earlier, defending me before I even noticed the attack, and I gave her a nod of thanks. That was exactly what was supposed to happen here.

Which was frustrating because now I couldn't tell if Abel was fucking with me to see me get my ass kicked or if he was actively doing his job. I was beginning to regret my decision to train with him. Abel was an effective fighter, but as a teacher, he was kind of an asshole. Alden was nowhere near this sadistic. Probably. Okay, I still didn't know how many of his training techniques were real and how many were just him messing with us. But if he was as sadistic, he was at least better at hiding it.

I lost myself in battle after that. At least, more than before. The feel of the occasional painful strike was enough to bring me back to myself enough to note when an hour passed here or there. I managed to fall into that meditative state Abel mentioned a few times, but whenever it happened, I noticed it and got excited, usually causing me to freeze up and get hit.

I really needed Jessie to patch me up, but Abel had forbidden us from using her ability, saying that the euphoria from the supercharge would unbalance us and skew the results of the training.

Finally he called a halt to the session. "Alright, that's enough." His voice rang out over the Pavilion ring with authority. Mel wasn't here for this part, having said she had paperwork to do and that she wasn't necessary here anyway.

As the fighters filed away, Abel jumped down and strolled over to look down at where Callie and I were slumped, panting, on the ground. "Decent effort, you two. I'd say at this rate, you'll need three more days of this before we move on to the next phase. You have the rest of the day off, but be back here at dawn tomorrow."

He turned and walked away, missing my middle finger being aimed at his back. I probably could have told him what an ass he was, but I was too tired to muster up a sentence, so I just let it go.

I slumped against Callie, who groaned lightly but didn't push me away. Then I just lay there, sore and exhausted as my girlfriend reached up to play with my hair. I smiled slightly. I had to admit, this part was kind of nice.

Chapter Seven

A WEEK. A week of constant ass-kicking. Three days of the group fights, then four more days of the same group fights with Abel doing his best to actively distract us. That week got me seventy points, as well as seven attacks to stockpile. Thirty-five wishes. The seventy points were distributed to my stats mostly evenly. Fifty to Fantasy, bringing it up to a hundred and one, and then ten each to Perception and Creation, bringing them to one hundred even and one hundred and two, respectively.

Knowing I could get to that point without dedicating every wish to stats, we started letting Callie make some of the wishes left after the contractually obligated three for the Beast Lord Garden. On the third-to-last day, she used three wishes, and for the last two days, she used both of the spares. The seven shadow attacks brought me to an even ten, and Callie dumped all thirty-five points into Fantasy as she'd been considering, bringing her to an even hundred and twenty.

It was a truly staggering windfall for us, rounding us out in multiple important ways, and we saw the benefit of almost none of it during our training. Abel refused to let us use Skills, and had made sure to engage suppression to prevent us from abusing our stats to compensate for the numbers, so while we were growing more powerful, it didn't have a pronounced effect on our combat abilities as it happened.

As we progressed, Abel started throwing curveballs to distract us. He made us switch to fighting alone against half the attackers, then staggered the numbers, and at one point threw *actual* curveballs at us from behind to ruin our focus mid-battle.

We reacted to everything as seamlessly as possible, making some mistakes at the beginning, but slowly growing more comfortable slipping into our "teamwork trance" and then back out of it. Even the curveballs weren't landing by the end of the week, Callie and I defending each other even from Abel's absolutely monstrous sense of spatial awareness and eye for weaknesses. He wasn't using his power to attack us or anything, but we had definitely come a long way and I was proud of our progress.

Which was why I was deeply concerned when we showed up to the Pavilion and I found not ten people, but two in the circle of dirt waiting for us. Mel and Abel were sitting relaxed at a small table, seemingly unconcerned with our arrival as they waved us over without looking up from a game of chess. Abel held up a finger to ask us to hold. He ignored us for about twenty minutes as the two of them finished up their game, not appearing to hurry at all.

When they finished, I expected them to stop, but again, I was thrown for a loop as they reset the pieces. This time, Abel began to speak. "We've been working with you for a bit over a week now, and you've gotten much better about your awareness. Your instinctive grasp on each other's positions is passable now, at least when you try. However, your combat styles have both changed from what they were. The version of you who fights next to your partner, and the version of you who fights *beside* them, react to things in different ways."

He made a move, and Mel clucked her tongue in annoyance before picking up the thread of the conversation. "What my cryptic ass of a boyfriend is trying to say, in the most pretentious way possible, is that you need to relearn each other's habits. You know how your partner fights, but that's changed. Proper cooperation is built with trust, and trust is built with knowledge and communication. The better you know someone, the more at ease you can feel when putting yourself in their hands."

I raised a skeptical eyebrow behind my mask. "So… you want us to play chess? I assume that's where this is going and that we aren't just here to spectate your own games? Because I don't think even you two can convince

34

me that watching you play a board game is a viable training method for team combat."

Mel glanced over at me with a chuckle, which faded into a curse as Abel made another move.

"No," she said. "You will be playing. As for the reason... well, chess has lots of correlations with real battle. It's limited and constrained enough not to be a great representation of combat, but that serves our purposes perfectly here. We *want* limited and constrained for this part. You need to build your understanding of each other back up slowly. Of course, you aren't going to be playing to a win. Beating another person is easy. Fuck, who uses an en passant anymore?" She cleared her throat as she realized she'd trailed off. "Sorry, as I was saying, easy. What we want you to do is play to a stalemate. Well, one of you. The other one will be trying for a win. That'll alternate."

That was... harder. I knew the rules for chess, my dad had taught me as a kid. He hadn't exactly been around, but he'd sent tasks for me to do and had contacted me remotely often enough as a child. Chess was easy to play over long distances, and had fit well with his mindset. Still, she was right. Winning a chess game was *much* easier than trying to force a draw. At least against an opponent trying to beat you.

I could already see how annoying this was going to be. Still, I saw the logic, at least, and I was pretty sure Callie did too.

It took about a half hour for their game to finish, and when it did, they stood up and gestured for us to sit down. "Okay," Abel said. "Solomon is up first, you're going to be the one trying for a draw. Let's see how well you know Nightstrike. Pay close attention to her playstyle and how it compares to the way she acts in combat. Learning the way that kind of thing translates is the key to being able to predict her moves. If you can't learn to do it with something as structured as chess, you have no shot in a real fight."

I sat down and started to play, going slowly and taking my time. Unsurprisingly, Abel didn't stop talking as we had our game, continuing to wax philosophical. "If it helps, this isn't just a benefit to combat. It's really good for your relationship to learn how the other person thinks. Being able to intuit your partner's emotions is the key to a successful courtship." His tone was distant in a way that implied he was trying for wisdom, but it was cut off by his ear being grabbed roughly. "Ow, ow, ow Mel, that hurts!"

The red-masked woman was glaring down at him. "Are you really in a position to be giving these kids relationship advice after running off on me for years? If so, maybe you can educate me too. Tell me, what kind of emotions are your intuition picking up right now?"

The half of Abel's face exposed by the mask paled as his eyes widened like a deer in headlights. Seeing a guy that powerful cowering like that was pretty pitiful. I would have laughed at him for it, but I felt like Callie might get upset at me for being petty.

I very deliberately ignored the irony and focused on helping Abel out. "So, is this the last step in this *hare*brained training you have us doing? Because I'm anxious to get to the point where we can train with actual Skills." I was lucky I had so many points to give to Callie actually, because I would need a *lot* of shadow attacks for all the training we were planning on doing. Just a shame she needed them more than the others, I really could have used some more fire attacks. I would be sure to get some from Cark before the tournament.

Abel's eyes snapped from fearful to suspicious so fast it became clear he had mostly been playing up the patheticness for Mel's amusement as he glared at me. "First of all, no rabbit jokes. You're better than that, and if you aren't, I have *much* more intense training I can subject you to until you are." He pulled away from Mel. "Second of all, no. There's another step after this before we allow Skill use. But it's combat-oriented, so I'm sure you'll enjoy it quite a bit." The way he was grinning at the thought made me pretty suspicious of that prediction, but I couldn't spend too much time watching because I was busy.

The game itself ran for about an hour. Playing for a stalemate was weird. I'd learned chess with the express purpose of victory, and playing so that no one won was a radically different mindset. Rather than vying for position, I was aiming to exchange as many pieces as possible just to free up the space to box her in. Lots of amateurs played that way even in serious games, but rapid trading was actually an incredibly stupid way to play in the early game, at least if you wanted to win.

Abel's nonsense turned out to be accurate again, because when I paid attention, I *could* see similarities between Callie's playstyle and her fighting style, and I could somewhat reverse engineer those similarities to predict her moves. Despite how weird and absurd that sounded, it was feasible now that I had over a hundred Focus, meaning my brain was processing approximately a hundred times faster than even a genius mortal.

Focus was… a weird stat. It came across in the day-to-day as improved memory. The rest of the time it wasn't usually obvious how it affected me save for offsetting Perception overload. It was just a ton of raw processing power, but I didn't *use* that much processing power most of the time.

At times like this though, when I was cranking my deductive reasoning as hard as I could, I really drew on those reserves. It showed me more than anything how deeply stats could affect you without you noticing. There were so many aspects of stat gain that I never bothered to try to tap into, still constrained by my mortal mindset. I suspected people like Abel had a much more holistic grasp on their stats and how to make the most of every point at all times. I made a mental note to put some effort into that when I finally got the chance, but I knew for the moment it was just another thing on the pile.

I lost the game, and Abel made us reset. This time, I was trying to win, which I did. We played back and forth for hours, constantly switching which of us would try to stall the other.

Once the training was done, Abel called a stop to it and began to put away the board. As he did, he gave us both an approving nod. "Good. You learned what you needed to. I want you to keep doing that exercise nightly, two games. As for here, though… well, like I said, the next step is a bit more physical. Make sure you wear your armor tomorrow." He gave us a wide grin. "It's time for me to take a personal hand in your sparring matches."

Chapter Eight

WE GOT in early the next day, as requested. Well, "day" is a strong word. We arrived in what was technically the morning, despite the lack of sun and any waking people to interact with. Catching the Beast Lord Garden initiates going *home* for the night, I had just used all five wishes to bump up my Perception, since it was my lowest stat. Fifteen points onto an even hundred was simple enough that I didn't have to actually think about it, which was good, because thinking wasn't really my strong suit right now.

The opposite of a morning person, Callie was *not* pleased with our training schedule. So, when we arrived to find Abel waiting for us alone, she had no patience whatsoever with the nonsense games he liked to play, and just flat-out asked, "Where is Mel? I thought we were supposed to be sparring with you two together?"

Abel chuckled at her waspish tone. "No. I said that I would be taking a personal hand in your training. Which I will. You're going to be getting that personal hand upside your heads for the rest of the day. Just me for now, though. Get out here and get in position to attack. No Skills or abilities."

We both groaned, shuffling out into the dirt ring to take up our place together across from our teacher. Once we were standing adjacent, he nodded. "Good. Now, fight me."

Then he just stood there. I blinked. "Okay. But… what do you want us to learn from this? We won't know what to take away from this fight if we don't know what aspect of teamwork we're supposed to be training. You can't just tell us to fight you and then not say why."

"Really?" he asked archly. "Why not?" I opened my mouth to respond and then trailed off, earning a smirk from Abel. "Exactly. This is training. It's my job to teach, and your job to learn. I don't need to spoon-feed you every lesson. This particular training has two purposes, actually, but I'm not telling you either of them. You need to figure it out yourself. Now, hurry the fuck up. I want to go and get some pancakes on our first break, and I won't be stopping until neither of you can stand."

That was annoying. Hell, much of what Abel did and said was annoying. Now we had a way to respond to that. He literally told us to beat his ass. So I shrugged and lashed out with a whirl of my cane. He stepped away, towards Callie, but came up short of entering her space. I started to react to his attack, but when he didn't actually make one, I kind of… froze up.

Abel just stood there, looking bored. "You figure some of it out yet?" His tone was dry and somewhat mocking.

I grimaced. "Well, fuck." Callie looked over at me quizzically, and I turned to her and sighed. "Reaction. He's trying to point out that as a team, our combat style is currently entirely reactive. It's instinctual, but instincts are responses. We don't know how to integrate in joint attacks except in response to openings we see during battle."

"See," Abel said, "I told Mel you weren't stupid. She gets caught up in that 'brains versus brawn' thing. Thought you wouldn't get it just because you let your girl do all the planning. I think you're a bit like me, though. Combat intelligence and day-to-day intelligence aren't the same thing. You're essentially correct, at least for the first part. You don't act, you react. Defense is great, but you need to be able to take the initiative. That *should* show you the second reason for this training, but somehow I doubt it will. Try again."

I looked over to Callie, gesturing subtly with a hand, and we started to circle. We might not have a way to integrate both of us into an attack directly, but some training with my wolf method could polish that weakness out. That was the reason Abel had banned Skills, I suspect. All of our combination attacks were Skill-based. He was right that we hadn't integrated physical combat initiative into our style. Luckily for us, if we both attacked together, anything he'd do in response would trigger our defensive instincts.

I lashed out at the back of his head with my cane, Callie whirling out one leg to sweep his feet out from under him at nearly the same instant. Abel ducked my blow without even looking, stepped over hers, and reached up to grab my cane, pulling it slightly forward and unbalancing me as he did. I started to fall and scrambled to catch myself by putting a foot forward, only to step into the way of Callie's foot and get my load-bearing leg taken out from under me, sending me spilling to the ground.

Instead of backing off this time, Abel stepped in and aimed a stomping kick at the back of my neck. Callie tried to intercept it with a kick of her own, but Abel shifted the position of his back foot slightly. He turned the stomping blow into a snap kick from the side, smashing it into Callie's head while I was on the ground, staggering her. He reached down and grabbed me by the jacket, picked me up, and physically fucking hurled me at my currently off-balance girlfriend without a second of hesitation.

He stared down at us dispassionately. "You figure it out yet? Because I just gave you like four hints." It was infuriating how casual he sounded, like he'd just come back from a nap rather than kicking the living shit out of us. I groaned as I stood, holding out a hand to help Callie to her feet.

She answered this time. "I got it." She was wincing and rubbing her head. Apparently Abel could hit like a truck even without his ability. Not exactly a shock. "It's cohesion. We know how the other person thinks, how to be aware of them, but now we need to put those things together. Uneven training in the two areas is making it impossible for us to operate smoothly, and you're exploiting the gaps." She sounded frustrated, but honestly I was just impressed she'd figured it out so easily. I would have needed much longer.

Abel had no problem confirming the lesson once we'd gotten the second one. "Exactly. The single biggest flaw in any team combat is lack of cohesion. The gaps between where your styles overlap. I'll even give you a freebie. The point of this training isn't just to make you aware of your limitations so you can fix them, it's also to teach you to spot that same kinds of gaps in other teams' cooperation. In this tournament, we'll be fighting plenty of them. Being able to break formations and cooperation is going to be vital."

40

We'd seen that before when dealing with opponents during the scavenger hunt, so I could definitely follow his train of thought, but it left one glaring flaw in this whole training regimen. "What about you guys? How are we supposed to work with you when all our training is going to be on working with each other? Can't they exploit those same weaknesses in our cooperation?"

Abel smiled at that. "Now you're thinking. And the answer is no. Or at least, not easily. For a few reasons. First of all, we're training you on how to work with each other, but you can apply these lessons to others. Since we've already learned all this, learning to cooperate with us will be simpler by far than learning to fight beside someone who wasn't your teacher in the first place.

"Secondly," he said with a grin, "you're neglecting to remember that we're actively watching you train and learning your combat styles. We have much more experience with this style of fighting, and after training you, we'll be able to integrate ourselves into your teamwork pretty easily. All you have to do is work with each other and trust us to handle the rest. Now, enough talking. Back to work. The lesson is far from ending just because you figured out how it works."

He stepped back, leaving himself open again, and I grimaced. This really was a pain in the ass.

I met Callie's eyes over his shoulder and made a circle with my hand. She cocked her head for a second, and then her eyes widened as I made a biting gesture with my hand. Wolves. She got it. With a solemn nod, the two of us began to circle. Abel didn't even react, seemingly staring casually off into the distance despite our obvious attack preparations.

We rotated for a while, gauging his reactions and waiting to see what he would do in response to the few feints we tried. Nothing.

Finally, after he ignored my feint three consecutive times, I drove my cane at the back of his knee in a stabbing blow meant to buckle his leg and dump him on his ass. As I did, Callie launched herself at his chest with a punishing strike aimed to plow her fist right into his sternum.

I was sure it was punishing, because it caught me right in the solar plexus as he neatly shifted his body on one foot. He leaned back a bit so her punch grazed past him even as my cane sailed through the spot his leg had been. I saw his hand snake out like a viper and clamp around Callie's wrist,

41

and barely had time to register it before he yanked her up and over his head, then brought her full weight down in an arc right on my back while I was still bent forward from my low blow.

I fell to my knees from the impact. Callie barely managed to yank me out of the way as he aimed a kick up at my chin from the ground like he was kicking a ball. We both stumbled back, and I shot her a nod of gratitude. I'd gotten so lost in the danger I'd let my instinctual defense of her slip. I should have deflected that grab. Abel watched us scramble away without any special interest.

Which was when it clicked. "Oh, you asshole!" I turned to Callie. "He isn't ignoring us, he unfocused his fucking eyes to take in more of the battlefield. He's probably hyperfocusing on Perception right now, processing every tiny indication of what we do to predict our attacks." Then I looked at him. "How did you see me coming from behind? Or did I make too much noise?"

That drew a snicker from our teacher as his eyes finally focused on us. "Reflection in the pupils. It's why we spent so much time teaching you to operate without looking at each other. When partners constantly track each other's movements, it makes it too easy to predict what they're going to do. You should really watch that."

I growled as I took up position next to Callie. Abel simply let his eyes unfocus and waited. Ready for anything and nothing all at the same time, body relaxed and hands hanging loosely at his sides. He looked like he was wide open, but having seen the bastard move, I knew that couldn't be further from the truth. Forget landing a hit, we would need perfect team-work to avoid getting brutalized.

I sighed before gesturing for Callie to circle around the other side. If at first you don't succeed, I supposed. Still, I had a feeling this was going to be a long fucking day.

Chapter Nine

I WAS IN PAIN. So very, very much pain. I was considering inventing a new word to describe this sensation, actually, because "pain" seemed like it was underselling exactly how much this sucked. Not even "agony" was enough. I raised my head from the dirt to glare at my tormentor, seeing his ever-present grin shining down at me as if in mockery of the state he'd left me in. I peeled my lip back in a snarl. "Die."

Well, I tried to say "die." It came out more like "duuuuuh." I liked to think my eyes made the message clear, though. My hatred was clearly visible. It had to be.

I rolled over as best I could to check on Callie, who was lying on the ground staring up at the ceiling. "Ugh," I moaned, before finally speaking language again, even if the attempt was hoarse and barely understandable. "How are we in this much pain? And why can't I heal us?"

The snicker Abel had been holding back finally burst forth, the rabbit-masked man howling with laughter at our pain. "Impact. Vitality has less effect against higher-ranked opponents. We're the same rank, so it's not so exaggerated, but there *is* a wait, and that shit adds up. I've just hit you so many times today that your bodies literally can't keep up with the repairs. I didn't use any Skills or anything, so it'll fade. As for healing, you can't because it disrupts the learning process. No pain, no gain, and all that."

"Listen," I said seriously, "I hate you." He glanced down at me quizzically, clearly expecting my declaration to have more to it. I just stared at him. "That's it. I hate you. Message over. Die."

That one started another howling attack of laughter as he turned to walk over to a table off to one side, picking up a bottle of water. My sore throat convulsed looking at it. "That looks… good. Can I have some?"

"What?" he said in a tone of innocent faux confusion. "But you hate me? I can't share water with you, since I'm supposed to be dead."

I just glared at him so viciously it probably would have killed him if it had been an attack.

He rolled his eyes. "Oh, fine, you huge baby. Here. Drink up." He walked over and stood above me. When I opened my mouth to ask what he was doing, he poured the water right down my damn throat.

I hacked and coughed and gagged, rolling over and pounding the ground as my soaked face dripped into the dirt. He sucked his teeth in sympathy. "Pretty sure you're supposed to swallow that stuff. Doesn't do much if you spit out. It's your show, though. You do you."

I turned to fix my furious gaze on him, only to see him walking away. I caught a slight smirk on his lips as he turned, but I knew that it didn't matter.

He came back a second later with a towel he tossed me, and I groaned hard as I sat up. Then I mopped my face clean as Callie sat up with another loud groan. Abel chuckled at the performance, but eventually trailed off. "Alright, you two. It's just after noon. I want you to go and have some fun. Enjoy your day. No training. As important as working is, you also need time to adapt to the changes. For your awareness of each other especially, spending time together casually will be a huge help as you learn. You earned some downtime anyway. Go enjoy yourselves."

That hadn't been what I was expecting him to say. "Oh. Um… okay? Sure. We can do that." I turned to look at Callie. "What do you say, babe? Want to go on a date today?"

Callie let out a wheezing puff of air that couldn't be described as a word or grunt of affirmation even by the most generous of people, but I decided to assume it was a yes.

I rolled over a few times, back and forth, building up momentum to get up on my hands and knees so I could crawl over to her. Slowly. I moaned. "Oh gods, please let me use some healing."

"Nope," said Abel callously. "Enjoy your downtime. I suggest going to get food. It should help. Trust me, you should be glad I didn't let you eat when I had breakfast. You'd have puked it all up ten times over by now. Never do really hardcore exercise on a full stomach. Anyway, I'll leave you to it. Meet me back here tomorrow. You should be healed up by then, and we can move on to fighting team versus team."

I refused to think about that as he left. The idea of Mel joining that beating was too awful.

I dragged myself over to Callie and pulled her head into my lap, stroking her hair. "Hey, love. How are you feeling?" She wheezed out another small sound that may have been the word "bad." I winced. "Yeah, I think he went harder on you to compensate for your higher Vitality. Never been so glad I don't focus on that stat enough." She glared at me. "Sorry. Here, let's sit you up, maybe that'll help."

I pulled on her, ignoring my body's groans of protest. Luckily, lifting something human-sized was literal child's play, even when I was this sore. It was such an infinitesimal effort that my condition literally didn't matter. Huh, I guessed the suppression was gone. Which made sense, since we were allowed to leave. Guess he wanted our Vitality patching us up so we didn't die.

"Ow," Callie said as I got her vertical. "Ow. Ow." She paused. "Ow, wait, no. I meant 'bastard.' I need to relearn the words for things. 'Ow' is for how I'm feeling, 'bastard' is for Abel. How about you, sweetie? How are you feeling? You don't look much better than me."

I grinned at her. "Well, you look like a goddess, so that leaves me in great shape. But to answer your question, 'ow' works for me too."

I forced myself to my feet with a wince, helping Callie up by the hand and letting her fall against me. I decided if we were going on a date, I didn't need my mask, and she didn't either if she didn't want to wear it.

"So, before we leave, I figure we split up and put on our civvie clothes. The Pavilion keeps workout gear around. We can change into that and take a walk around the circus. What do you think?"

Callie was thrilled at the idea, even if the execution was tough, and we both hobbled off to the locker rooms to get showered off and changed. With this place being a giant clubhouse for battle maniacs, an area to change and clean up was essential. It was one of the many spots we'd discovered when we first toured the Pavilion after we took control of it. The place was much bigger than it looked at first glance, with large sections underground (well, all of it was technically underground since it was in the WCP, but large chunks were under *this* ground).

So I knew where to find the shower and rinse off. It only took me fifteen or twenty minutes to get ready, stash my gear in a gym bag, and bring everything back up to the ring to meet up with Callie, who looked... amazing. Granted, Callie always looked amazing, and whether it was an Ascendant thing or she was just naturally beautiful, my girlfriend was kind of a shock every time I looked at her. Something about her now, though, in workout clothes with her wet hair up in a ponytail, just made me stop and stare.

She noticed me there and raised an eyebrow. "Come on, I don't look that gross, do I? I cleaned up, at least, so I know I don't smell." She gave a sniff. "Neither do you, which is impressive. They must have good soap here. You usually smell like guy." At my offended gasp, she just gave me a warm smile. "Downsides of high Perception. It's not noticeable unless you look for it. But we should find out what kind of soap they use. Most of the ones that are thorough enough to counter high Perception are overwhelming. This is kind of neutral, I like it."

"Okay," I said helplessly. "I'll see if I can get a few bars. For the record, though, *you* don't smell, and you look gorgeous, that's why I was staring." I frowned down at myself. "You could really smell me all this time? I don't see how that could not be in a bad way. Nobody wants to smell."

She limped over, wincing at the motion, before standing on her tiptoes to give me a quick kiss. "Stop that. It's not some sort of weird character defect. Everyone smells like something, unless they use special soap like I mentioned. Your scent isn't bad or anything. Kind of... papery. With some ink, maybe? And leather from the armor. It's hard to explain if you aren't at the point where you pick it up. Scents are kind of unique. I don't focus on it much. I know people who literally track using scent, but I'm definitely not one of them."

I waved her off. "Okay, this is getting off track. We can do the smell lesson later if you want. For now, I'm clean and showered and ready for a day out at the circus with my girlfriend." I put an arm around her, starting us toward the entrance. "You got the worst of it today, so why don't you pick what we do? Anything you want. As long as I'm spending time with you, I don't care one bit." I paused. "Well, nothing physical, obviously. But other than that."

She let her head slump against my shoulder softly as we walked. "I don't care much either. It'll just be nice to be together. But I am pretty hungry. How about we hit the corn dog stand? They have those pancake-and-sausage ones. I know it isn't exactly breakfast time, but who cares?"

"Seriously," I said with derision. "I'll eat breakfast whenever I want. Anyone who has something to say about that can suck it. I'm a grown-ass man, no one but me decides the timing with which I consume whatever food I see fit at the moment." I gazed off into the distance stoically for a second before winking at her.

She rolled her eyes, but her lips were quirked in a smile. "You aren't nearly as funny as you think you are. But despite what a huge nerd you are, I still love you." She poked my side. "Being a giant wall of muscle *does* kind of offset the terrible sense of humor, though. Just don't start making bad puns and we should be fine."

I gave her a scandalized look. "There are no such things as *bad* puns, you philistine. But fine, I see how it is. I can lower myself to your level for the sake of my affection for you." She giggled at that, and I pulled her close, reveling in the sense of serenity in my heart. Something about being here with her, especially when I was so fresh from training, just felt... right. This was where I was supposed to be.

I'd expected to be nervous or anxious about the coming tournament, but oddly, I wasn't. I'd been training my ass off nonstop, and I hadn't even realized how exhausting it was because it had been so engaging. But this... this was relaxing in a way I hadn't know I needed until now.

I smiled down at Callie and then around at the busy circus as a whole. The tournament was months away. For now, time with my girlfriend was the order of the day, and I had absolutely no problem with that at all.

My stomach grumbled a bit.

Those corn dogs were definitely the first thing on my list, though. I wondered if they had syrup for dipping?

Chapter Ten

"Ow. ow. ow." I punctuated each step with the word as we limped away from the corn dog stand, laden down with pancake-and-sausage stick treats, as well as large cups of syrup. We staggered over to a picnic table nearby, slumping down onto the peeling and cracking wood with a groan as we let our food drop onto the table. We had paper plates, so I wasn't worried too much about it being dirty, and I was able to leave it there as I let my head slam into the wood, no longer strong enough to stay upright. "Ow."

Callie giggled, a sound which cut off with a whimper as the motion jostled her sore ribs. "Ow," she echoed. "Don't make me laugh. Or cry." She paused. "Wait, am I already crying? I can't tell."

I cracked open an eye and looked up at her questioningly, but confirmed she wasn't and shook my head. I didn't raise it before shaking, so my face scraped across the surface of the table. I didn't care.

She sighed in relief. "Oh, good. That would have been humiliating. Crying from just a little workout."

I snorted at that. "'A little workout.' I've been hit full-force by a Dullahan that was trying to kill me, and this was so much worse than that. Abel is a sadist." I forced myself to sit upright, since I had to eat anyway. "Still. I feel like it's getting results, don't you? Like, there's no way we would have lasted that long if we fought him a week ago. He would have crushed us. I never realized how lucky we were that the vision of him down in the labyrinth was so bored. Or maybe the years made him tougher? I have no idea."

Callie gave a vague nod as she dipped a corn dog in syrup and took a hearty bite, moaning in joy at the taste. I decided that seemed like a good idea, and picked up one of mine, biting into it with gusto. I groaned in ecstasy as the sweet syrupy flavor melted into the fluffy pancakes and the steaming sausage. "Oh gods," I said through a mouthful of food. "How is this so good? What rank is this food?"

Having better manners than me despite eating much more voraciously, Callie finished chewing and swallowed with a groan. "G-rank, of course. It just tastes better because we're both starving. Still, that is delicious." She finished the first corn dog and started on the second, talking between bites. "So, aside from insane hardcore training, what do you think we should do with our time until the tournament? Abel was right, downtime is a necessity."

I nodded, choosing to swallow before responding this time. "Well," I said, "I was thinking we could do some bonding with the wolves. They've been kind of backburnered since we got back. We can go camping and take them with us, just enjoy the outdoors with puppies. Benny and I used to go camping in Valen, or at least nearby. It was always a lot of fun."

Callie bit her lip. "I mean... we could try it I guess. Especially if we invite Grimmengap. Their wolves would probably enjoy it, and having an elf along in the woods is bound to make things easier."

I nodded enthusiastically at that. She seemed uncertain, though. I didn't feel the need to push, just waited.

Eventually she flushed and admitted in a low voice, "I've never really been camping. I don't count the hunt, because we had a building. Real camping, though? Like with tents and stuff? I never had anyone to take me."

Her eyes were distant as she stared off into the crowd. She clearly had something she wanted to talk about, so I didn't interrupt. "My dad was never really around," she finally said. "You know about that. Spent all his time at the office or out on patrol. It was just me and Mom, and she never had any abilities. The wilderness isn't *all* too dangerous for mortals, I think you and Benny were mortals when you went, but Mom... my dad did a number on her.

"Not physically," she hurried to say. She sounded like that mattered to her. I was starting to get really pissed off, but obviously not at her, so I kept quiet as she continued. "It was more like... dismissal. He acted like she was less than he was. He was mostly patronizing about it, making comments about how mortals never understood, or how her ideas were bad but it wasn't her fault. Looking back, I see how completely toxic he was to her all the time."

I reached out and put my hand over hers. Her eyes snapped to mine, and she coughed. "Oh. Sorry. Camping. Sounds fun. We should go. I was just thinking about that offer you made. About my mom. I just... Gods, Shane, I can't tell you what that would mean. How important it would be."

I leaned over the table to give her a quick kiss and pulled back with a big smile.

"It makes you happy," I said firmly. "It's worth it. Besides, it's not like I'm giving her something for free. My power doesn't work like that. She'll need to come up with some kind of payment. I can't really be involved, but I'm sure you can help her think of something that would work." I didn't want to make too big a deal about the gratitude. It was nice that she was happy, but I didn't do things for her because I wanted her to be grateful.

She seemed to sense that, because she shifted to the subject I brought up. "Payment will be tricky for sure. I'm positive we can figure something out, though. And it's a mortal wish, maybe she can pay in credits or something? Never mind, not involved. Point is, it's something I'm excited about. Maybe we can make our visit back before the tournament, provided we manage to get all our training done early."

Callie sounded excited about that, and I didn't mind. "If we get our goals met, no reason not to take a break," I said. "Hell, we can ask Abel to arrange it for us ahead of time if you want. I'm sure he could squeeze it in between our training without messing up our schedule too much. He seems like he would be good at finding time to be lazy when he wants it." I said that last bit with a snicker.

When we finished eating, we decided to go for a walk. It wasn't as crazy as it sounded. The pain was worse when we were sitting still, and we figured a nice leisurely stroll would get the blood pumping. Well, "leisurely" in this case being an arctic crawl as we dragged our dead limbs across the grounds, but to be fair, we were both tough enough to hide the signs and make it at least look like we were walking casually.

As we strolled arm in arm around the circus, I took a long, deep breath. The smell of the food and the rides and sounds of excitement were everywhere, and I loved it. The lights burned in the darkness, creating a tapestry of emotion and sensation I had never seen anywhere else. I was just as poleaxed by this place as I had been the very first time I'd come here. Maybe more.

"You know," I said, "I really love this place. Just being here makes me happy. Doesn't it just make you feel so… alive?"

Callie laid her head on my shoulder. "Yeah. I've always felt comfortable in the WCP, honestly, but more than that, this place is ours. At least part of it. I've never had anything like that before. Something permanent and mine. Like, I know we won't be staying forever, but still, it's like we own our own house." She flushed a bit. "Or whatever. That sounds weird. But you know what I mean."

And I did. I'd lived with Zeke in our apartment in Valen for ages, and now we had the house in Rajak, but neither of those were mine. There was something really amazing about having a home that belonged only to you, about being able to do whatever you wanted to a place because you felt like it. Growing up, I'd been able to decorate my room however I wanted, but it wasn't mine completely. It was an apartment, and it was Zeke's. I could paint my walls, but I couldn't rip them out or install a nice shower in the bathroom.

Not that I wanted to do either of those things at the Pavilion. But I *could* do them. It was a heady feeling. Having a place that I controlled completely and that no one could take away from me. Once again, Callie and I were on the same page here. I pulled her closer to me.

I loved the atmosphere of our talk right now, but I'd been wondering about something and I thought talking about it would be good. "So, have you talked to your uncle lately? You never mentioned how things went there."

The two of us spent a ton of time together, but we weren't around each other twenty-four hours a day. Well, not usually—the training had us bonding more. Still, she had tons of time to herself, and I wasn't sure if she'd ever called her father's twin, also known as the Nothing, the E-ranked leader of Silent Dagger. We'd only recently found out he existed.

Callie stiffened a bit before relaxing, letting out a long sigh. "I haven't been in touch. I've considered it a few times, but it's… hard. He looks like my dad, obviously, and there are so many issues there. I know that's not really fair to him, but I can't help it."

I blew out a breath. "I can't claim to get how that feels. I'm not sure how I'd react if I met my dad's twin. Granted, the situation isn't the same anyway. Still, if you don't mind me giving my two cents, I do have an opinion." I shot her a searching look, and she gave a solemn nod. "I think you should reach out. If it's too much, you can always just cut contact, I'm sure he would understand, but if you don't at least try, I think you'll regret it for a long time."

Looking down, I saw her glaring at me. There wasn't much heat in it, but she looked annoyed. "You know, you aren't always supposed to give me good advice. Sometimes you're just supposed to say 'yes, dear, I think you have the right idea.' Just because I'm doing something dumb doesn't mean I want you to correct me." Her tone wasn't harsh or anything, just a little sulky, and I could tell she was half joking, though not completely.

"Yes, dear," I said woodenly, my voice deadpan. "I think you have the right idea." I looked her right in the eyes as I said it, making sure to keep my voice as devoid of inflection as possible.

Her glare intensified for a second, but I saw her lips twitching a bit at the edges until she finally broke down and lost it, bursting out laughing so hard I had to actually hold her up.

She finally got control over herself with a marked effort, and still took a moment of gasping to regain her ability to speak. "You're such an asshole sometimes. Fine, I'm being stupid, I'll call him and at least say hi, happy?" I grinned at her and leaned down for a kiss, which she accepted with an eye roll. "I have to admit, you're weirdly good at cheering me up. I'm already feeling better."

Then she paused. "Although… not that much better." She stopped and looked up at me ponderingly before walking around behind me, and without any warning, jumping on my back. I caught her, hands under her knees as she forced me to carry her. "Okay, *now* I feel all the way better."

Chapter Eleven

ABEL HAD BEEN RIGHT. The next morning, we both felt so much better. Eight hours of healing was enough to fix us up, and I was good as new when I got out of bed. I headed to the kitchen to cook breakfast for everyone while I considered exactly what we would be doing today. More fighting with Abel, if I had to guess. We usually didn't move on until we'd learned our lesson at each step, and we were nowhere close to keeping up with that monster as a duo. Even without his Skills or abilities, his raw stats and sheer combat prowess let him pick us apart.

Still, it wasn't hopeless. Abel had been teaching us for over a week now, and we'd gotten markedly better. At this rate, we might be up to snuff for this tournament.

I'd made the mistake of thinking the tournament would be easy with Abel's help, at the start, but he had quickly disabused me of that notion. Even if he and Mel were the two strongest of their generation, number three hadn't been that far behind, and their teamwork, while impressive, had never been the best among the Titan Twenty. Not that we would be fighting their peers for the most part (it had been years) but still. This would be far from easy, and that was without acknowledging that the people we were up against were from all over the Gloryfire System.

Which meant we really needed to know as much as possible about this whole thing. As I started cooking, I spun up my scan ring and placed a call to a number I'd never used before. My cousin picked up, saying, "Hey, little cousin, to what do I owe this pleasant surprise? I figured you would be too busy with training for the tourney to call upon little old me? Hoping for some words of wisdom to help you get closer to that smokeshow you're dating?"

I rolled my eyes, having to fight back a smile at how... normal this felt. "No, Nat. I don't need your advice on my dating life. Callie and I are doing great. Sadly I'm calling about business. Though we could catch up first, if you want? Our teacher is letting us come in late today because he kicked the shit out of us so hard yesterday." That actually wasn't the real reason. It was more that Abel had overestimated the amount of time we could last in one-on-one training with him, and adjusted the time we needed to arrive to compensate. He didn't like waking up at dawn either, and since we'd ended up with half a day leftover, he just figured he'd let us sleep. We'd gotten the text about it on the way home.

The image of my cousin pouted. "Lame. I totally have sage wisdom to share. But oh well, we can talk about boring stuff, I guess. I assume you're calling about the tournament?" I nodded. "Well, I'm not sure how much I can help. I don't have the sources to suss out all the players showing up, though I suspect I do know enough to tell you who everyone is once we meet them. The layout itself is pretty simple. Team elimination matches until there are only 160 fighters left, and then it's a single-elimination bracket. Winner gets all ten slots to distribute themselves."

I whistled at that. "Holy shit, final 160? How many contestants are there going to be in this thing? Also, wait, single elimination? Does that mean I'm going to have to fight my teammates?" Because there was no way in hell I was going to be able to beat Abel. I *might* be able to pull off something against Mel, if I managed to pick up an appropriate set of attacks before the tournament. But I had no clue what ability I could stockpile to help me counter whatever spatial nonsense my rabbit-masked teacher used.

"Yup." She popped the p as she said that. "Which is why I made my alliance with you. My chances were originally three in 128, now they're seven in 128. Well... probably a lot higher, actually. Between my guards, your girl, and that monster in the rabbit mask and his partner, I don't hate our chances of scraping out a win no matter who shows up. Hell, even you'll probably put up a good showing. Though I admit, you took a different route than most of us do."

That was intriguing to hear. "I figured I wasn't the first to stockpile attacks, but why isn't it more common? It's damn effective." It had seemed like such a perfect idea for me that it was hard to understand why any of my relatives wouldn't use the same strategy.

She chuckled. "Because it requires an absurd amount of soul strength, and training that hurts like a bitch. The attacks are all pretty static, and using them strains your soul, which most of us don't bother to improve. It's much easier and less painful to just contract a bunch of minions you can boost, or to get paid in cash or artifacts and show up ass-deep in firepower. Most of us aren't the hands-on type. Don't get me wrong, we're all dangerous as hell, and most of us have trump cards you won't find anywhere else, but still, we aren't the 'punch it till it dies' type."

I blinked. That made sense. My soul strength was high because of my DS Mastery Skill. It *did* suck to train it, and if I weren't so pumped about the Skill itself, I might not have gotten into the habit. I remembered how muddled and pained I felt after my fight with Beat. I could definitely see the advantage of just buffing a bunch of guards. Still, it wasn't my style. I liked being in battle—micromanaging everything from the back would drive me nuts. Plus, it was one of the factors in punching up ranks.

More than that though, it felt... important. The strength of our souls grew when we ranked up, sure, but I couldn't help but think that more of it would be better. I was pretty sure having a strong soul would be useful later on, even if I didn't know why. Maybe it was Fantasy pushing my instincts, or maybe it was wishful thinking.

I grimaced at the unintentional mental pun and Natalie raised an eyebrow at me. "I mean, it seems to work for you," she said. "But not all of us like getting up close and personal."

Realizing she thought I was grimacing at the fact that more of us didn't use my style, I chuckled and shook my head. "Not that, sorry. Got lost in my own thoughts. I do that. I used to be pretty sure it was a factor of my Perception being much higher than my Focus, but apparently it's also just part of my personality. Remind me to make sure word of that doesn't get out. I'll end up having some nonsense 'wisdom' aspect added to my legend and spend all my time daydreaming. It would be thematic, at least, if nothing else."

She snickered at that. "The Focus will probably help, but yeah, I'd keep a lid on that around enemies. I think you should be fine, though, unless you go into a daze mid-fight, in which case we might need to have a discussion about our alliance." She winked to let me know she was kidding. "Anyway, don't worry too much about the tournament. Not that it isn't a big deal, but I can tell you're working your ass off, and you can't do more than your best. We'll win or we won't. That's the best part of living in this crazy universe of ours. Even if we miss out, there's always another big event somewhere else, if you're willing to look for it."

That actually made me curious about something else. "Do many of us travel like you do? Not the usual upward trajectory, but moving around on D-ranked planets like this one looking for interesting things and people? I never really considered leaving Callus just to go to another planet at the same level. It just seems like a waste not to get as much as I can from here and then head up."

She shrugged. "You aren't the first to think so. And no, it's not common. But I'm in no real hurry. We grow the fastest out of all the divine clans, it's what we're known for. The Wyndham clan has the most S-rankers, though ours don't tend to be as powerful in a straight fight. I can always catch up later, but making sure to get as much as I can out of this System, hell, this Star Cluster, is bound to pay off down the line. People forget that this competition is aimed at building connections. People tend to be easier to befriend when they're in the early stages of growth."

There was so much information in that statement I didn't know where the hell to start. I could guess at some of it. I knew clans were a thing, divine clans obviously being the clans founded by the six gods. I hadn't known we had the most S-rankers, though it made sense, given my own growth. I was pretty sure I was growing faster than most because of my starting point having all my stats unlocked, but still, I had no illusions about the usefulness of my power in encouraging growth. But there were so many smaller, less obvious questions I had.

"Okay. That's... wow. How many clans are there, exactly?"

"Who knows. A few dozen. The universe is a big place, and anyone who makes it to S-rank can found a clan. Though if it's an inherited power like ours, they have to make do with a branch clan or oust the original founder. The branch founders are all on a clan council that makes decisions absent the founder's decree in our clan. Our grandfather is on the council, actually. Not that we ever see him. Grandpa Malachai rarely interacts with anyone below S-rank himself. Once you hit that point, you don't need renown to grow anymore."

I wondered what that really meant, but it didn't seem like the time to get into it. She'd already given me this much to think about. I resolved to ask her later about the divine clans and any others she knew about, but I had a feeling it would be a long conversation, and we *did* still have training today. It would need to wait.

I had the information I wanted about the tournament, and I'd finished cooking as I talked (cooking one-handed was remarkably easy with stats like mine), so I went ahead and said goodbye.

Then I called everyone else in to come eat, and sat down to enjoy the cheese blintzes I made. I ate next to Callie, but didn't talk much. I was thinking over my conversation and how much information I still didn't have. I could always find out that stuff later, and most of it probably wouldn't be relevant for a while, but still. There was so much in this world that I hadn't even scratched the surface of.

Oddly, that didn't upset me at all. It excited me. So much to do, so much to see. I had so many things to learn and experience.

I put an arm around Callie, who leaned into me a bit while still shoveling food into her mouth. I gave her a kiss on the top of the head, chuckling at the fervor with which she was eating. Yeah, the world was big, but if you had the right people to see it with you, the journey was probably the best part.

Chapter Twelve

BETWEEN THE DATE and the conversation with my cousin, I was feeling recharged enough after breakfast to get back to training. I decided to forego doing the extra wishes for the Beast Lord Garden folks, and knocked out one of them with Cark before we left so I could top up my fire attacks at least a bit. The best part was that Cark exclusively cared about Might, and that increased his firepower, so the attacks got stronger with every wish, and since it was entirely to his benefit, it was totally valid.

I saved one wish and did the three contractually obligated ones for Sloane, topping up my Fantasy to an even 110 before going to find Alden. Our mentor was sitting in the stands in the Pavilion, relaxing as he waited for our training to start. I waved to him as we approached. "Hey, old man, haven't seen you around here for a week or so. Why didn't you sit in earlier?" I dropped onto the seat next to him, reclining to watch the mostly empty ring.

"Watch?" He snorted. "Watch what? The two of you getting your fool arses kicked in creative ways by the boy? This training course was my creation, lad, I know what the first week or so is like. Today is the sweet spot. First time against your real instructor after you've had the humility beaten into you. Mel and the boy couldn't even walk by the time they gave in on that first day. The next day, though... that's when you see something. Have all the stupid smacked out of you enough to be halfway competent."

I was beginning to see how Abel had ended up the charming and compassionate person that he was. The poisoned apple didn't fall far from the man-eating tree. Rolling my eyes at the bearded man, I stopped to have Callie put up one of her stealthed shadow domes. Most people here knew, but no point in advertising. He arched an eyebrow in concern when the dome went up, but didn't complain, just waited for us to explain.

After mulling over how best to phrase this, I decided to just come out and say it. "I can offer you a WCP wish. I have access to a source." I very carefully did *not* mention or look at his leg. It was obvious what he would wish for, and I didn't want to invalidate the wish by tampering with the compensation. "So…" I said lamely. "Do you want a wish?"

Alden burst out laughing. "Lad, that was the worst sales pitch I've ever heard, but I suppose when you're selling gold, you ain't gotta hype the merchandise. Am I to assume this source is the reasoning behind all the support from the Beast Lord Garden? E-rankers don't much go in for lavishing gifts and aid on little do-nothing outfits like this. I was wondering how you got them to commit so many resources."

He looked down at his leg. "Now, forgive me, but wishes take payment, right? What might this old man have that would be worth a new limb? I already work for you, lad, and I don't have much money to offer. The boy is already training you, and I trust him to do that much properly."

Callie, knowing I was reticent to comment on wishes and potentially skew the results, cut in from where she had been quietly holding the shield. "Well, you could pay with some of your attacks. Regrowing a limb for someone at our rank isn't just about normal stats, though. It would require Impact. The payment for something like that would probably be more than just one attack."

That was true. I'd used Impact in most of my wishes as a stand-in for other stats I was lacking, but I'd only ever granted an Impact-related wish once: when I gave Benny his powers. I was pretty sure I had the stats to do it, but even I was under the impression that it would take more than one attack, even one as impressive as Alden's, to offset that cost. It was just a matter of how I perceived things. A few points were fine for an attack because attacks were made up of hundreds of points. The raw value was there, and then modified by my need for combat ability.

Alden didn't seem worried. "Alright, then. If I do this the way I think, then I wish for my leg to regrow. I'm willing to pay with ten attacks, paid out over ten days. Does that work? I figure the delay means I should pay more of them, and it'll be a hefty price for a leg, in any case." He raised an eyebrow at me questioningly.

Wish detected. Grant wish?

I confirmed. I was interested to see if this worked. It would be less of a priority day-to-day, since points only took one attack to pay off, but it would give options for things like Skills if my friends needed them.

Stat points sufficient. Requirements: 36 Impact, 330 Vitality, 350 Might, 306 Creation.

Damn. Though I'd seen more expensive wishes, that was a hefty chunk. Granted, this was essentially a Beginner-rank limb. I wondered if soul strength played a role in determining the value or even affected it at all.

With the dome still up, I decided to just get on with it. I reached out and put a hand on Alden's shoulder as I accepted. "I have a sneaking suspicion this is going to hurt really badly," I said apologetically. Big changes made to others usually hurt, and a physical one like this was bound to be even worse. Alden just nodded as the purple electricity began to build along my skin, until finally it hit a breaking point and rolled out of me and into the other man with the force of a tidal wave.

His body locked up, and I saw his jaw clamp shut tightly to prevent a scream as all his muscles tightened. The electricity gathered in the stump of his leg, funneling down to where it was needed. As we watched, the bone speared out of the flesh, growing into the smaller bones of a foot, held together by tendons, with muscles knitting themselves together down the length as skin split and then grew down over the appendage. Finally, nails popped out of the toes and Alden was sitting there with a fully grown, if completely hairless, leg.

The electricity faded, and Alden slumped back against the seat, panting in exhaustion and pain. Before he could really relax, the still-fading electricity gathered in his hand and Gravity started to warp into a sphere of disrupted space. The power condensed for a minute, electric arcs of purple dancing over the outside, before it popped like a soap bubble, and the electricity arced to me. It ran through my body, though not nearly as painfully.

I was kind of shocked. That was a pretty unique way of transferring an attack. It was different than Benny's physical attack, or Callie's semicorporeal shadows, or even Jessie's life energy. Regardless, it was done, and

Alden groaned slightly as he lay there, still panting. "Okay. Ow. You might've undersold it a bit with 'hurt really badly,' lad." He grinned tiredly. "Pain isn't much, though. Thank you for this. It means a lot that you would trust me with this, and I know you did it because I was injured and needed it, which means even more."

Me and Callie helped him sit up. "No problem," I said cheerfully. "Also, that was fucking gross. I've regrown limbs before, but it's usually faster than that. Watching it in slow motion was weird. Not sure why it was like that. Maybe because the limb was higher-Impact, so it needed more time to form. Still, glad I could fix it."

He snickered a bit at that. "Yeah, well, I didn't have much time for admirin', what with being paralyzed with mind-searing agony, but I don't doubt you." He looked at Callie. "You can let down the shield now, lass. If anyone asks about the leg, I'll just tell them you got some kind of medicine from the Beast Lord Garden for me. Don't you worry. I won't let on you have connections to the WCP."

Callie let the shadows drop, and I was pleased to see she hardly seemed affected by the effort. She must have been working on her soul strength.

We both stood up, stretching. I wasn't tired from the wishes. I rarely got exhausted from the easy ones, and it took more than one huge wish to wear me out with my current Vitality. With Callie still feeling fine, the two of us were more than ready to get back to our training with Abel. Well... physically. Mentally we weren't ever going to be prepared for that sadism, but oh well.

When we reached the ring, Abel was waiting for us. He'd seen us come in and watched the dome go up, but hadn't seen the need to bother us. "You fixed his leg." His voice was quiet. "I... appreciate that. We were already planning to arrange it, but it would have taken time. Regrowing Ascendant limbs isn't a common ability, and tech that can do it is expensive, especially for someone as high up in the G-ranks as the old man."

"Of course," I said stoically. "He's done a lot for us, even before he really had a reason to. I'm glad we could help." I grinned unapologetically behind my mask, humor leaking into my voice. "Don't suppose this means that you're going to go easy on us today? Give us a break on the ass-kicking as a thank-you for helping him out?" My tone was wry, because I had no illusions of that happening. Still, phrasing it as a joke meant asking was pretty much nothing but potential gain.

Abel just chuckled warmly. "Oh, buddy. No. We're training. Taking it easy on you isn't a favor, it's a disservice. The less I push you, the less you grow. You don't want me to hold back. We're already on a tight schedule." His grin became sharper. "In fact, I think that this favor is going to earn you a more… thorough training session. I'll be sure to put my all into making you the best fighters you can possibly be. Doesn't that sound nice?"

It did not, as a matter of fact, sound nice. It sounded terrifying. But under the sadism, I could tell he really was trying to help, even if I wished he didn't enjoy it so much. Besides, I was pretty sure trying to talk him out of it would only make things worse.

I gave him a weak thumbs-up as I sighed tiredly. "Oh, sure. Sounds like a party." I chuckled uneasily to match his own enthusiasm, shooting a side-long glance at Callie, who met my eyes worriedly.

Abel huffed. "Oh, don't be such babies. I'll even let Agria heal you up after. The point of the first day's training was to leave an impression. Now that you've had your ineptness drilled into you, just the pain of actually fighting me should be enough for you to learn from. Normally I would have waited another two days to allow healing, but since I'm doubling down today, I'll be nice and allow it early." We both relaxed a bit at that.

We went into position across from Abel, about to try our hardest not to get demolished. I adjusted my stance to complement Callie's, ready to intercept any attacks that came her way as we both lapsed into that special state where we fought as one. As Abel blurred toward us, my last coherent thought before violence overtook us was, "Gods, this fucking dungeon better be amazing."

Chapter Thirteen

It took several hours before we were beaten enough to be considered finished. Abel apparently didn't subscribe to Alden's theory that giving up was enough, and forced us to keep going. Luckily we had Jessie to heal us up after he crushed us. Despite being crushed, we were substantially better prepared than last time, and did pretty well for the first hour or so. But eventually the damage started to add up, and slowing down produced a vicious cycle.

Once we finished our day up, we headed home, and I proposed probably the weirdest possible date. "Hey, I was thinking of logging in to Doom Sovereign," I said in a faux-casual tone. "I'm hoping that playing a bit will help me get some ideas for alterations to my subskills to help me rank it up. Do you want to try it out?"

Callie had never played, to my knowledge, which made sense. I'd mostly played as an escape. Callie had reasons to dislike her life when she was younger, but she'd just *literally* escaped from them rather than playing video games. I kind of thought her way was better.

She chewed her lip. "Oh yeah, I've heard Benny and you talking about playing that a few times. I haven't heard you mention it lately, though, so I kind of assumed you quit. You were pretty into the game before ascending, right? Why hasn't it come up before?" Her tone was curious, but also sort of flippant, like she was letting me know I could blow it off or change the subject if I wanted to.

I smiled at her softly. "Mostly a mix of not having time and not really having a reason. I can use most of those abilities in real life now. I played it for adventure and fun, but my life is plenty adventurous now, and I have fun with you. I've also been, like… on the edge of death for a large portion of the last few months, so there wasn't a ton of spare time. I still won't get much from it, granted, given my Beginner Skill makes me the best player who has ever lived, but I want to see if I can get ideas on how to guide my subskills as I upgrade them."

"Huh," she said, interested. "Virtual reality date. I can dig it. Sure. I'm in." She shot me a huge grin. "But you can't peek when I design my character. I want to have fun with it." I agreed, and she hopped up from the couch and ran off to find one of the scan boxes around the house.

I considered inviting Benny, but he was at the Academy with Celine, and I doubted he wanted me interrupting girlfriend time any more than I wanted to give up time with Callie. I promised myself we would do something with just the two of us soon.

I waited about ten minutes before I got a text with Callie's screen name and headed to my room to boot up my own scan box. I booted up the game and waited, logging in to my old character for the first time. The world of Doom Sovereign faded in around me, and I found myself standing in a familiar house. I pulled out a magic mirror and contacted Callie at the address she gave me, giving her directions to get here. It didn't take too long—she skipped the tutorial under my instructions. I could give her lessons better than the game itself at this point.

When she finally knocked on the door, I let her in with a smile that froze on my face when I saw her. I tried my hardest to suppress a huge grin, but failed as I took in her avatar.

"You're playing a giantess? Really?" Callie looked… well, like Callie, only about twice her size. She had to stoop to come into the house. I groaned. "Did you specifically agree to this so you could be taller than me? I thought you liked the height difference."

She snickered. "I do, but this is fun. I wanted to be the one towering over you for a change." She grunted. "Callie want manling. Callie drag manling

64

back to cave." Her gruff, faux-cavewoman voice was ridiculous, and I rolled my eyes so hard I briefly worried they would get stuck that way.

I turned to head back into the house. "Okay, first of all, I think that's speciesist. Not that I know if giants are real. But if they are, not cool. Second of all, I was planning to give you Rogue lessons, but it doesn't work so well if your physical dimensions are dramatically altered. Your legs go up to my collarbone. Anything I show you is going to be completely useless."

She snorted. "Um, no? These are my actual dimensions, just doubled. The giant race on here has, like, a thousand different physical modification options. Seriously, if I didn't have the Focus I do, I'd have spent about an hour going through the options. Regardless, I'm the same size I am normally, just... like, bigger. Anything I learn will still be applicable. But why teach me Rogue Skills? Do you think I can get the DS Mastery Skill?"

I shrugged. "The Minor Skill, maybe. It's kind of personalized past that. Might not even work, I've never asked anyone if you can teach Unique Skills. I feel like you have to be able to, but most of my knowledge won't translate up to Lesser for you. Still, I mostly just want to have some fun, and teaching can be a great way to understand the finer points of your abilities, right?"

"Well." She sounded contemplative. "I guess that's true. Learning seems like it might be neat, and even if I don't get the Skill, it'll help me understand your abilities better, which should help with team combat." She shrugged. "I'm in. Show me what I'm doing, little guy."

I glared up at her. Oh, I was not enjoying this at all. I made a note to never grant her any more height wishes. I *also* liked the height difference.

So we spent the next hour or two working on Rogue Skills. I taught her some of my basics (Touch of Tears, Double Trouble, just whatever came to mind) and as I went, I paid more attention to how my subskills built on each other. How they interacted and how those interactions played into my fighting style.

I started to alter my Skills slowly like I'd been planning, letting Callie practice on her own as I worked on them. First up was Mercy Kill. As a finisher, it was strong, but it was also limited. It was useful as an add-on, but it wasn't the final blow it used to be.

65

Considering how to make it more useful, I decided to extend the time. I started warping the Skill, its soul weight difficult to manage, but not impossible. I had plenty of charges, forty-eight of them at the moment, and I took my time, trying different configurations. I tried making it a persistent effect, but it almost crippled the boost. I tried increasing the boost. I tried doing both, but the soul weight was too much for me and the Skill, and I had a feeling if I kept pushing, I might break one of us.

I cast it again and again and again, I lost myself in the pain and the concentration, until finally, I found a configuration that worked. Once I'd done that, I started spamming it. Each time was painful and difficult, but got progressively easier until finally, I could cast it with no weight on my soul, and I felt that click of recognition. Mercy Kill had changed. Instead of using one bulk attack, I'd managed to split it into three separate fifty-percent-boosted attacks.

As soon as I finished it, I dropped to the ground, exhausted, head swimming with pain. I might have rushed it a bit. Callie said my name a few times, but I couldn't respond. She cut the game off to run across the house and check on me.

I closed my own game down and lay there on my hands and knees, eyes closed as I tried to make the pain go away. She arrived and held me as I shook on the ground. I needed to be careful. Having more charges meant more chances to strain my soul, but it didn't mean my soul was up to that strain in the first place.

Eventually, the pain receded, and I was lying there in Callie's lap as she shushed me and stroked my hair, telling me things would be okay. I opened my eyes with a groan. "I resent past me for agreeing to wake up today. Existing hurts. I think my hair aches." My voice was rough. Even my own words sent spikes of agony through my head, but they lessened in severity as I went. I hadn't pushed *too* far past my limits. Just a bit. It was a relief feeling myself recover.

Callie chuckled quietly, which felt like knives in my brain, and helped me sit up. She kept her voice quiet as she responded. "Alright, you giant baby. You're okay. You had me worried there, you know. I've never seen it that bad before. What the hell happened? Your head gets a bit sensitive when you work on your soul strength, but you don't black out from the pain." Her blue eyes bored into mine intensely, as if trying to scan my brain for damage, and I felt like shit for making her worry.

I leaned down to kiss her gently for a minute, pulling back with a tender smile. "I just misjudged something after a rank up. It was my bad and it won't happen again. I'm sorry to worry you, but I'm glad to know how much you care." I pulled her against me and she rested her head on my shoulder, closing her eyes as she sat there and drank in my presence.

I'd really scared her this time. She'd seen me hurt before, but we had a healer for that. Soul damage wasn't something you could heal. If I accidentally shattered my soul, I'd be fucked, and there'd be nothing Jessie could do. Seeing me black out like that must have been terrifying.

She took a deep breath and opened her eyes, apparently ready to resume talking. Her eyes pinned me in a harsh stare. "Be more careful in the future. Ass. I love you, and…" She looked away shyly. "I don't know what I'd do without you." She cleared her throat. "So I can keep an eye on you, I think you should sleep in my room tonight."

I gave her a lopsided grin. "Hey, don't worry so much, I'll be fine. I'm right down the hall and… oh." I froze as the meaningful look she was giving me sank in. She meant for me to sleep in her room. Or like. Not sleep. That was… well, my headache was suddenly much less of a priority.

I swallowed hard. "I… um, are you sure? Or like… not that there's anything you need to be sure about if you don't want to be sure or anything because we're just going to be sleeping unless sleeping isn't what you mean—"

She reached up and put a finger to my lips, then tried not to snicker as she stood up and strolled over to the door. "Well? Are you coming or not? As for sleeping…" She shrugged, shooting me a wicked grin. "We don't have training until later tomorrow. We can afford to sleep in."

I blame the pain for me tripping as I scrambled to my feet and bolted after her. That was definitely the reason.

Chapter Fourteen

I STEPPED out of Callie's room the next day around eleven in the morning and was immediately assailed by the sound of clapping. I sighed as I turned to glare at Benny. "Can you keep it down, please? It's early." I was blushing a bit, which he had wanted, because he was my best friend and he knew how to get a rise out of me. Making a big show of my first time was one such way, and I absolutely did *not* like giving him the satisfaction of letting him know it was working.

He leered at me anyway. "What's wrong. The blushing virgin can't bear to face the consequences of his carnal shame?" I grimaced. Benny always got extra wordy when he was smug. Which he wasn't for much longer, because Jessie reached out and smacked him upside the head.

He yelped and shot her a betrayed look, only to get an eye roll. "My gods, are you five? 'Oooh, Shane likes a giiiiirl, girls are gross.' Stop being a dick or I'm going to tell Celine about your apparent distaste for people hooking up out of wedlock."

Benny's face drained of blood and his mouth snapped shut, which was a hilarious sight. I shot Jessie a thumbs-up and she returned it with a wink.

The door behind me opened, and my previously sleeping girlfriend came out wearing one of my shirts, which kind of looked like a dress on her five-foot five frame. "What's going on here?" she demanded imperiously. She put an arm around my waist, pulling me against her. "You giving my man a hard time, Benicio?" Jessie made an "ooooh" sound as Benny recoiled from someone using his full name.

I rolled my eyes at my friends' antics. Cark just sat to one side and snickered. Right up until Cass looked at Callie and cocked her head. "How come Callie is wearing your clothes? Did you guys have a sleepover? That's her room, though? Shouldn't she have clothes in there?" We all froze like statues, looking down at the small girl who gazed up at us with innocent confusion.

Zeke, who was seated nearby eating cereal, snorted the milk out of his nose as he tried to choke down his snickers. Cark glared at my uncle, who didn't seem to actually care but at least had the good grace to pretend to be cowed. He raked us all with his glare and we just kind of stood there, waiting to see what he'd do.

He shot Cass a wide, strained smile. "Well, I think today is Callie's laundry day. She must have spilled something on her last outfit, so Shane lent her his shirt. That's why he was in her room."

I gave him a thumbs-up for quick thinking as Callie started nodding frantically. "Yeah, that's right! I'm super lazy about doing my laundry. I'm just lucky Shane has such big shirts, or I'd have to hide in my room all day while I washed my clothes." She gave me a squeeze. "He's such a good friend." I was having trouble not bursting out laughing, but Cark's face promised murder if we didn't stick the landing on this, so I just nodded along amiably.

Cass gave an "ohhh" of understanding, and the realization dawning on her face was so perfect that I would have assumed she was fucking with us if she hadn't been mortal and in a room full of people with Perception in the hundreds. If Cass was trolling us, she was so good at it that the rest of the universe should be quaking in fear because this girl was going to be the most terrifying spy who ever lived.

I cleared my throat. "Anyway, I feel like making breakfast. How does everyone feel about French toast? If enough people want some, I'll even throw in some bacon."

Cass was distracted from her line of questioning by the promise of sweet breakfast foods, as I've found most people to be. She cheered in excitement, requesting powdered sugar on her toast, a request I obviously already planned to fulfill.

I headed for the stove as Callie dipped back into her room to put on pants and conveniently avoid the death glares from the only person in the house who could literally light us both on fire with his mind. When she came back, she grabbed Jessie and pulled her off for a conversation I very deliberately avoided listening in on.

Benny came over to lean against the counter next to me. "You know, as much as I like to give you shit, I just wanted you to know. I'm happy for you. Not just last night, but just… in general. She's good for you. I've never seen you as alive as you are around her."

"Well… thanks," I said awkwardly. "I mean, yeah. She makes me happy. Just being around her is like being on an adventure. Even when we're just sitting around and doing nothing. We're just so in sync with each other, and it's… nice. Having someone who understands me and who makes me so excited to start my day." I cut my eyes at him, narrowing them in annoyance. "And what the fuck do you mean alive? You saying I was dead before?"

He snorted. "Only socially, you shut-in. I just mean that you seem to have an excitement you didn't before. A sense of anticipation. It's nice to see you getting so worked up over things. I love you like family, man, but you were so damn passive before you got your powers. Things happened *to* you. She's made you more assertive. Bolder. You happen to things. It's cool. I always knew you had that in you. Seeing it is nice."

I gave him a smile, but inside, my heart clenched. I knew what he meant, and I wasn't totally sure it had much to do with Callie. It seemed to be more recursion than relationship, but I didn't want to say that out loud. Besides, I was pretty sure I had a handle on it, and I didn't want to ruin a nice moment with my best friend over nothing.

"So, how have things been with Celine? Are you two actually officially dating yet?"

Despite my tone being neutral and interested, he scowled at me. "Don't you dare become one of those guys who gets all preachy about relationships because yours is going well. Yes, we're dating. Sort of. Elves are weirdly formal about this stuff. She's accepted my intentions, but I'm supposed to write to her mom and make an official request to court her. I did, and I haven't heard back, but Cel says that elves don't tend to rush in matters of politics. Which this apparently is, despite me not being politically motivated in the least. Fucking nobles, man."

Wincing, I clapped him on the shoulder in commiseration. In a way, I was lucky Callie and I bonded over having shitty absentee dads. Meant I had one less parent to meet. Her mom also sounded really sweet, so I wasn't as worried about that as I could be, and that was without the whole "giving her superpowers" thing.

I gave his shoulder a squeeze and got back to cooking. "Have you talked to Maria lately? I haven't heard from her, but I've been busy as hell. I really need to make time."

He sighed, letting his head drop back against the wall. "Yeah, she's been chafing at being stuck back home. She and Zach broke up, so that's good. Apparently she's been carrying a torch for Jessie, and they talk when possible, though that hasn't been as much as either of them likes. She did mention you not calling, and says if you don't get around to it soon, she's going to come down here and break the water heater. See how you like taking your showers cold."

I flinched in disgust at the heresy he'd just spouted. "Cold? She... she would make me shower in the cold? That's sick. Your sister needs help, Benny. What kind of deviant would interfere with a man's shower time? I've never had anyone threaten to do anything as heinous as that to me. If she gets abilities, she'd better be watched. She clearly has a twisted and ruthless mind that the rest of us can only dread."

Benny rolled his eyes. Hard. "Shane, a group of fanatical sleeper assassins literally threatened to murder you. I can't describe to you how stupid it is that the idea of cold showers scares you so much. Hell, knowing you, cold isn't even the worst. Lukewarm is probably your nightmare."

I nodded, shuddering. He was right. Showers should be so hot they almost hurt. Lukewarm showers were even worse than cold ones. At least with cold, there were health benefits. A lukewarm shower was just a heartless taunt to the person taking it.

"You know, it's nice to see," said Benny. "As much as you've changed since meeting Callie and getting your ability, plenty of parts of you are still the same old weirdo I made friends with when we were kids. I'm glad you've grown into yourself a bit, but I'm also glad you're still you. Oh, speaking of growing, any chance I can come watch your training today? Jessie said you guys are basically just being beaten mercilessly for hours, and that makes me smile."

I groaned. "You were doing so well there for a second. But fine, I guess you can tag along. It's not like we'll be any more injured with you watching. Plus, I can be happy knowing you couldn't possibly do any better. Maybe I can even talk Abel into giving you some... 'lessons' of your own." I gave him a vicious grin, and it was his turn to shudder.

"No thanks," he said forcefully. "I might do some work with Alden today, but I've seen Abel fight. Some things just aren't worth the price of admission. I'd love to be an invincible badass, but there are limits to what I'll do to get there." He smirked at me. "Besides, you nerds might need your big muscles and combat ability, but brilliant Inventing geniuses like myself know that knowledge is power. Also trial and error. Trial and error is power too."

Hearing my childhood friend sound like a proper mad scientist made me want to laugh, and I turned to focus on the French toast so he wouldn't see that his stupid humor was getting a rise out of me.

Last night had been... crazy. I felt so damn serene it was absurd, and I was honestly a little worried I'd lose my edge against Abel, or I would be if I didn't feel more in sync with Callie than ever. Still, it was like this constant knot of fear and worry had just melted away. It would be back, I was sure, but for now, it was nice not to feel literal months of stress piling onto me, a burden I hadn't even really noticed until it was gone.

I whisked some cinnamon and sugar into the eggs for dipping the toast in, along with a bit of cream, and pulled the bacon from the pan, using the leftover grease to keep it from sticking. For the moment, I was happy, relaxed, and looking forward to the future in a way that was altogether different from how I had for a while. Callie came back in with Jessie, both of them chuckling about something I had no desire to learn about, and sent me a soft smile.

Once I finished cooking, we all sat down and ate together, and Cass told us about the most recent episode of one of her cartoons as we all made fascinated noises and smiled at each other about how cute the kid was. Finally, though, our family breakfast was over, and it was time to get back to work.

I donned my costume and we headed down to G district to meet up with Abel at the Pavilion. Unlike yesterday, I was looking forward to my training. It was going to be a good day.

Chapter Fifteen

THE NEXT THREE weeks were more of the same. 105 wishes, sixty-three of them being given over to the Beast Lord Garden and forty-two of them for personal use, all of which I traded for attacks. I'd started pacing myself on stats, given the cap coming up. I was already starting to get close to it. For the stats, I gained 189 points from those sixty-three wishes: twenty to Vitality, forty to Focus, forty to Creation, forty-nine to Fantasy, twenty to Might, and twenty to Perception.

A total of 859 points across all my stats wasn't bad. We rotated through all twelve of the Beast Lord Garden elites that had been sent out, since Sloane, Beric, and Croll only had so many points to give, but that had always been the plan. The forty-two other wishes I'd traded for attacks. Ten healing bursts (I'd used up the two I had), nine fire attacks, five more triple-strength tranq blows from Benny, eight more triple-strength density-shifted attacks, nine more spider leg attacks, and Callie had even given me access to one of her shadow clones made to look like me.

I'd also collected all ten of Alden's gravity attacks, so I was pretty much completely stocked up in the direct stuff, though the shadow clone thing had opened up the possibility of Jessie giving me taming or animation abilities, something I was eager to look into in the coming days. All the attacks had really helped my friends out too. Benny had put thirty of his sixty-six points into Might, thirty into Focus, and six in Fantasy just because it was so damn low. That brought them up to 114, 105, and sixteen, respectively.

All twenty-seven of Jessie's points went in Vitality, of course. Callie put her three into Creation, bringing it up to 135, and Cark put all his into Might, though I still hadn't really asked what his stats were.

I'd even gotten three of my subskills modified over time. Touch of Tears and Consecration of Flame had both been boosted to ten-minute durations instead of five, and Double Trouble didn't require me to be restrained anymore.

I'd been insanely busy the whole three weeks. We'd spent the first getting our asses kicked by just Abel, and when we could finally take some of the punishment and even land glancing blows back, he brought Mel in to "really" start our training, and we officially began the brutalizing. They didn't use Skills, which was the only reason we were probably still alive, but they put us through the wringer.

Shockingly, we actually had this week off from training. There were three weeks left before our two-month deadline (a few days had passed before and after our first week, and then there were the three we'd just done), and when I brought this up, my teacher shrugged.

"You can't train nonstop, I told you that. Everyone burns out, even Ascendants. Plus, you don't want to get a rep for being a grinder. That shit follows you for life. But you also don't want your edge to be dull when you get to the actual tournament. Take the week off now, and the last two weeks before showtime we'll drill you into the ground."

Despite his wolfish grin, which normally would have terrified me, I actually smiled back. I turned to Callie. "So, I'm thinking we might be able to take that trip back home we've been talking about, if you think it's a good time." I'd considered that this might come up and talked to Melinda about maintaining my deal with Beast Lord Garden during the trip. We'd agreed that any wishes I'd done for them past my contractually obligated three would roll over. With about ten days of those and one spare, I was at twenty-one extra, which would give me a week off from that too, so it worked out.

Callie hadn't been granting wishes, but she'd been constantly training with her shadow manipulation, and had actually reached out to her uncle a few times. She was running on fumes too, and it occurred to me that Abel had a pretty decent grasp on what we were up for.

Her shoulders sagged in profound relief. "Oh gods, yes. That sounds amazing. I'm so damn tired. Not physically, obviously, but… mentally I'm just fried. Healing just doesn't do anything for mental fatigue."

It didn't. My own stomach was unclenching at the sudden lack of the stress that had been plaguing me for weeks. Sometimes you couldn't even feel the weight crushing down on you until it was gone. I honestly thought if it wasn't for my time with Callie after training (I'd taken to sleeping in her room pretty much every night now, though most nights it really was just sleeping, given the exhaustion), I'd have probably snapped. The more I thought about this, the better it sounded for everyone. We could all use some downtime.

Callie stepped up and pulled me against her, happier than I had seen her in a while, at least at the Pavilion. "I'm sure Mom would be so excited to have us. She's been talking about you visiting for ages. She really wants to meet my first serious boyfriend. It's honestly been getting kind of annoying lately, so this will really help me out." She winked up at me, her beaming smile more than enough to make the whole idea worth it. I loved seeing her smile like that, and loved being the cause even more.

I paused as I had another thought. "Wait… why the hell did you make us come all the way down here to tell us we didn't have to come in? You couldn't have just texted us this?" I was wearing my mask, but my annoyance must have been audible, because Abel's smug grin made it clear he knew he'd gotten to me. This asshole.

Even Callie turned and glared at him a little as Mel lounged at the table they'd been playing chess at. She was trying not to snicker at us too obviously, and failing even while wearing a mask of her own.

Abel said, "Because it was funny? Honestly, how was I supposed to know you were going to take a vacation? Still, if you're leaving, there are a few things you should iron out here anyway, so it's not too bad you came." He looked over at Mel. "You had paperwork for them to sign, right? Might be your last chance to get anything done if they're going out of town." I grimaced as he clearly just came up with a reason off the top of his head, and even more as he tried to make work for me.

I reached up and placed a finger to the middle of my mask. "Not it," I said seriously. Callie's eyes widened with shock which quickly turned to annoyance. She glared at me, but I just waved it off. "Don't be a spoilsport. Nose goes is a sacred code of honor. It's not my fault that you weren't fast

75

enough to notice what I was doing. Aren't you supposed to be trained to be attuned to every movement I make?"

She growled at me, which was more cute than scary, since I knew she wouldn't hurt me. "Only during combat. You're a bastard. But fine, you called it so I suppose I have no choice. I'll have my revenge someday, though. Be on your guard."

I snickered as Mel led her away. Abel was just looking at me quizzically. "What? Nose goes is sacred. It's like dibs, or shotgun. They're the basis of the modern concept of honor."

Chuffing out a laugh, my teacher shook his head. "You kids are all crazy. But whatever. Since I don't have to train you today, I'm going to go take a nap on top of one of the tents. No one ever finds me up there." He shot me a grin and a cheery wave and headed off to find some building-sized circus tent to climb. I assumed he was using his ability to get up there, but still, it was an impressive amount of effort to avoid being woken up.

I stopped to let Alden know we would be gone for a while, and he waved with congratulations on my vacation. Once that was done, I let Sloane and the rest of Beast Lord Garden know I'd be gone a week, and to tell Melinda when I'd be back.

Then I tracked down the others to let them know what was going on. Jessie was excited to go home and visit, and happy for the opportunity to see Maria and to check in with her brother's old teammate Lindsey, with whom she was extremely close.

Benny was the last person I went to talk to, and I found my best friend relaxing on the benches. He hadn't gone to visit Celine today, luckily, and I sat down next to him, staring out at the Pavilion.

"Hey, man, you look bored," I said. "You didn't have to come with today. Could have gone to hang out with your girl." I poked him in the ribs, earning a light grunt and an annoyed glare before he backed off with a chuckle.

"I could have," he said easily. "But absence makes the heart grow fonder. Not all of us are part of a co-dependent battle couple who spend all their time together. It works for you and Callie and that's great, but Cel likes her privacy too. Being underfoot all the time would only bug her. Not that she would ever actually *say* anything about it, but still. Me taking some time to hang with you guys lets her decompress, and makes our next time hanging out more fun. Don't want her to get sick of me."

I shrugged. "We're not codependent, we just love each other's company. I spent years alone. It was fine, I guess, but Callie... being with her doesn't feel like being in a crowd. We're both happy to be alone sometimes, but we can be alone together if we want to." Benny just rolled his eyes good-naturedly. "Anyway, I didn't come over here for your opinion on my relationship. I wanted to let you know that we're planning a trip back to Valen. I wasn't sure if you were in. You can bring Celine if you want."

He jerked upright. "Wait. Really? Fuck yes I want to go home! I've been missing my family like crazy, and I want to introduce them to Cel. When did you want to leave?" He stood up and started to pace. "Shit, I have to get presents for Mom and Dad, and something for Maria to shut her up so she doesn't bitch I skipped her. Plus, I need to buy something nice to wear. I've been in my costume for ages, and Mom will expect me to be dressed to impress when I introduce my girlfriend."

It was hard not to chuckle at his frantic muttering, given his lackadaisical attitude just a minute ago. I didn't think he had much to worry about. Amber was a social butterfly and a big fan of high society. Bringing home a pretty, noble elf girl would thrill her. If anything, Benny would have trouble convincing her to leave them alone.

Still, I let him ramble, enjoying the comfort of the familiar voice of my best friend. Pretty soon I would be home again. I wondered how everyone was doing. It would be nice to see them all.

Chapter Sixteen

GETTING BACK to Valen was shockingly easy. We had the money to hire an air shuttle, not to mention being the winners of the freshman treasure hunt had everyone hoping to get in good with us. We avoided using the Unity's in-house shuttles, and that way avoided Midknight and Annie. There were a lot of options, but in the end, we got a ride from Callie's uncle, Alexander, who decided to come back for a visit once he heard we were going and offered us use of his personal air shuttle for the trip.

I expected Callie to shut that down fast, but apparently their calls had been going well, because she seemed fine with it, and was even excited to have him along. And she was in a good mood for the whole day until we finally met up. As we arrived at the landing site, I was forced to stop and stare at the conveyance we were going to be using to get back home. "Okay." I pointed at it. "Why the hell is that thing so... that." Words failed me as I gestured at the air shuttle dismissively.

Alexander, who was out of costume like the rest of us, just snickered. "Well, I have something of a reputation to maintain, after all. Besides, it's not *that* bad." He cast a contemplative gaze to the air shuttle, which in his defense wasn't *bad*, so much as just... a lot. Though it had a similar shape to the last one, that was where the similarities ended.

The E-ranker's shuttle was made of pitch-black metal that was jagged and dramatic, and scrolled through with traceries of gold, making its shape all the more striking. We could see from out here that the inside was plush and lined with red velvet, and it had dark, thick red curtains blocking off the empty spaces on the sides, also velvet, with gold pull ropes. It was basically the most over-the-top thing I'd ever seen in my life, and that was a pretty big list, considering all the places I'd been as an Ascendant.

Callie snickered. "Sorry, Uncle Alex. It's just kind of much. But it's fine, we know that your people are more likely to get something like this for you to use. We just appreciate not having to spend chits to get back. We have cash on hand, but trips like this are damn expensive, and it's better to save the money when we can." She looked him over with amusement. "So, you seem a bit dressed up for a trip back home. Looking forward to seeing anyone special?"

Alexander cleared his throat. "Not at all, it's just been years since I've seen Amelia. I don't want her to think I've become some kind of layabout."

Callie and I did our best not to snicker at the obvious crush he had on her mother. I wasn't sure exactly how that would work out, given his identical features to her cheating ex-husband, but she'd known them both for years, so maybe it wouldn't be a problem for her.

We turned to see the others approaching to climb inside. Benny, Jessie, Zeke, Cark, Cass, Celine, and six wolves. We'd brought Cark and his sister along because Callie had mentioned the little girl to her mother, who'd apparently insisted. I'd have been down to invite them either way. Cark was a great guy and Cass was a blast to have around. Plus, having the kid around was a breath of fresh air. Kept us all a little more human.

Celine waved slightly. I couldn't tell if she was shy about riding home with all of us, or just being her normal taciturn self.

Benny looked over the moon that she'd agreed to come with. He put an arm over her shoulder. "Hey, guys, hope we aren't late. Had to grab some things. So what kind of time are we looking at for travel here? I remember it was crazy fast last time. Like two hours or so. Will this one be as fast?" He sounded excited for the trip, which I got. The last ride had been pretty intense. I wondered if the drapes would make it better or worse?

We all climbed in, and as usual, the space inside wasn't cramped at all. This thing was swanky. It had all the same spatial expansions as the elevator compartments in the WCP, even better than most of the cars we'd been in.

We all took seats on the plush black sofas. Alexander gave an expansive gesture. "Sit wherever you like. Anyone who wants to can open the curtains. There are barriers to prevent windburn and stop falling, but honestly, past the first ride, watching countryside blur past too quickly to see gets pretty old."

I slumped into the comfortable couch and smiled at Alexander, who'd chosen to sit nearby. Callie had gone to talk with Jessie, so it was just us.

He cleared his throat again, then lowered his voice. "Shane. I'd like to thank you. Calliope mentioned you were the one who suggested she give me a call. Getting to know her has been… nice. I never got to know her when she was a girl, my relationship with my brother being what it is. I never thought I would have the chance to spend time with her like this." We both knew that lowering his voice did nothing, but all of our Focus was decent enough that we could avoid constantly hearing everything with supernatural levels of fidelity.

"It's fine," I assured him, my smile turning wry. "If it makes you feel better, you don't owe me anything for it. I did it for Callie. I was pretty sure she would regret not getting to know you just because of her dad. She hates letting him control her, and that's what it would have been. She deserved to make her own choice, and you deserved a chance to prove your intentions. Seems like it worked out well for everyone. I should be thanking you for training her. She's mentioned you've been giving her some exercises to do and they've been helping her polish her shadow combat skills."

He just shook his head. "That isn't training. Just offering advice. It's quite literally the least I could do. She's been improving rapidly, from what I saw when I arrived, though. You both have. I'd heard some rumors floating around E district about you, but I hadn't believed them. It seems they were accurate after all. Still, it's not just stat gain. You both walk like completely different people. You must be working hard."

Gesturing over at Callie, who saw me and raised an eyebrow, I smiled. "She's the one who's been working the hardest. I've just been trying to keep up. She's absolutely brilliant in battle. Her instincts are fantastic, and she seems to be able to pick up when I'm in trouble like a sixth sense."

We'd been doing so much work, it was nice to finally have a chance to brag a bit, even if I wasn't bragging about me. It was also nice to talk Callie up while she and her uncle were still getting acquainted, and I really was insanely proud of her.

She, as it turned out, felt the same way. "Oh, none of that," I heard her say as she stepped up behind me. She fell sideways over the couch arm, flopping over into my lap without any sort of warning or hesitation. I grinned at her and kissed the top of her head.

"He's being modest," she told her uncle. "Like… to a stupid degree. We've both improved a ton, but he started literal years after I did. Stat-wise, we're about even, and in terms of combat prowess, I'm probably a bit ahead because of my Skills and build, but that is pretty fucking amazing on its own."

I just shrugged. "It's not the same."

I was kind of cheating. Sure, Callie's stats were rising, but she had made as much progress as I had. The only big difference was that she hadn't managed to get DS Mastery past Minor. That wasn't a shock, really. It was a unique Skill no one else that I knew of had ever managed to gain. She could have wished for it, but decided against it, saying she already had too much to work on, and had another Skill to synergize next rank already anyway.

She just rolled her eyes. "I appreciate the hype, but I'm not going to let you pretend you're not turning into a total beast yourself." She paused, then shouted over to Rellia. "No offense, Rel." The wolf just ignored her, which I took to be a dismissal. "Anyway, your combat senses have been growing dramatically. I almost never worry about getting hit anymore."

I tried to protest, but she leaned up to kiss me to shut me up. "Okay, that's enough, my uncle doesn't need to hear us argue about which one of us is a better fighter." She cut her eyes at him mischievously. "He needs to tell me more about that bottle of wine I noticed stashed in one of the cupboards with a bow on it."

That drew a loud sigh from Alexander. "Damn. I thought it was hidden well enough not to draw attention. It's nothing. Just a hostess gift. It's good manners to bring a bottle of wine when someone allows you into their home." He showed absolutely no sign of distress or discomfort when saying that, which would have been much more impressive if I didn't know how absolutely monstrous his Perception had to be. He could have been openly weeping on the inside and not shown even a hint of it as far as we could tell.

Callie looked dubious, but let it go in the end. She didn't want to make him uncomfortable, even if I imagined she was kind of protective about her mother.

Alexander seemed to have made a good impression on his niece. The guy was just so damned polite and formal, though. Callie and I weren't formal people, so we tried our hardest to get him to loosen up as we talked, to little success. Still, it was a nice way to kill the time, enjoying the conversation as we sped through the air. Occasionally one of the others would come over to chat, but they mostly kept to themselves, with Cass excitedly watching the passing countryside once Cark was reassured about the barriers being secure.

In what felt like no time at all we began our final approach. Everyone stood up to watch the descent, pushing aside the curtains as we slowed down to land on the roof of the guild building. I felt lighter than I had in months, and I saw Stella (the Valen Guild Master), her son Ian (Captain Polaris), Lindsey (Jessie's brother's friend), and to my surprise, Benny's sister Maria, all waiting for us on the rooftop.

Once we had stopped and the barriers dropped, I grinned and bolted from the shuttle. I headed for Maria first, scooping up my annoying surrogate sister in a huge hug and spinning her in a circle.

She squeaked in outrage. "Shane, you beast! Put me down! Did you get taller somehow? This is ridiculous—why are you and Benny so damn big? I demand you stop growing and possibly drop an inch or two." Her voice was rough with happiness as I put her down, only for her to get snatched up and put through the same thing by Benny, and she groaned in annoyance and gave him a similar speech.

In the old days I might have been irritated, but this time I wasn't upset at all. I was finally home, and that was all that mattered. It was good to be back.

Chapter Seventeen

WHILE BENNY HEADED home to see his parents, taking Celine with him and planning to meet up with the rest of us later, we all headed into Valen proper. We were staying with Callie's mom during the visit, and I was a bit worried she wouldn't have the space for us until Callie reassured me that her mom had gotten the house in the divorce, and that the place was absurdly big for a single-family home. Amelia apparently lived alone at the moment, though she had several dogs.

Arriving at the house, I had to admit that I saw what Callie meant about the absurdity. Callie's mom didn't live in a mansion, she lived in a fucking compound. It was stunning, but also very defensible. Despite being huge in terms of surface area, all the buildings were single-story. The house was laid out in an interesting style I hadn't seen before. Short, reddish-brown walls made of sandy stone were topped with sloped rooftops of terracotta tiles and lined with pretty stained-glass windows that were tall and thin enough that they wouldn't provide an entrance even if broken.

Ivy grew along the walls, especially near the tops, and I could see roses blooming within the climbing vines, so subtly entwined they looked like they were the same plant unless you paid attention. The mosaic-tiled court-yard at the entrance had a single large clay fountain inset with opals that shimmered in the sunlight, the light playing over the clear water as it poured forth from the spouts. It was pretty much the homiest and most welcoming fortress I had ever seen in my life.

I turned to Callie, my jaw dropping. "You grew up *here?*" Despite being a potential heir to a universal syndicate, I hadn't had access to much more than a comfortable level of wealth as a kid. Benny's family was incredibly well-off, however, and even he would have been a bit blown away by this place. I supposed it shouldn't surprise me after all I had seen, but Callie's mom was a mortal. Her scale for wealth should be closer to Benny's than ours. I mean, we could have a house like this built with our current funds, but we were *really* rich for G-rankers.

She shrugged. "My father had it built for her when they got married. I think he wanted to make sure she stayed out of his hair. She adores this place. Spends almost all her time cleaning and maintaining it. There's a built-in greenhouse in the center that acts as a sort of courtyard, where she keeps her garden. It's a pretty place, I admit, but I have mixed feelings about it. I'd be fine if she just moved, but she has a lot of good memories of me growing up here, and she's attached." Her voice lowered a notch. "She got a bit clingy with my childhood stuff when I ran away. That's on me, so I can't really complain about it."

I could hear the shame and discomfort in her voice when she said that, but it was subtle enough that even with my Perception, I wouldn't have noticed if I hadn't known her so well. Her expression melted into one of joy, however, as she glanced over at the gate, which was now opening to reveal a gorgeous dark-haired woman with bright blue eyes that were the same shade as Callie's. The woman, presumably Amelia, looked about thirty, as opposed to the early forties I expected from someone with a daughter who was nearly twenty.

"Baby girl!" she squealed happily, her arms flung wide for her daughter. Callie bolted across the courtyard and threw herself at Amelia, wrapping her up in a tight hug. Amelia was taller than Callie, though that wasn't hard, especially since Cal had traded me an inch of height and gone down to five foot five.

"Look at you. You look wonderful." She pushed her back, gripping her shoulders as she raked her eyes over her daughter critically. "A bit smaller, though. Did you lose weight..." She paused. "Or height somehow?" She shook off the thought after a moment. "Not important, how was the trip?"

Callie smiled at her mother, and the expression was beautiful for how relaxed and joyful it was. "It was fine, Mom. Uncle Alex gave us a lift. He came with us for the visit, actually." She raised an eyebrow. "Speaking of

Uncle Alex, we should have a talk later about keeping important information from your daughter. I can't believe you never told me I had an uncle on Dad's side of the family. Any other secrets you're keeping?"

Most people would have wilted under Callie's glare (my girlfriend had a formidable presence), but Amelia just raised a nearly identical eyebrow. "Darling, I was married to a Unity Guild Master for over a decade. I know more secrets than you can imagine. As for Alexander... we hadn't spoken to him in a long time. I suspected he wanted to distance himself from Paul and I, and I respected that." She shifted her gaze over to where the man himself stood. "Though it appears his desire for distance has eroded with time. How have you been, Alex?"

Alexander looked... flustered. Which was a fucking weird thing to think about an E-ranker. "I've been well, Amy. You look good. Haven't aged a day since I last saw you." There was some weird subtext in that statement that I couldn't and didn't really want to parse, but Amelia blushed slightly when he said it. Callie gave the two of them a suspicious look, and Alexander changed the subject quickly, striding across the courtyard to present the wine. "I brought this, by the way. Claren Fal 4683. I know it's your favorite. A gift for my generous hostess." He smiled warmly, offering her the bottle with both hands, one around the base and one cradling the neck.

She gave him a wry smile, along with that same raised eyebrow that looked so much like Callie's it was almost eerie. "Yes," she said dryly as she took the gift, "this one bottle of wine is definitely enough to make up for your nearly two decades of avoiding me. I'm glad you're treating your actions with the gravity that they deserve." Her voice was as icy and poisonous as a cyanide popsicle, and just as sweet. Alexander paled slightly under her glare.

For a second it looked like she would glare him into a puddle, but then, as suddenly as it came, the icy rage melted into a sunny smile as she turned to me. "Now, then, this must be the boy my daughter can't stop gushing about." She completely ignored Callie's mortified "Mom!" in the background as she took my arm and hauled me toward the entrance to the house. "I want to hear all about your relationship. Dates, social outings, embarrassing stories I may have missed while she was away, spare no details. I assure you, I have plenty of stories to trade."

Callie's expression was no longer a raised eyebrow. Her face had taken on the same petrified expression Alexander was wearing as I looked back at her. I could only give in as her mother dragged me away. Amelia was pretty scary for a mortal, and I was lucky she seemed to like me.

As she dragged me inside, I did my due diligence as a guest. "You have a lovely home, by the way, ma'am."

She patted me on the arm with amusement. "Yes, dear, I know, I designed it. But thank you for the kind words. And please, call me Amy, I insist. My daughter has mentioned how close you two are, and how far out of your way you go to take care of her." She smirked at me. "She's also mentioned that you're a better cook than I am, which I hope I'll get to see for myself while you're here. Not tonight, of course, you've only just arrived, so I'll be preparing dinner this evening."

I chuckled at that. Something about Amy put me at ease. Probably the similarity to my girlfriend. Her mannerisms were all extremely close to her daughter's, and I could see how big of an impact she'd had on raising Callie. It shouldn't have been a surprise. I somehow doubted Midknight had been a hands-on parent even before he'd left, so she must have basically raised Callie on her own.

Smiling down at her, I gave a nod. "I'd be happy to cook for you sometime. As for taking care of her... Well, I'd be dead a hundred times over without Callie. It would be more accurate to say I returned the favor. She means the world to me. She also *thinks* the world of you. Callie was really nervous about us meeting, though also really excited. I can see why. She's a lot like you. You two must be close for her to have picked up so many of your mannerisms."

That got a smile. "Good catch. Yes, we have a close relationship. We've always had a very special bond. Well, except..." She trailed off, her smile growing brittle for a moment. "Anyway, yes, we're very close. I'm glad to see you're so invested in her feelings on the matter. Most boys your age would have just assumed this was a 'meet the parents' thing and put in a token effort. Or been too nervous to talk properly. It's good to see you're made of sterner stuff than that." She gave me a smirk and poked my side. "Quite a bit of it, by the looks of things. What do they feed you kids these days?"

There was no logical reason for me to blush, but I did anyway, which got a giggle from Amelia. She dragged me through the house, showing me various rooms and hallways, commenting on the places Callie had liked to spend time as a kid, and the others caught up with us, following along. She showed me the greenhouse (which was gorgeous) and Jessie excitedly began asking her questions about nitrate levels in her fertilizers or some other gardening shit (no pun intended) that I tuned out.

Jessie loved plants and gardening, but she spent all her time with Ascendants now, and they went more for the super than the natural aspect of supernatural plant growth. It was easy to forget my blonde teammate had grown up working with flowers before she ever had her ability.

As soon as Amelia was distracted with Jessie, Callie swooped in and dragged me away, effectively putting herself between her mother and me to prevent any embarrassing stories from being told. Like she could physically stop me from hearing her dirty laundry by standing in front of me. It was unspeakably cute.

After a few hours, in which we were shown our rooms (mine was the guest room right next to Callie's childhood bedroom, where she was staying, and Amelia's wink when she mentioned that made my girlfriend turn a shade of red I suspected to be unhealthy), we all headed into the kitchen, and Amelia made us all dinner. She had one of those flat grill surfaces you see in some restaurants, and she cooked us meat and vegetables and fried rice as we watched. Her knife work was actually pretty impressive for a mortal.

All in all, it was a fantastic day, and exactly what we needed. The feeling of relaxing without needing to worry about anything was just amazing. After dinner, we arranged to meet up with Benny, Celine, and Maria the next day, which Jessie seemed excited about, and explore the city. Our elf friend and the Cark siblings had never been to Valen, and we wanted to show them all the sights, as well as possibly throw our weight around a bit since G-rankers were rare here, and there were only a few people higher than that in the whole city.

I fell asleep smiling. This vacation had been a great idea.

Chapter Eighteen

WAKING up the next morning was so relaxing. We slept in, which should have been routine, since we'd been doing it for a while, but there was something different about a day when you had training later and a day when you were just doing whatever you wanted. I rolled over and was greeted with a grunt of annoyance and a hand shoving my face away sleepily. I sputtered a bit, and then started laughing, sitting up to look down at my girlfriend, who was never in a good mood when someone woke her up.

She opened one eye, glaring at me balefully. "S'bright. N'cold. Lay down." She'd somehow managed to slip in here after I went to bed and burrow under me like I was a giant blanket. The bleary, squinting annoyance of someone who wished they were still sleeping was adorable on her.

I raised an eyebrow. "I'm pretty sure we need to go down for breakfast. I smell bacon. I bet your mom made us some food. We can't just stay up here forever. Also, how did you even get in here without waking me up? My Perception is pretty high. Did you use Stealth or something?" I didn't try to hide the laughter in my voice at the fact that she wasn't comfortable staying in separate rooms for even a day. Or the happiness. It made me smile.

The other eye creaked open as she glared hard at me. "Ugh." She was clearly forcing her vocal cords to warm up and actually function. "My bed is too big. And cold. It was annoying. I *was* perfectly warm here until you got up like a jerk. But fine. If bacon is more important to you than your beloved girlfriend, I see how it is." She turned her head away, too lazy to get up and roll over to shun me. "You can just leave me here to freeze."

I grinned and hopped out of bed, pulling on a shirt to go with the sweats I'd been sleeping in. "Oh, okay. Glad you understand. Can't expect a man not to prioritize his bacon. Well… if there's any left once I'm finished with it. I love me some bacon." I turned to leave with a snicker, planning to wait outside for her.

Apparently I underestimated her, as I felt a slipper smack into the back of my head. I turned in shock to glare, but barely managed to catch sight of her as she pushed her ridiculously high Might to blitz past me and make it to the door before I could. "You asshole!" I yelped, turning to bolt after her. She wasn't going all out, since she didn't want to shatter the floors or anything. Fantasy could warp the world a bit to allow us to use our power without some of the inconveniences, but hers wasn't as high as her Might.

Little things like that were part of our training over the last few weeks. Learning to harness our abilities better and use our stats to the fullest. At the beginning of last month, I wouldn't have been able to bolt down the hall after her at top speed without breaking anything. I'd have shattered the floor or run into a wall. Both of us were so much more than we had been.

She got to the kitchen a second before me, and I scooped her up by the waist and spun her around, dropping her outside the doorway as I bolted for the plate with the bacon on it. She gave an offended squawk and made to follow, but we both stopped when we heard a loud throat-clearing noise from one side. Frozen and caught, I slowly turned to regard an amused-looking Alexander, who was sitting next to an annoyed-seeming Amelia.

Our hostess smiled archly. "You two seem spirited."

Turning to Callie, I was shocked to see my usually unflappable girlfriend looking like she was caught with her hand in the cookie jar. We were so used to our mornings together that we'd gotten a bit lost on what would happen if I chased her down the stairs and into the kitchen. She cleared her throat, looking just like Alexander for a second. "Ah. Hello. Fancy seeing you all here. Lovely morning, isn't it?"

It was probably the most blatant attempt to ignore reality I'd ever seen, and Callie could literally make fake copies of herself from pure darkness.

Amelia smirked. "Yes, fancy seeing me in my own kitchen." She stared for a minute, then sighed and rolled her eyes, breaking eye contact before she looked back to her plate. "And yes, Calliope, it is a lovely morning. Or what's left of it. It's almost noon." Her smirk became sly. "The two of you must have been comfortable."

Callie's expression became semi-panicked. She stalked over and grabbed a plate from the cabinet, slammed it down on the counter, and started shoveling food onto it, proclaiming loudly, "*So*, what are everyone's plans for today?! Are you all coming with us to show the Cark siblings around town and meet up with Benny?" Her obvious change of subject wasn't commented on, though there were more than a few muffled snickers from around the full table. Mostly Cark and Jessie.

Zeke shook his head. "Nah, I've seen the whole town. Amy said I could relax in the garden, and I'm getting some of my favorite lager delivered. It's a local microbrew you can't get in Rajak. Damn brewer won't export it. Says it's meant to bolster the local economy or some nonsense. A beer maker who won't sell beer. What is the world coming to, I ask you?" He looked to the other two older members of the breakfast group. "Amy, Alex, are you two going to tag along with the kids? I imagine it'll be nice spending time with Callie, at the very least."

I was pretty sure he just wanted the house to himself to get drunk. Though I had become less sure he could actually *get* drunk from anything he could find here, as much as he liked to act sloppy and ridiculous when drinking. His Vitality had to be high enough to make that nearly impossible.

Amelia smiled at him. "I might just do that, Ezekial, thank you. Alex, do you want to join me?" Her face was oddly bashful, like she was talking about a date, and Alexander swallowed hard before replying with a grin that he would love to.

My uncle clicked his tongue, then surprised me by saying, "In that case, it might be bad form to get the beer delivered. I can just go pick it up myself. I can stock up. I didn't bother last time I was in town because we left in a hurry and I didn't know they wouldn't ship." He smiled nostalgically. "Maybe I'll bring some to Stella as a peace offering. She might be willing to actually speak to me, since I've been gone for a while. Maybe she's finally figured out that she misses me."

Jessie shrugged. "I'll tag along. I want to visit with Maria. She broke up with her boyfriend and I think she's feeling down about it, but she doesn't feel comfortable sharing that with Shane or Benny because she knows they both hated him." I shrugged at that. It was true. Her smile became softer. "Plus, we haven't talked as much, since we've all been busy." She raised an eyebrow at me. "On that note. I don't suppose you're planning to offer her the same choice you're giving Amelia?"

That... hadn't really occurred to me. Maria was like a little sister to me, but she was still sixteen. Only two years younger than us, sure, but I'd seen what that kind of attention had done to Callie so early. It was a huge amount of pressure. On the other hand, the earlier she got her ability, the more sought-after she would be when she managed to get to higher ranks. G-rankers under twenty got poached for the Academy for a reason. Younger people who reached higher ranks experienced a much faster swell in reputation. Everyone loved hearing about prodigies, after all.

She'd *also* see a massive bump in lifespan. Impact reduced aging by one physical year for every point. That meant if you had another eighty physical years to age, you would enjoy potentially hundreds of extra years of living. There were good and bad aspects of it, and in the end, Jessie was right. Maria was the only one who could make that call for herself.

I nodded. "I'll make the offer. You aren't wrong, I probably should have considered that. It's just not something that popped into my head until you mentioned it." I gave her a grateful smile, before turning to Amelia. "While we're on the subject, is there a specific time you'd like to talk that over? I'm sure Callie mentioned it to you, and I'm happy to make the time whenever."

For the first time since I'd met her, Amelia looked... uncertain. I knew from talking to Callie that this was a tougher decision for her than it seemed. "Do you want superpowers?" might seem like a no-brainer at first glance, but Amelia had been married to an Ascendant for years, and had serious and justified issues with the culture. She wouldn't dismiss it out of hand, if only because her daughter was the one pushing for it and the lifespan it promised would let her stay with her child for much longer, but still, it wasn't a simple question.

I'd known that when I asked it, of course, but just because someone doesn't know the answer doesn't mean you don't still have to ask. She needed to think this through, and her indecision just made it clear she'd been putting it off. Still, I held up my hands placatingly. "No rush or anything. It's something you need to think about and I get that, but I wanted to at least put the thought in your head. Just let me know when you're ready to at least discuss it."

Callie didn't look happy at that, but she was more upset at the situation than anything. She wasn't angry at me for giving her mom time, or her mom for taking it, she just didn't want to wait. It was understandable.

Amelia noticed and reached out to take her daughter's hand. "No," she said after some hesitation. "No I don't need time. I'll take you up on that. We can do it later tonight, if you'd like." She offered Callie a strained smile.

My girlfriend bolted out of her seat and threw her arms around her mother, smiling brightly. "Oh, thank you, Mom! I promise you're going to love it. You don't need to rush or anything. We can push you up to G-rank before we leave, and you can take your time from there. No need to go to Rajak or involve yourself in politics. I just… I want you around for as long as possible? We could have so many more years together this way!"

She completely ignored Alexander, who didn't seem surprised anyway. I wasn't sure if that was stoicism or really good information-gathering, but either way, he knew the truth now. With Zeke here, he wasn't a threat, and I doubted he would screw up Amelia's chances of living longer.

After Callie released her mother and sat back down, she turned to address the table. "Well, seems like we all have our plans for the day lined up. Let's enjoy this delicious breakfast Mom made, and we can all head out. I'm sure Benny is excited to show Celine around town. There's definitely plenty to see."

She flashed us all a wild grin. "I personally want to drop in on some old friends if we have time. It'll be so good to see them." From her smile, I was guessing "friend" was a strong word, and I wasn't sure they were going to feel the same about seeing her.

Chapter Nineteen

IT FELT weird to be walking around out of costume for extended periods of time. It felt even weirder knowing that we didn't need to *worry* about walking around in costume for extended periods of time. With three F-rankers and probably less than a dozen or two G-rankers around here, there weren't many things that could threaten us. We weren't equipped to punch up ranks, but we were probably just barely Titan Twenty-level on our own now. Which meant basically no G-ranker in the city should be a real threat, even if we didn't have Alexander with us.

We had our costumes on hand since Callie was planning some kind of vengeance spree later after we all hung out, but honestly I wasn't too worried about that. I was interested to see some more of the local criminal element from this civilian side of things, and I knew Callie well enough to trust she wasn't planning something too over-the-top. She wasn't the "kill 'em all and let the gods sort them out" type. For now though, we were sticking with the civilian side of things, since we had her mom and uncle with us, not to mention Cass.

By the time we met up with Benny, Celine, and Maria, it was about 2 PM. My best friend looked more relaxed and at peace than I had seen him in a long time. I hardly recognized him when I spotted him sitting on a bench next to Celine. Something about him had changed. It took me a minute to figure out that my Perception was picking up things like body language and microexpressions subconsciously and my Focus was processing them.

I waved when he looked up, and he grinned at us, popping to his feet. "Hey, guys, you made it. And you brought Callie's uncle and... her sister?" He looked semi-confused, and I realized that we hadn't mentioned Amelia would be coming. The older woman looked good for her age. She didn't seem out of place next to Alexander, who only looked a bit older than the rest of us.

Amelia giggled a bit, brushing a lock of hair behind her ear. "Calliope, your friends are so sweet. I like this one." She held out a hand to shake Benny's with a smile. "Amelia Reynolds. I'm Callie's mother. It's nice to meet another of her team members. You must be Benicio. She didn't mention how tall you were. What *do* they feed you boys? You're all practically giants." Her eyes shone with good humor as she made the comment, so no one had the heart to point out that she and Callie were mostly just short.

I was surprised at the introduction, though. Amelia hadn't given her last name in the time we had been staying with her, and I hadn't expected her to keep her married name. I supposed she wanted to keep it for Callie's sake.

Benny's eyes went wide, and he gestured toward her on reflex, looking shocked. "You're... her mother? I thought her mother was mortal? You look so young."

Amelia laughed at that, and Benny grunted as Maria elbowed him in the ribs as she went past. Not hard, thankfully, though I saw her rubbing her elbow a bit as she smiled welcomingly at Amelia.

"Sorry about my brother," she said sincerely. "He can be a bit prone to foot in mouth. It's really nice to meet you. I'm Maria Cortez. This is my brother's girlfriend, who is way out of his league, Celine." The elf girl gave a graceful wave I was sure she had practiced in the mirror.

Maria turned to the rest of us. "Most of you I know, since I saw you in passing when everyone arrived. It's nice to see you all." Her eyes locked on Cass, and she strolled over to offer a hand. "Hi there, I'm Maria. Sorry to say you're the youngest now. It can be a pain dealing with all these older types, but I'm glad it's not me anymore." She winked at the younger girl.

Cass, for her part, just giggled in amusement and took her hand. "Cassidy. You're still pretty old, but I guess you're not as bad as the rest of them. I can put up with the adults for you if you need me to. I'm used to dealing with it from my big brother." She shot Cark an annoyed glance that was softened with a fond smile. "He's always trying to act like he knows better than me and I should just shut up and listen."

That got a surprised laugh from Maria. "Trust me, I know." She shot her own annoyed glance at Benny and me. "I have my own big brothers, and they always think they know better. It's not all bad, though, it helps me keep them in line. They can be kind of dumb sometimes, so they really need it." The two of them shared a commiserating nod that should probably have worried me somewhat before Benny cut in.

"As much fun as this little pow-wow *isn't*," he said with exasperation, "I was pretty sure we were going to show everyone around the city? Any of you guys have any ideas for a first stop? The Night Market is a no-go for a family trip, not that it's even open this early, and the WCP doesn't exactly seem like the best place to take them. Vengiello's might work, but I don't really think Cass would enjoy it."

Callie bit her lip. "We could go to the Druid's Grove? Mom loves that place, and it's gorgeous. Have you guys ever been?" Benny and I shook our heads. Jessie looked excited, and Callie just chuckled. "Yeah, I figured it would be your scene, Jess. The Druid's Grove is the local Ascendant Farmer's Market. It's mostly H-rankers there, though the owner is a Unity executive. They sell mortal fruit too, but they grow most of it there and it's absolutely beautiful."

I'd never heard of it, but then, I hadn't really interacted much with Ascendant culture here when I'd lived in town, and it was a big city. I was only eighteen, so there was no reason to expect I'd seen it all here. It sounded like fun to me, and I was looking forward to picking up some ingredients, so there was no reason to refuse. "Well, I'm in," I said. "I don't know about everyone else, but weird fruits and veggies sounds entertaining to me."

Jessie snickered. "It's not just fruits and veggies. They have flowers there too, and other interesting plants. Nothing as impressive or powerful as Melinda's garden, but plenty of things that are pretty to look at, plus I know the owner. I used to work there sometimes before I got my ability. My mom was friendly with Harvest, the executive Callie mentioned, and she was kind of my mentor in flower arranging when I was a kid." She smiled sadly. "I haven't seen her in years, though. Once Mom and Dad died, we stopped going. Reminded us of them too much."

Maria put a hand on her shoulder and squeezed. I was honestly just surprised. Jessie never talked about her parents, I knew they'd died when she was young, and Alan had basically raised her. Other than that I realized I'd never heard her say much of anything about them. This was the first time I'd heard her imply that they might have been Ascendants, and it would explain how she and her brother both got powers. I knew because of my own parents that Ascendant traits could carry over, though not much until you hit the higher ranks.

Seeing our friend lost in her own thoughts, Callie cleared her throat. "Anyway, Druid's Grove it is. I haven't been in a while either. I really love the apples there." She nodded to Amelia. "Mom used to take me all the time as a kid, she and Harvest are friends." She got an odd look on her face, glancing to Jessie and then her mother. "Actually, I don't think it's ever come up, but did you know Jessie's mom? I didn't realize you guys were both friends of Aunt Alyssa until just now."

Amelia smiled softly. "Not really. I think I knew her in passing, though. If she's who I'm thinking of, she was always a kind woman. I hadn't realized Jessica was her daughter until you mentioned it, but I see the resemblance. Piper had black hair, but there's a lot of similarity in the eyes." She gave Jessie a warm smile. "I didn't know her well, but she and Alyssa were very close, and I heard nothing but wonderful things. She spoke about you and your brother often on the few occasions I did meet her. She was very proud of your talent for flower arranging."

My teammate swallowed hard, her emerald eyes swimming for a second with emotion before she pushed it all down. Jessie was much better at controlling her emotions than her generally happy demeanor would let on.

With everything decided, though, we headed out, deciding to take the bus to our destination. There was a stop nearby (it was at the same park where Benny and I had met back when I first found out about my power), and Benny and I knew the schedule by heart.

Being back on a Valen bus with my best friend was a bit surreal. It felt like it had been so long since we'd done so, and being with new faces made it all the stranger. We all chatted back and forth, Amelia asking about the Academy, Rajak in general, and our adventures in the capital. Maria caught us up on how things had been back home, her breakup with Zack, and how things had been since M-Jack left. It had been both more and less peaceful, with no lunatic shenanigans but plenty of turf wars, even if the Unity mostly kept them from affecting the mortals.

Finally, we arrived at the Druid's Grove. We climbed out of the bus and walked for about two miles before we came to the right place. Jessie stopped first, having run ahead a bit, and took a deep, happy breath. "Oh wow, I forgot how much I love the smell of this place. Like earth and fresh fruit and growing things." She spun around a few times, eyes closed, and just luxuriated in the atmosphere. Then she stopped and gave us an embarrassed grin. "Sorry, bit distracted. Welcome to the Druid's Grove."

She gestured around us, and I could see why they wanted to come here. The place was a park in its own right, but where others were green and lush, this one was shades of red, orange, and yellow. It was autumn here somehow, and the ground was thick with leaves that crunched underfoot. Among the trees were wooden tables that had an almost boxlike top, each holding different fruits, vegetables, or even packed-in dirt which grew beautiful plants.

I chuckled a bit as Callie grabbed my hand, dragging me along with her toward the tables. She seemed so excited to be here, and Amelia's smile told me that she loved seeing her daughter so happy just as much as I did. As Callie began to drag me toward a table filled with dark-red juicy-looking apples, I began to understand where my girlfriend's appetite came from. If I'd grown up coming here, I'd be hungry all the time too. I was definitely going to try one of those apples. They looked delicious.

Chapter Twenty

I NEVER GOT to grab an apple. I tried to head in that direction, but was tugged insistently away by my girlfriend and joined by the rest. We walked past most of the tables, ignoring them, as Callie led us into the deeper portions of the park, where the yellow and orange trees were crowded closer together. After several copses of trees, we finally came to a small wood cabin tucked back out of sight. It was a homey-looking place made of lightly colored wooden beams that had seasoned to a golden color reminiscent of sunlight in the last minutes of the day.

On the porch of the cabin sat a woman elbow-deep in mud, seated in front of a pottery wheel as she worked on what looked like a huge vase. Her hands pressed forcefully into the clay as she worked it, and I watched the porch buckle slightly under the wheel before she eased up. Whatever that clay was, it was clearly much harder to work than one would expect. It was G-ranked material at least, and the woman working it was the same.

She had a wide smile on her lips as she molded the clay, obviously lost in her joy in creating something, and she didn't seem to hear us at all, implying she was throwing all her Focus into whatever crafting she was doing. We stood to the side and waited as she worked, no one daring to interrupt, and I had my first look at the woman I could only assume was Harvest, the executive who owned the Grove.

Her hair was green. Not emerald, but more of a seaweed. A darker green that somehow seemed more natural, and it fell in wild curls down her shoulders. Her face was delicate, almost fragile, with high cheekbones, and golden eyes that seemed to play off her brilliant smile like sunlight on water. She was tall for a woman, six feet if I had to guess (I couldn't tell perfectly with her sitting) but she had long graceful limbs and thin artistic fingers. Between the hair and eyes, she was one of the most otherworldly looking ascendants I'd seen in some ways.

We watched for about thirty minutes as she molded the clay, pushing and pulling and slapping the material, tracing fingers over it with runes I recognized as Enchantments, though I didn't recognize what kind. She was using another Skill alongside Enchanting, probably some kind of pottery Skill, and I wasn't familiar enough with the technique to figure out how one affected the other.

Eventually though, she finished the last of the work, and lowered her hands with a happy sigh. Her amber eyes rose from the pot and she jumped slightly in surprise, hand going to her chest in a gesture of shock. "Oh! Guests. Sorry about that. I was a bit focused." Her eyes fell on Callie standing next to me, and her smile widened into an affectionate grin. "Calliope!" She was up in a flash, blurring over to sweep my girlfriend up into a crushing hug. "Darling girl. It's so good to see you back." She put Callie down, hands clasping her shoulders before she looked conspiratorially around, leaning in to stage-whisper. "Your poor mother has been going spare worrying about you up in the big city."

Amelia cleared her throat, glaring at her friend. "Oh, are we telling secrets, Aly? Is that what we're doing? Because I seem to remember a certain someone having a rather strong reaction to a batch of hard cider she made a few years ago. If we're sharing, maybe I should tell everyone what happened. It's such an entertaining story." Her eyebrow was arched in threatening annoyance, but the small smirk pulling at her lips gave lie to the threat.

Harvest, or Alyssa, raised her hands in surrender. "Don't shoot. Down, girl. No need to get nasty. Your daughter knows you missed her. She's hardly—" She stopped talking, and her eyes locked onto the pale face of my teammate, who looked almost afraid of how her childhood mentor would react to seeing her.

If Alyssa's hug rush toward Callie had been a blur, she practically teleported to Jessie. My blonde teammate started to flinch back, but barely had time before she was captured in a hug so tight it looked like she might snap in half. Alyssa buried her head in the green cloak of our healer, squeezing for all she was worth. "Jessica," she murmured, voice muffled against Jessie's shoulder. "Sweetie, I am so glad to see you! Are you alright? I tried to come see you when I heard what happened, but you weren't taking visitors except for Lindsey, and then you were gone."

Her voice was thick with unshed tears, raw and painful and vulnerable in a way that made me deeply uncomfortable to hear from a complete stranger. At last she put Jessie down, and I only noticed then that my friend's feet had left the ground when she was pulled against the much taller woman. Jessie's eyes looked about to overflow with tears, shimmering green like the sun through a glass bottle in the ocean's depths.

She took a long, slow breath, calming down as she forced a smile onto her face. "I'm fine, Aunt Alyssa. Really. I've…" She looked over at us. "I've made good friends. They've been helping me a lot. It's been hard sometimes, a lot of times, even, but I'm getting through it. I don't feel like I can't get out of bed in the mornings anymore. Some days are worse than others, but my friends are there with me. I've met so many interesting people and seen so many amazing things. I-I don't think I would be anywhere near this stable if I'd stayed. Coming back has felt strange, but it's let me see how much good my time away did, if that makes sense."

Jessie was talking fast and without breath as she filled her mother's friend in on how things had been, but she didn't seem to have any trouble getting through it.

Alyssa looked at her with a conflicted expression and stepped back, offering a caring smile. "That… that sounds nice. Gods you look so much like Piper now. I haven't seen you since you were a gap-toothed little pipsqueak. Those eyes, though. Look at you." She shook off her daze. "Sorry, sorry, all of you come inside, please."

She walked over to the door, kicked it twice at the base and then bumped the middle with her elbow. It popped open, and when she saw some of us looking confused, she grinned, holding up her hands. "I got sick of cleaning my doorknob, so I set up a catch plate in the door I could hit to open it. The lock shifts it out of place, so it only works when the door is already open, but it's been a massive time-saver for me." She nodded us in.

"Here, let me clean up first, and then I'll get everyone some drinks. I have a new honey apple cider if you'd like?" She smirked at Amelia. "No booze in this one."

She headed over to a small sink to wash up as we looked around the inside of the cabin, taking in the small but cozy space. The whole living room area was full of furniture, two couches, three chairs, all squeezed into the space and showing that Alyssa loved having guests even if she didn't have much room for them. The kitchen had a small round wooden table with four chairs around it, a much less open place where we wouldn't be able to crowd in, and somewhere I pegged as being for close friends.

The floor was a much darker wood, but there were brightly colored yellow, orange, and red throw rugs at various spots that reminded me of the leaves outside, almost creating a canopy effect on the floor of the house. The windows, with their drapes drawn back, let golden light spill in from multiple spots, giving a nice cross-illumination effect. The house smelled like mulled cider, too, and I smiled and closed my eyes, taking a deep whiff.

Alyssa was in the kitchen, where a small sink sat unobtrusively to one side of a wood-burning stove. "Let me wash my hands and I'll get anyone who wants one a mug. Amy? Jessie? Callie? Anything for you all? How about—" She stopped, frozen again, and turned to narrow her eyes at Alexander. "See… I got so distracted by Jessica I didn't even notice someone else was here. I'm assuming that's you, Alex, because Paul isn't stupid enough to walk into my house after that stunt he pulled."

With a grimace, Alexander waved. "Hello, Aly. Been a few years." She glared at him. "I… like what you've done with the place?" More glaring. Son of Glaring. Glaring Returns. "You look fantastic, by the way," he offered weakly. She just turned and stalked into the kitchen, summarily ignoring the now-cringing E-ranker.

That was a surprise, but it also kind of made sense. Amelia seemed to be an old friend of Alyssa, and the G-ranker would naturally have known Midknight, so it made sense she'd grown up with the twins too, or at least been aware of them. I hadn't really taken that far enough to figure out they might have grown up together. Amelia didn't *look* like she was in her forties, even for a mortal, and naturally the rest of them all looked early- to mid-twenties, given their Impact. They'd aged four or five years max.

She took her time cleaning her hands, seeming very focused on scrubbing all the clay off and out from under her nail beds especially, and she didn't acknowledge anyone as she did it. Once she was done, she started taking incredibly delicate pottery mugs with very smooth glazes from the cabinet above the stove and set them all on the table, before pulling a clay jug from the same cabinet (which shouldn't have had the room—I was guessing spatial expansion) and pouring a healthy dose into each glass.

Alyssa picked one up, walked over to Alexander, and held it out. When he reached for it, she then proceeded to throw the whole mug full of apple cider right into his face. Then she placed the empty cup in his hand and turned to go back to the table, picking up a few more and giving them to each of us in turn. Amelia was trying her hardest not to smirk.

Once she passed out all the cups, she walked back to the cabinet, pulled out a towel, and threw it to Alexander, who began to clean himself and then the floor. Then she sat down on one of the couches, took a long sip of cider, and smiled dazzlingly. "Well. I feel better." Callie looked like she was having almost as hard a time not laughing as Amelia. Alyssa gestured us all over to sit on the couch. "Please, have a seat." Her eyes locked on Alexander. "Not you, Alex. I don't want my couches to get wet."

Then she turned back to Jessie. "Now, Jessica. I insist you tell me all about your adventures. I knew you had gone to Rajak, but I never realized you were part of Callie's party. I should have introduced you two years ago, but I just never thought of it. I'm glad you became friends, though. You're both such special girls."

Her golden eyes shifted to me. "Oh, and speaking of how special Callie is, this must be the boyfriend." She patted the couch right next to her, smile turning wolfish. "How about you come sit over here. I have so many questions."

I looked over at the soaking wet E-ranker mopping up spilled cider on the floor as it dripped off his face. Gulp.

Chapter Twenty-One

THE REST of the day passed in a blur. We spent the time talking to Alyssa, who told us stories about her time growing up with Amelia, Alexander, and (though she rarely mentioned him at length) Paul, Callie's dad. She avoided mentioning Midknight as much as possible, though she talked enough about his twin that he came up incidentally a few times.

She also talked at length about Piper, Jessie's mom, and how they knew each other. It turned out that Alyssa's family were old Valen money, as were Piper's. The two of them grew up going to the same social functions and had become fast friends. She'd met Amelia and the twins fairly young as well, but she'd gotten to know them through the Unity, rather than the older families I hadn't even known existed in Valen.

Piper hadn't been interested in joining the Unity as a hero, and had gone through intake and then into the private sector, an option that had been mentioned when I'd tested my own powers so long ago, but one I'd never considered. Despite their different paths, the two had remained friends for most of their lives, even if Alyssa kept her two social circles mostly separate.

By the time night fell, Jessie was enjoying talking to her old mentor so much that she'd decided to stick around, and most of the others did the same, wanting to see the Druid's Grove at night. But Callie and I decided to go our own way, since my girlfriend had somewhere she was planning to be tonight. We said our goodbyes to the others and then suited up, taking the bus downtown.

"So," I said as we lounged on the bus bench, "where is this mysterious destination, and exactly why are we heading there? Are you going to let me in on the plan? Or am I just following along?" I cracked a smile. "Not that I mind in either case. I did tell you that you should do more selfish stuff that you want to do, and this feels like it might qualify." I kept my tone teasing so she didn't take my probing as some kind of complaint. Still, I was sure I'd be amused by whatever she had planned, based on the grin from the day before.

Luckily, she didn't take offense and grinned back. "Oh, definitely selfish. We're heading to the Shuffle Masquerade. I don't think you've ever been. It's the Queen of Hearts' biggest earner. A dance club run by her most influential lieutenants, triplets named Calamity, Disaster, and Despair. They're all G-rankers, and they've been a constant annoyance for pretty much the entire time I've been an Ascendant."

I chuckled darkly. "So we're going to start some trouble, then? I'm figuring attacking without provocation is a no-go, but it should be easy enough to act up a bit and bait them into a fight. Assuming the Queen isn't going to get involved? We have literally no shot at beating an F-ranker, especially not one with probably decades of experience under her belt." I was down for a little mayhem, but I wasn't going to get my ass kicked just to amuse Callie.

The shake of her head was a relief. "We won't need to. As long as we don't take it too far, she won't get involved. The Queen is tough, but she doesn't cross Stella lightly, not to mention we're members of the main branch. The mortals may be cut off, but you can bet your ass that the bigger gangs here have connections in the capital, and there's no way they didn't clock us showing up. It's going to be just us and them, especially since it'll be two-on-three. If Mommy has to save their bony asses, it'll ruin their rep, and you know how much that means to an Ascendant."

I had to concede that. Strength was a big deal for people like us. Losing was fine, but getting humiliated could seriously fuck up your future. Things like the tournament were opportunities, but also dangers, and picking this fight in their center of power would make that even more effective.

So I shrugged. As long as we had a legit reason, I didn't mind starting a bar fight. From the sound of it, these girls hated Callie, so they'd be willing to oblige and mess with us.

"Alright," I said. "I'm down for a night out with a few punches thrown. I could use some more info, though. What exactly did these three do to you, and what are their powers? You said they're the Queen's daughters? They don't have her ability, do they?"

The Queen might not be at Stella's level, but she was a genuinely terrifying person for anyone below F-rank. From the research I'd done, she was the kind of person who would have conquered this whole fucking city if this wasn't a Unity planet.

The Queen's ability wasn't a secret, though most people who were lower-ranked didn't know it for the simple reason that the Unity didn't want to cause a panic. Her power was called Touch of the Heart. The Queen could literally reach into a willing target's chest and touch their heart. When she did, they became stronger, slightly upgrading their ability at the cost of allowing the Queen influence over them. She left a mark on them that allowed her access at any time.

Heart touched were the eyes and ears of the Queen of Hearts, as well as being her hands in the world. She could alter their thoughts and goals and sense them at all times. Some people even claimed she could draw power from them. Last I'd heard, she could make a hundred of them at F-rank, so the slots were exclusive.

Callie just laughed. "Gods no. They wish. They can imbue other people with powerful energy. Calamity can imbue strength, Disaster grace, and Despair induces a sort of crazy battle confidence that increases the efficiency of Skills. They wouldn't be quite so dangerous, but they're glued to each other almost all the time, and when they get into fights, they stack their powers across each other. It's an annoying combination, especially since as triplets, they're freakishly good at communicating in combat."

That I wasn't worried about. However good their natural rapport was, I was sure that we were better after our training. I had to ask the obvious, though. "Are they heart touched? I know she only gets a certain amount, but they're her daughters, so I figure there's a solid chance they were selected."

Callie grimaced. "Yeah. All three of them. The upgrade makes their abilities much more effective, and since each of them gets it, the stacking effect amplifies the difference. They aren't at a level we'll have trouble with, though. They have a lot of raw power, and I've never been able to take them head-on, but that was back when I lived here. Some of the people we've seen in Rajak could turn them inside out, and we can beat most of those by now. This shouldn't be a problem."

She bit her lip, seemingly having talked herself out of the plan more than me into it. Her eyes swam with indecision. "I… I guess it is a bit reckless. If you don't want to do this, that's fine. We can do a patrol or something. The more I think about it, the less of a good idea this sounds like." She nodded after a second. "Yeah, let's ju—"

I cut her off with a kiss, the bottom of my mask opening the same way it did when I needed to eat. I made a note of that trick for later.

When I pulled back, I left the mask open so she could see me grinning. "Nope," I said firmly. She raised an eyebrow in confusion. "No dice. This sounds like fun, and I insist we go. If things go wrong, we can figure it out. The Queen won't kill us anyway, so the stakes aren't that high. We can escape a few souped-up G-rankers if needed. You want to do this, I can tell, and if you want it, I'm going to make it happen. If it's stupid, all the better. You're making me look bad with all your maturity and forward thinking." I put on a faux-reprimanding tone. "I'm sick of it."

She giggled at my absurdity, narrowing her eyes a bit in contemplation as she decided whether or not to fight me on this. Finally, she just sighed and leaned against me. "Okay, you're right. There isn't too much room for real trouble. And I really hate those three. Especially Disaster. She's been a pain in my ass for literal years. The triplets got their abilities around the same time I did, and Disaster decided she was going to be my nemesis. She's sent more than a few of her goon squads after me."

I shrugged. "Just tell me what to do. Like I said, I'm not really down to attack someone for no reason or anything, but since you said they're bound to start shit if we piss them off I have no problem running my mouth a bit."

She smiled up at me softly, and we both jumped a bit as the bus pulled to a stop. We'd been too distracted by each other to notice we were coming to our destination.

As we hopped off, I looked around at the neighborhood, trying to get a feel for the place. It was nice. Upscale in a downtown-hotspot kind of way. The

Shuffle Masquerade was a gorgeous black-paneled building that looked more like an opera house than a nightclub. But there was a line outside, a bouncer, and music I could hear thumping from inside. Not to mention the illumination peeking out between panels and through thin slits of unobscured windows, I saw multicolored neon strobing into the evening air.

Callie saw me staring and smiled. "Ah, wow, I guess this is your first nightclub, huh? I didn't even consider that. You going to be okay?" I nodded decisively, and she pulled me into a hug. "Now, how did I know you would say that? Just stick close, I'll help you navigate, and if you start to get overwhelmed, tell me. We can always leave if you're uncomfortable." She winked up at me. "I want my guy to be happy, call me selfish."

I squeezed her back with a chuckle. "I'm fine. This isn't my scene, but being basically invincible in Valen helps. At least aside from a few threats. Whatever you need, I'm down for." I stepped away from her, formally offering my elbow. "Now, if you might accompany me inside, milady. I believe we have some trouble to start. We should scope out the club to see how we can get some attention without being dicks about it."

That got a laugh from Callie. "Fair enough. We aren't just going to punch a civvie or something—we'll need to come up with a plan." She took my arm, and we headed for the door.

As we got in line, I took a deep breath. Walking in here would be more stressful than I was letting on, but I was happy to do it. This was Callie's night, and I'd make sure she had fun. Besides, this sounded like it might be a good fight, so I was probably going to enjoy myself too.

Chapter Twenty-Two

I EXPECTED to be stopped at the door of the Shuffle Masquerade, given Callie was with me and apparently the triplets hated her, but to my surprise, the bouncer just waved us both through. Once we got inside, I stuck close to her so we didn't get separated. It was… a lot. I wasn't overly fond of places like this. It wasn't just the crowds, I'd dealt with those before. It was more that the sensation of churning bodies packed into a small building like this made me feel like I was in a pressure cooker.

Callie knew me well enough to know I'd be uncomfortable here, hence her offer to back out, but I was able to ignore the feeling by leaning a bit harder on my Focus than was normal. In the state of logic processing that was Focus, it was easy to hyperconcentrate on just one thing and let the rest of it fall away. I focused on Callie, making sure she was safe and nearby, and it wasn't as hard to block everything out.

It certainly helped that it was so much fun to watch her like this. She was practically buzzing with excitement, and constantly looking around like she expected to get caught with her hand in the cookie jar any moment now. She didn't seem anxious. Just energized.

This was a bad idea. She knew it, I knew it, but neither of us cared. She wanted to do it, and I wanted her to make a couple mistakes. She spent so much time focused on others, on being the perfect leader. She deserved to do something dumb just because she felt like it.

Despite watching her with all my Focus, I wasn't able to completely block out everything else. My Perception still mapped the room around us, even as an afterthought, so I was able to both avoid tripping over my own feet and have an idea of what this place was like. The masquerade was, in a word, strange. The theme here seemed to be black-and-white marble with splashes of red. The tiles were all different sizes, the furniture of different designs, and even the layout looked chaotic and haphazard in a way that somehow gave the impression of being intentional.

The Masquerade was a gestalt of chaos, but the sheer variety created an almost homogeneous impression. The people certainly seemed to enjoy it, and I could see dozens of people in a combination of cape outfits and formal party clothes dancing and writhing, with a few small areas of calm amidst the tumult. A table with ropes around it, a bar, and a door leading up to a second level of the club that overlooked the entire dance floor.

We, of course, headed for the latter. That door was where the triplets were most likely to be spending time, and Callie wanted to bait the three of them. I probably should have been nervous about that part, but between the churning cauldron of discomfort I was avoiding with my Focus and the excitement of a fight, not to mention happiness that Callie was doing something for herself, I almost didn't have room to think or worry about the possible negative ramifications of my actions.

Plus, and I couldn't stress this enough. I was *not* afraid of these people. If spending three weeks in daily sparring with Abel did one thing, it was normalize power. I was so used to brawling with someone who might as well be an F-ranker that nothing short of that could scare me anymore. It was like spending almost a month being chased around by a terrifying monster. Jump scares kind of lose their effect in comparison to the real deal. That might be presumptuous and a bit cocky, and it might be proven wrong soon enough, but somehow I doubted it tonight—the triplets were basically our age.

It took less time than I'd expected to make it through the crowd. The man standing guard at the door was colossal, even by my standards, probably a full seven feet tall. He was only H-rank, which muted most of that impression, but still, big guy. When he saw us, he crossed his arms over his chest and glared down at us menacingly. Or rather, at Callie.

"Nightstrike." His voice was much higher pitched than expected from such a huge man. "Do you have an invitation?"

Callie just gave him a big smile. "Nope. I've been out of town, so I didn't have a chance to set up this little visit. Tell Disaster I'm here to see her." Then she just turned back to me, effectively ignoring the big man. He looked annoyed, but also wary, and turned around to stalk upstairs, presumably to inform his boss of who was asking for her.

I cocked my head at Callie and she grinned, twining her arms around me as we waited. "The triplets outnumber me three to one. If I show up and ask to come in and they say no, I can just leave, but it tells everyone else that they're too scared to face me, even with a numbers advantage. Granted, he'll have noticed you too. But even two-on-three, not letting us in sends the message that they're worried about us, which they really can't afford." She smirked at me. "You didn't think I'd come here just to get chased off, did you?"

"I have no clue," I said with a small shrug. "I'm just following your lead. The details are all you, just tell me where to stand." The mouth of my mask opened, large enough for me to press a kiss to her forehead. "This is your show." I pulled back out of her embrace regretfully. "And speaking of shows, seems this one is set to continue. That guy is coming back, we'd better get ready for the big event."

Sure enough, less than a minute later, the towering form of the bouncer returned, glowering down at us. "Disaster says I should let you in." He grimaced. "Your... friend... can come too." The glower seemed even more extreme when aimed at me, presumably because Callie was perceived as a legitimate threat after her years in the spotlight and I was just a big dude in a mask. Still, I *was* G-rank, so the guy didn't actually say anything to me. The chances of this random bouncer being able to punch up ranks were minimal. Hell, I doubted anyone in the city could manage it, and even if they could, they wouldn't be able to do it with Callie and me. We weren't your average G-rankers.

Turning and gesturing for us to follow, the large man led us up the steps and into the second floor of the club. To my complete lack of surprise, the second floor, which looked like a small balcony from downstairs, was much bigger on the inside. Entering the top level, we emerged onto a huge dance floor easily equal in size to the bottom layer of the building, albeit much less fancy and refined.

The top floor was much more of a stereotypical nightclub in terms of design, at least from what I'd come to expect from movies and books. The dance floor in the middle was a series of glowing blue cubes pressed together to create a square grid. Around the edges were railings and decks made from some sort of opaque dark-blue gemstone, with strange zaps of electricity arcing through the material at irregular intervals that seemed to somehow line up with the music.

Much like the lower floor, this place had plenty of people, though it wasn't quite as packed. I noticed several suited forms wearing the masks that denoted the Queen's people, just not the usual ones I saw in the streets. Most of the heart masks I saw on random thugs were ten masks, with the number signifying their place in the organization. The people here, however, were mostly sixes and sevens, from what I could see, with the sole exception of the three women sitting at the large table in the back corner.

The three of them were wearing what looked like corseted dresses with wavy skirts, each a different color. They all had heart masks with the letter *A* on them, something I'd never seen before. Aces, I supposed, which made sense, since the ace was simultaneously the highest and lowest value card in the deck. If these were the Queen's daughters, the Ace designation was probably how she marked them as second-in-command.

As I drew closer, I was able to see them more clearly. A brunette, a blonde, and a redhead, all with long, nearly identical haircuts. We made our way straight towards the table, Callie dragging me by the hand to approach the three women. I didn't think we were going to fight so soon. They wouldn't be stupid enough to get baited into attacking within seconds of our arrival, right?

Soon I could see the identical green eyes behind the masks fixed on us. "Nightstrike," they said in unison, "to what do we owe the pleasure?"

I winced. That was really creepy. They almost had to practice that. Callie's grimace showed she didn't like it either, but she wasn't going to give them the satisfaction of admitting it. She just raised an eyebrow, her eyes fixed on the redhead. "Disaster. Thanks for the invite. Always nice to see you. Hope your mother is well, I haven't seen her in quite a while."

Politics made my head hurt. Everything Callie had just said was pleasant and polite, but I could tell from her tone she'd been taking some sort of potshot at the trio and the Queen herself. I personally preferred the direct approach. Whatever happened to just calling someone an asshole to their face?

On the upside, it seemed to break them out of their weird unison talking thing, because the redhead, Disaster, looked over to me in interest. "And who is your friend? I didn't realize we were in such esteemed company. A G-ranker from the capital, I take it?"

I was kind of bummed she didn't recognize me, if only because I'd thought my reputation in Valen had been pretty good since beating Stricture. Still, it was kind of cool to be taken seriously.

Callie didn't seem to share that impression, and I winced a bit as her hand tightened around mine in annoyance. Not hard enough to crush my fingers or anything, but tight enough to be momentarily uncomfortable. "You know very well who he is," she said, in a calm, measured voice. "This is my boyfriend Solomon."

Ah, it had just been more political bullshit. Fair enough. I raised my non-crushed hand and waved. "Hi."

All three of them looked at me intently, and Callie glared. I slowly put my hand down. Right, I was clearly missing some of the not-so-subtle under-tones here.

"Hey, Nightstrike, why don't we go get something to drink," I said as cheerfully as possible. Fighting I was fine with, but this was just uncomfortable. I wanted to leave.

That seemed to be the right thing to say, because Callie smiled brightly. "That's a great idea!"

She turned to the other girls with an extremely fake grin on her face. "We're going to go enjoy the festivities, thanks again for the invite. We'll see you all later."

Then she dragged me away, off toward the small bar that the second floor had available. I breathed a sigh of relief as soon as we were clear. That had been so awkward. I hoped the rest of the night would be much less passive-aggressive. I was just here to support my girlfriend and punch things. Why did people have to be so aggressive?

Chapter Twenty-Three

CALLIE WAS STILL FUMING when we made to the bar. I, as an experienced boyfriend, did *not* bug her about what was making her angry until she decided to talk about it herself. We just ordered our drinks (I got a smoothie with blueberries and banana) and found a table to sit down at. Once we made it to the table, I took my seat and waited patiently for her to process, letting the bottom of my mask open into a mouth so I could take a long pull of my delicious drink.

After sipping her own beverage (some kind of weird oversized blue concoction with an umbrella that, based on the small taste I'd stolen, had surprisingly little alcohol by volume), she finally sighed and let her head slam down on the table in annoyance. "Ugh! I hate her so much." She looked up at me sadly. "I'm sorry. That was shitty. Putting you in the middle of that. I should have figured she would try to get a rise out of me by drooling over you. I swear I'm not all insecure about that kind of thing, she just brings out that side of me."

I shrugged it off. "It's fine, Cal, I didn't even notice, really. Besides, I know you aren't all crazy jealous. Saffron was way more in-your-face about flirting and you only reacted a little bit." I paused in contemplation. "I'm still missing the actual flirting, though. Are you sure she wasn't just making small talk? I wasn't picking up any kind of a vibe. With my Perception, I'd have expected to at least notice."

"No, sweetie." She smiled. "She was *not* just making small talk. I've known her for years. She was trying to piss me off by leering. As for Perception, aside from the Focus you've been employing to block out everything except for me, all the Perception in the world can't let you pick up something you don't know to look for. I love you to pieces, Shane, but you aren't exactly a people person. Not that I dislike that—it's sweet how straightforward you are—but you tend to miss out on some subtler undertones."

That was fair. "I've never really been too social," I said with a shrug. "I spent most of my time with Benny and Maria growing up. Aside from video games like DS, I didn't interact with a lot of strangers. Especially not women, so it makes sense I'd miss out on certain signals. I'm not a moron, so overt flirting like Saffron was doing is obvious enough, but it's easy not to get the context behind certain looks or tones, especially from people I don't know."

She held up both hands. "Whoa there. I wasn't saying you're dense or anything. Just that you tend to leave more nuanced communication to me. Outside of a weirdly sneaky streak when it comes to contracts, I mean. Still, that's hardly a bad thing. It's why we make such a great team. You tend to just come out and say what needs saying, leaving me to wade around in the murky waters of interpersonal politics."

I chuckled, sipping my smoothie. I didn't hate that idea. It wasn't like I couldn't have tried harder to understand people or work on my political savvy. I just had no real interest in it. It was much simpler and more relaxing to just say what I meant all the time. Not that I used it as an excuse to be an asshole, but subtext and doublespeak sounded exhausting. I'd leave that shit to Callie.

That thought gave me the sudden insight that I had based a large portion of my worldview off of Zeke, who seemed to follow the same train of thought, and I tried not to have a negative knee-jerk reaction to that. I loved my uncle, but having grown up with him, I was more than aware of his many flaws as a person. Once I moved past the initial resistance, though, I kind of liked the concept.

Zeke was a badass, and clearly his personality was conducive to being a powerful Ascendant, since he was a fucking B-ranker. I wasn't going to turn into him anytime soon, but picking up a few of his habits wouldn't be the worst thing in the world.

I must have trailed off for a bit, because I felt a plink on my forehead, and looked up to see my girlfriend smirking at me. "A credit for your thoughts? I'd love to know where your head goes when you do that."

With an embarrassed chuckle, I shrugged again. "I just drift off sometimes. I thought it was a Perception overload thing, but I think it's partly just how my brain works. I like to think I'm getting better, at least. Having so much more Focus seems to make my tangents shorter because I can run through them more quickly. As for this one, I was just thinking about how much like Zeke I'm becoming, and how that's not exactly a bad thing."

Grimacing, Callie recoiled a bit. "Ew! No thank you. If you start coming home smelling like a brewery, I'm making you sleep on the couch. Zeke's drinking isn't too inconvenient, since we don't need him to do much, but I don't want my boyfriend constantly guzzling liquor."

I snickered at that. "Oh, I see how it is, it's only a problem if it impacts you? Don't worry, though, I don't have any interest in drinking. The idea of being drunk is weird to me. I don't like the lack of control. Then again, Zeke is too high-ranked to really get buzzed off the stuff he drinks, I think. Maybe he just enjoys the taste." I cocked my head in faux thought. "Maybe I should start drinking after all."

"On. The. Couch." Callie poked her finger into my chest with each word. "I don't mean your bed, either. The couch. In the living room." Her eyes were narrowed in an imitation of annoyance, but I could see the twitch of her lips making it clear she was kind of amused. I held both hands up in surrender, and she gave a pleased nod that was way too stuck-up to be anything but a joke before we both burst out laughing.

"Alright," I said as we stopped. "As much fun as this is, I think we need to figure out how to start that fight you were itching for. I don't know enough about this place or how it works to have a decent idea how to piss people off. So what are we supposed to do to get them riled?"

This had been Callie's idea, so I was sure she had some kind of plan in mind. I didn't know anything much about the Queen's organization. We'd mostly avoided it when I'd been here, focusing on the Jerks, who were the far more outspoken and attention-grabbing targets.

"Easiest way I can think of is to just start bad-mouthing them. Disaster in particular has a nasty temper. I'll just start telling stories, maybe exaggerate a few of her more embarrassing moments, and I doubt it'll take her more than a few minutes to start something. In case you missed it, she knows how to push my buttons, and I'm just as good at making her angry. It comes from being someone's archenemy for years." She shot me a wink when she said "archenemy," clearly knowing how silly and dramatic it sounded, even if it was also a weirdly appropriate term, from what I could see.

Picking up her drink, she gestured for me to follow, and we made our way to the bigger tables beside the dance floor. The big tables seemed to be a place for groups to mingle and socialize, and we slid into a booth easily. We dropped in to listen to a pair of bickering Ascendants, who were apparently just back from a trip into the deeper parts of the wilderness.

The big man with bright-yellow hair and dark skin was glaring accusingly at his smaller female companion, whose freckled face was beet red. "And all I'm saying is that you clearly knew that I misheard you, Candle! I was under the impression that you said those goats *spat* fire. You had to have figured that out when I announced that plan was to sneak up behind them!"

Candle, whose red hair was every bit as bright as her name suggested, just shrugged helplessly. "Well, I'm sorry you don't listen when I talk, Volt. I assumed that sneaking up behind them was only *part* of the plan. Besides, it's not like anyone was hurt. They were only H-rank goats, and our armor wasn't too badly burned. The smell will probably even wash out after a few years."

Callie and I gave each other wide-eyed looks and slightly scooted down the bench away from the pair, and we definitely weren't the only ones to do so. The red-haired girl noticed that and snapped her mouth closed, her face flushing as the yellow-haired guy pinched the bridge of his nose in exasperation.

Callie, half to save them the embarrassment and half to put the attention on us, cleared her throat. "Well, that sounds dramatic. Glad you're both safe, though." It was impressive how she managed to say that while sounding sympathetic yet avoiding coming across as condescending. I was pretty sure I couldn't have managed it.

Everyone turned to her, and she smiled disarmingly. "Hi there, I'm Nightstrike, and this is my boyfriend Solomon." No one looked surprised, which wasn't a shock. Callie was one of the most famous members of the younger generation in Valen. "It's nice to meet everyone. I've heard of most of you, of course."

I wasn't sure that was true. There were a few G-rankers mixed in here, and every G-ranker in Valen was well-known enough to be recognized on sight. There weren't that many of them around. But there were H-rankers among them too, and it would be odd for her to know them all.

Still, nobody called her on it as she continued in a friendly tone. "Are we telling stories? Because I have a few good ones."

She then launched into a series of carefully chosen anecdotes. The early ones were about her adventures when she first gained her abilities: some embarrassing moments, but mostly cute-embarrassing rather than genuinely reputation-damaging. As she went on, she transitioned into subtle bragging, and then slowly started to work Disaster into her stories. Just a mention here or there, until she was finally telling stories exclusively about the two of them.

I was blown away. Callie was shifting the topic of conversation so subtly I'd barely noticed, and I was actively looking for it. Her stories were just the right mix of funny, sympathetic, and mildly embarrassing to suck people in as quickly as possible.

By the time she got to the Disaster stories, everyone was completely hooked, laughing along with her narrative and hanging on her every word. She was an absolute genius at controlling the crowd, and I finally started to get an idea about how Callie had become one of the youngest G-rankers in the whole city.

Finally, when Callie was halfway through a story where Disaster had accidentally ended up in the sewer after a particularly long chase, I heard glass shatter on the other side of the room. Everyone looked over at the same time, to see the redhead in the Ace of Hearts mask holding a shattered champagne flute and stalking over to us.

"Bullshit!" she screamed at Callie. "You tricked me into taking that turn! You think you can tell lies about me in my own club?"

Huh. Callie had been right. That actually was pretty easy. Now for the fun part.

Chapter Twenty-Four

DISASTER, unsurprisingly, was quickly followed by her sisters, and the rest of the people at our table were clear within seconds. From what Callie told me, Ascendant clubs tended to be incredibly dramatic by nature. Random brawls weren't unusual at places like this, and everyone knew exactly what to do in the event of a fight. They couldn't have been gone faster if they had teleported.

The triplets stalked across the intervening space, eyes glued to Callie, who was smiling quizzically at them, head cocked in a textbook expression of puzzled confusion.

We left the table, since having it in the way wasn't likely to help much, and stepped out to face them in the empty space between it and the dance floor. I didn't really feel like bickering, so I just stood behind Callie and crossed my arms, trying to look menacing, which was admittedly not hard when you're six foot four and made of solid muscle covered in expensive, powerful armor.

Stopping a few feet short of us, Disaster glared at Callie. "I am so fucking glad you took your boy toy and fucked off to the capital, you holier-than-thou bitch. Do you know how nice it's been not having to deal with your constant showboating and cries for attention?" She put on a high-pitched voice. "'Oh, I'm Nightstrike, and people fear me because I'm such a badass, they definitely don't pay attention to me because of my ridiculous oversized ass and skimpy leotard. I'm the strongest heroine in the city.' Fucking gag me, Calliope! We were all so relieved you were gone and you had to ruin it by showing your snooty face again."

Callie's puzzled frown melted into an angry sneer. Using real names was considered terrible form. Callie's identity wasn't really a secret, considering her parentage, but it was still an asshole thing to do. "Oh, how shocking, the perpetual second-place doesn't like how much attention I get. Grow up, Ashley. We're Ascendants. We're all trying to get attention. And I'm not even going to dignify that costume remark with a response. Maybe if you spent half the time you waste throwing tantrums about how people should care more about you actually trying to improve, you wouldn't be so far behind."

I was starting to really dislike this girl. The insistence that Callie was coasting on her looks was insulting as hell, especially to someone like me who trained with her constantly. No one put in as much effort as my girl-friend—she was the most driven person I knew.

The two sisters stood back, watching carefully but not actually moving. The redhead jerked her eyes to me. "Oh, and how about the arm candy. You do know she's only with you for the glory, right? How convenient that you got together right after you got famous and got a ride out of this dump. Or did you think she actually liked you?"

My mask was convenient in this case because it hid the barely contained laughter on my face, which probably would have made things worse. Callie could have gone to Rajak any time she wanted. She was furious about needing to give in to her dad's pressure, and had only gone because she cared about the team. If Disaster wanted to sow dissent, she had picked the exact wrong string to pull on. It was actually kind of funny seeing her misread the situation so badly.

Despite the wild inaccuracy, though, Callie seemed to be furious at the accusation, and I saw the shadows around us start to literally bubble as her ability reached out to take hold of them. My eyes widened and I put a warning hand on her shoulder. "Honey. I think maybe using our abilities on them directly is a bit overkill. We're not here to hurt anyone, and that seems like it might be a step too far."

It was the subtlest way I could say "what are you doing, we don't want to kill them." After studying the triplets a bit, I'd concluded that they were low-tier G-rankers who couldn't have been on that level more than a year

119

at most. Without our advantages in training and stats, I doubted any of them had a specialized stat that equaled even one of my evenly distributed ones. After weeks of training against Abel, we could probably take the three of them with barely any Skill use and a bit of elbow grease. Using Callie's shadows directly was like swatting a fly by collapsing a building on it.

Releasing a deep breath, Callie relaxed, and the shadows pacified. She'd definitely done that on purpose, but I wasn't sure if she was showing off to make a point or was genuinely so angry she'd been about to hurt them.

Disaster, for her part, didn't seem to care. She snarled at the pretension of my comment and Callie's concession, and blurred forward toward us without a second of warning.

Unfortunately for her, "without a second of warning," from someone at her level, might as well have come with an engraved invitation to a fight with a time and date stamp attached. Disaster was not only glowing with green energy, but shot through with the blue glow surrounding the dark-haired one, and the red glow surrounding the blonde. Calamity and Despair, though I didn't know which was which.

Whatever the order was, they had clearly juiced her up already, and while it didn't bridge the gap between us stat-wise, it gave her enough of a bump that I could see her doing alright against some of the lower-level Pavilion members. Unfortunately, it was *only* the lower-level members, and I groaned in annoyance as I stepped back. Callie didn't need help with this. As much as I'd been itching for a fight, I'd just be stepping on her moment.

I wasn't really sure what the beef between these two was, but Callie clearly hated Disaster enough to fight all three of them alone. She wanted to work out some aggression, and the point of this whole thing was for her to have fun and do something stupid and selfish for a change.

I backed up and sat down at the table again, picking up my blueberry smoothie and taking a long sip as I watched the show. Seeing Callie fight was always amazing.

Disaster, for her part, was pretty impressive. Her hands came up and she lashed out with a pair of punches crackling with green flame, which made my eyebrows shoot up. Since I knew her ability, that was either a trick she managed through synergizing or she had an actual fucking fire fist Skill. I knew Skills like that existed, but they were insanely rare on Callus, Unique Skills like my DS Mastery notwithstanding.

Callie was surprised too, but to her credit, she also had much higher Might and Perception than I did. Picking up, processing, and then reacting to that attack was child's play for her, and she barely hesitated for an instant as Disaster came in at her. Dropping to a one-legged crouch, Callie planted a hand flat on the floor and spun herself in a circle, using the circular momentum and her Balam skills to take Disaster's feet right out from under her.

She rolled to the side just fast enough to avoid Calamity's stomping attempt to smash her face in, went up onto her hands, and arched into a graceful backbend to get back to her feet. I had to stifle a laugh because it was such a showy and obviously frivolous move that literally no one could mistake it for anything but blatant mockery. She was playing with them, and she wanted them all to know it.

With Disaster coming back to her feet, the triplets all took a moment to stop and reorient themselves before spreading out around her in a loose triangle formation. The next attack, when it came, was a perfectly synchronized assault from three directions that was much more difficult to dodge than any of the singular attacks would have been. I could see what Callie meant: the three of them had good synergy. Seems like I'd underestimated their strength. If we hadn't been undergoing the training we had, I'd probably have needed to help her out of this.

We had trained, however. These three rookies were probably about as good as we were after the first week of Abel beating our mistakes into us. Still, that wasn't good enough. Callie was easily able to identify the small gaps in their cooperative assault and slip through them. Even if she hadn't been more skilled, she had a stat advantage they just weren't good enough to compensate for.

Disaster came at her from the front, aiming to lock her up. The one I suspected was Calamity (red, blonde) came from behind on the left, aiming low, and Despair (blue, brunette) from behind on the right, driving the first blazing kick at the back of her head. I watched with interest to see if the hits would land. With Callie's armor it wasn't like the attacks could do any real damage. Might hurt a bit, but she wasn't going to get injured.

It never even got that far. As Despair's foot swung at her head, my girl-friend spun in place. One hand lashed out, using the momentum of a full rotation to lift the blue-glowing Ascendant off her feet, as the other clamped down on her thigh, lifting her bodily off the ground and swinging her along the trajectory of the kick. Calamity noticed the move too late and tried to pull out of her attack, but had already committed too much, and her low blow slammed into her sister as she was swung around along the ground, tangling the two of them up and sending her sprawling.

Callie, no longer in the same spot after the movement, avoided the direct assault from Disaster by putting the tangled forms of her sisters in her way with a quick yank, and the three of them ended up in a heap on the floor, groaning at the impact. Callie casually strolled over to where I was sitting, plopping down in my lap and snatching up my smoothie to take a long sip as I yelped in protest.

Of course, they weren't down and out or anything. She hadn't seriously hurt them, even if I doubted that had been much fun. She was just giving them time to sort themselves out and make a plan, or decide not to engage again. Her display just now had effectively proved that she was *way* out of their league. If they were smart, they would back off. This had been their own idea anyway, at least from an outside perspective.

Disaster looked just about ready to explode, but her sisters were whispering to her hurriedly, clearly trying to avoid letting the whole mess escalate. She forced herself to take a breath, but once she did, she started to calm down a bit. She'd been outmaneuvered here, and so she needed something to help her save face, but she knew she couldn't win a direct fight. I couldn't hear what they were saying, so they must have been using some kind of Stealth Skill.

She strode forward, shoulders back, head high, and stalked up to point at Callie. "Okay, that was kind of impressive, but really, this isn't the place for combat anyway. We wouldn't be able to let loose for fear of damaging our business, you understand." That was a decent excuse, but they weren't going to leave it at that. I was sure of it. They needed a way to change the narrative.

I considered dozens of scenarios, but in the end, I was absolutely floored when Disaster pointed directly at us and shouted, "We challenge you to a dance-off!"

Wait... what?

Chapter Twenty-Five

APPARENTLY THERE WERE preparations necessary for the "dance-off," so I was able to steal Callie away before the competition actually started. I dragged her back to the table, and she covered us with a film of shadow that muted our words.

As soon as the bubble went up, she started cursing. "That bitch! She completely outmaneuvered me. How did I not see that coming?"

I just kind of... stared. Finally my brain started working enough for me to speak. "Okay, what the actual fuck? How was that even a viable challenge, much less a masterstroke that destroyed all your plans? She challenged you to a dance-off. That's, like... Jerk-level stupid."

Callie growled in annoyance. "If you recall, the Jerks partially ran this town for years. But the stupidity is *why* it's genius. Ascendant interactions, politics specifically, are all about perception. Lowercase-*p* perception, as in the way people see you. The reason this whole plan was viable was because baiting them into attacking and kicking their asses in their own club made them look like incompetent morons. Being seen as a hero, or even as an evil bastard, these things all have value... being seen as a useless idiot, less so."

I opened my mouth to mention the Jerks again, and she held up a finger to cut me off. "The Jerks were morons, but they weren't useless. They got things done, so the stupidity got them more buzz, not less. Which is why *this*"—she gestured over her shoulder with a thumb—"is such a good move. Challenging me to a dance-off effectively neutralizes any weight this had. It's turned the whole thing into a game. Win or lose, nothing we do now matters. We come out looking like squabbling kids either way."

"Ah," I said. "If we try to fight them anyway, we look like aggro assholes, which runs counter to our image and would hurt us more than help. We have to be careful about our reputation so we don't pile negative recursion on ourselves. Whereas if we accept, this is just silly nonsense. They put us in a box." I groaned. "This kind of shit makes my head hurt. I just wanted to fight somebody. This is why I prefer the WCP. At least down there, people just try to straight-up murder you. Dealing with Unity bullshit is so complicated."

Callie just waved me off. "It's fine. You won't be participating. The initial challenge was a big sweeping declaration because it grabbed attention. She's going to realize it would be two-on-three, and needing an extra person to beat me makes her look bad, even if it is a joke. She'll tell her sisters to back off and the two of us will take each other on head-to-head. It's not like I don't know how to dance. I took like... four years of ballet when I was younger. It's not exactly the right style for this, but I have a few other moves."

I reached out to take her hand and gave it a squeeze. "Really? Yet another thing I didn't know about you. Will you ever stop surprising me?" I paused after I said that. "Although thinking back, the leotard probably would have been a decent clue if I'd thought about it. I admit, I mostly just got distracted by your legs though." She rolled her eyes at that, and I slid back down into the booth. "Alright. Well, go kick her ass... through dance. Nope, that just isn't getting less stupid. Weird, I thought I'd get used to it."

She just laughed as she got up and dismissed the bubble. Sure enough, Disaster was standing alone in the middle of the floor, and as Callie walked out to face her, she loudly announced that it would be one-on-one to make things fair.

To my surprise, Despair and Calamity plopped down in the other side of the booth, giving me friendly nods. I cocked my head, the universal symbol for "confused masked guy." "Um... hello? It's nice to meet you?"

The blonde one (Despair, I thought), just chuckled. "You too. You and Callie seem close. I think it's nice she found someone. She always had trouble meeting guys. They were almost all asshole Ascendants who wanted to ride the fame train up to the next rank. You seem really sweet, though. It's nice." At my stunned silence, she just laughed again. "Sorry. You must be confused. I'm Lauren. This is Amber. We've known Callie for years."

"Um... okay?" I said, completely thrown. "But doesn't she, like... hate you guys? No offense, you seem nice enough so far, but you seem more at ease with this situation than I expected. I figured you would be shit-talking her or trying to sow seeds of doubt or doing something..."

"Villainous?" chimed in Amber, amused. "Not really. Most villains and heroes get along fine outside actual combat. Unless there's a personal grudge. We grew up in the same social circles as Callie. You have to remember that abilities don't manifest until usually late puberty. Sometimes a few years earlier, like with Callie, but that means that Ascendant kids tend to mix and match before they figure out if they'll get abilities. Hell, half of us change sides when we do, because we'd rather not work for our parents."

That made a lot of sense, actually. Except one thing. "So why didn't you do that, then? Switch sides, I mean. The three of you work for your mom, right? Also, if you grew up together, why does Callie hate Disaster so much, and vice versa? There seems to be a lot of animosity for childhood friends." At least I assumed so. I didn't really have any childhood friends but Benny, but their dynamic still seemed odd.

Lauren giggled. "Making a *lot* of assumptions there. But mostly it's jealousy. Callie developed her powers early, and we got ours just slightly later. Unfortunately, augmentation is pretty shit at low ranks, and ours only scaled with stats. So while Callie got to be the superstar with her dramatic shadow powers, we all had to grind our way up slow. We were still able to take her as a group, of course, but we never had the same buzz as she did. The two of us didn't care too much, but Ash was Mom's golden girl. It drove her nuts."

As I took in all the information, the music finally started. The whole dance-off thing was silly, but I wasn't about to let Callie down by not showing support. When she started, I whooped and cheered, clapping in the loudest and most obnoxious way possible. I saw her stiffen up as she tried desperately not to burst into giggles. But when the song started to play in earnest, she began to move.

I'd expected something... flowery. Based on her ballet training. But I should have known better. My Callie wasn't one to lean on style over substance, outside the odd illusion. When she started moving, it took me a second to place what she was doing, and when I did, I had to hold back a booming laugh of my own. As she began to wind and twirl in complex rhythms, slowly shifting in circular movements, it was easy to recognize the forms of Balam, as they were executed in time to the music.

Callie had been training her ass off for months now to grasp her Beginner Skill in Balam, learning the moves, learning to integrate them into her combat style and her motions. She'd spent night after night training with me, Abel, Mel, and sometimes on her own when she had the free time. Callie's grasp on the Balam forms was absolutely flawless, and at Beginner level, she was able to apply them in any way she saw fit. Even artistically.

I'd noted before how beautiful she looked doing the forms, how graceful and ethereal and deadly. Seeing them to music just amped that up to eleven. There are some songs you can do any repetitive motion to and look like you're dancing. The forms were concise, fluid, and repetitive in the perfect way to fit to music, and between that and Callie's mastery over them, it was staggering how amazing she looked performing them to the beat.

It wasn't a club dance, or ballet, but it was thrilling and dangerous and powerful, and everyone in the club was as entranced as I was. I could see her plan here, too. Demonstrating her combat ability within the meta of the dance battle. She would come out of this looking badass even if she barely showed off her fighting, and I couldn't have been prouder.

Amber whistled. "Well, shit. That's definitely not a Minor Skill. I didn't know Callie was that into martial arts. Hell of an ace up her sleeve." She winked. "No pun intended." I had to roll my eyes at that, considering her mask.

The song ended, and there was a thundering round of applause as every single person in the club let her know how impressive that had been.

Disaster, for her part, didn't give up. She started a new song and did her best to dance back. It looked pretty sad in comparison though, and I think even she knew that, because I got the impression she just wanted to get through it. When she finished, Disaster announced Callie was the winner through gritted teeth, and Amber stood up to inform everyone that Callie's drinks would be on the house tonight, further decreasing the stakes of this and making sure anyone who heard this story would definitely forget it in minutes.

Callie walked over and plopped down in my lap as Disaster, or rather Ashley, slid in next to her sisters. A server came over, and Callie ordered another fishbowl drink before turning to grin at Disaster. "Nice move there with the dance battle, but you ended up losing anyway. Ass." Her tone was malicious as she needled her rival, who literally growled in annoyance.

"I hate you so fucking much," Ashley hissed. "I hope you know that. If you weren't some kind of freak who obviously cheated to get stronger, I would have kicked your ass. You're way too powerful compared to when you left." She didn't ask how that happened. It was poor form to question how another Ascendant gained their stats unless you were close. She probably just wrote it off as a result of being in the capital, which I doubted helped.

Amber just snickered. "Oh, stop it, you two. You take yourselves far too seriously when it comes to this little rivalry. This is officially over. So stop being assholes and let your boyfriend enjoy his night out, Callie."

Being alone in a group of people who knew the truth meant there was no problem with the whole secret identity thing. Still, I didn't know what to make of them, so I didn't give out my own name. No need to expose myself to risk for no reason, and they didn't seem to mind me keeping it to myself.

I ordered another smoothie and we started talking about Callie. Her child-hood before her powers and shortly after, more about how they all knew each other (in a more specific sense than they'd mentioned so far) and just generally whatever else we could think of. The triplets were actually pretty chill people.

The only real downside of the night was Ashley and Callie taking potshots at each other, but we eventually separated them and forbade them from speaking to one another directly. After ten minutes of trying to get us to pass insulting messages we all knew they could both hear fine, they started ignoring each other.

By the time we stood up to leave, I was more grateful than ever that I'd convinced Callie to come out tonight like she'd planned, even if the way things had gone down was a huge shock. This had been good for both of us, and I couldn't wait to see what this vacation had in store next.

Chapter Twenty-Six

WE HEADED HOME a few hours later, both in a surprisingly good mood. Lauren and Amber had actually gotten Callie to be pretty friendly once she and Ashley were banned from speaking to each other, and by the end of the night, everyone had fun. I'd have expected the attempted ass-kicking and reputation bomb to have stepped on toes, but everyone just kind of blew it off as the cost of doing business. Heroes versus villains. I really didn't get the way the Unity worked. But if it was good for them, they were welcome to the weirdness.

When we got back to the house, Amelia was waiting up for us. For a second, I thought this might be a parent thing. I read that moms did that after a long night? I wasn't sure, I'd never really had a long night, and the very few things that might count Zeke hadn't cared much about. He wasn't the helicopter type.

I soon realized that this wasn't some curfew policing weirdness. She was staying up to talk to me about her wish. She was finally ready to get powers.

She gestured for both of us to sit in the living room. "Hey, you two. Good to see you. I wanted to talk to Shane. Cal, you're free to stay, but try not to weigh in too much. This is between me and him, okay?" Her tone was gentle, but very firm, and Callie nodded solemnly at the statement, just excited that her mom was stepping on the path.

Amelia turned back to me. "So, how much control do I get here? Can I wish for a specific power?"

I gave a shrug. "All wishes depend on what you can pay. I can't really give much advice without compromising the process. I can say that I can give you most abilities at this point, I expect. Probably nothing, like... clan-specific, because of the perception of exclusivity, but if you want a particular power, as long as it's Minor, it should be fine. I can give you a shadow power, if that's what you mean."

"Oh, gods, no!" Amelia said, with a loud snort. At Callie's hurt look, she winced at her own outburst. "Sweetie. I love you, you know that. But I'm perfectly aware of why your father left. Don't get me wrong, the man was miserable to live with, and I'm well past being bitter about it, but I have no desire to invite him back into my life by becoming a part of his twisted dynastic fantasies. I can't think of a faster way to make Paul show up at my door than to awaken a shadow ability. I literally want to get as far away from that as I possibly can."

Callie's hurt faded a bit into resignation. "That's... fair. He really has zero concern for other people, I could see him showing up to try to get you back if you got shadow abilities. I'm already getting stronger, so in his mind, you developing abilities would make you even more suited to be the mother of his child. I wouldn't wish that on my worst enemy. So, the opposite, then? Maybe some kind of light-based power?"

She seemed to be warming to the idea now that she knew it was about hating on her dad. I had to fight down a snicker as I saw them bonding over mutual dislike. I'd never met Midknight, and honestly at this point, I hoped that streak continued. It seemed like everyone was just better off when he was avoided. It was pretty much a moot point right now anyway with him in Rajak. I was just glad we moved out of the Unity building. I didn't think Callie could have opened up like she had while she was under her dad's thumb (or that's how she'd seen it).

Amelia was looking intrigued by her suggestion. "Light-based might be nice. I was kind of thinking about healing? I've always liked caring for things, and I bet it would work on my garden. I'm guessing whatever power Jessie has is out. Even if I got her same starting ability and synergized the same Skills with it, if I didn't have the same stat distribution and knowledge base, I'd end up with something else. Better to just aim for my own thing. What do you think?"

They were talking like I wasn't there, which was good, because for the purposes of this conversation, I kind of wasn't. I just let Callie advise her. She knew more about my power than almost anyone except for me and, like... Zeke. Plus, like I'd said, I could grant basically any Minor ability they could think of. How useful any given ability was at Minor was a different story. Plus she had to be able to pay for it.

Callie had considered that too, because she bit her lip worriedly as she thought out loud. "Healing would be nice. Healers are hard to come by, and even if you ever headed to the capital I doubt Uncle Alex would let the Peace Lord anywhere near you. It would probably be expensive to pay for though. What are you planning to offer for your power? A Minor ability has little value to Shane, so that'll bring down the cost, but Impact is a valuable commodity to anyone even if he can only do the partial point."

I'd expected worry, but Amelia didn't look bothered. "I considered that. I talked to Ezekial a bit about it, he's something of an expert, and I thought over what you told me about the ability. I think some kind of contract would be the best bet. Something like a promise of a safe haven here if it's ever needed for a certain number of years, maybe? As long as I make sure Shane is always welcome in our home, I feel like that's something of significant value, given his feelings for you."

That... certainly had value to me. I was pretty sure it would work. Wishes on mortals tended to be cheaper since they were easier to affect, in any case, and I'd been paid in credits for mortal wishes before, which set a standard of value. Plus, it really was important to me that Callie's mom liked me and was okay having me here. I couldn't comment, of course, so I just waited as she formulated her wish.

She gave it substantial thought before finally putting it into words. "I wish that I had the best possible light-based power for me that you have the power to grant at this moment."

I grinned. She really had been listening to Callie. That was an excellent wish.

"In return, you will be welcome in my home at any time for the rest of my life, even if things don't work out between you and my daughter."

Wish detected. Grant wish?

I didn't love the caveat, but I saw the need for it. There was a possibility

Callie and I would break up. It was nice of her to offer to shelter me even if that happened, as much as I hoped it wouldn't come up. I confirmed.

Stat points sufficient. Requirements: 10 Impact, 100 Creation, 100 Vitality, 100 Might.

I felt the familiar static begin to build in my body, though it was *much* weaker than usual.

For a mortal wish, this was actually pretty pricey, but the low Impact cost was what really told me how low-level it was. When I was running up against the edge of my ability, it used all my potential Impact to patch up any shortages I had in the required points. This one, despite costing a pretty large amount in terms of individual stats, only cost ten Impact .

I reached out my hand for Amelia to take, and she did. As per usual, the electricity arced into her, and Callie appeared behind her mother to hold her up as the power coursed through her.

This was a much bigger change than Benny had, because I let his ability come to the surface on its own. This time I was literally molding a power, which had to be more invasive. Luckily I was also much higher-ranked, and rank differences seemed to make everything easier. Kind of explained some of the things the current Wishmaster could do.

It took about five minutes, which was a while for something like this, before Amelia was finished with her ascension. When it was done, she fell back onto the couch and groaned.

She looked different. She had already looked pretty young for her age, but she definitely seemed more youthful even than that. I remembered the original description I'd had of Vitality, that it kept you in increasingly good health for your age, while Impact was the deciding factor of how long you lived. I was pretty sure Amelia was starting the clock on her Impact-based aging late, but I was also sure that just becoming an Ascendant had helped.

Her eyes snapped open, taking a second to focus. "Oh… okay, wow. That was pretty crazy. Oh! And I have three stats active. Might, Vitality, and Creation. Vitality is even at two!" She sounded giddy. Almost childlike in a way, and I totally got it. I'd been just as excited about my abilities when I gained them. For someone who spent her life seeing her loved ones use powers she thought she'd never have, this must be absolutely enthralling.

Callie laughed and pulled her mother into a tight hug, eyes swimming with unshed tears. "Gods, Mom, I'm so happy you're an Ascendant now! We'll get you up a few ranks and make sure you can live a nice long life. I don't want to turn around one day and find you gone. I couldn't stand it. What ability did you get, anyway? You didn't say."

"First of all," Amelia wheezed, "ribs, dear."

Callie blushed and let her go, getting a wide grin in return. Amelia might be an Ascendant now, but she was also only I-rank, which barely counted. That must have been why I was able to even do this at all. I wasn't giving a point of Impact (which I had tried with Benny and the others and couldn't do) I was pushing someone's natural partial point of Impact to a whole one.

Amelia stretched a bit to work out the soreness. "Secondly, I got a power called Minor Lay on Hands. It scans any living thing I touch and lets me mend small injuries. I suspect higher levels will let me do more, but for now, it's mostly cuts and scrapes. Not a surprise, Minor abilities are pretty weak most of the time. Still, a combination scanning and healing ability is very useful. It also works on plants and animals, which is pretty versatile."

She stood up and walked over to me, pulling me into a tight hug. "I love it. Thank you so much, Shane. As I said, you're always welcome here."

Callie crashed into her from the other side, her arms wrapping around us both and squeezing us in a bear hug as she buried her face in her mother's shoulder. Her voice came out muffled as she added, "Seriously, Shane, you have no idea what this means to me. I can never thank you enough."

I just shook my head with a laugh. "Please. I love you. We don't need to keep score. If we did, you'd be way ahead just because of how grateful I am to have you in my life." She rolled her eyes at my sappiness, but I saw a big smile on her face as she pulled back.

"Now. I still have four wishes today, so once you're feeling up to it, maybe we can get you up to H-rank. I could definitely use the scanning aspect of that ability. I have my own healing, but I can't really see what I'm doing."

It was a good thing Amelia slipped out of the hold before I said that. I was pretty sure Callie cracked *my* ribs that time.

Chapter Twenty-Seven

I COULD NOT, as it turned out, trade three points for an all-out attack from an I-ranker, regardless of the utility or how much I valued its usefulness. I managed to barely squeak by at one point per wish for the attacks, and Amelia had to promise me ten attacks per wish to even justify that. It was annoying that *this* was when I found out the limits of how far I could push things, but I'd known there had to be one. No matter how much I valued something, base value *did* come into effect, and Minor attacks just couldn't make the jump as they were.

Still, with a contract to give me forty of her "attacks" (read: healing scans), I managed to give her four points, one for each wish remaining today. She put two in Vitality and two in Perception, which she assumed would affect the scanning abilities of her power. With her original four points from her breakthrough, that put her at nine, counting Impact. That was... frustrating. Still, it wasn't the end of the world. She would probably earn a point from the rep of ascending so late in life anyway, so she would be at H-rank soon enough.

Callie seemed completely unbothered, peppering my face with kisses as she told me how amazing I was, and I couldn't stop smiling all the way to bed as we headed to sleep. Amelia told us to be ready for a delicious breakfast, since it was the least she could do. I tried to tell her it wasn't necessary, but she insisted, planning to make biscuits and gravy. I couldn't have brought myself to turn that down even if Callie wouldn't have shivved me in my sleep for denying her a delicious meal.

We both headed to our own rooms and passed out after a long night, and I slept like a rock knowing that things were so good.

Once again, I woke up with a face full of long black hair, and had to fight back a laugh as I realized Callie had snuck back into my room. I shifted slightly, apparently letting the light hit her face, which drew a groan from her as she grabbed a pillow and shoved it over her head.

I pulled it away. "Nope. I'm awake now, and I refuse to allow you peace while I must suffer. Wake up."

She pawed at my hand a few times, weakly trying to grab the pillow, and then flopped back to throw her arm over her eyes. "Stop. It's too bright." Her voice was hoarse, but the complete sentences were a good sign.

I debated tickling her or something, but this early, she was liable to throw me out of bed at the attempt. Size difference or not, she was much stronger than me.

Finally, she groaned again and sat up. "Fine, I'm up. What time is it, even? If you woke me up too long before breakfast, I'm going to be pissed."

I looked at her flatly. "Yes, how dare I move in my own bed that I went to sleep in alone. What's next? Wearing my own clothes to bed instead of letting you use them?" I looked down meaningfully at the oversized T-shirt she'd stolen from me and worn to sleep. "I'm a lunatic. Who will end my reign of terror?"

She pouted up at me. "In case you're wondering, you're not cute when I'm tired. Also, you didn't answer my question about what time it was. Avoidance is the first sign of a guilty conscience." She sighed theatrically and waved off the thought. "Oh well, you can make it up to me. You mentioned cooking for my mom while we were here. As restitution for disturbing my slumber, you can let me pick the meal. We can stop at the market today and pick up the stuff. I figure we can get some cheese, and bread and butter, maybe some tomato soup. I want you to make—"

"Grilled cheese," I cut in dryly. "Yeah, I cracked that code. But sure. I can make grilled cheese for dinner for my night cooking. We can do all your favorite cheeses. Some smoked gouda and maybe a little Monterey Jack." I leaned down to kiss her. "And we can pretend you didn't ask for that to make the dinner thing easier on me because you know how simple grilled cheese is, if you want."

She snorted and looked away to hide her smirk. "Whatever, egomaniac. I just like fried cheese." She leaned over me to see the clock and then squealed in excitement. "Oh! Also, breakfast should be ready soon. I'm going to go shower before we eat. Mom's biscuits and gravy are amazing. They might be almost as good as your food." With that, she hopped out of bed and bolted for the bathroom. I just smiled, rolled my eyes, and got up to get dressed. I preferred to shower at the end of the day rather than the beginning.

The food actually did smell amazing. I wondered if now that she had Impact, Amelia qualified for the Minor Cooking Mastery Skill. I'd never been sure how that worked. Most people broke through in their teens when they didn't have developed Skills yet, so it would be interesting to see how things worked out.

Knowing I might not get much to eat if Callie made it downstairs first, I decided to leave her to her shower and try to get my food before her. She might sulk, but she wouldn't be too mad as long as I didn't eat it all, and considering how much Amelia cooked last time, I doubted I would.

As I headed downstairs, I tried to think through everything we needed to do while we were here.

We had the guild to visit, Maria and Benny to spend time with (as well as Maria to offer a wish to), and only four days or so left here to do all that in. It seemed like both plenty of time and not enough. At least Maria would have Amelia entering the world of capes at the same time, and she already knew all about Ascendant life. Having a friend who could guide her would be a huge help to my surrogate little sister.

When I arrived at the kitchen, breakfast was just about ready, and Amelia was putting out plates. She was talking to Alexander, who was smiling noticeably. The normally taciturn and formal man looked absolutely ecstatic at the change in Amelia's lifespan, and brightened more when he saw me. "Shane! Good morning. Amy was just catching me up on her evening. I can't thank you enough for everything you've done. I sent for a few of my F-rankers to come and help her with things around the house and ranking up. She doesn't want to relocate to Rajak for several reasons."

"I can speak for myself, thank you," said Amelia with good humor. "But yes. I'd rather avoid my ex-husband's city. I'm more suited to the Unity, and if I went to the capital, I'd be forced to interact with him quite a bit. Stella has a large amount of control over this branch, and I've known her for quite some time. I'm not entirely sold on the idea of a bunch of F-rankers coming to babysit me, but Alex is insistent, and I figure I can have them run errands, if nothing else."

It made me smile to think of dangerous WCP assassins, and F-rankers at that, being forced to go buy groceries and water plants by an I-ranker. I knew from seeing them together that Alexander cared deeply about Amelia, and I had no doubt he'd make sure his people were on their best behavior.

"In that case," I said, "you might be able to help me out with something, actually. If you wouldn't mind."

Amelia raised an eyebrow good-naturedly. "I'm happy to hear you out. I won't promise you my firstborn or anything. Oh, no, wait, you've already got her." I stifled a groan at the terrible mom joke, but couldn't fight down a smile. "Jokes aside, I'm sure I can help. What did you need?"

I composed myself before responding. "Maria—that's Benny's sister, who I grew up with—is probably going to be getting an ability. If you're going to have F-rankers in town to power-level you or even just keep an eye out, could you include her in your plans? Nothing crazy, just let her tag along when possible. It would be a huge leg up for her, I think. Plus, you know a ton about Ascendant life and she's a complete rookie. I trust Stella to help her out if not. I just figured I'd ask."

To my surprise, Amelia looked thrilled. "That sounds lovely! It's been too quiet since Calliope moved away. Having a new face around will really brighten my day. I'd love to show her the ropes, it'll make my own journey starting out so much less monotonous. Early Ascendant grinding can be fairly tedious even to watch after seeing it often enough."

That worked out well for me. I gave her a grateful smile. "That would be awesome, thank you. I'm not positive she's going to decide to unlock an ability, but if she does, I feel a lot better knowing she has you looking out for her. Stella and Ian would help her for sure, but they have work and Unity business. Another rookie would be ideal. I owe you one." Before she could protest, I changed the subject. "Now, I'd love to try some of these biscuits and gravy before your daughter shows up and devours most of them, though I don't think she'd finish all of it before everyone else eats. Where is everyone else, actually?"

Amelia smiled ruefully. "We stayed late at the Druid's Grove. Ezekial actually ended up staying after we left. He and Alyssa hit it off. She's an old friend of Stella, and she'd heard of him even before they officially met. Alyssa never really bothered with the WCP. Anyway, short answer is they're all asleep still. It's not actually that late. Still nine or so. I was planning to let the biscuits and gravy warm in the oven while I waited for everyone to wake up." She chuckled. "I should have figured Callie's boyfriend would have some sort of psychic food sense."

I laughed off the joke and sat down, eager to try the food. Thick, buttery biscuits with heavy sausage gravy were heaped onto the plate, as well as a side of homemade hashbrown casserole with cheese and bacon that I hadn't even noticed, but that smelled absolutely amazing. I shoveled a huge forkful of each into my mouth and almost groaned with appreciation. The biscuits were soft and springy and the casserole was perfectly cooked to bring out the underlying crispiness of the hash browns, which I was pretty sure she had fried first before making the dish.

"Hash browns, score!" came Callie's shout of delight as she practically dove into the seat next to me, heaping a few biscuits and a generous spoonful of hashbrown casserole onto her plate. Without looking, she also stabbed her fork onto my plate to steal a bit of my own hash browns, shooting me a grin as she stuffed them in her mouth. Her vengeance at me for coming down early satisfied, she dug in.

I snickered at that, and went back to eating. I finished up shortly and leaned back, satisfied. Amelia handed me a glass of fresh-squeezed orange juice that smelled so good I physically couldn't turn it down, so I sipped on that and relaxed.

As Callie ate, I considered where to spend our day. She'd picked yesterday, so I didn't think she'd mind a suggestion. Besides, I figured she was as excited as I was to see what ability Maria ended up with.

Chapter Twenty-Eight

WE ALL TALKED over meeting with Maria about the wish, but I realized no one had explained to her how it worked, and if I offered her one, I couldn't tell her to wish for an ability without compromising it. We decided to make that a tomorrow plan. Today we were going in to see Stella and Cap at the guild. Amelia was coming with us to do her intake, but other than that, it was just Jessie, Callie, Benny, Celine, and I. Cass and Cark decided to sit things out with Zeke and Alexander at home, since they weren't Unity.

Celine, as a member of the Academy, was welcome, of course, and Benny seemed excited to see the Valen branch of the Unity as much as to show it to her. As we all sat together on the bus, he said, "This is going to be amazing! I've never really spent time at the guild, except for that time you got kidnapped by a psychopath and we were waiting for you to wake up." He turned to me cheerfully. "Understandably I didn't do much sightseeing there at the time."

I rolled my eyes. "Sorry my near-death experience ruined your day trip. I'm sure this one will be better." I briefly worried Jessie might be upset at the flippant joke about Stricture, given what he'd done, but apparently a combination of the fact that he was dead now and the fact that we were planning to bring back her brother made it much less stressful to think about.

Speaking of Jessie. "Oh hey, Agria, are we meeting Sparkdove here? I figured she'd want to spend time with you while we're in town."

Sparkdove was Jessie's friend Lindsey, and had been among those waiting for us when we'd arrived in Velan the other day. She'd been on a team with Jessie's Brother before his death. After he'd died, Lindsey had taken it upon herself to look after Jessie as best she could. They'd kept in touch via scan ring after we headed to Rajak, as far as I knew, though Jessie didn't talk about their conversations much. I had a feeling she confided many of the things she liked to push down to her childhood friend. She'd been a lot better since we'd talked about bringing Alan back, but everyone had bad days.

Our blonde teammate lit up at the question. "She is! She's been taking a more active role in the guild since we left. I was so happy to see her when we touched down, but we didn't get to spend much time together, so this will be awesome. Cap is going to be meeting us there too, right?"

Callie answered this one with a grin. "Yup, and not just him. He's been spending all his time with Blue Fox since we left. I think those two are *finally* dating. Honestly, watching them dance around each other for years was getting frustrating for pretty much everyone. I was beginning to think Stella would have to assign him a mission to finally ask her out before he would get around to it."

Amelia just laughed. "Oh gods, I remember those two coming over to the house. It's nice to know they ended up together. Ian was always a good boy. I liked his mother quite a bit. I always thought picking her as successor was the only thing your father did right when he was in charge here. Paul was hopeless at paperwork. Stella did all of that for him anyway. She deserved to be recognized for her contributions to the guild."

It was weird to hear about Stella when she was younger, but thinking about it, despite her youthful appearance (especially now), Amelia was in her forties. She was part of the generation before Stella took over.

That brought to mind another question I'd had. "Why didn't Harvest take over? She's G-rank, but I'm pretty sure she's at the higher end. I bet if she became Guild Master, she could have broken through, and since she grew up with you, she'd have had seniority, right? Why did Stella get tapped?"

"Oh, that." Amelia sounded dismissive. "Paul didn't ask because he knew Alyssa would say no. Hell, if she wanted, she could have taken over before he did. Alyssa has always been good with people, but she's also not an ambitious person. She likes her woods and interacting with people at the Grove. She doesn't want to be in charge of anything. She just wants to enjoy her life."

Jessie nodded. "That's true. Alan mentioned a few times that he wished she'd be more active in the field. It just isn't her scene, though. I think she bowed out partly because she didn't want to rank up. F-rank comes with a lot of attention in Valen. If she got there, she would be forced to interact with the higher-level factions whether she liked it or not. I got the impression while catching up with her that she's more than happy to stay where she is."

That almost reminded me of Abel in some ways. It was interesting how many reasons some people found not to rank up. It was a good reminder that not everything in life was about progression.

Finally, the bus made it to the guild hall, and we climbed out. I stopped outside, staring up at the building with a smile. It had only been a few months since I'd first stood here for my intake, and so many things had changed. I had new friends, a girlfriend, power, and I knew things about myself and my family I never could have imagined.

It looked so different now, having seen what I'd seen. Smaller and less impressive in some ways, but more special in others because this was where I came from. It still looked like a courthouse, with columns and a marble facade, but it didn't seem nearly as large or imposing as it had the first time. Not with buildings like the Unity headquarters in Rajak to compare it to.

We headed inside, Callie pointing things out to Celine and Benny, since this was her first visit, and Benny's first real one. Callie seemed just as excited to be back as I was.

Ian met us downstairs in costume, alongside Blue Fox, who I didn't know very well. A tall, friendly girl with bright blue streaks in her blonde hair that matched her cerulean eyes, along with a wide infectious smile. She cheered in excitement as she saw us, or rather, one of us in particular.

She slammed into Callie, sweeping my girlfriend up in a crushing hug. "Nightstrike! It's so good to have you back, we really missed you." While Blue Fox was pretty tall for a woman at five foot ten, Callie was half a foot shorter than the other woman.

It was amusing to see my kickass girlfriend who was on the high end of G-rank manhandled by an H-ranker, but Callie just smiled fondly and squeezed her back. "Nice to see you too, Fox." She nodded over to Ian. "Cap, I see the two of you are as close as ever. Did you actually bite the bullet and finally ask her out? I was almost positive, but it's hard to tell with you two, so I figured I'd ask."

Ian just rolled his eyes, giving me a handshake before getting an enthusiastic hug from Jessie, and then a more measured one from Amelia. "Yes. We're dating. We started going out last month, and not that it's any of your business, but *she* asked me."

Callie spat a curse. "Shit. I owe Stella five chits. I had you being the one to finally get up the guts to ask. Why must you always find new ways to hurt me?" She shot Blue Fox a wide smile. "Not that I'm not happy for you guys, I'm glad one of you has a spine, at least. I'm just annoyed at losing the money. So, why don't we show Celine and Clockwork around? Actually…" She paused, turning to Celine. "Do you not have a codename? I just realized that."

Celine chuckled. "No. I don't use the Heroic Cultivation system. Where I'm from, we don't really use codenames. I just go by my regular name, same as I don't use a mask. Still, I'm on good terms with the Unity branches on this planet, so a tour should be fine. I'm interested to see how things work here."

"Wait," Ian said, eyes widening. "Are you an elf? Like a real one? I saw the ears, but I figured it was some kind of Skill- or ability-based change. Like some people have oddly colored hair. That's so cool!" We all looked at him in amusement, and he flushed. "I've never met an elf before, okay? Only low-level fae like Suki. Elves are cool." He stood there awkwardly for a beat as we stared at him, then huffed. "Oh, shut up, let's just go."

Blue Fox (or rather, Clarissa) snickered and put an arm over his shoulder. "It's okay, sweetie. I'm sure you aren't the first nerd Celine has met." She kissed him on the cheek, smiling softly at Ian as he gaped in betrayal, and then grabbed Callie and dragged her ahead of us into the building.

I stepped up next to my former team leader. "Oh, I like her. Just sorry I didn't get to meet her when I was in town the first time. How've you been, boss man? You seem happy, mortification at being a 'nerd' notwithstanding. Things been going okay here? With the Jerks gone, I bet the city has been quieter."

We started walking, Celine and Benny catching up with Callie, with Jessie trailing behind. Ian grimaced. "Less than you would think. Mr. Jack-tastic was a lunatic, but his whole brand was being *mostly* non-threatening. There were a few psychos like Ronnie mixed in there, but for the most part, the Jerks were more zany than actually dangerous. With him gone, other gangs in the city have been moving to hold some of that territory."

I hadn't been expecting that. "Can they even manage that? Without an F-ranker, how would they be able to keep up with the Queen of Hearts or the Nobody Man? I'd have figured the bigger factions would be snatching up the free territory to split between them."

"Some of it." He sighed. "But there are limits to what they can comfortably hold. They're fighting over the prime real estate, but that leaves turf wars popping up in the smaller and less important parts of open territory. Granted, the bigger gangs will probably just annex anything that gets taken later, but that's its own kind of benefit." He shook his head absently. "Not your problem, kid. You have stuff to worry about already. Leave that to us."

I nodded. With the F-rankers from the capital coming to support Amelia, I doubted the political situation would stay too unsteady.

"Mom is excited to see you," Ian continued. "Her little investment. She was over the moon when you won the freshman scavenger hunt at the Academy. Hasn't stopped bragging about it since."

I flushed. "Wait, bragging? About me? I mean, that's really nice, but I didn't know she cared that much."

He just laughed and clapped me on the back. "Of course. You and Callie represent Valen on the world stage. Now she gets to tell everyone how she has such a good eye for talent because she got you into that contract early. Plus a not-insubstantial amount of gratitude mixed in for catching Stricture, and a bit of guilt. She's definitely Team Solomon, though, and she's glad to see you home."

I smiled a bit under my mask. Not just because Stella was proud of me, which felt... weird, but good, but also because he was right. I did feel like I was home.

Chapter Twenty-Nine

STELLA DIDN'T COME down to meet us, because she was busy and also in charge. She *did* call us up to her office to say hello, which was nice, and it was fun to see Celine and Benny awed.

Her office was as impressive as I remembered. Billowing smoke parted to reveal what looked like a surreal illusion of a miniature universe, complete with tiny glowing stars and planets, with a cosmic dust floor. It occurred to me that as a Guild Master of one of the branches, Stella would have access to resources that an F-ranker in Valen might not. I'd only ever met with E-rankers in official faction headquarters. It was probable people like Alexander had crazy rooms like this squirreled away somewhere to meet with other big names.

The Guild Master looked the same as I remembered: no-nonsense bun, well-tailored suit, sitting at a huge wooden desk. Unlike the first time I'd seen her though, she was smiling warmly when she saw us. "Hail the conquering heroes." She chuckled. "My budget has nearly tripled because of you two, you know? Between your win and the nonsense Mr. Jack-tastic has been getting up to, Valen's star is on the rise, so to speak." She gave a wink so subtle that I almost missed it when she dropped the pun.

"That was bad," said Callie, deadpan. "And you should feel bad for saying it. Is this what you do when I'm not here? Spend your time coming up with bad celestial puns? I need to visit more often, I guess. I should have known nothing gets done around here without me."

Snorting, Stella looked over her glasses at my girlfriend. "Little girl, you've bulked up a decent amount in Rajak, but the day I need a G-ranked baby telling me my business is the day I retire. Especially a G-ranked baby who needed her auntie to cover for her when she slept through patrol rotation eight times in the first year she was on the job." The two of them had teasing smiles tugging at their lips as they bantered.

I gave a wave. "Nice to see you, boss. Hope things have been quiet. Glad we could drop in and say hi." I leaned forward, lowering my voice. "Now that the pleasantries are out of the way, maybe you can tell me more about these missed rotations. I'm always looking for good material to keep her humble."

Callie glared and elbowed me in the ribs pointedly, which didn't do much, given she wasn't trying to hurt me and I was in F-ranked armor.

"I think," said Stella with a smirk, "you are pretty much the worst possible influence on her humility. Or did someone forget asking me to partner him with Nightstrike when we were working up his contract?"

My eyes widened because I *had* forgotten that. My Focus had been ridiculously low when that happened. I very carefully kept my eyes on Stella as I felt my cheeks burn.

Callie smiled broadly like a shark scenting blood as she cooed, "Oh, sweetie. That's so cute. I was like your mortal crush. Did you collect my merchandise? I still have a full set of those Nightstrike novelty mugs lying around somewhere. Do you need any of the holiday run? Those can be hard to find." I could hear suppressed laughter in her voice as I did my best to completely ignore her comments.

"I was hardly the only person to have a crush on you," I said with faux dignity. "And no. I have them all," I mumbled. "But my two-hundredth-anniversary Unity mug is cracked. I wouldn't say no to swapping it out with one in mint condition."

They both just stared at me, and I felt everyone who wasn't Benny swing around to look at me in disbelief.

"They're a good investment!" I cried. "Those mugs are worth forty six percent more than they were when I bought them! Plus, Callie has been crushing it in Rajak. Joke's on you, when we hit S-rank I'll auction the damn things at the WCP headquarters."

Giggling musically, Callie buried her face in my shoulder as she pulled me into a hug. "It's okay. I know you're a huge nerd. I love you anyway. She's right, though. You are the worst possible thing for my humility. Teasing not withstanding, you're the most supportive boyfriend I can imagine."

"Okay." I was irrationally offended that I was being told I was a good boyfriend. "Can we get back to the meeting, please? This is about catching up with Stella, not putting my collecting habits under a microscope." I turned to the side, looking for someone else to take the spotlight. "Amelia! Aren't you and Stella old friends? It's been a pretty big week for you, right? So much to fill her in on, don't you think?" I said almost desperately. Literally anything to change the damn subject.

Amelia just clucked her tongue. "Honestly, Shane. Even I didn't buy the novelty mugs," she said judgmentally, ignoring my glare. "But yes, hello, Stacy, wonderful to see you again. You look like you've fit into your role here perfectly. I've had a certain former paramour of yours staying at my home recently. He talks about you when he isn't paying attention to guarding his tongue. We all do so love our masks, don't we?" She gave a subtle wink of her own.

Unlike Stella's joke, Amelia's produced visible results, and the Guild Master's face lit up tomato red as she squeaked, "Amy! Don't talk about my romantic history in front of the kids!" She averted her eyes and sniffed. "And I know he's here. If he wants to see me, he can get off his lazy ass and come visit. I'm not his nanny. I don't need to go running every time he shows up in town."

"Well, if you're going to tease my daughter and my poor little future son-in-law..." Amelia said, ignoring the wide-eyed squawks of shock and yelps of mortification from Callie and me. That was moving *way* too fast. "I'm going to poke fun." She arched an eyebrow in challenge. "Now, why don't you climb out from behind that absurd desk and come with us to meet with Benjamin. I haven't seen the boy in years, and I want to make sure he hasn't blown himself up in any permanent fashion." It took me a second to realize who she was probably talking about—Beaker, the Mad Scientist who'd conducted me and Jessie's Unity intake.

Seeing the normally implacable Guild Master look like a chastised teenager made this entire thing worth it. As she climbed down, Amelia shot me a conspiratorial wink, and I had to fight a smile. It was nice to know she liked me, at least.

As we met Stella at the other side of the desk (which had an entire set of stairs for descending), Amelia smiled at the younger woman. "Jokes aside, though, I'm here to register for intake. I've recently developed an ability of my own, much to everyone's surprise."

Stella actually tripped when she heard that, turning to stare in shock at Amelia. "I... what? At forty? That is... so rare. I mean, dear gods, I can count the number of times I've heard of that happening on one hand with fingers left over." She paused, looking suspicious. "Wait, you said Zeke was staying with you?"

She came to pretty much the exact wrong conclusion, but I decided to play into it. The WCP knew about my ability, and that would eventually spread to the Unity, but for now, having an alibi might keep the information away from people like Midknight for just a bit longer.

I raised my hand. "I asked Zeke to get a wish for her. He had some favors to call in, and he was drunk for my last, like... eleven birthdays, so I figured he owed me one."

Though I felt a bit bad lying to Stella about this when she'd been so nice, worst-case I could apologize and offer her a wish or something later to make up for it.

At the mention of Zeke's drinking she just rolled her eyes with a huff, clearly too distracted by my uncle's alcohol intake to think past the easy answer I'd given her. Callie twined her hand in mine and squeezed, which I knew was a thank-you, but which fit with the story well enough anyway. I still felt a warmth in the pit of my stomach at the gesture.

We headed down the steps to Beaker's lab, Amelia telling Stella all about her new abilities as best she knew them. She didn't bother filling her in on stats, since she had to do the intake anyway and we would all see them then. I snickered internally when I remembered how impressed Stella had been that I'd managed to hit H-rank before coming in. Amelia wasn't quite there, but she was damn close. I foresaw a pretty lucrative contract in her future.

We remounted the spiraling crystalline stairs, and when we got a certain part of the way down, Stella stopped and fished a key from her suit pocket. I recognized it as the one Stricture had used all those months ago. She slipped it into a spot midair (one that with my current Perception I could *barely* see shimmering) and turned it with a click, letting the same door we'd seen at my own intake swing open. She gestured us all in, and Amelia took the lead.

Entering with a sniff of disapproval, Amelia looked around and shook her head. "That boy. Functionally incapable of not making a mess." She looked around only briefly before calling out impatiently. "Benjamin! You have guests, dear. Be polite and come say hello." It occurred to me that Beaker, being F-rank himself, was probably older than he looked, and much closer to Stella's age than the twenty years he appeared. He'd probably just ranked up early.

Beaker came stumbling out of a side room, carrying a glass tube full of bubbling neon-pink liquid, eyes bleary behind his glasses. He froze when he saw Amelia, and I saw the carefree attitude melt from him as he stood up straight, looking like a deer in the headlights. "Miss. Amy! It's... so good to see you. What brings you to my study? I haven't seen you in quite some time."

Out of all the reactions I'd seen from other people, this was the first one that seemed more afraid than fond. Not in the genuine way you might see from someone who had been bullied, but in the sheepish way you'd see from someone talking to a strict mother. Stella's generation had been kids when Paul was active, so I guessed that made sense, but it was a weird thing to see from Beaker of all people. Especially knowing how things ended up. I remembered Callie saying that her mother spent most of her time at the house when she was growing up. I supposed Amelia had stopped coming around after Stella and Beaker's time, maybe when Callie was born.

Amelia gave him a fond smile. "It's nice to see you too, Benjamin. I see you've managed to confine your messes to an appropriate work area. That's excellent to see." She gestured down at herself. "As for why I'm here, well... I'll be needing one of your intake devices. I've recently developed an Ascendant ability of my own. I'm here to register my stats for the first time."

Rather than being shocked, Beaker looked excited. "Oh, really? That is *fascinating*. You hardly ever see older people awakening an ability. I've never gotten to process one before." He bustled off to one side of the room to look for the device, breaking off conversation without any acknowledge-

147

ment as the same old manic energy reignited in the spectacled man. He paused after he got about five feet, looking over his shoulder. "Well... are you coming or not? I believe we have a test to run."

We all followed him with a chuckle. It was nice to see Beaker had stayed the same. Visiting him was never boring, at least.

Chapter Thirty

THE REST of the visit home went by in a blur. Between finally giving Maria her ability (magnetism, of all things), hanging out around town with Callie, spending time with Amelia, and catching up with Maria while she got to know Celine, the days just flew past. By the time we were ready to head home, I had to basically force myself to leave. It had been so relaxing and peaceful since we got here that the thought of returning to Rajak to deal with the tournament nonsense almost wasn't worth it.

In the end though, I knew that none of us would be happy long-term just lounging around. As nice as it was to decompress, we all loved getting stronger and having adventures. We'd just been a bit burned out on training, and this trip had certainly helped.

Of course, I kept up my wishes, gaining another nine clone charges from Callie and granting one last wish for Amelia to bump her to H-rank before we left (since she was I-rank and it was a single point, she was able to pay me promises to cook us a bunch of snacks for the return trip). I still had today's wishes, but I'd deal with those later. For now, we were in Alex's air shuttle and heading back to the capital.

Callie sighed heavily as she looked through the curtains at the rapidly shrinking city. "I'm going to miss it. Being home. It was... fun. Hell, even seeing Ashley was kind of nice. Granted, mostly I just enjoyed rubbing my growth in her face. We've been at each other's throats since we were both twelve, though. She's... like my nemesis. It's really kind of sad she isn't getting strong as fast as me." Her eyes snapped to mine. "Don't you dare tell anyone I said that."

I held up both hands placatingly. "Whoa, no sharing secrets, I've got it. I don't think it's that weird, though. She's been on your heels for more than half a decade. That's an important relationship. Just because someone is kind of an asshole doesn't mean they aren't a big part of your life. Nobody likes leaving people they care about behind." I reached out to take her hand and squeeze it. "If it helps, we're not going anywhere. This team will be sticking together for the long haul, at least as long as everyone wants to stay."

Jessie, who was lying on a couch across from us with her feet up, cheered. "Hell yeah! You aren't getting rid of us that easy. Just watch, you'll be sick of us before long." She winked at her slightly teary friend, who chuckled at our healer's enthusiasm. "Anyway, I feel you. I'm going to miss it too. Honestly, Shane, I'm surprised you didn't bring Maria with us. She could totally keep up, especially with your help."

Benny cut in. "No." Jessie looked surprised at the vehemence in his voice. He just gave her an apologetic smile. "Sorry, Jess, but I don't want my sixteen-year-old sister in the fast lane. She's only a couple years younger, sure, but so much of the shit we've gone through has been insane. We could have all died multiple times over."

He looked at me. "I love you like a brother, man, and I'm happy to stick it out, but I don't want Maria in this shit. She can go slow and steady and work with Amelia."

Callie sighed. "Honestly, I get it. It's kind of condescending, but based on the things we've seen and done, it isn't exactly crazy. She's in a better spot than I was at sixteen for sure. Mom will help her out, and she has those F-rankers Uncle Alex is sending to look after her. She's arguably in a better position to grow than we are. She doesn't have wishes, but she'll have powerful team members to boost her up, plus none of your enemies trying to murder her."

At my hurt look, she leaned up to kiss me softly. I wasn't wearing my mask on the trip, but at the moment, I wished I had. She gave me a soft smile. "Hey, we all know what we're doing. I'm not saying anything that has happened was on you. I'm just saying you tend to attract trouble, and while that's great for fast cultivation, it's less than ideal for slow and steady progress."

Zeke snorted from off to one side. "She's right, kid. Any shortcut to the peak will draw ire. Her current advantages are good, for the moment. If it helps, you can always come back and give her a hand once you get higher-ranked and can more easily protect people. It should be insanely easy to help her rank up with that kind of power. Speaking of easier rank ups, how are you feeling about this tournament?"

Blowing out a breath, I let myself relax into the seat. "I feel... good. The downtime definitely helped clear my head. I'm still a bit nervous, but I think time away has helped some of it sink in. I know that Abel is going to kick our asses for the next two weeks, but still, making it this far into the training gives me a serious sense of accomplishment. Especially seeing how Callie did in her dustup at the club."

"Dustup?" Callie snorted out a laugh. "Are you six hundred years old? Admittedly, it wasn't much of a fight. But yeah, comparing myself to other G-rankers definitely helped me realize how far we've come. We're nowhere close to done, obviously, but it feels good. I can't wait to win and get that bump to Impact. Imagine being just that much tougher than any other person your rank." She paused. "Actually, Zeke, have you ever gotten extra Impact?"

That surprised a laugh from my uncle. "Oh, sure. Not many times, but I've gotten a few points. Comes in handy at higher ranks, and it sets a founda-tion. You'll learn about why later. It's definitely worth doing, and it has compounding effects. The more you demonstrate capabilities beyond your rank, even slightly, the more you stand out. People who can buff Impact early tend to build up a lot of momentum. It's not universal, but it happens more often than not."

I had figured that would be the case. Having that little bit of extra dura-bility against others of your rank would mean the weaker ones wouldn't really be able to do much of anything to you and even middling Ascen-dants would have to put in effort. Not as good as a full rank difference, but also not nearly as obvious.

Though that little tidbit about Zeke brought to mind a question I hadn't considered. "So wait, are you watching our training? I never bothered to ask. If so, I'm curious about your feedback."

Zeke grinned widely at me. "That is a fantastic question. The answer is... kind of? I keep an eye on you most of the time, but it's vague. Just a general sense for anyone E-ranked or higher who might be nearby. If you're in proximity to someone strong enough to need my intervention, I'll focus a bit harder. I try not to intrude too much, since I can't help with lower-ranked enemies either way. I did check out your training when you mentioned it, though."

It made me feel so much better that he wasn't just watching me all the time. The idea had only just occurred to me, but it was creepy as hell.

I looked at him expectantly. "Well? What did you think? Was it impressive? Mediocre? You've seen what things are like at the top, so I'm damn curious what you think of the whole thing. How does Abel measure up to the big dogs in the universe? I think he's the strongest I've seen here level for level, though I'm not exactly an expert, so some of the E-rankers might be better."

"Oh," Zeke said. "That's what you wanted to know. Figured you were fishing for sympathy. He's decent. He's not the first battle nut to try to perfect his own heritage. His is pretty incomplete, but it's better than most of what you would find on this backwater. He's not exactly the strongest for his level, per se. But he's definitely powerful for his age. There are some E-rankers that could keep up if they were at the same rank because of their rich experience, though not all of them by any means. In the wider universe, I'd call him mediocre, probably. For a world at this level, he's a top-tier talent though."

That kind of scared me honestly. The idea that Abel, who was damn near invincible as far as I was concerned, was mediocre in terms of combat standards. I had the feeling that Zeke was counting those huge forces with a heritage, though, and that was definitely a factor to take into consideration.

I shook off that thought though. We'd deal with what came as it came. For now we just needed to focus on the tournament. I had to trust anyone coming to an event at this level would be something we could deal with at least with Mel and Abel's help.

Not wanting to get sucked back into tournament prep before we got home and were forced into it, I turned to Benny. He seemed quiet on his couch with Celine, and had been staring into space for a bit. Aside from his comment about not wanting Maria to be on the team he'd been silent, and it struck me now how out-of-character that was. I waved a hand to try to get his attention.

"Hey, man, you doing alright? You seem out of it."

He started a bit. "Huh? Oh, sorry. When you guys got back onto the tournament, I sort of spaced out. I'm fine. Just weird seeing my parents. I spent so much time growing up in my dad's shadow. I didn't mind it, even—it was comfortable and I wasn't really ambitious. I liked being able to relax and just let my family name help me coast. Then I started doing this and you guys all outpaced me so fast. I had to buckle down and work my ass off to catch up. Now I've been doing that so long I don't even recognize myself."

I got where he was coming from, but I also knew he wasn't done, so I just waited for him to continue venting. He stopped to think for a bit before he went on. "Now, though... seeing my dad, who was this larger-than-life person, and comparing him to some of the people I've seen... it just kind of highlights the huge differences. Part of me envies him for being able to stay the same, but I know I couldn't go back to who I used to be with what I've seen." He sighed. "I don't know. I guess I'm just having an existential crisis."

Celine smiled and put a hand on his. "Introspection is hardly a flaw. Seeing one's roots can make a person rethink their path, or affirm it. It's not a bad thing that you're choosing to mull over where you are in life. Just know that no matter what conclusion you come to, I'll be here to listen."

We all turned and blinked at her in shock. That was... a lot of emotion for Celine. The taciturn elf was intentionally closed off most of the time, a side effect of her upbringing. Hearing her express that level of fondness and support was jarring, to say the least.

I had to wonder, though, if Benny wouldn't be a bit less down if he had something else to focus on. I couldn't exactly find him a teacher, since he was kind of doing his own thing, but we could look into buying him some more Inventing materials. Maybe an upgrade would help him find a bit of purpose. If not, it might help him break stuff more effectively. That always made me feel better.

Either way, it was something to think about as we started to descend. We were finally back.

Chapter Thirty-One

WE HEADED STRAIGHT for the Pavilion when we touched down. There was no rush to go home, at least not for the four of us. Zeke headed back with Cass and Cark, and Celine said goodbye to Benny and headed for the Academy to meet up with her team.

When Benny, Jessie, Callie and I reached the Pavilion, it was mostly empty. We'd gotten there around mid-morning, and Abel and Mel were relaxing in the stands, sharing cups of something hot with Alden and chatting as they watched the Pavilion members train.

As we walked in, their eyes all flicked to us, and I raised my hand in a wave. "Hey there!" I called over. "We just got back in, so we aren't here to train right now, but I wanted to stop in, check up on Pavilion business, see how everyone was." I held up a bag. "I also brought presents!"

Callie and I'd discussed it and figured bringing even lame gifts would make Abel more likely to leave us alone the first day back. Sure enough, at the mention of presents, the rabbit-masked man's head perked up and he practically teleported to the space in front of us. Or literally teleported. It was hard to tell with Abel. Still, it made me smile to see my teacher so excited.

"Presents? See, this is why you two are my favorite students. None of my other disciples bring me presents." He was practically bouncing in place. Mel laughed behind him, striding down the stands with wide steps that covered several benches at a time.

I rolled my eyes. "We're your only students, so that isn't saying much, but yes, we brought you presents." I reached into the bag and pulled out... a huge paper package full of meat. "We figured you might enjoy some new cuts to test out for the cart. We hit up Rantano's in the WCP over in Valen and got samples of all their regularly accessible premium meats. We talked over some terms with Suki, and if you're interested, she's willing to set up shipments of whichever ones you like best, for some... small considerations."

Which meant money, but buying in bulk, she had assured us, he would still be able to turn a nice profit.

I'd expected derision or an eye roll, but to my surprise, Abel looked touched. It was hard to tell through the mask, but I was pretty sure the man was completely dumbstruck.

Mel, who had only gotten close as I explained it, gave me a warm smile. "That was very thoughtful, Solomon. Abel has been missing his sausage cart. He hasn't really had time to get a new one set up here with all the Pavilion business and the training, but it's been on his mind."

"Yeah." His eyes were fixed on the package in his hands. "I... thanks, kid. That means a lot. Most people assumed I'd give up on the cart when I came back. Said it wasn't dignified for a powerful G-ranker to run a food stand." His voice was bitter, and I was pretty sure I knew who told him that. Fucking Cicero. He was pretty much incapable of not being an unmitigated bastard.

Mel's jaw tightening up at the comment solidified that for me. I just shook my head. "Fuck those guys. I love to cook." I put my arm around Callie's shoulders. "You think a giant thug like me gets a woman like this without serious culinary skills? If I didn't feed her, there's no way she would stick around." I caught a sharp elbow in the ribs for that, but she was smirking a bit under the glare. She knew I was just trying to cheer Abel up.

The rabbit-masked asshole nodded sagely. "We were wondering. You aren't good for much else." I flipped him off, and his serious expression melted into a snicker. "Seriously, though, this is going to be great. I recognize a few of these meats, but I haven't had a chance to work with them much. After I left the circus, I was on my own, and I didn't have much in the way of funds. The only Skill I had that I could market was fighting, which sort of defeated the purpose. I worked my way up to the cuts I'm able to afford now, but they weren't anything this quality."

It made me think well of him that he put so much work into his passion, and I was glad I'd been able to help.

I reached back into the bag. "Mel, I'm afraid this gift is slightly less meaningful, though no less heartfelt." I passed her a shining red sphere. "It's a focus crystal. The ruby was mixed with a drop of blood from an Ifrit. Not enough to make it higher than F-rank, but it amplifies the heat of flames by a quarter, and lowers the cost by a flat ten percent. We weren't sure if you had something better, but we figured it would be of some use as an off-hand weapon either way."

She tossed it effortlessly into the air, catching it on a fingertip and setting it to spin. An Ascendant dropping an object that size and *not* being able to pick it out of the air was pretty much impossible at our rank, so no one batted an eye as she tested the balance and the weight. As she focused, a candle flame bloomed in front of her, shifting shapes into a snake that wrapped her arm.

Mel nodded. "This is fantastic. I'll need to do some training with it, but it should complement my current weapon pretty well. Thanks, both of you." Her warm tone was enough to convey her appreciation even through the mask.

We passed Alden his present (a selection of Valen microbrews) before I turned to face Abel with the question that had been on my mind almost since we left. "So. What is in store for the last two weeks?" I asked with a forced casual tone. "I know we aren't training today, but I figure knowing what's coming will help us prepare."

To my surprise, the grin I saw this time wasn't entirely malicious. There was a hint of the usual sadism, but the face was also part genuine excitement.

"Well, I was planning to have it be a surprise, but we're going to take a trip down to one of the dark districts. It's one of the more out-of-the-way ones, so we won't be running into anyone too powerful. No E-rankers will be there, and any F-rankers, Mel and I should be able to handle between us. But it'll be a live combat situation that we aren't likely to be able to recreate."

I froze. That was... terrifying and amazing at the same time. Even an out-of-the-way dark district seemed dangerous as hell, but the chance to experience that kind of environment was definitely exciting.

"Wow. Really?" I said. "But isn't the whole thing with the dark districts that anyone can show up there? What if we run into someone too strong for us?" I knew that they wouldn't be able to take every F-ranker, or even a bunch of them together. E-rankers I was less worried about with Zeke around.

Abel just shrugged. "It's unlikely this territory will have too many people with real potential. There's almost nothing valuable there. It's kind of an agreed-on newbie spot. Not just G-rankers, or there would be no point, but anyone with real power and experience will be in one of the other districts. Plus, the Beast Lord Garden should have people down there who can help you out. Hell, Sloane and the other two will probably be sent along with you."

Mel held up a hand. "Listen. This isn't going to be entirely safe. We'll do our best to watch out for you, but there will be real danger in these next two weeks of training. We won't force you to do this part. You can always say no and stick with sparring. We just thought live combat would help temper you guys some, and you've been learning quite a few things that you could use experience putting into practice."

"That does sound useful," Callie said uncertainly. "I definitely see why it would be helpful. Can we get back to you? I want to talk it over with our team first, if that's okay."

I hadn't even really considered discussing it with them. Leaving the others up here as we put ourselves in horrible danger would definitely suck for them, and no way was I okay taking them with us, knowing what we knew. Talking it out was a smart plan, even if I really hoped we ended up going.

Abel just waved the question off. "Of course. Like you said, it's not a today problem. Think it over. Just know that you two are more than good enough for us to be comfortable taking you down there. Your teamwork is extremely refined, and both of you are dangerous in your own right after so much training. We wouldn't have suggested it if we didn't think you were ready."

"For now, you're all home and it's good to see you," Mel added. She turned to yell over the Pavilion members training. "Hey, can you lunatics take a break for a bit? We haven't had a good party in weeks, might as well celebrate the kids' homecoming."

Then she turned to Alden, who was seated nearby and cracking into a microbrew that Zeke had mentioned was pretty decent. "Hey, old man. You have enough refreshments stocked around here for a spur-of-the-moment bash?"

The bearded man looked contemplative. "I… don't know. I'd have to check my stashes. I'm probably good on booze, but my soda stores have been running low. Someone keeps raiding them. I have no clue who, but probably someone with high Perception, because I keep them stashed away pretty well. Anyway, give me a minute to grab what I've got." He looked at Abel. "What about food? You think you can handle that?"

My masked teacher grinned. "Obviously." He looked down at the meat in his hands. "I don't really want to waste the time making new sausages during a party, but even if I haven't had the time to open my shop, I still have some stock on ice I can use." He grinned at Mel. "I'll take the money out of Pavilion funds, but don't worry, I'll only charge at cost, since this is a party for my favorite disciples."

Mel rolled her eyes, waving him off, but didn't argue as the three of them scattered to get ready. After Callie and I watched them leave, I turned to blink at her in surprise. That had escalated quickly.

She grinned and shrugged. "From our first night here, I can assume they like to throw parties. I guess we've kept them too busy during training, so having one now seems like as good an idea as any. Besides, I think they want to make sure we end our vacation on a good note." She looked around in amusement. "I'd be shocked if it takes them more than an hour to get set up."

I admitted she had a point, and we headed over to talk to Jessie. If we were going to party, we should have the whole team around.

Chapter Thirty-Two

I HAD ASSUMED, based on prior experience, that the trip to the dark district would be accomplished through an elevator, but here we were in Abel's car, speeding down the road.

I'd used my five wishes all on Sloane and the others yesterday, netting myself another fifteen points of Perception and getting that stat to an even 150. And I had plans to do the same today if I didn't need them in the dark district.

We'd been told to show up at the Pavilion early. We arrived to find Abel and Mel dressed in sturdy, functional clothes, and gesturing us towards a car, telling us we would be driving to the entrance. At our surprise, Abel smiled. "The dark districts are considered restricted to civilians, so making them accessible through the upper terminal would be a bad decision. We'll be taking a series of tunnels, and will be walking most of the way."

The biggest surprise of the morning was Abel. My teacher had replaced his signature rabbit mask with a stylized silver one that covered half his face. I assumed it was the mask he'd worn as Apollyon.

As we drove, Abel filled us in on more of the reasoning for this trip. "Alright, the dark district we're heading to is specifically known as Doom-town. It's a relatively out of the way spot that, as I mentioned, is mostly aimed at newbies. Different forces send their youngsters there to get them some combat experience before dropping them in the deep end, though there are also several unique forces that have formed there over the years. Doomtown is, as the name implies, dangerous and cutthroat. Aside from the basic courtesy of higher-end F-rankers and E-rankers staying out of there, don't expect any rules or protection to be in place. Which is why we had you leave behind Clockwork and Agria."

Benny and Jessie had been understanding (if a bit annoyed) about the need to stay behind, but once we passed some cash to Benny and told him he should work on his Inventing, he perked up quite a bit. Jessie had headed for the Beast Lord Garden with most of the wolves to say hello to Melinda and get in some training, with only Rellia and Jin accompanying us for this particular trip.

"So," I asked with some trepidation. "Are we... supposed to just randomly kill people down here? Because I'm not really okay with that. Even if they're trying to kill us first, it just seems kind of wrong defaulting to murder. If we're expected to just wantonly slaughter anyone we meet, I'd rather avoid the whole mess. We can just work on the normal training we've been doing."

Mel and Abel looked at each other, but my teacher finally just shrugged. "It's not really anyone's default down there. While there's definitely a 'what happens in Doomtown stays in Doomtown' mentality, it isn't unheard-of for people to declare vendettas if someone they love is killed. Most of these people are younger-generation members of bigger factions, so wanton slaughter is usually avoided. Not that someone won't murder you if they can get away with it out of sight, but most public brawls lack a killing edge. Most. There are some straight-up psychos down there, so be aware we may not always have a choice."

I still wasn't okay with killing, but I could handle it if someone forced the issue, especially if they were some mass-murdering lunatic, and I told him as much.

He nodded in relief. "Fair. I wasn't sure where your line was on that. The Unity tends to be more inflexible about that than pretty much any other faction in the wider universe because of the nature of Heroic Cultivation. As Ascendants who grew up in the WCP, we're a bit less persnickety about ending problems, but we aren't here to force you to do anything."

That was a whole can of worms I wasn't going to open. It wasn't my job to try to convince Abel and Mel killing was wrong. The whole "live by the sword" mentality was pretty common in the WCP and I figured you took your life into your own hands when you went down there, even if that might make me a bit of a hypocrite for refusing to actually kill anyone unless I had to.

Callie, seeing my thoughtful silence, decided to pick up the conversation herself. "So, you implied there were other reasons to go down there. Is there some unique aspect of this place that's relevant to us right now?"

Clearly happy for a return to the subject at hand, Abel cleared his throat. "Right. That. Like I said, Doomtown is where most of the bigwigs send their juniors. We're likely to run into several of our competitors down there. You'll get a chance to match yourselves against other people in the same general strength bracket and see how you stack up. We're G-rankers, but we aren't exactly considered your average combatants, and while training against strong opponents is great, actually being able to *win* some training matches is also kind of necessary."

From anyone else, that would have sounded like hubris, but thinking about how they'd spent the month before our vacation bouncing us off every surface in the Pavilion, it was tough to argue. Without the worry about killing someone (past any accidents we would do our best to avoid obviously) it sounded like a ton of fun to see how we measured up before the big tournament.

Although... "Wait," I said. "Isn't the main difficulty in the tournament likely to come from outsiders coming over from other parts of the star cluster? I mean, I guess the Titan Twenty are a concern, but will those other forces send their people down there when it's such a disadvantage that they do so? Like, their juniors could get hurt before the tournament and then they would be out of the running."

The look Abel and Mel shot me made me feel like a total idiot, though I didn't really know why until Abel spoke. "Yes, Shane. They *will* send them down to feel out the opponents. Anyone that they consider top-tier will be strong enough not to worry about, and anyone who gets killed or injured fighting G-rankers from a backwater planet like this isn't worth their time. I forget sometimes how sheltered you guys are in the Unity."

Zeke had said similar things a time or two, though he'd also implied even the Unity wasn't as cuddly as it pretended to be for the most part. Still, it stung to have that condescending look turned my way.

That must have been clear in my body language, because Abel sighed. "Look, it won't be all of them. There's a spectrum out there. Some factions, like the Beast Lord Garden here, are more concerned with their juniors than others. Some do the law of the jungle thing. There will be a few scary outsiders running around, I'm sure, though plenty we won't see until the tournament."

I sighed. "Yeah, I get it. It's just hard for me to think in terms of, 'well, if you're good enough, you won't die in the first place.'"

My experience with the WCP hadn't been *great*, but they'd at least left Zeke to watch my back against high-level people. Thinking it through, the Black Sorrow Cult was probably more cutthroat than the WCP in that regard.

I remained silent as we arrived at the tunnels to Doomtown and climbed out of the car to begin our walk.

It took a few hours to get down there. We talked a bit, but mostly I just thought over what I knew, came to terms with how things worked, and chose to focus on my excitement. As we started to get closer though, I tuned back in to the conversation around me just in time to hear Callie asking something extremely relevant.

"By the way, how common are attacks? Should we expect to be assaulted as soon as we get down there? Will they try to catch us somewhere secluded? What should we expect?"

Abel, who was walking ahead of us, turned around to walk backwards, still easily keeping pace with Mel, who was out in front. "Depends on who we meet. Some of the factions native to the place are less restrained. Since they never leave, they don't worry as much about politics. Those are the ones more likely to just attack when your back is turned. Larger factions usually try to make a pretense, but it's often bullshit. Bumping into you and accusing you of spilling their drink, shit like that. Best to just assume you're always in danger of an attack and act accordingly. Everyone else will."

Tightening my grip on my cane, I nodded as we finally emerged from the tunnel, and into... well, a town. Not a huge one, but not as run-down and shitty as I expected from the name. The buildings were squat, made of sturdy dark stone, and the light was mostly shades of red. It gave the place a sinister, hellish vibe, and despite being unlike what I had thought I'd see, it was pretty fitting for a place called Doomtown.

I turned to Abel, who was still walking backwards. "Okay, we're here. Where are we heading to get some training in?"

That got a laugh from my teacher. "Where else? A bar. If you want to get into stupid fights, there's nowhere like a drinking spot to get them started. The Raving Baby is still around, I think. I haven't been down here in years, so I'm kind of behind the times. But if we can't find a fight there, we can at least ask around. In either case, it's that way." He pointed off in a direction that looked the same as all the other directions, finally resuming a forward gait as we headed off down the road.

Before we had walked fifty feet, though, a series of forms melted out of the shadows, all dressed in identical brown-and-black dog masks with bright red eyes. Their clothes were a variety of black leather articles covered in chains and studs of different kinds, and they surrounded us quickly and silently.

Once they had us encircled, the leader spoke. "Well, well, well, boys. What do we have here? Looks like fresh meat to me. And here I was getting hungry." He grinned nastily at us. "The question is which of you are snacks and which are trash for us to toss?"

Mel glared at him, taking a deep breath and reaching into a pocket for a jingling bag that I was pretty sure contained chits. "You indescribable assholes. You couldn't have waited for the next group? This is my pocket money for the whole month." She turned and passed it to Abel, who deftly caught it and jingled it beside his ear with a happy sigh. "Don't gloat. It's unattractive." I could almost hear the sulk in her voice as she pretty much ignored the men standing around us.

Abel chuckled at her. "No one likes a sore loser, dear heart." He shook his head derisively. "Betting we would make it to the bar before we got attacked. Honestly, it's like you *wanted* to lose your money. I have to say, though, getting surrounded by *literal* rabid dogs is a bit on the nose. Good to see Doomtown doesn't disappoint after my time away." He turned to us, his grin taking on a brutal edge. "Well then, kids, looks like we're in for a practical lesson. Pick your dance partners fast, or all the good ones will be taken."

Chapter Thirty-Three

THERE WERE ten of the dog-masked men. I didn't even consciously count them, my Focus and Perception synergizing to grant me an innate sense of the number of enemies and where they were standing based on the various inputs. I wasn't sure whether that was some kind of side effect of my training with Callie or just a factor of surpassing some threshold of either stat.

Abel and Mel were letting us take priority, since they were much more experienced and would have an easy time working themselves into our cooperation. So Callie and I shifted into our teamwork trance and blitzed forward, instinctively knowing we were going to take the four directly in front of us and leave the rest to the others. Rellia and Jin each jumped one, leaving two each for Mel and Abel as well, and it was nice to be able to trust our team enough to just ignore our backs as we attacked, knowing they had us covered.

The four men in front of us barely seemed surprised by our decision to fight. I considered using some of my stored attacks on them, but after I gamed it out in my head, I decided to stick with my DS subskills. These were random G-rankers attacking newcomers, they wouldn't be too strong. Callie and I both had the same thought, which wasn't unusual, and we closed the distance, ready to work together as we'd been taught.

As we came near them, I layered a Touch of Tears and Consecration of Flame on my cane, and then let my left leg drop out as I fell into a shoulder roll toward Callie.

Being able to sense me and instinctually react to my moves, she stepped off my shoulder mid-roll, splitting into a trio of clones as her body was cloaked in darkness. The two she'd been approaching froze at the sight of a foot and a half more Ascendant than they had been expecting swinging a green flaming cane at them, and I was able to stack a Mercy Kill and Flurry of Blows to tag both of them several times. One in the ribs, knee and shoulder, and one in the hip, elbow, and collarbone.

As soon as I landed the blows, I turned to swing overhand at full extension, smashing an ice attack aimed at Callie's temple out of the air even as one of the clones slipped out of my own shadow to tank a burst of lightning from one of my two foes. Callie, who had been backing away after landing a series of light cuts on the legs of her opponents, hit my back and we switched places.

I choked up on my cane and swung it like a bat, unleashing the force stored so far along with a Mercy Kill to smash what looked like a ball of super-heated rock straight at the ice user, who squeaked and dove out of the way of the attack, not having expected it. The meteor (basically) attack had been aimed at Callie's head, which, considering her height, meant it had been coming right up the middle for me, perfect for a proper swing.

As soon as I made the hit, I used Sucking Mud, then switched with Callie again, taking advantage of a shadowy smoke screen she had put up to attack Lightning Guy, hitting his other knee and dropping him before changing directions and attacking the other guy, who was trying to use a wall of water to protect himself from all sides. I could see why those two worked beside each other, water and lightning was a good combo. But unfortunately for him, whereas *my* mask had a filtration function, his didn't, and the steam that came off my cane as the poison fire hit the wall of liquid was definitely not healthy to inhale.

I tapped a sharp series of beats on the ground with my cane to let Callie know the situation as I changed targets to Meteor Guy, since Lightning Guy and Water Guy were submerged in a cloud of poisoned steam that they inhaled even as they tried to scream. It wouldn't kill them, but burned, poisoned lungs had to fucking suck. Callie was engaging Ice Guy with her clones, leaving me with just Meteor Guy, as well as a quick deflection of an ice spear aimed at her back, which had come from one of the puddles Water Guy had left behind. Another solid bit of synergy.

Meteor Guy had tanked quite a few hits and seemed sturdier for G-rank than most, probably thanks to an ability, so as I came close, I stopped, letting him notice his feet currently beginning to submerge in mud. The distraction gave enough time to use my improved Stone Limb (only took a second to cast now), and another Consecration of Flame on my leg.

Then I did something I had decided against before. I stacked on a triple-strength density-shifted blow and tossed on a Mercy Kill, before spinning off my other leg and smashing into his side with a super-dense triple-stacked Mercy Kill-empowered magma spin kick.

My head spun a bit as the soul weight of that much mid-combat fuckery slammed into my brain, but not nearly as hard as my suped up kick slammed into that guy's ribs (which I could literally hear crack under the blow, even if they didn't break). He went sailing off in the opposite direction, smashing into the wall behind him hard enough to leave a crater, and only the groaning made me sure I hadn't accidentally killed him. That fucking magma leg combo was nuts, and I made a mental note to add it to my permanent loadout against opponents with defensive abilities.

Turning to deal with Ice Guy, I realized Callie had already dropped him. She was leaning against a wall petting Rellia because the wolves (one of whom looked a bit singed) had taken down their two and Mel and Abel had made short work of the other four.

Abel, who was walking over, whistled as he looked at the broken wall where Meteor Guy had landed. "Holy shit, kid, that was a rough one. I think even I would have trouble tanking that. Of course, it would never hit me—way too slow—but still, hell of a finisher."

I groaned, putting a hand to my head. "Yeah, but I'm going to need to practice it some more to get used to the strain. That kind of soul weight is no joke. I was doing way too much at once during that attack." I paused, letting the pain slightly recede. "Although if I can get used to it, a Flurry of Blows tacked on would take care of the speed issue. That move would be even scarier at a faster speed. Remind me to give that a shot."

"You will do no such thing," snapped Callie, "especially not mid-combat. Are you insane? You don't test theoretical move combos with unknown costs to your soul mid-battle. What is wrong with you?" She marched up to me, yanking my head down to look into my eyes as if checking for a concussion. "You seem like you're okay, but you need to be more careful, Solomon. I know it's been a while since you were able to really cut loose with Skills like this, but doing things like that is dangerous without testing. Promise me you won't do that again."

I winced at the tone, but nodded. She was right. I'd been sidelined in Valen, and we hadn't been using Skills in training with Abel and Mel, so I'd been antsy and done something stupid.

I held up both hands with a sigh. "Sorry. You're right. Got a bit excited and took a stupid risk. It won't happen again, I promise."

Her shoulders relaxed, and she stepped up to wrap her arms around me, resting her head on my chest. "Good. Sorry, I just saw you start to wobble like that and kind of freaked out. It wasn't that big of a deal. You made sure it was your last opponent, at least. Still not smart, but you put some thought into it."

She stepped back, clearing her throat as she turned to the others. "Speaking of putting thought into things, you couldn't have warned us about a potential attack? You clearly thought it was likely enough to bet on it."

Abel just shrugged. "We did warn you. What part of 'be ready to be attacked at all times' was unclear? Besides, you're all fine. Jin looks a little toasty, but he and Rellia were acting in perfect sync, it was impressive. Some of that was probably just wolf instinct, but I'm pretty sure they've been learning from some of the lessons, which is kind of crazy. Who says you can't teach an old dog new tricks?"

I turned at a sudden realization to see Sloane and the other G-rankers from the Beast Lord Garden stepping out of an alley.

Callie shot them a "what the fuck?" look, and Sloane just shrugged. "Sorry, we were following a bit behind you. By the time we showed up, they had already surrounded you. We figured we would jump in if you needed it, but that clearly wasn't necessary."

Come to think of it, I hadn't seen them during the last portion of the walk down, but I'd been too distracted to notice it. Maybe they had stopped for a break or something? Whatever the case, they didn't really owe us backup, and the chance to make our reps here was appreciated. A few windows closed along the street, and I was pretty sure we had been noticed during our little spat.

Abel seemed to think nothing of it, telling the new arrivals to keep up because things were going to get a bit dicier here soon enough, so we just shrugged it off and resumed our walk. With a full fifteen people, we weren't stopped again. Mel looked kind of annoyed that Sloane and the others hadn't show up earlier and saved her some money, though she didn't say anything to them. The Beast Lord Garden initiates were along for the ride as an allied force, but they weren't Pavilion. Mel wasn't in charge of them, and while I kind of was, she couldn't really use that authority.

Finally, we made it to an old, run-down black stone building. There was a sign out front showing a cigar-smoking baby in a spiky black leather jacket and a mohawk that read "The Raving Baby," which I thought was awesome. When he saw it, Abel gave a whoop of joy. "It's still here! Fantastic! I wonder who's running the place. No way Taggert hasn't outleveled this place by now. Maybe his nephew Owen?" He shook his head. "Oh well, doesn't matter, lets head in and see if we can get the lay of the land."

I made to follow after him, but he stopped after a few steps, turning to us. "Oh, one more thing. Alliances down here get complicated. Don't make waves until we can figure out who stands where in terms of local powers. Not to say bar fights aren't fine, but try to keep things one-on-one until we get some answers. Once we know who is who we can pick our targets, maybe get you acquainted with some of the Titan Twenty." He shot me a wink to let me know he meant violence, then turned to head inside.

I looked at Callie and shrugged, stepping close enough that I felt like I could help her if someone attacked and vice versa. We trailed Mel and Abel into the bar, the Beast Lord Garden crew behind us and our wolves covering the flanks.

We were going to be down here for the next few weeks. Time to learn exactly what we would be dealing with, and how to best use it to our advantage.

Chapter Thirty-Four

THE RAVING BABY was pretty much exactly what you would expect a dive bar to be. Low light, smoky air, pool table, old worn chairs and tables. It looked like someone had written up a "seedy dive bar" checklist and gone through one item at a time just to make sure it was as authentic as possible.

Abel was scanning the room, but rather than showing serious worry, his eyes were wide and excited. "It hasn't changed a bit! And that smell! I missed that smell so bad."

Mel sighed dramatically. "Oh gods, I forgot about the enchiladas." At our confused looks, she rolled her eyes and pointed across the room. Opposite the entrance was a huge wall of hanging pictures, above which was written "Enchilada Avalanche Challenge." Each picture had a paper star with a number hanging from it, and all the way at the top was a photo of a clearly recognizable Abel, in the same silver mask he wore now, with the number eighty-seven pinned to it.

I froze, blinking in shock at the number. "Okay, we can come back to everything else in a minute, but I have to ask, is that label implying that Abel ate *eighty-seven* enchiladas in one sitting? How is that even possible? Like, I know Ascendants tend to eat heavy, but stomachs still have limited space in them, that's what higher-ranking food is for. How do you physically *fit* eighty-seven enchiladas in a human body?"

Ignoring me completely, Abel bolted for the bar. "Rudy!" he crowed happily. "You're still here! I figured Taggert would be gone, but I'm glad at least you're still around. How's my favorite bartender?" Abel managed to cross the crowded bar without actually bumping into anyone, the space around him warping to allow him to slip between other people and around tables so quickly and seamlessly it was almost hard to see it happening.

He appeared in front of a seven-foot-tall man with maroon hair and a goatee who was cleaning a glass. When his eyes, which had jerked up at the sound of his name, found Abel, they widened. For a second I thought it was surprise, but it only took me a second to register the expression of existential *dread* on the face of the huge bartender as he looked down at my teacher. "Sweet revenant, *no!* You can't be here! You're dead! Everyone said so!"

Abel frowned sulkily. "Hey now, that's not nice. I was one of your best customers. I spent tons of money here when I used to visit, if you'll remember. Did anyone else ever buy as many enchiladas as I did?" He sounded genuinely offended by the clear distress the other man was showing, but the big bartender was too busy having a small panic attack at the sight of him to acknowledge it.

"Yes, but we *spent* about twice that much on repairs whenever you showed up," Rudy almost wailed. "Taggert only let you come back because he was too scared to ban you. We threw a party the day we heard you weren't coming back. The stone here is so expensive, do you know how much effort it is to repair buildings in Doomtown? And you literally never failed to break *something.*"

A new voice cut in. "Enough, Rudy." The bartender turned to see another man, much shorter and with seaweed-green hair. He shot the bartender a wry smile. "Go work on inventory in the back for a while and collect yourself. I'll handle the bar."

Watching the massive form of the red-haired man blur out from behind the bar and into a door in the back, the man shook his head with a chuckle before turning to Abel. "Must you make a ruckus every time you go anywhere, Pol?"

Despite his words, he held out a hand with a grin and he and Abel clasped wrists, pulling each other into a quick one-armed hug as they smacked each other on the back. My mentor looked thrilled once again as he pulled back. "Owen, good to see you. I figured Taggert would leave the place to you. He was already early F-rank when I stopped coming. How long since you took over?"

The green-haired man gestured for us to take a seat at the bar as he slipped behind it, then filled up glasses for each of us with some local beer. "Oh, it's been a few years now. For the record, I never thought you were dead, and neither did my uncle. It's why he insisted on keeping the insurance policy he took out on the bar for you active. Still can't believe they made him pay for you as a separate policy. To be fair, though, the premiums have gone *way* down since you vanished."

Mel clicked her tongue as she took the offered beer, along with the rest of us. I was *not* a beer guy, but it seemed rude to refuse, so I decided to just nurse it (which, spoiler alert, makes beer *so* much worse). She raised an eyebrow at the green-haired man. "I'm surprised Taggert got you to retire and take over. Taurus was almost as famous as the two of us back in the day. You were responsible for half the trouble my idiot"—she nudged Abel —"got into when we were younger, though granted, he probably got you into just as much."

Owen shrugged. "I kind of retired when you two left the scene. It just wasn't fun anymore. I considered ranking up and leaving, but it had just lost the appeal." His eyes flicked to us. "Who are the new kids? You two finally pick up some apprentices? I heard there's a big tourney coming up, and introducing a couple of newbies would be a great way to make a splash. If so, let me know. I'll make sure to get my bets in on them early while the odds are still good."

Abel raised an eyebrow. "See, you say that, but it kind of sounds like you're feeling out whether the kids are going to be entering the tournament. I don't suppose there's been some sort of bounty offer going around for contestant information, by any chance? Because I could see some of the bigger factions putting out a standing offer for the lowdown on who they'll be up against."

The shameless grin Owen fired back made it clear he had indeed been fishing. "Well, maybe. Though that answer is just as good for confirmation as telling me yes would be, isn't it? Of course, I don't know their names or who they represent, but the others you came in with are Beast Lord Garden, and one of them is the Beast Queen's personal disciple. I bet if I look around for information on new Beast Lord initiates, I can find *something* out. The question is what it's worth to you for me to keep quiet."

I expected Abel to be upset, but he just shook his head ruefully. "That would be a mistake on your part. The kids *are* entering, but they're going to be entering with the two of us. Anyone you pass their information to is bound to get dinged out anyway. It would be a better investment to pass us the information you have so far and then actually place those bets."

The casual way they were discussing us being sold out was... weird to me. Owen seemed like an old friend of Abel's, but Abel barely even flinched at the idea that he might sell off our information. Apparently, down here that kind of thing was commonplace.

For his part, Owen seemed shocked by the fact that Abel was going to be entering. "Wait... you're fighting? Personally? *Both* of you? That's... Shit, yeah, okay, give me their names so I can put money on them before that comes out. The odds on the two of them will nosedive when it comes out you two are on their team. I'll pass you what I've learned so far on the house, as long as you promise not to spread your participation for at least two days."

Abel looked interested. "That does seem like it would be a good deal, but we could get that information somewhere else. I think we need you to sweeten the pot a bit. You're getting a chance to make a shitload of money. Granted, we can put money on the two of them too, and we will, but if we're helping you, I want to get something out of it." He planted both hands on the counter and gave the other man a bloodthirsty grin. "I want free enchiladas for traveling companions for a month. *Regardless* of quantity."

I expected an eye roll or some kind of dismissal, but Owen's face paled immediately. "A-a month? Pol, that's crazy. You eat at least fifty per sitting even when you aren't trying. Sure, the meat is only H-rank, but in those quantities, you'll be seriously cutting into my bottom line. I'm running a business here. I don't even know how much the others might eat. A month is way too long."

Mel reached out and smacked Abel in the back of the head. "We aren't here to feed your enchilada addiction, you lunatic." She glared at Owen. "A week, because if he doesn't get *something*, he'll never shut up about it. Agree so we can move on to the business at hand." The last part wasn't a plea or a question, it was a command, and the glare in her orange eyes was enough to make me want to take a step back.

At least some of Owen's reticence had clearly been for show, because his already pale face completely drained of blood as he cleared his throat and looked away. "Right. Yes. A week. I can do a week."

He reached out and he and Abel shook to confirm the deal. "Let me get you all set up with a plate on the house to get you started, and we can talk shop." He looked over his shoulder. "Rudy! Break's over, I'm going to make some food and then eat with my friends. Get your ass back behind the bar."

There was a loud groan from inside the door we'd seen Rudy flee through. "Do I have to?" he called hesitantly. Owen didn't even bother to respond, glaring through the door as if Rudy could see him. A weary sigh echoed out, and the big man slunk out of the back and took his place behind the bar, glaring distrustfully at all four of us from his spot in front of the bottles as Owen headed for the kitchen.

"Alright, you folks go sit down and I'll get your food," Owen called over his shoulder. "Then we can go over the details of what I know and you can let me in on who our new wonder team is so I can get my bets in. Four plates of enchiladas coming up. No charge." Despite his supposed resistance to the idea, he seemed to be almost skipping with happiness as he headed for the kitchen, clearly feeling like he'd pulled one over on us with how little he'd been forced to concede.

Or at least, he was pulling one over until Abel called him to a stop. "Hey Owen, aren't you forgetting something?"

The green-haired man froze, turning suspiciously as Abel raised a hand and pointed over to the table with our Beast Lord Garden allies. Owen's eyes grew with horror even before the other man spoke, but he clearly noticed the loophole in his earlier agreement at the same time I did.

Abel's grin was positively vulpine as he asked, "Aren't you going to go ask if any of them are hungry?" Admittedly the evil laughter after he said it might have been a touch over-the-top, but I couldn't say it wasn't satisfying.

Chapter Thirty-Five

"DEAR GODS," I said through a mouthful of rice and cheese and sauce. "These enchiladas are amazing. Like, top five of all time in terms of sheer deliciousness. These are only H-rank?" I shoveled in another bite happily, ignoring the blistering glare Owen was shooting all of us as we scarfed down free enchiladas for almost twenty people. I was planning to eat here every meal for the week they were free. Though they weren't even that expensive, it would add up because I couldn't stop eating them.

Abel, who was polishing off his fiftieth somehow, nodded without looking up. "Yeah. The original recipe was created by some D-rank chef Taggert met ages ago. He pulled some kind of high-ranking nonsense and figured out how to make the ingredients harmonize perfectly to boost the flavor profile. Still only H-rank materials and results, but the taste is G-ranked in quality somehow. Gods I forgot how good these are. I didn't see the chef. Who is cooking these things anyway? They must hate me." He laughed after he said it like it was a joke, but I was pretty sure he was right about that.

Owen actually smirked. "Cherry took over as chef ages ago. And yes, she hates you, but to be fair, she's hated you for years. My sister always could hold a grudge, and she never forgave you for winning her motorcycle in that poker game and then crashing it. I think she might have tried to have you killed if anyone would have been willing to take the bounty." He stared fondly off into the distance, but at that last word, shook his head to clear it. "Ah, right, bounties. You wanted to hear about all the contestants I've met so far."

I fixed my eyes on him, waiting expectantly as I continued eating enchiladas. There was a pair of big platters in the center of the table, and Rudy kept bringing out a fresh one to swap for whichever emptied first. Apparently deciding he might as well enjoy the expense, Owen grabbed a plate and started packing in enchiladas himself, eating as he decided where to begin.

"Well," he said between bites. "I think the first thing to mention is that while I was only planning to collect the information bounty, most of the local factions are taking out legitimate contracts on the known contestants. Once you're all noticed, you'll undoubtedly have a few taken out on you too. There's a whole pre-tournament war game type thing going on down here, and the biggest names are all paying the most. The outsider factions don't have as much in the way of connections, but most of them are making offers where they can, so just being down here is dangerous as hell."

Abel swallowed a bite and actually stopped eating. "Really? That sounds fun. Anyone we would know participating? We can't be the only ones from the old days that held out at G-rank for whatever reason. I know some of the old Twenty were almost as into combat specialization as I was. Granted, they'd be too old for the list now, but still, they would be decent competition."

That got a chuckle for Owen. "Just two. Rayka Vale and Helix. Vale has been running a bounty hunting business down here for years now. Never felt the need to jump up ranks because she didn't want to lose her cash cow. Word on the street is she's finally ready to make the jump up to F-rank after the tournament. Helix disappeared for a few years there. No one is sure where he went, but I heard rumors he ended up in one of Mad Madigan's lost mazes and got stuck there for a while. He came out... weird. I'd avoid him. It's not common for Ascendants to go crazy for non-recursion reasons, but I'm pretty sure Helix did."

Abel actually cringed at that. "That's... not ideal. Helix was a scary bastard even back in the day. That transmutation power of his is nasty, and he was always good at coming up with creative ways to use it. Sad to hear he's had such a bad time. He wasn't very talkative, but I always liked him well enough. I remember Rayka too, but she made less of an impression. Something about energy constructs, I think? I'll keep an eye out for them. What about the new blood? Anyone with potential or just the usual legacies?"

"Most of the E-rankers have kids going in, but not too many of them are notable." Owen said. "We've got them coming in from both sides, too. The Unity and WCP both. Screaming Stevie has a kid entering who seems to be pretty competent. Sonic powers are always a pain in the ass to deal with, so he's under scrutiny. Dread's daughter is going to be in it, to no one's surprise. The entire Titan Twenty is going to be competing, though only those few are really notable. Well, Beat and Sever are supposed to be solid, and they've been seen around with Serenity, the Peace Lord's daughter, though all three vanished for a while."

I shared a look with Callie, who smirked slightly at the mention of our defeated enemies. Good to know that was going around.

Abel, on the other hand, looked annoyed. "Food aside, this isn't really worth much, man. You've told me about a few people I could have heard about elsewhere. You made it sound like you had the inside line on anyone we might be meeting. I assume that you can at least give us the details on the outsider factions?"

The eye roll Owen gave my teacher reminded me so much of something Benny would do that I had to stop myself from choking on my food. "Impatient ass," he said fondly. "Yes, I have the details on most of the recent arrivals. I also have my sources still scrounging and have my ear to the ground. I'll get you the new information as it becomes available too. We're in this together now, so I want the four of you to place well. How else will I get paid?"

"We appreciate the help either way," Callie cut in with a reproachful glare at Abel. "Any information is better than none, and this food is delicious." I tried not to snicker at that. Callie was obsessed with good food, so this deal was already a good investment as far as she was concerned. Abel knew her well enough to know the same, and just scoffed at her predictable reaction. "In any case, any info on the outsiders is bound to be useful. We can find out about the locals from anywhere, but knowledge about the new arrivals is sure to be sparse."

Even Abel couldn't argue that, and he raised an eyebrow at Owen, silently prompting the green-haired man to continue.

With a victorious smirk at my silver-masked teacher, he did so. "There are a few of them that I've heard about. Mostly bigger factions from the nearby star systems. The Twilight Order is here. They're Monk-types, and most of them use some variation of light and shadow powers, sometimes both. Big on tricks and illusions and *super* pretentious. Their contender's name is Macgregor. Big blonde bastard with a beard who prefers light-based attacks. Heard he burns out people's eyes sometimes."

He looked around quickly before continuing, lowering his voice. "The Darkling Institute use some weird combination of necromancy and mad science to create minions. They're pretty scary, but the most dangerous is a girl named Mordaunt. Dark-blue hair and dark skin, travels with a huge bandaged guy in manacles. Has the creepiest glowing green eyes. The minion's name is Malgrim and he's got a freaky level of regeneration. Some kind of Vitality multiplier ability, I think, because he straight-up knits back together as you watch."

I shuddered a bit at what kind of abominations necromancy and Mad Science could produce in conjunction. Mad Science could seemingly bend or even break the rules that governed most ranks out of sheer randomness, and necromancy created powerful undead servants. The last thing I felt like running into was some kind of super corpse with rule-bending abilities, and I made a note to avoid the Institute's people if possible.

But I had to ask. "Are there any less… creepy options? Someone more into direct combat?"

He smirked at that. "Well, the Spear Legion is here. They all have the same ability, actually, or versions of it. Spear Mastery. They tend to synergize it with odd stuff, but their whole thing is just being really good at stabbing stuff with a spear. It's less straightforward than it sounds, though. Weapon masters are nasty in a fight. They only have the one trick, but they're damn good at it." He gestured at Abel. "This scary bastard could technically be considered an unarmed combat specialist, to give you a bit of context."

That did give me a bit of an idea about how versatile some of those spear users might be, but far from scaring me off, it made me even more excited. I hadn't ever fought a spear user before, and I was betting they had some fantastic martial arts. I wanted to see how they would measure up against our Balam Mastery, not to mention my combination style with Callie.

"Who did the Spear Legion send?" I asked. "Most of the system factions have a primary inheritor, right? They must have some really impressive contestant lined up as their primary."

"Got it in one." He nodded. "Lament is their main contender. That girl basically breathes the spear, from what I've heard. She's spent twenty-five years in G-rank, just polishing her spear Skill to the peak of Intermediate."

At the mention of a peak Intermediate Skill, I just blinked in shock. The absurd amount of dedication that had to have taken at G-rank boggled the mind. If her Spear Mastery Skill was peak Intermediate and she was still at G-rank, it also meant that wasn't her actual ability, either. Probably a synergized Skill. Someone that scary having an unknown ability thrilled me, and even Abel looked intrigued.

My mentor's eyes lit up at the mention, and he looked at Owen intensely. "Peak Intermediate? My Ragam is peak Intermediate. Managing to get a Skill more than a single rank above your current ability rank is difficult, bordering on impossible. The soul weight is too much for most people to take. If she's planning to break through to Expert as soon as she hits F-rank, she must be a monster."

I was curious about that, actually. The news that Skills ranked above your standard had more soul weight made sense when I thought about it, considering how elixirs and such worked, but it opened up many questions.

"Does combat mastery have a high requirement for soul strength? I know that any alterations to a technique strain the soul, and combat specialists are all about maximizing usage. Do you and Mel have high soul strength?"

Abel nodded absently. "Yeah, any decent combat specialist has a strong soul. Soul strength is pretty important for any decent elite, it's much more common on higher-ranked planets." He glanced at Mel. "We need to feel out some of the competition. Most of them will probably be holed up scheming, but the Spear Legion sound like they're the kind to prefer a straight fight."

"If you go after them, keep an eye out for the other three members of Lament's team," Owen cautioned. "They're no slouches either. Her second is a guy named Wren who uses an absolutely gigantic spear made from some oversized animal bone."

Abel turned his predatory grin on Owen. "I only have one more question. What are the chances the Spear Legion fighters are at the Bone Arena?"

Owen's answering smirk was all the confirmation I needed. Guess I knew where we were heading next.

Chapter Thirty-Six

OWEN WAS INCREDIBLY RELIEVED to see us go. Sloane and the others were disappointed to leave, but when they heard we were heading for an arena, they perked up. Arenas were pretty popular among Ascendants, I'd found. We were all show-offs who loved to make a scene, and making flashy moves in an open space against a strong enemy while potentially thousands of people watched was a popular pastime.

I couldn't pretend to be any different. I'd gotten excited as soon as I'd heard about the Bone Arena, and I was *definitely* going to fight someone there. Maybe not Lament, since I didn't want any part of a combatant someone would equate to Abel in terms of power, especially not someone who knew and had fought with him. Granted, from what I could tell, Abel had gotten exponentially scarier after years of being a sausage-selling hermit who presumably trained constantly because he had no social life, but still.

So we were all in a pretty good mood as we headed for the Bone Arena, Doomtown's answer to the unspoken questions on every Ascendant's mind: "Is there something stupid and violent we can do today, and how many people will watch?" As expected, traveling with our full contingent was more than most people wanted to bite into, so we weren't attacked again, and we made good time. The arena was a massive black stone coliseum that somehow managed to look squat and dark despite being ten times the size of every other building here.

When we got to the Arena, Mel was the one who took the lead, stepping past Abel and waving jovially to the dark-armored woman standing to the left of the entrance. "Ceras! I thought that was you. I haven't seen you in years. They have you on door duty, huh? You still fighting? Or is this your usual gig?" She stepped up to hug the surprised guardswoman, shooting a perfunctory nod to the man on the other side but otherwise ignoring him in favor of an old friend.

As Ceras responded and the two began catching up, Abel stepped up to us and leaned in to murmur. "Mel was always much more interested in the arena than I was. Don't get me wrong, I came here often enough, but I've always preferred a spontaneous battle to scripted combat. Mel practically lived at this place during our time in the Twenty, though. Starbreaker was the queen of the Bone Arena for years, so don't be surprised if she seems to know more than a few of the people here."

As if on cue, Mel waved us all over. "Alright, you lot, Ceras says there are a few fights on the card for the evening, but we still have time for the open bouts. Some of the Spear Legion are here. That Wren guy that Owen mentioned is around, but Lament doesn't show up until right before her matches. They have her up against the reigning champion tonight."

She turned to Abel. "Apparently Blight is still fighting here. He moved up after I left and has been undefeated for quite a while recently."

Abel snorted out a laugh. "Blight? That super pale kid with the long hair and the skinny chest who only wore leather pants and a vest and followed you around like a puppy? I forgot that kid even existed. Oh wow, this place has slipped since we left." He shot her a wolfish grin. "Though I suppose it became obvious when we first arrived that this place had... gone to the dogs."

We all groaned at that, and one of the Beast Lord Garden initiates actually booed loudly, though when Abel turned to see who it was, he didn't seem to be able to tell. Shame, I'd have liked to tell them how funny I thought it was.

Mel just rolled her eyes and ignored her boyfriend. "Anyway, there are still plenty of matches open for sign-up if you two want to fight against Wren. If he accepts, you can try challenging him two-on-one. There aren't a lot of limits in the arena, aside from what the contestants agree on."

I turned to shoot Callie a pleading look, which she saw immediately, prompting an eye roll and a giggle. "Oh, stop it. I'm fine with a fight. Even if this guy is too tough for us, it'll be good practice for the tournament and give us something to work off of. If he isn't, we can put the fear of us into the Spear Legion, so really it's a win-win."

She looked at Mel. "Do we have to pay for this?" We had some money, but most of it had gone into expanding the Pavilion, so we weren't carrying much on hand.

Luckily, Mel just shook her head. "Not directly. They charge to watch the fights, but it's sort of an all-access pass for the open challenges, and fighters are exempted. The rest of us will be fine, Ceras will let us in just this once. The owner, Melkar, is an old friend, and he won't mind her letting me in for free with some friends.

"So, are you going to challenge Wren? Because if so I have bets to place."

I snickered at that. "Place some for us too, then, because yes. Most of our liquid cash is in the Pavilion, so just take it out of there. Though I'm not quite as confident as you are that we'll win. We've been training our asses off, but competing against someone like this is a level of combat we haven't ever really experienced. Beat and Sever were the closest, but they were distracted, and they're locals anyway. This is a guy from a force considered powerful in the star system as a whole. I have a feeling he won't be an easy mark."

Mel shrugged. "If you lose, you lose. It's not like I'm betting my life savings on you. Besides, if he's been doing well, the odds should be pretty good. I'll make sure not to put too much of your own cash on you, either. I figure ten G-ranked chits or so."

As Ceras brought the group into the arena, the unnamed guard led Callie and I away and down a side hallway. We had to stop to do a bit of paper-work before being led to a waiting area with more than a few other Ascendants in it.

We'd signed up for pairs, with the option to fight singles as a team, and when we arrived, we sought out Wren, who was actually really easy to find. A huge man with olive skin and long red hair, he was easily identifiable by the absolutely colossal bone spear leaning against the wall next to him. Made from what appeared to be a femur the size of a person, the thing had been shaved down to be grippable by Wren's dinner plate-sized hands (seriously, he was at least seven feet tall) and had a single steel-coated tooth molded seamlessly into the end, honed to a razor's edge.

We stopped in front of the big man, whose amber eyes remained closed as he reclined in his seat, at least until he heard us stop. They creaked open slightly. "What do you want?" he said in perhaps the most relaxed voice I'd ever heard. "I'm trying to nap before my next match." He yawned expansively, but despite the relaxation and laziness, I noted that his hand was never more than a full arm's extension from grabbing the spear. He might be napping, but if he was, he wasn't stupid enough to leave any openings.

Callie cheerfully held out her hand to shake. "Hi there! I'm Nightstrike and this is Solomon. Can we both fight you at once?" Her tone was upbeat and entirely without shame for how unbalanced the match was, and everyone in the room turned to look at us in confusion. They had all been sitting quietly, staring down opponents or trying to look disaffected and tough.

Wren's eyes opened completely, focusing on Callie, before his lips twitched into a wide grin and he burst out laughing. "That... that was the weirdest challenge I've had since I got here. Wow. No posturing or excuses, huh? Just 'let us gang up on you so we can kick your ass'?" He paused in contemplation before standing up, cracking his neck and hoisting the spear up over his shoulder. "You know what? Sure. What the hell. I was going to let them do a random match thing, but why the hell not?"

He strolled over to the window on one end of the room to ask a clerk, who had been quietly doing paperwork, to officiate a challenge.

I turned to Callie. She'd been smiling widely at his acceptance, but as soon as he was out of range, her face turned serious. "I'm assuming you noticed that?"

I nodded grimly. "He was straining to lift that spear. Not a lot, but anyone at peak G-rank in a physical combat style should have absurdly high Might. Whatever the fuck that thing is made from, it's *heavy*." I wasn't sure what the weight ratio was on bone, but since Ascendants in the G-rank clocked lifting power in the *tons*, I was pretty sure that thing wasn't any normal type of bone. It seemed to be made from F-ranked materials, if the Impact was anything to go by, but it was probably on the high end of that scale.

Instead of coming back, Wren gave us a broad wave and gestured over to a hallway across the room with a sign next to it saying 'left gate enclosure.'

He turned and vanished into the one on the right, and I caught on to the obvious idea. Callie and I moved down a hall lit with widely spaced torches, their flames the same red we saw in most of Doomtown.

We ended up in a small stone room with a dark metal gate on one side. Seeing the closed gate, Callie and I took up a position nearby.

I turned to cock my head at her. "You ready for this? Our first taste of real combat at the star system level? I'm pretty psyched myself." My hands were basically shaking with anticipation. One slipped down to my coat to slide my cane free, twirling it between my fingers so fast the sand at our feet was blown around.

"I can tell," Callie said fondly. "But yeah. This will be fun. How is your Balam Skill, by the way? We've been training a while, and I forgot to ask. I know you're at Lesser, but with all the nonstop work we've put in, I'm assuming you're coming close to Beginner?" She sounded hopeful, which made sense. Even if it wasn't much of a restriction, the geas was inconvenient, and I would be just as glad when it was gone.

I shook my head sadly, but before I could answer, a loud voice rang through the stone. "Ladies and gentlemen! Our next match is going to be a special treat: a two-on-one showcase against Wren, who you've all seen in here the last few days." The gate began to rise. "Now, coming in from the left gate, put your hands together for *Nightstrike* and *Solomon!*" Taking that as a cue, we headed out into the massive expanse of sand that was the arena proper.

Seeing us enter, Wren gave a cheerful wave before gripping his spear one-handed and whipping it through the air around him. The weight and force caused small explosions of air and sound as the thing broke the sound barrier, blowing the nearby sand around in a storm of motion. "Well!" he called across the sand. "Hope you two can give me a decent workout. I haven't had a solid fight since I got to this mudhole." There was an explosion of sand as he rocketed himself forward, moving so fast I wouldn't have been able to move out of the way if I hadn't been expecting it. Guess we were starting.

Chapter Thirty-Seven

AVOIDING Wren's wrecking-ball charge didn't mean that we'd escaped it. As he landed from what I now saw had been an incredibly long, low leap, the impact sent sand geysering up into the air and shook the ground beneath us, displacing our footing. Unfortunately for Wren, he made the immense mistake of picking the wrong one of us to prioritize. Or rather, picking the *right* one to prioritize, leaving the other open to defend.

On landing, his spear lashed out at Callie, who, having much more impressive stats due to specialization, was a bigger threat. I had no clue how he could *tell* that, but he clearly had some way of doing so, and he went right for her. Sadly for him, Callie had zero defense during our combat trance. She left that up to me.

Making a sharp gesture with one hand, I pointed at a spot in the air near her, triggering Cloud Step. While her footing had been disturbed, I'd made sure to put it close enough to plant her hands on the surface, allowing her to arch up into a backbend handstand.

The spear smashed through the space where Callie's ribs had been with bone-crushing force, but failed to find any purchase as she pushed off and sent herself flying out of range, at an angle that kept her close to me. During this whole mess, I regained my footing easily enough. As she distracted Wren with her acrobatics, I used Sucking Mud on the sand to prevent the shifting ground from being as big of a problem, then layered

Consecration of Flame and Touch of Tears on my cane as I lashed it out at the side of Wren's knee.

To my surprise, Wren choked up on his grip, smashing the butt of his spear into the mud and using the ground to create a blockade between my cane and his leg. My blow bounced harmlessly off, not even managing to corrode the bone. He barely showed any strain yanking the spear from the mud, but before he could turn to attack, he was forced to wheel in place and swing the spear to deflect a massive pitch-black ball of shadow swinging at his head on a wide chain.

Balam and the combat trance combined to show me exactly where I needed to attack, and I silently activated my overlay, resonating it with my Balam Skill to find the perfect trajectory to attack from. Selecting the option that best mirrored Callie's own attack, I rolled sideways through the mud, smashing out at Wren's lower spine with a vicious blow that would leave me in his blind spot provided he was focused on Callie.

It… sort of worked. He didn't notice the attack until the last second, and avoided it by pivoting his body around the spear he'd driven into the mud again to fend off Callie's offensive. That took his feet off the ground for a second, and as he came down, a barrage of shadow spikes lashed up from the ground.

He'd slipped on the mud, but I was doing the same damn thing. This mud was vaguely better than sand, but not by much.

With the split second of distraction the shadow blades bought me, I used Consecration of Flame again, but this time, I strained my soul to force it to treat Sucking Mud's area of effect as a focus, causing the mud to harden as it was imbued with the same magma-like properties my Stone Limb could get. I dropped the Skill near-instantly, then used Mistwalking, creating a bank of mist around us which quickly turned into hissing steam.

Wren's frustrated growl was music to my ears as I used Seek Hidden, then winced a bit at so much soul weight so quickly. Still, he came into view perfectly and my mask kept the steam from bothering me. Callie wasn't inside the bank of mist, since she'd been attacking from a distance. I activated Stealth as I walked, keeping my footsteps silent as I circled in the obstruction, looking for an opening.

"Okay," Wren snarled. "I admit, that's really fucking annoying. What the hell is your ability? Fire, water, earth, some weird poison shit if that cane glowing was anything to go by. You're not exactly super powerful, but you're versatile as hell."

I snickered at that internally, though I didn't let out a noise. He had no clue how powerful I was. I hadn't used a single stored attack yet.

There were two reasons for this. Firstly, we were trying to see where we stood against an opponent from the star system. Second, the less of our tricks we used here, the less we gave away for the tournament. And finally, this was *great* training for our dual combat style. This guy was absurdly good with his weapon. I didn't know how he was picking up our attacks so quickly (maybe a Perception specialization), but his ability to react to them without leaving openings was first-class.

Sadly for him, that lack of openings didn't extend to his monologue, because as he vented his frustration, I finally noticed a gap in his guard. I flashed in, triggering Flurry of Blows to massively speed up my attack, and swung for his hip joint in what should have been a blind spot. I was kind of suspicious, so I didn't commit too heavily, and that turned out to be a life-saver. I could barely react to the shift in his center of gravity and dodge the blazingly fast attack he launched because I was staring at his midsection for the attack.

The boom of displaced air crashed into the mist, dispersing it as I landed after a handspring. Wren grinned at me viciously, opening his mouth to speak, but was interrupted by having to dive sideways to avoid a massive black hammer Callie brought down right on top of him. The impact compacted the ground, which had been sort of loose after being quenched by magma and heated by sand, flattening out a section of it. I considered using my magma leg combo, but it seemed stupid this early in the fight, so instead I quietly slipped around to join up with Callie, who was in her dark distorted form and taking advantage of her armor's disguise features.

She'd been waiting for the opening he made with that strike, preparing to cover me if I was in trouble, and I gave her a grateful nod, which earned me a happy smile, one with a violent edge I only saw in fights, which made me all the more aware of how well we fit sometimes.

She raised an eyebrow at Wren. "You're pretty good. I heard you're the second-in-command of the Spear Legion's team. Is Lament really that much better than you?" While it seemed like info gathering or smack talk, I could tell she was just genuinely curious.

Wren's laugh was good-natured and rolling. "Are you kidding? Lament is a monster. Three of me would have trouble taking her. You two are damn impressive for such a backwater. Your cooperation is seamless and it's incredibly irritating, and all those fun tricks and the shaping power make you a versatile and surprising team. That said, Lament would pulp you both in a single blow. That's not to denigrate your capabilities. She'd kill me just as easily. Some people can't be described with common sense."

That was... unfortunate. But then again, she wasn't the only monster. If we couldn't take her, maybe Abel could. Of course, considering how fucking scary Wren was turning out to be, both Callie and I would need to handle him, or we'd have to let Mel do it while we'd handle the other two. Assuming they were fielding a four-man team (I wasn't sure if teams could be smaller).

Either way, no use worrying about it now. We had a fight to win.

I spun up my cane as he spoke, easing myself into a circling movement to get to the other side of the disk of solid earth we were using for the fight. Wren noticed, but rather than follow, he stepped back to let his eyes take in more of the circle. They unfocused the same way Abel had done in training, expanding his field of view so he could react more quickly.

He was not, however, watching behind him. Which was why he didn't notice Callie rise from the sand in one smooth motion and launch a cascade of shadow spears up from his back. I dove forward in a quick juke before withdrawing, and Wren reacted, tensing up and staring with confusion before his eyes widened in understanding. He spun on his heel, lashing out with another air-smashing strike that dispersed the shadows and hit Callie directly.

My eyes widened in horror until she started to dissolve, and I grinned. She'd used the cover of the mist to make a clone, but had sent the clone around for the sneak attack instead of going herself. Wren's distracted state left him open, with his back to both of us, and we flickered forward as a single unit, coming around from opposite sides. My cane flashed out for his ankle layered with a Mercy Kill as she swung another massive hammer construct almost as tall as she was right at his head.

Between the shock and the perfect timing, he didn't have time to block both, and dug the butt of his spear in to stop the hammer. It was an understandable move (the head was the most vulnerable part of the body) but he left himself open, and I took advantage. Unlike my shadow strikes or flame attacks, the triple-strength density shift was completely viable without drawing attention. I layered that one onto the cane along with a Mercy Kill to boost it even higher, and unleashed every bit of stored force along with the strike as the head of my cane smashed into Wren's ankle.

There was a loud crack as the bone shattered, prevented from regenerating by the creeping poison fire that I heavily suspected hurt *way* worse when it was getting into broken bone.

Wren roared in pain, forced to shift onto his other foot and effectively ruin his footing. I spun off the strike, reversing to spin out into a blow aimed at the back of the man's head as Callie attacked his ribs with a pair of condensed shadow tonfas, even as the hammer dispersed into a concealing shadow fog.

That was a new trick, and my Seek Hidden let me see right through it just as Callie could. We spent the next five minutes whittling him down. Cracking his ankle broke his concentration, and as the pain and damage from the poison fire mounted every time I managed a hit, he got slower and slower, our teamwork chipping away at him.

Finally he roared out. "Enough!" Swinging his spear in a full circle to drive us back, he then drove it into the ground to lean on. "That's enough. I concede."

My body relaxed, feeling relieved, as the constant Skill use had been slowly cranking up the pain in my head. I held up a fist in triumph.

As the match ended, an arena healer scurried out onto the field to treat Wren, who grinned at us widely. "Well, you two are certainly worth watching." He let the healer patch him up as I allowed the poison fire to dissipate from his body.

As he turned to walk away, he looked back over his shoulder, still with that same grin. "Don't lose too quickly in the tournament. I want a rematch."

It was only after he disappeared behind the gate that I realized that he hadn't used his ability once in the battle. He'd been holding back as much as we had, maybe more. I mirrored his grin, my mouth stretched wide behind my mask. This tournament was going to be so much fun.

Chapter Thirty-Eight

WHEN WE GOT BACK to the waiting room, Wren was gone, but Abel, Mel, and Sloane were there waiting. Sloane was particularly impressed, cheering loudly when we came within range.

"That was *fantastic!* That guy was a monster, his Might must be insane. I was afraid he'd kill one of you by mistake, but you kept him off-balance the whole time. He never even had a chance!"

Abel sighed, holding up a hand. "Alright, let's not take this too far. It was a decent fight, but he wasn't going all-in. He never even used his ability. Granted, you kept plenty of your tricks in reserve, which I approve of, but you had plenty of room for improvement. Either Mel or I could have taken him one-on-one pretty easily. It's fine to recognize your strengths, but don't let it go to your heads. These next two weeks are for training, and if you lose motivation, you'll stall out."

"He's not wrong." Mel's tone was conciliatory. "But still, I do think you two did a damn good job for your first major fight against an outsider. With the caveat that you can still learn plenty, it's not a problem to be proud of your battle. In that vein, though, why don't you point out some of the things you did wrong? It'll help to contextualize where you can improve in the future." She gestured over to the nearby seats. "We can wait over here. Sloane signed up for the singles matches, but she needs to wait until her name is called."

Callie, as usual, picked up the inconsistency first. "Wait, where are Beric and Croll and the other Beast Lord Initiates?" she asked. "Also, what are you all doing down here? Weren't you being escorted to, like, an observation deck or something?" Thinking about it that way, I was pretty curious too.

"We were," answered Abel. "It was more of a VIP box. But the part-time fleabag decided she wanted to fight, and Mel and I know this place pretty well. The others are up in the box watching the fights, but we figured coming with Sloane would be a good chance to give you some feedback." He pointed to the back corner of the room where a scan box was projecting an image of a currently starting match onto the wall. "We can watch her match over there when it starts. Now, like Mel said, what did you do wrong? Solomon, you go first."

I wasn't sure if he decided that because Callie was better able to note details or because I was more in tune with combat, but it didn't really matter.

Thinking, I cocked my head slightly. "Off the top of my head, using my triple strike on his ankle might have been sloppy. I was trying not to use any of my powerful tricks before the tournament. It might have been noticed and given away some more of my abilities."

To my surprise, Abel shook his head. "Nah. It was a physical attack, hard to tell when those are more than they seem. And you showed enough variety with DS Mastery to make it unlikely for anyone to catch the slip. It was a measured risk that you put thought into. I'd say it worked out fine, given the overturn in the combat dynamic when it happened. Try again."

That had been the most obvious slip, and I had to dig a bit deeper to find something else. "The mist?" He raised an eyebrow over his mask, gesturing for me to continue. "I used it without warning Callie it was going to happen. She adapted on the fly, but it was a stupid slip to make, cutting off her view of me without letting her know." It was sometimes hard to remember that while we were incredibly in sync, we couldn't read each other's minds. Trust could become a liability if it wasn't tempered with knowledge.

Abel smiled. "Good. The hardest part of perfecting a team dynamic is finding your partner's limits. You two did well taking advantage of the mistake, but it still happened. You count on your partner in all things when in battle, which means you need to be able to estimate how much information they can glean. Without knowing what they know, you can't predict what they'll do, and someone you can't predict isn't an asset in a battle, they're a liability."

"I guess," Callie said thoughtfully. "I feel like that was a good move, though. Using that combo to take care of the sand. He communicated some of it with hand signs. I wasn't expecting the mist, but it didn't seem to hurt us. Are you saying we can't improvise? Because that doesn't sound like you." I smiled a bit at how defensive she sounded for my sake. It was sweet how much she cared.

Abel shrugged. "Not at all. I'm saying you need to game out these combinations and responses beforehand and have contingencies for them. It's not a matter of never reacting, it's a matter of making sure your partner has a frame of reference for every action you take. The whole magma mist combo was a smart way to solidify the ground, but it was *new*. Trying new moves outside your partner's grasp on your abilities creates gaps."

"So… more training?" I asked wryly. His answering grin was response enough, and I groaned. "Fair enough. I can't imagine how many years you two trained together when you were younger to have as good a grasp on your combat styles as you do. How did you even maintain that level of cooperation for such a long time? Even after Apollyon was gone for a while, you just fell right back into it."

Mel just waved that off. "Once you hit a certain point, your combat style tends to solidify. I was able to predict how he fights because he hasn't changed it much. He still uses the same martial art, the same ability, he just uses them more smoothly. It's a benefit of developing your cooperation this late. Less change at this point in your journey, at least in terms of combat. Not that no one ever pivots or changes their style, but most people tend to stay on brand. Consistency helps build a more lasting impression."

That made sense with how most people gained stats. Less of a priority for me, honestly, but I could see how even without that factor, specializing in a certain kind of combat and sharpening that skill set would be a big help. Hell, I'd been doing exactly that lately.

Deciding to do the rest of the "what did you do wrong" exercise later and in private, I turned to Sloane. "So, you decided to fight next? I haven't seen too much of your serious combat abilities beyond the siege."

I knew she could merge with her animals somehow. She had bird wings and... fox ears? I guessed foxes had good ears, since they were so big. It would be interesting to see what else she could do with them. Earlier, she hadn't had a chance to shine.

She certainly looked excited enough. Sloane was one of the many WCP residents that didn't bother with a mask. Some of the kids of the E-rankers, like Sage, figured there was no reason for a second identity, given who their parents were. I wasn't sure if Sloane was Melinda's daughter or just her apprentice, but she seemed to have gone with the same general aesthetic. No mask made it incredibly easy to see the energy and anticipation on her face as she spoke.

"Hell yes! I saw your fight and it got me pretty pumped. I hope I get someone that strong!"

Mel chuckled. "You won't. None of the regulars are that powerful, but you might get someone with a power drastically opposed to yours. Those are always fun. I remember one time I got matched against an opponent who absorbed fire and converted it to physical strength. That fight was annoying."

Callie nodded fervently. "I'm lucky my constructs are dense enough that normal light doesn't affect them much. I've run into a few counterpowers and they are absolutely awful to deal with. Unless you work with a team, the easiest way to deal with them is to have some kind of combat Skill."

She tilted her head. "Although, actually, I don't think I've ever asked if you have a martial art Skill. Being the direct disciple of an E-ranker, I figure you probably do, though, right?"

"No spoilers." Sloane snickered. "You'll have to wait and see like everyone else. Don't forget that the Beast Lord Garden is entering the tournament too. If you can figure some things out from watching me fight, that's fine, but I'm not giving any hints." She gave a mysterious smirk, making it clear she'd be holding back just as much as we had.

We talked for a bit longer before a voice called for Sloane and she headed out to prepare for her fight. I raised an eyebrow at that and turned to Mel. "Wait, why did she get called but we didn't? We were able to just head out when we were ready, is that not how it usually goes?"

"Nah," Mel said casually. "You were benefiting from Wren's status. He's been tearing into their best for days, and while he isn't at the same level as

Lament, he's got quite a rep at this point. If there wasn't a qualitative difference in renown at higher levels, I don't doubt factions like the Spear Legion would just send all their kids to backwaters to crush everyone else. Hell, some of them probably do that anyway, though thankfully it's not common."

That made sense. "So he was just allowed to go up whenever he wanted and he took us along? I'll have to thank him when we see him again." I switched topics. "Can we place bets down here? Also, how much did we win off the last bet? I'm pretty confident in Sloane, and if we got a bunch of extra cash anyway might as well keep it going." I wasn't sure how much Mel had put up for us, but our odds had probably been decent if Wren was so well-known here.

My enthusiasm got a chuckle from Mel. "I figured you'd say that. I put some of your winnings on Sloane, though the odds were much less favorable for her. I figured if you decided not to bet, I could just take it out of my personal account instead to cover the difference. You won about a hundred G-ranked chits. I put twenty down from your Pavilion account and you got five-to-one odds. Pretty decent, though I doubt it'll be anywhere near as much if you do it again. I put twenty-five on her for you, but it's only two-to-one odds."

"If?" I asked in confusion. "I figured we'd be spending most of our trip down here. Seems like a great place to train. We need to polish our combat skills don't we?" I'd been looking forward to possibly becoming a champion pit fighter. It seemed like such a cool accomplishment.

Abel answered with a laugh. "Kid, most people aren't responsible enough to come to a fighting pit in Doomtown. We'll get in just as many fights out in the wild, and under plenty more circumstances. Besides, it'll be a good idea to establish your brand a bit around here. Aside from learning about your opponents, you'll have plenty of opportunities to expand your reputation."

Before I could respond, he held up a hand and pointed over to the screen. "We can talk about it later. First lesson of the arena, kid: always watch matches you bet on." And with that bit of wisdom, we turned to see Sloane's fight.

Chapter Thirty-Nine

SLOANE HAD ALREADY MERGED with her companions by the time she reached the sand. They had somehow restored the arena to its original state, sans big circle of rock, but I noted with interest that her feet seemed to skim over the ground without imprinting too deeply. I wasn't sure whether it was an effect of the silver wings or some kind of light step fox ability, but it was an interesting detail to note.

I turned to Mel. "So," I said, "who exactly is she fighting? I don't think they said. Do either of you know?"

Having details on the other fighter for comparison would give me a better idea of what Sloane could do, since we were apparently going to be fighting her in the tournament. Or more realistically, I might be fighting her. If our team ran into the Beast Lord Garden's crew, Abel and Mel would crush them, but the team competition was only the preliminary stage of the event.

Mel shook her head. "Not sure, but they usually do some kind of announcement." Even as she spoke, the announcer bellowed Sloane's name and affiliation before moving on to introduce the dark-cloth-wrapped form slinking from the other gate. When Mel heard the enemy's name, she winced. "Ah. That's not going to be an easy fight. I've never fought Shale, but I got a quick rundown of the big names from Ceras."

"Shale?" I asked suspiciously. "That's a type of rock, right? Some kind of earth manipulator? I could see how that might be a pain in the ass."

As the battle started, Sloane pivoted forward, her wings cracking the air as they drove her straight at the other fighter, almost too fast to follow. The glow of the wings made it clear there was more at work than just muscle, and I whistled at the speed on display.

Still, it wasn't too fast for someone like me to dodge, so I assumed Shale would move. I assumed wrong. Not only did Shale not move, Shale didn't do *anything*. They just stood there as Sloane smashed into them at top speed… and bounced off, skidding across the sand with a scream of pain, holding the shoulder she had led with. She staggered to her feet, giving a quick jerk of her arm to pop it back into place as she glared at the other fighter.

The cloth across Shale's chest had been shredded slightly by the wings, in some kind of split-second slashing attack I hadn't even seen in the moment after Sloane bounced off, but the flesh under the wrapping didn't seem to be bleeding. Hell, it didn't seem to be flesh. Shale shook their head, reaching up to unwind the cloth from their face and rebind it over their chest.

The revealed face was masculine and rough. Not like some people use that phrase to mean worn or hard-won, but *literally* rough. Also grey. Because the form under the wrappings was made of solid rock.

Mel snickered slightly. "Earth manipulation-adjacent." I turned to cock my head at her. "He's a golem. It's a relatively rare racial trait. They're pretty environmentally specific, but in an arena like this, he's going to be a beast to get by. Most of them have a few earth manipulation Skills."

I winced. "That sounds… unfortunate. I take it from that blow he tanked that they're relatively sturdy for their level of Impact?" I knew that some abilities could make people more durable within their rank. Rock with twelve Impact was tougher than wood with twelve Impact, and they were both tougher than flesh. That was how defensive abilities worked, and Shale's seemed like a pretty good one based on the attack he just took.

Rather than answer, she gestured to the screen, where Sloane was climbing to her feet. "Okay," she growled, "that hurt." Her voice was rough and animalistic as she slowly stalked forward. "I admit, I wasn't expecting that. Don't suppose I actually did any damage?"

"Not much." Shale chuckled. If Sloane's voice was the growl of an animal, Shale's was the crashing of falling rocks. It was so bassy it was almost hard to discern the words. "Still, that's better than most manage. You definitely cut into me a bit. I'm curious to see if you can do it again." As he finished speaking, he stripped the sleeves off his arms and knelt down, pressing a fist to the sand. The earth crawled up his grey stone flesh, thickening and expanding his arms and then moving to his chest, stretching its wrapping to the limit but not breaking it.

I could see why he used the wraps instead of normal clothes now. The bandages expanded as he did, preventing rips and tears. By the time he was done and stood back up, his upper body had almost doubled in muscle mass. The sand had condensed into something halfway between armor and a body modification.

I grimaced. Mel had been right. Earth-based Skill. Racial traits shifted the primary ability to a Skill when a transformation was activated, just like Jobs. This was probably his ability before he became a Golem.

Sloane looked conflicted. She was clearly unhappy to just sit and watch him buff up, but this was such an obvious opening that actually attacking probably felt like a trap. I knew I probably wouldn't have closed during that little show. Maybe I'd have tried some kind of ranged attack, but I didn't know if Sloane even *had* any of those.

She seemed indecisive for a minute, before eventually deciding to just bite the bullet and attack again, flashing forward in another blur of silver wings.

I was confused as to what she was going to do, but she seemed to have taken into account the new information. Instead of slamming into Shale, when she got in close this time, she juked sideways, spinning out on her wings to circle behind him. As she pirouetted in the air, her wings lashed out like blades, scoring along the exterior of Shale's enhanced body and flitting away too quickly to grab.

Despite the wings' versatility, I was ninety percent sure that some of the movements Sloane was making shouldn't be physically possible. Not for lack of power or anything like that, but because the smooth shifts in momentum were antithetical to how force and inertia should work. In some strange way, it reminded me a bit of the weird lack of impression her feet had left when she entered the arena. While the wings clearly gave her some kind of massive speed boost and could carve into the stone that way,

I figured the fox aspect of her transformation was giving her access to impossible agility and maneuverability.

The combination was absolutely brutal, and despite Shale's incredibly powerful form, she was functionally untouchable as he lashed out at her with short, precise jabs and grabs. Despite the huge disadvantage of his speed, the Golem was doing an amazing job of keeping damage low by assuming an extremely tight defensive stance and focusing the slicing attacks at non vital areas.

I could see grey metallic blood begin to leak from some of the slashes, but only a trickle, and Shale remained as composed and unmoving as his rock-like exterior implied as he patiently waited for her to show an opening. Sloane, for her part, was looking a bit tired after a few minutes of the stalemate. She began to slow down, and finally, after three minutes of the attack blitz, she desperately dove for a low sweeping cut that left her open to the Golem's retaliation.

He lashed out with all the speed his immense Might could manage, snapping out a grab at her wing with the speed of a striking snake. Unfortunately for him, she had expected that. Her "accidental" slip hadn't been an accident at all. She'd been setting up an opening to exploit in return. As he dove forward in a split-second grab, the wings turned into silver mist in his grip.

Eyes the color of granite widened in shock as he overbalanced slightly when he grabbed nothing but air. It was only a split second, but it was enough. As the wings faded, birdlike talons tore free of the shoes on Sloane's feet as she planted her hands in the sand and kicked out at Shale's exposed body. One claw raked over an eye, another opening his throat, both vulnerable spots he'd been protecting with his defensive stance.

The gouges weren't crippling or life-threatening, she didn't have enough force for that. But they were distracting and painful and kept him preoccupied enough for her to swing around and start lashing out with more blows. The claws were much better suited for cutting than the feathers, and they tore holes in several vulnerable places, cutting into the underarms, the pecs, and even the thighs. Sloane had unleashed a blistering storm of slashing kicks on her enemy, who stumbled back blindly to get away.

A back handspring up to her feet followed by a scything flip that brought her legs up and over again in another assault pressed the attack, and Shale desperately tried to regain his footing to defend. It looked like she was going to pull off the win for a minute, until Shale managed to find a small gap in her attacks and post up again.

With his defense in place, her attacks started doing far less damage than they had been up to this point. No vitals on display meant no obvious strike points, and aside from being durable, Golems were apparently tough as nails, because the damage he'd taken up to now didn't seem to be slowing him down much. Sloane's earlier exhaustion had been a feint, and she had been going all out in this attack blitz, but after another minute or two, she actually started to flag for real.

Having learned his lesson, Shale didn't go for the opening. He just stayed posted in place, feet sunk deep into the sand as he endured the slowly flagging wave of attacks. In the end, Sloane just wasn't able to put him down, and after she had thoroughly exhausted herself and slowed down immensely, he started taking cautious shots at her. She avoided some of them, but not all, and slowly but surely he chipped away at her until she left herself open for a finishing blow.

The punch that he landed to her jaw snapped her head to the side sharply, and she was unconscious by the time she hit the sand.

Mel cursed. "Shit. I should have quit while I was ahead." She looked guilty. "Sorry about that. You want me to cover the bet? I didn't ask you, so I won't be too bothered to handle the payment."

Callie just waved her off. "Nah. It's fine. You won us seventy-five chits on top of the loss, so we'll cover it. Cost of doing business." Seventy-five G-ranked chits was a decent windfall anyway, so I wasn't too worried about it either. Glancing at the screen, Callie winced as some guard hopped into the pit and started dragging Sloane out by her ankle. "Wow. She's going to have sand in so many uncomfortable places."

That surprised a laugh out of me.

On that note we headed for the tunnel to meet Sloane when she was dropped off. Might as well save her some annoyance by picking her up. I was a guest elder, after all.

Once that was done we headed back up to meet with the rest of the Beast Lord initiates, who all seemed a bit sulky, probably having bet on their boss like we had. I tried my hardest not to snicker at the expressions. At least Doomtown hadn't been boring so far.

Chapter Forty

SLOANE WAS UNDERSTANDABLY upset about losing, but we made sure to let her know how well she'd done. "You were awesome," Callie stated with finality. "Seriously. You were so fast. You just met the exact wrong opponent. Solomon or I would have had a hard time beating you and you're going to do great in the tournament." I wasn't really sure that was true, but I decided not to get involved. She was trying to help Sloane feel better more than anything.

"That's not the point!" cried Sloane in frustration. "I barely put up a fight. Not to mention everyone bet on the match. If I get back to the Garden missing that much money, I'm going to be in so much trouble. Since the two of you kicked the shit out of the big guy, I can't even bet on you both to make it back, because no one is going to give either of you decent odds in any of your fights now."

Abel snickered a bit at her frenzied tone. "Well, I was planning a trip to the Burning Rain Casino next. If you really want to make money, you can always do some gambling. Sadly, the games are all luck-based, so enhanced stats don't do much good, but still, it's not a bad place to make a few bucks if you're having a good day." He paused. "Or lose a few. It's pretty hit-or-miss, but you're already behind quite a few bucks anyway. Might as well give it a shot."

"That's…" Mel sighed, putting her hand to her mask in annoyance. "We aren't really trying to get them all to gamble away their… And you're gone. Fantastic."

Abel, apparently not in the mood for a lecture, had turned and wandered off when she started talking. That was the most proactive I'd seen him about ignoring anyone.

I expected Mel to be offended, but she just sighed. "Right, I forgot how he gets down here. Honestly surprised he stuck around for that much of the conversation. Oh well, you kids coming?"

Apparently deciding to follow him to wherever the Burning Rain Casino was, Mel just set off after Abel.

Callie and I shared a look and then shrugged. We still had seventy-five G-ranked chits' worth of profit here, so a few bets wouldn't be a big deal. Besides, I was curious to see more of Doomtown. Sloane and the others all trailed behind us, Beric and Croll trying to reassure their team leader as we went.

The wolves prowled in the back, and it struck me that I hadn't really noticed them around for a while. I wondered where they'd gone or when we'd lost them, but they were still fine, so it didn't really matter, I guessed. They were smart enough not to go around eating random people.

They caught up to us, and I scratched Jin behind the ears. Rellia snuggled up to Callie as we walked, following our mentors as they led us back out onto the road.

It didn't take long to reach the casino. Much like the rest of Doomtown, the building was dark stone, but unlike the other places we'd seen, the rock was slick and reflective. The tall building had hundreds of windows, each shining one of a half-dozen colors and creating a sort of absurd, fantastical effect as the mixture of colored light poured down on the entrance. At the end of a line, a pair of double doors lay open, blocked off by a rope attended by a pair of hulking guards in suits and featureless black full-face masks.

I caught up to Abel with a grin as he stopped to take the place in. "Another old haunt? Do you or Mel know the guys at the door here too?" I could understand why they might have old friends all over at the places they brought us, since they were pretty impressive and they'd taken us to places they knew best, but eventually they were going to have to run out of places where everyone knew them on sight.

To my surprise, Abel just shrugged. "Who the hell knows. It's not like I can tell them apart. They're just door guards." He strolled forward with purpose, coming to a stop in front of the guards. Instead of telling them who he was or bullying them, he reached into his pocket and pulled out a gold casino chip, holding it up to show the guys at the door. As soon as they saw it, they opened the rope to let him in, ignoring the boos of the people in line that we'd walked right past.

Mel snickered at that. "He was never close to anyone here, but he came by a lot. The arena has built-in bets, but Doomtown as a whole tends to attract lots of fights. You can place prop bets on the outcome of fights between certain big-name players. Apollyon used to come here to bet on himself and then hunt down all the strongest fighters." Then she sighed. "He *also* has an extreme fondness for roulette, and he ended up feeding them back most of his winnings. That's why he has the golden chip, it's a high-roller token. He's never really worried much about money. Easy come, easy go."

I could kind of see that, really. He definitely seemed like the type to ignore anything that didn't suit him. If he needed money, he'd just go get some. It put his sausage stand into a different context. I knew he'd worked his way up, but it was a lot more impressive knowing he could have solved any money problems even easier than I thought.

Noticing them closing the ropes, I hurried forward, not wanting to get left behind. Shockingly, even the wolves were allowed in. I wasn't sure whether it was a factor of Abel having a gold token or the guards just not caring, but it was a relief we didn't have to find somewhere to board them while we went inside.

The inside of the Burning Rain was, if anything, even more chaotic than the outside. The multicolored swirl of lights was still present, and the carpets and furniture had patterns of black and white that caught and twisted the colors in ways that probably would have made a mortal pass out.

Even I, with a surplus of Perception and plenty of Focus to block this out, was feeling a bit disoriented. I turned to look at Abel, who at the very least was less dizzying than the surroundings, and found him rolling his eyes. "They haven't changed. Same nonsense games to throw people off." He turned to Mel, giving her a charming grin. "Honey, do you happen to have some pocket money we can use? I want to try the roulette table." He literally folded his hands under his chin and pouted as he asked, like a puppy dog begging for a treat.

Mel just snickered at her boyfriend. "Oh, now you listen to me? Not going to just wander off?"

Abel had the good sense to look abashed and began to apologize (probably a bit too vehemently to be serious), wrapping Mel in his arms and expounding at length about how heartbroken he was to have offended her. The whole performance carried over into blatant sarcasm after a bit, but Mel was giggling too hard to be annoyed, finally putting her hand over his mouth. "Enough! You lunatic. Fine, take some money and go."

"Fantastic!" Abel cheered. He leaned down to peck Mel on the side of her mask. "Thanks, honey, have fun!"

Then he turned to us. "If you kids want to have some fun, might want to come with me. Knowing Mel, she'll probably go relax at the bar or something, though she might hit the prop bet table and try to get in some odds on the lot of us before people start adjusting for your fight with Wren. Either way, it'll be boring, so come on."

He didn't bother waiting as he took off into the crowd, energetically bulling past everyone around him in his hurry. I shrugged at Callie, and she and Sloane both trailed after us. The rest of the Beast Lord initiates didn't follow, probably because they cleaned themselves out betting on Sloane. Sloane herself was hoping to make some money back, so she should have at least something to bet. The wolves followed, moving through the dizzying crowd like sharks through a neon ocean.

I couldn't even find Abel for a second, but luckily his silver mask stood out in this light, so I caught a trace of him. We pushed through the crowd to reach him and found him standing at a table in front of a diminutive woman in the same nondescript mask as the guards. The colors of her clothes were almost imperceptible under so many lights, but she was wearing what I suspected was a white shirt and red vest, and standing in front of a huge roulette wheel, which lit up in a riot of colors.

"Whooo!" Abel cheered. "Rainbow wheel! Guys, come over here!" He waved to us, shoving a few nearby forms aside to make room. "This is awesome. It's rainbow wheel. Unlike boring roulette, where there's two colors and a bunch of numbers, rainbow wheel is way more fun! The wheel is covered with numbers, but the numbers are in grey screens, As the wheel spins, the colors flicker randomly across the tiles, and when the ball stops, they all lock into place. Don't worry, though, rainbow wheel is watched over by high-Perception reps from the WCP to make sure they don't monkey with the color change."

That was... insane. "So you just pick a random color and number and hope it hits? Is this the game you always play? Also, what are the odds on this?" I kind of wished someone had thought to do a luck wish before coming here, and I made a note to bring Benny back once he was strong enough to survive down here.

"A thousand to one," came a smooth, lackadaisical voice from the other side of the table. I turned to find a girl with dark skin and glowing green eyes staring back at me. I couldn't see her hair color with all the light pollution, but my guess was that it was dark blue. Of course, the hulking bandaged form with wrist manacles and a long coat standing behind her kind of gave it away. This would be Mordaunt, then.

She smiled widely when she caught our gazes. "But no, rainbow wheel isn't a consistent thing. They only spin once a night."

Abel nodded excitedly. "It's true! Sadly we can't play tonight. For rainbow wheel, you can only bet money you won *at* the table. It stops people from just dumping all their cash on it. Shame, I love rainbow wheel. I've played four times. Never won, but it's always a blast."

I could see how they would be able to afford thousand-to-one odds under those conditions. It was probably a huge draw. Quite a spectacle.

Mordaunt chuckled, the sound somehow audible despite all the noise around us. "I'd be happy to let you watch my spin. There's only a one-in-ten-thousand chance of triggering a rainbow wheel spin on a winning bet, or at least so I was told when we began."

Abel nodded enthusiastically, and I shrugged. It sounded like a fun time, and it wasn't like it would cost anything. We'd obviously stick around.

Mordaunt turned to the woman in the vest. "Forty-six, red." It seemed she just picked a random number-and-color combination, not that I imagined there was a much better way. With seven potential colors on each number the chance of hitting was absurdly low. No way they could afford to pay so much out unless the odds were freakishly slim.

Before the woman could spin, though, we heard a new voice cut through the din. A haughty sneering tone that boomed across the space around us. "Why am I not surprised the abominations are engaged in such depravity? I suspected I'd find you here, monster maker."

We all turned to take in the hulking form of the blonde-haired man in the brown robes sneering through his bushy beard. The game was forgotten as Mordaunt turned to face Macgregor, two of the outsider factions squaring off against each other. Why did I think this was going to get messy?

Chapter Forty-One

SINCE WE WEREN'T the ones spinning the rainbow wheel, I wasn't too worried about missing out (I doubted Mordaunt would allow the casino to screw her over by canceling it anyway), but this was much more interesting. Macgregor was clearly here to start trouble.

To her credit, the Darkling Institute elite didn't seem too pressured by the big Monk. She just shot him a charming smile. "Macgregor, always good to see you. Were you looking for me for some reason?"

The Monk (seriously, he was wearing roughspun brown robes tied with a rope and everything) sneered down at her. "You know why I'm here, witch. The Moonsong Glade entry slots will belong to the Twilight Order. Your abominable freak show has one chance to withdraw."

Mordaunt's charming smile turned sharp. "Or... what? Are you going to fight me, Macgregor? Going to kill the monster maker?" She casually tilted her head, calling over her shoulder. "Rahm, darling, be a dear and protect your mistress."

The massive bandaged form of her attendant appeared in front of her without hesitation, blurring forward so fast I had trouble tracking him.

Rahm was at least as fast as Sloane with her wings out. His speed wasn't the all-time fastest thing I'd ever seen, but he was also *huge*. When he appeared in front of Mordaunt, he let both arms hang loosely at his sides, ready to engage as he straightened his back, glaring down at Macgregor. Rahm was at least seven and a half feet, and made even the Monk, who was taller than I was, seem small.

Macgregor sneered harder. He was pretty good at that. Lots of practice, probably, and he made the expression really obvious even through the thick beard. "You think I fear your creature, witch?" His hands started to glow with an uncomfortably white light, but before he could act, a smaller man with plain features and dark hair who I hadn't even noticed in his shadow stepped up and put a hand on his arm.

To my surprise, rather than just dismiss the other Monk, Macgregor actually backed down. I found that odd, based on what I'd seen from him so far, but it *had* only been a minute or two.

Mordaunt smirked. "As your minder no doubt reminded you, this is a pseudo D-ranked planet. If we start trouble, we'll be forced to deal with the Unity or, gods forbid, the Wish Curse Palace themselves. Even you rabid animals can't possibly be that stupid. Present company excepted." She said the last part with a sickly sweet smile, and Macgregor's hands started to glow brighter before flickering out a moment later.

"Fine," he hissed between clenched teeth. "Then accompany me outside so we might solve this once and for all. It should be no problem if you have as much confidence in your creature as you claim." It was easy to hear the goading in his tone, and apparently I wasn't the only one who thought so.

Mordaunt just snorted. "Do you think everyone is as predictable and stupid as the lot of you? I'm not going to fight you, I have no reason to risk that. I won't follow you outside because you said mean things about me either. I'm going to stay here and gamble. You're free to stay and enjoy a few games, assuming you know what that word even means." She turned her back on him, facing the rainbow wheel again and dismissing him wordlessly from her notice. I snickered at the expression on his face, but kept it internal so he didn't notice.

"Coward," Macgregor bit out. "Fine. I suppose it isn't necessary anyway. A sniveling wretch like you won't be an obstacle in the tournament. You'd best watch yourself in the future—if we catch you outside, we'll destroy you and your monstrosity as surely as you deserve." He turned, his fucking robe actually snapping dramatically as he strode purposefully from the casino.

"Well," I said in confusion. "That was... pointless. Did he really track you down just to snipe at you and then leave?" I could have sworn he wanted to actually fight, but he'd retreated way too easily. This whole thing seemed like a waste of time in every conceivable way.

Mordaunt rolled her eyes. "He'd have fought me here if he could have, but since I wouldn't accept the challenge, he decided to try to recursion lock me. Enough people hear about the fight and they'll start talking about it like it's definitely going to happen, and both of us will start making decisions that skew us toward eventual combat. It's not foolproof or anything, you can still avoid it, but the more the story grows, the harder it is to stay away from it. Fucking Monks." She waved to the woman behind the table. "Go ahead and spin it."

She did, and the ball landed on forty-six blue. With a shrug, Mordaunt turned away from the table. "Shame. But oh well. I'm done playing anyway. I'd much rather focus on making some local friends. I take it you're all going to be entering the tournament as well?" Her eyes skimmed over us all clinically, seeming to memorize as much about us as she possibly could.

Abel glanced longingly at the wheel, then sighed and nodded, gesturing for us to follow before he led us off to a side room where we could sit and talk.

The room was much calmer, with no crazy lights or furniture. Just leather chairs and a nice fireplace with a flame already crackling. We slumped down into the chairs. I was kind of glad to be away from the dizzying background.

"So," Callie said, getting to the real reason we'd followed Mordaunt in here. "What's the deal with you and Macgregor?" Given we'd be fighting these people, there was no way we were leaving information on the table. The more we knew about the outsider forces the better.

"Oh, that." Mordaunt sniffed derisively. "The Twilight Order are holier-than-thou busybodies. Just because we use human parts in our experiments, they get all bent out of shape. Our corpses are all ethically sourced from donations and criminals. It's not like we just snatch people off the street." She paused. "Well, except for that one guy, but we kicked him out as soon as we noticed he was doing it."

That was... kind of unsettling. I hadn't considered where they might be finding the parts. If people were donating, that was their business. The criminal thing was murky, but it wasn't like I could do much about what their local government decided to allow. Still, it made me wary of Mordaunt.

Callie looked a bit unsettled too, but she knew we could still get some information. "So why are you down here if you aren't looking to fight. Doomtown isn't exactly safe. You could find some nicer places to relax if you were looking for entertainment." Thinking about it, she wasn't wrong. We were down here to start fights and get information. If Macgregor had challenged us, we'd probably have accepted.

Mordaunt's smile was mysterious this time. "Well, I guess I can let you know. We're here for the Walking Silence Auction. The Institute is using the influx of forces from all over the star system to put on a bit of an exhibition. They've been stockpiling stuff for months in preparation. Even we haven't been able to get access to some of the premium goods. It's going to be held in Doomtown, since while the red zones are open for violence, this one is limited to prevent any overpowered participants."

I perked up at that. Auctions could be fun, from what I'd heard. I'd never been to a proper Ascendant auction. "Really? What kind of stuff will they have?" I paused for a second in distaste. "It's not all going to be body parts, is it?" I was definitely interested, but there was no reason to go if we couldn't get anything useful.

Luckily Mordaunt just waved off my concerns. "Of course not. No point in waiting to hold a large-scale auction when we're the only customers. There will be some experimental materials, but also plenty of artifacts and medicines for people to pick up. I'm sure you could find something you like. Do you want to come along? I have some guest spots and I'd be happy to bring you four with me?"

That seemed weird to me. "Okay, but why? You don't know us, and inviting random strangers to your Institute's super high-profile event seems… weird." I looked at the others. "This isn't just me, right? Like, this whole thing is super suspicious." I tried not to get in the way when we were planning things out, Callie had a good head on her shoulders, but this girl gave me the creeps. She'd been nice enough so far, but the casual talk of body parts just rubbed me the wrong way.

To my surprise, the question seemed to amuse her. "Oh, it's totally suspicious. But I'm mostly doing it for the same reason you're having this conversation right now. I need more information on the local landscape and you all are obviously locals. Silver mask over there is clearly comfortable here, and if he has info that I can use, it's worth burning some invitation slots I wasn't going to use anyway."

Callie shot me a questioning look. I was guessing that since I'd had the objection, she wanted to make sure I was satisfied with the explanation. I wasn't really, but it was the same kind of political nonsense I heard from everyone else, so it was probably legit.

I gave her a subtle nod and she turned a beaming smile on Mordaunt. "We'd love to come along. I take it the event isn't going to be for a few days at least?"

Mordaunt seemed amused by our dynamic, but I got the feeling she was amused by most things. Another check on the list of reasons she bothered me. Ultimately, I was probably biased. Having an undead with her kind of bugged me, given our time in the necropolis, and that wasn't really fair. I wasn't in a hurry to trust her, but if Callie wanted to go to the auction, I was down with that. Some gear for our friends would really help them out.

We'd need to boost them up during the tournament to be ready for the trip to Moonsong Glade if we managed to win, and better gear would mean they could show off a bunch in public for compounding gains.

We talked for another fifteen minutes about local nonsense, us trying to avoid giving away too much and her trying to pry, but eventually we ran dry. Seeing that all of the business stuff was out of the way, Mordaunt popped to her feet. "Well, I'm bored now. How about we go out and do some more gambling? We can talk about boring stuff later."

She hurried out of the room with all the focus of a toddler on a sugar high, and we all just shrugged and followed along. We could try to get more information from her later, but for now, we *had* come here to have fun.

I wanted to check out that betting table, hoping we could pick up a prop bet for our rematch with Wren. I was looking forward to seeing what he could do with his ability in use, and if I could make some money while I did, all the better.

Chapter Forty-Two

AFTER WE LEFT THE CASINO, Abel and Mel brought us deeper into Doomtown. In the inner reaches of the city, the lights weren't quite as red, bleached out by streetlamps glowing a blinding white. I noticed as we walked that the neighborhood seemed much more relaxed here. Not completely safe, but at the very least, people seemed less likely to jump out and kill us.

I was so surprised by the shift in atmosphere I had to bring it up. "What's the deal with this place? It seems so much quieter and more restful than the rest of the town."

Abel chuckled. "This is Sunshine Boulevard. It's... not exactly a neutral zone, but open conflict is discouraged. Be careful about eating anything you didn't see prepared in front of you, but yeah, you're not likely to get stabbed from behind. Even the outsiders probably won't start anything direct here. Of course, there are stealthier methods of killing and those are still more than possible, but there's far less benefit to that unless you build a rep for it over time. This is one of the few places where it's safe to sleep down here."

That was something I'd been wondering about. "So we're staying down here for the whole two weeks? Admittedly, walking back up those damn tunnels every night sounds annoying. Do you guys have some old friend around here we can stay with or something?" I gestured behind me to where Sloane was leading the Beast Lord crew. "Because I'll be honest, I don't think we're going to fit in someone's spare room."

"Not at all," said Mel. "We don't really know anyone who hangs out in places like Sunshine Boulevard. We *do* know of a reputable inn around here, though. Even we need somewhere to sleep. We never spent enough time here to get to know the owners or anything, but the Blue Robin Tavern has rooms for rent and is pretty much the closest thing to guaranteed safety in Doomtown."

The dark stone buildings had the same designs as the rest of the town, but the change in lighting made them seem much different. The red lighting had given the buildings a squat, devilish appearance, but in the much brighter (albeit still pink-tinged) light from the mixed streetlamps and overhead illumination of the city, the stone seemed sturdy and reliable, and all the buildings seemed just a bit taller, even if I knew they weren't.

What was more, as we walked down Sunshine Boulevard, I began to see bright green ivy climbing up the stone walls, artfully spread across the outside of the buildings in beautiful patterns that I was positive weren't natural. Callie smiled happily at the relaxing view and leaned against me, seemingly losing herself in the laid-back atmosphere. Despite that, I could feel just a bit of tension in her shoulder where it pressed against my side. She might seem relaxed, but she was too smart to let her guard down completely here.

After walking for about twenty minutes, we stopped at a building made of the same black stone, and with the same ivy, while being larger than any of the nearby structures. At two stories tall and twice as wide, the Blue Robin Inn (there was a sign above the front door) stood out starkly from everything around it. The owners had clearly put plenty of time and effort into building it up.

Abel clicked his tongue. "Ugh. It's all boring and idyllic. I forgot how lame this place was. Aside from someone trying to slip me shadeviper venom in a glass of beer once, I've never had any fun at this place. They even cook the food right in front of you so people don't have to worry as much."

Patting him on the shoulder, Mel said gently, "Yes, but most people like that, sweetie. Besides, don't pretend you never enjoy any downtime. You ran that sausage cart for years, are you telling me you got regular assassination attempts on you during that whole time?"

"Well, no," complained Abel. "But that's not the same. This is Doomtown. It's like going to an amusement park and not getting on the rides. Attempted murder is part of the fun. I'm not here for a peaceful meal and a nice rest." He sighed. "Still, I guess the kids could use the break." He turned to us. "Plus, this place is a great location to farm intel. People come from all over Doomtown to stay here, so it's got a good cross section of potential sources."

Callie perked up a bit at that, but I was pretty ambivalent. Constantly trying to squeeze information out of everyone was starting to bore me. I knew it was important, but it just didn't amuse me much. "Do they have anything interesting to do here?" I knew fighting was a no-go, but there had to be *some* form of entertainment.

"Of course," Mel reassured me. "Don't listen to him. Even I'm not as battle crazy as he is. There are a bunch of things to do. They even have a special pool table that weights your stats like our obstacle course. Beating more powerful Ascendants is always fun. You can bet on the outcomes, but you don't have to."

That *did* sound like fun, actually. I had enjoyed playing pool sometimes as a mortal, though I hadn't played in ages. It made me think of Benny. His dad and grandfather both played when they were young, and he was kind of raised to it. I'd gone with him and his father a few times, and I'd really enjoyed it.

"Sounds like a blast. I'll give it a try when we get in there." I glanced at Callie. "Want to try a game?"

She shook her head. "Nah. I'd rather ask around about some of the local players. You go ahead, we can meet up to go get something to eat after."

I shrugged. That was fair. We spent a lot of time together, but it wasn't like we were attached at the hip. I could find someone else to play a game with.

So I turned to Abel. "You down for a game of pool? If you're going to sit around and sulk about not fighting anyway, might as well enjoy yourself while you're at it."

"That doesn't sound too bad," he mused aloud. "I don't hate *everything* about this place. The food and drink is solid. You can even get Moontear Brandy here. Granted, it's stupid expensive, but it's just about the best F-rank drink you can find on Callus. I haven't had any in ages."

He shot Mel a pleading glance. "You think I could get the kid a glass of the good stuff? To celebrate how far he's gotten in training?"

Mel's voice as she responded was icy. "No, Abel. You cannot buy yourself and one of our students a snifter of brandy that costs eight E-ranked chits per glass. We'd have to clean out the whole Pavilion. If it wasn't so expensive, why do you think the Robin would still have that bottle after all these years? You're the only person I've heard of crazy enough to buy a glass of it."

"It's not like I didn't share," sulked Abel. "I let you have a sip, didn't I?"

Despite his tone, my brain was still frozen on the price. I'd bought a fucking *car* that could *fly* for less than an F-ranked chit. In fact, I had very little understanding of what Ascendant money was actually worth. I mean, I knew each level of chit was worth ten times the lower levels, but I didn't know what that entailed in practical terms.

I should probably get a better grip on how the economy functioned, given my position of power in the Pavilion. Sure, I had other people for that, but it wasn't like I would always have people like Mel around. My massive windfalls and quick jumps between ranks had kind of skewed my understanding of how money worked.

Despite his obvious unhappiness, Abel didn't dwell on things. He strolled up to the Blue Robin's front door and rapped on it a few times. The door opened to show a squat, dark-skinned man with broad shoulders and blonde hair, a permanent scowl etched on his features. "Why are there so many of ye?" he said, in a thick accent that reminded me quite a bit of Alden. "We don't have the rooms for ye each to get one."

His steel-grey eyes bored into us harshly, as if we were offending him by even standing here when there were clearly too many of us.

Mel put up both hands placatingly. "Not a problem. We only need…" She turned to look at us. "Four rooms?" Sloane nodded, unbothered to be sharing a room with some of her initiates. We obviously wouldn't stuff twelve people in a room together, but six was less of a problem. "Yeah, we'll take four rooms. Do you have enough openings?"

The scowling man narrowed his eyes like he thought she was trying to trick her way past, but slowly turned his gaze to the side, clearly reading something in his mind's eye. "Aye," he said grudgingly. "We're close to capacity, but we can accommodate ye for four rooms. I'll remind ye that this is a neutral location and that troublemakers will be punished. We have an F-ranker standing watch, so no funny business. We have enough trouble with some of the outsiders here for that blasted tournament."

We all gave serious nods, and the man stared hard at us for a minute before stepping back, opening the door.

Once we were inside, Abel leaned in to murmur in Mel's ear. "Wow. This place is way less friendly than I remember. Last time we were here, they had a pixie at the door. She was much more welcoming."

The small, broad-shouldered man spun and smacked a palm into the wall. "No complaining! Or ye'll sleep on the street!"

Abel shut up, but not without a quiet snicker that I was sure the man had heard. Still, my teacher wasn't wrong. This guy wasn't exactly a customer service elite.

Once we were inside we split up. Abel and I headed for the pool table, Callie and Mel for the bar, and Sloane to figure out the distribution of rooms for her crew. I was happy to see that they had a nice selection of custom cues available to use, and all of them seemed incredibly sturdy and well-made. Sure enough, as soon as Abel and I picked them up, we felt ourselves become restricted, our bodies and minds slowing down to nearly mortal levels. I knew our Impact would remain untouched—it took more than some random table to suppress that stat, so we weren't in any danger. This would just make the game more fair.

There was a sign-up sheet to one side of the table with some illegible names, and we wrote ours down. We were signed up for a game of doubles. Since the place was so busy, one-on-one games were scheduled for later in the night. We wouldn't get to play against each other but that was fine. This was mostly just for amusement and to kill time.

When we arrived at the table, though, I froze, a familiar pair of amber eyes meeting mine from across the surface. "Well," said Wren of the Spear Legion, "this is certainly a quicker meeting than I was expecting. Do you think this counts as a rematch?"

Chapter Forty-Three

I'D LIKE to say I was surprised to see Wren. But after only a split second of thinking, I kind of wasn't. Weird coincidences are part and parcel of being an Ascendant, at least in my experience. Whether I was guided to exciting things by my Fantasy stat or this was some kind of grand recursive effect of all mortals idealizing the nonsense we go through, I'd probably never know, but if something could go weird, it would go weird.

Still, in terms of surprises, this one wasn't too bad. Wren was a big scary badass with a giant spear (which he wasn't carrying), but he seemed like an okay guy for the most part. I'd shattered his ankle with poison fire and he'd just seemed excited for the rematch. Which... I guessed was now?

I grinned at him. "Sure, but only because I want a chance to dunk on you again before the tournament. I'm a big believer in the rule of three."

He barked out a laugh. "Cocky little shit, aren't you? But I don't mind. You and your partner earned that much. Your level of coordination isn't something I expected from a couple backwater natives." His eyes flicked to Abel. "Though it looks like you have a new companion."

The laughter faded from Wren's face as his eyes bored into Abel. "You... are very dangerous. You remind me of Lament. I'm not sure why, but I trust my instincts."

I leaned in between them. "This is my mentor, Apollyon. But no more talking about that. You don't want me to think you're fishing for information, do you?" He snorted at that, dragging his eyes away, and I gestured to the table. "Now, I believe a rematch was mentioned? Do you want to break, or should I?" I didn't fancy trying to find a new place to sleep if they got into a dustup and destroyed half of this room. I had seen Abel fight, and if I didn't know he was human, I'd have suspected someone summoned him from the elemental plane of property damage.

Wren grinned wryly. "Going right for the throat, eh? Fine. You can break. Winner should get first shot." He winked. "Just be sure to keep that in mind for our next fight after I beat your ass at pool." He gestured down to the table, where I quickly racked the balls and then set up my shot. Pausing, I turned to Abel, but he just waved me on, and I took a shot.

The break was clean. I was working with mortal stats, so no crazy perfect shot that sunk all the balls, but I managed to get at least one in. "Solids," I proclaimed smugly, then set up for a second shot. I felt like showing off, so I hit a double bank off the far corner and tapped in another solid, a green this time. My third shot, sadly, ended the streak, but at least I didn't scratch.

Abel strolled up to stand next to me as Wren lined up his own shot. I hadn't left him with much. "That was better than I expected," my mentor said. "Most Ascendants are useless if you strip away their stats. You play this when you were mortal?"

"Yeah, Clockwork's dad used to take us when I was younger. I'm not as good as he is, but I do okay. It's a fun game."

My reminiscing was cut short by a perfect triple bank from Wren as he smoothly deposited a striped ball in one of the pockets. He lined up and pulled off three more shots in quick succession, and I winced.

Wren was a master martial artist. He spent all his time working with a spear. I wouldn't say that a spear and a pool cue are the same thing, but control of point of impact and more was ingrained in him even without his stats. He couldn't mobilize his Skills without stats to use, not past the Minor level anyway, but he still had the knowledge and control that gave him those Skills in the first place.

I expected him to completely clean us up, but luckily he was distracted for a second by an argument nearby and scratched. I exhaled with relief. It was odd not having the same level of Focus as usual, even for me. My brain didn't feel sluggish or anything, but my thoughts were definitely more scattered. Focus gave raw processing power, but it also helped concentration, and clearly Wren wasn't any more used to losing that than I was.

Without any hesitation, I passed the cue to Abel. I might not be a master of bodily control with a genius grasp on physical movement, but he was. He grinned at me smugly. "Don't feel too bad. You are pretty good. I hadn't really counted on the crossover either. Damn weapons masters. Let me give it a shot." He winked and walked over to the table. He started pacing around it, looking at angles and setting up shots he never took.

After a minute or two, Wren looked annoyed, but didn't say anything. Abel finally stopped, picking a specific spot and lining it up, then snapped off a single stroke. I watched in shock as the cue ball rocketed across the table, knocking off nearly every single ball. The solids remaining headed right for the pockets, and the few that couldn't be directly hit were banked or knocked on course by the stripes. Any stripes too close to the holes were knocked away by the solids.

Abel waited for a minute for them all to fall in. The eight ball came to a slow stop right on the rim of the pocket, with the cue ball about a foot away and lined up clearly. My teacher grinned over at Wren and said, "Eight ball, corner pocket." Then leisurely tapped it in. He turned to me and his grin widened. "Fun fact. Learning to manipulate space makes you *really* good at geometry and angles. Even without stats."

I hadn't considered that. I'd been paying attention to Abel's martial skills, but the stuff he did with his spatial lubrication must require an insane amount of spatial awareness. Some of that must be Focus, but the skills would be there anyway.

"Well, looks like we won." I smiled at Wren. "We gonna do a rematch? Or do you want to get a drink or something?"

Despite not being a big drinker, I didn't mind a bit of alcohol in a social setting. I'd ended up drinking some beer recently, and assuming I didn't get something high-ranking and expensive, my Vitality made it impossible to get drunk. I didn't *love* the taste, but if I didn't need to worry about getting tipsy because I couldn't hold my booze and acting like an idiot, there was no reason not to be polite. Plus, I knew from Callie's fishbowl thing that there were drinks that didn't taste as bad. Luckily for me, lower-ranked drinks would be cheaper anyway, so this was a win-win, as far as I was concerned.

Wren looked annoyed, but he blew out a breath. "Fine. But nothing crazy. I can see your buddy looking all shifty, and I am *not* paying for Moontear Brandy. Even I don't have the money to throw around to buy a round of that stuff. And even if I did, I wouldn't do it for a lost game of pool with no stakes."

I snickered at Abel's curse of annoyance, and then held up a hand. "Why don't we play a few more friendly games. No need to put reputation on the line this time, no rematch. But maybe me and your buddy there can do some shooting." I gestured at a smaller man with shaggy blue hair and a goatee the same color. I held out a hand. "Sorry, got caught up with Wren there, didn't catch your name."

He grabbed my hand and shook. "Vector. And don't sweat it. None of us expect to be first priority when either of the bosses are in the room. Wren is huge and Lament is... Lament." I cocked my head in confusion, and Vector just gave a rueful chuckle. "You'll see when you meet her. It's hard to describe." He sized up Abel. "For Wren to mention a similar vibe from you is interesting. I don't feel it myself."

Wren shook his head. "He's more restrained, but there's a sort of aura of violence that people develop when they're competent enough in combat. It's not really an Ascendant thing. Mortals can have it too. It's a surety of movement and purpose. Lament's is aggressive, like she's ten seconds from butchering you. His is more... smug. It kind of makes me want to punch him in the face."

Despite the hostile comment, his tone was more introspective than anything, as if he was trying to talk out a puzzle. I had to suppress a snicker as Abel held up both hands in a "what the hell?" gesture.

"Anyway," I said decisively, cutting off a potential fight that Wren would definitely lose. "I'd love to play against Vector a bit. I refuse to believe both of you have managed to translate your spear mastery into perfect pool cue use."

We played another four games. Vector and I both shot, and I won two while he won two. But it became obvious that once I shook the rust off regular rules wouldn't work, since you could keep taking shots when you sunk one and we were both hitting every shot. We started swapping back and forth, which dragged the games out, but it kind of stopped being fun because of how good we were.

Eventually we decided to abandon the pool table, heading to the bar for a drink, and we ran into Callie and Mel up there when we arrived. Callie was happily enjoying something brightly colored in an oddly shaped glass. I suspected most Ascendants liked lower-ranked drinks more for taste than inebriation, given how high their Vitality was. Clearly some of them had interest in getting drunk given the high ranked liquor I'd seen and heard of, but if you were drinking something that physically couldn't get you buzzed, there didn't seem a reason not to make sure it was tasty.

Callie called me over, waving wildly to get my attention. She stopped when she realized what she was doing and where, and leaned back against the bar, nonchalantly beckoning us like she hadn't done anything a second ago. When we got close, though, she grinned. "Oh wow, what a coincidence. Wren, good to see you. I should have guessed you might be staying here when they mentioned the outsider factions."

Wren chuckled. "Yeah, not many viable accommodations down here. Surprised to see you around, though. Locals and all. Anyway, luckily you have a drink already. I owe your partner some libations after losing to him and his buddy at pool." He rapped on the wood surface of the bar. "Hey, barkeep. Pair of drinks for my friends. Put whatever they get on my tab, but no top-shelf stuff."

The taciturn bartender with a shaved head and nose ring nodded solemnly, raising her eyebrow at the two of us. I ordered a milkshake, which drew a small huff of laughter, and Abel ordered a brandy (the non-wallet-destroying kind). She brought us our drinks and we settled in to enjoy.

We ended up staying up to talk to Wren and Vector for quite a while, learning more about the Spear Legion. Not information gathering or anything, but just the normal "getting to know you" stuff you talk to new friends about. What it was like there, what they did for fun, et cetera. They were both pretty chill guys, and I felt relaxed as we headed to bed after a night just hanging out.

Of course, that was only for tonight. Tomorrow we would need to figure out our next move, but so far, I was enjoying my time down here in Doomtown.

Chapter Forty-Four

THE NEXT DAY, we didn't end up going to some gambling den or fighting pit. Instead, Abel brought us out to a corner of Doomtown where a large cavern lake sat, and paid a guy in a small shack a few chits to rent us a boat. As he was doing this, Wren, Vector, Sloane, the other Beast Lord Initiates, Callie, and I all stood nearby looking confused.

I glanced over at Mel. "Is this… fishing? Is he taking us fishing? Because honestly, I didn't think he'd scheduled leisure activities. Like… I guess the inn was one, but that's more necessity than anything."

I'd almost started talking myself into the idea when Mel started to snicker. "Yes and no. Riot Bay *is* a fishing spot, but it isn't the kind that you go to when you want to relax. This place is going to be good training." She stepped meaningfully away. "For you. I'm not going into that fucking lake again for as long as I live. It's wet and it smells awful. Enjoy your training, though, kids—here comes Apollyon with the boat keys!"

Sure enough, Abel was on his way over with a few pairs of keys. He held up one, tossing the others to Wren and Sloane, and addressed the latter casually. "I'm not buying boats for all your minions. You can all squeeze into one, or some of them can stay with Mel. I don't really care. I'd recommend not packing in too tight, though. Room to move is key in Riot Bay." He gestured to the boats docked at the shore, all of which were surprisingly roomy.

He pointed to me and Callie. "You two are with me. Mostly because I want to watch you flounder." He snickered at his own joke (or at least I assumed it was a joke, since we were next to a lake) and then turned and strolled away. Before he got too far, he turned his head, calling over his shoulder. "Big man, you and your buddy should be fine on your own, but probably stick close to our boat if you can. Worst case, I can probably get over to save you if you need it."

Wren glared at him, muttering under his breath. "I don't even know what the hell is out there, but I already want to kill it just to prove to that asshole I can." He paused. "Probably not the most sensible instinct, but oh well." With a shrug, he headed for the shore, clicking the fob on his boat keys. There was a loud chirp like a car door unlocking, and one of the boats shuddered slightly. He nodded to us. "See you both out there, I guess... probably."

Heading for the boats, he dragged Vector along. Abel was already aboard what I assumed was our boat. I turned to Sloane, who was only bringing Beric and Croll and leaving all the randoms behind. "You have any idea what this is about?" she asked. "Because whatever it is, I have a bad feeling about it."

I did too, but I didn't bother saying so, since it wouldn't change anything. If Abel thought this would be helpful, we'd do it.

With a nonchalant shrug, I informed her I had no clue, and we separated from her and the other two to meet Abel on the boat. Climbing aboard, I could see further out into the lake, and I couldn't help but be struck by its beauty. The water of the lake was a flowing, opaque liquid. Superficially, it was like what you would find in common glow tubes. Still, there was something entrancing about the swirl of the softly glowing blue substance. Looking back as our boat idled, I could see it rolling up and down the black sand beach beside us, and the image was extremely soothing.

Callie smiled out at the lake, eyes closed as she inhaled deeply. "Okay. This is really nice. Kind of curious how it's going to try to kill us, but for the moment, I'm enjoying the trip."

I chuckled at that, not able to disagree on either count, and slipped a hand into hers. After a minute or two staring off into the distance, though, we heard a loud noise. Abel cleared his throat.

"Hey," he said lazily. "It's nice that you two are bonding, but I need some help to steer this thing. A ship this size can't be crewed by one person." He paused. "Well, I guess it *could* if I was willing to actually work at it, but I'm not, so you're going to help." He pointed me over to the jutting spear of wood in the middle of the deck. "Solomon, go unfurl the light sail. There's no wind down here, but the ships use an invisible energy screen that harvests the light from the lake."

It took me a second to find the controls, but they were surprisingly uncomplicated. I pressed the button, and missed what he told Callie to do as I stared in awe at the sheet of glowing blue energy. It unfurled along the length of the mast, and I watched it pulse slightly brighter every few seconds as it absorbed more energy from below.

Abel walked over. Knocking on the mast, he nodded amiably. "Good, still works. These things are discount transportation at best. They cost almost nothing to maintain, so they're profitable as hell, but they do break down regularly."

Shaking off the sight of the pulsing energy screen, I turned to Abel, who kicked the deck and stood by, watching a podium rise from the wood. Once it was up, he fiddled with the controls a bit and we began to smoothly glide through the water, going from stationary on the beach to mid-motion so suddenly that I had trouble isolating when the motion began.

"Alright," I said, tired of waiting, "what the hell are we doing here?"

Abel just chuckled, not bothering to take his eyes from the distant skyline... Lakeline? Caveline? From the horizon. "We're here for the Riot Tide," he said casually. "It's an excellent training tool. Basically, when we reach the deeper parts of the lake, we'll stay put. After an hour or so, the tide will come in. A wave of lake water will carry hundreds of fish right over the surface of the boat. We should be able to stay planted fine, but the fish will pummel everything on deck."

He pointed down into the opaque water. "You can't see them, but they're pretty big. They're all G-rank... well, mostly. The F-ranked ones only come up deeper into the lake, they're too big for the smaller waves here to lift. Anyway, the value of the fish varies based on color. They come fast and hard, and your job is to punch them out as they attack and then grab the tails to chuck them into a basket you'll keep at your side. The fish change color as they climb higher up G-rank, with red being the lowest and purple being the highest."

That sounded... insane. "So you want us to what? Catch a bunch of fish? How exactly will this help us progress?" This could be fun, and I wouldn't complain if we were just screwing around, but I definitely didn't want to miss the point and lose out on valuable training if it was there. I came down here to improve, and I wasn't confident yet we could achieve decent results in the tournament.

"Good question," Abel said approvingly. "The answer is simple. You're being graded. I'll be assigning points based on the fish you catch. Minus two for red, minus one for orange. Yellows are nothing. Green is one point, blue is two. Purple is three, but those are stupid rare, so I wouldn't hold my breath. This exercise is to help you judge the danger of incoming attacks for your partner without looking. It'll help with recognizing feints and things like that. Plus, we can cook or sell the fish. They taste great."

Huh, that was fair enough. I could see the usefulness. Plus, I hadn't had much of a chance to work with fish in the kitchen. Might be fun to take some home to make fish tacos for Callie or something.

I turned to see her smirking with anticipation and rolled my eyes. It was nice to know I could read her so well, at least.

"Alright," I said, liking the idea. "What do we need to do to get ready? You said we shouldn't get washed off the boat. I don't know exactly what that means, but I'd prefer not to fall in."

"Good call," said Abel blandly. "If you swim too deep, you can run into the F-rank fish. They're mean bastards. Plus, you can drown, but that's rare. Because of our higher Might, we can condense way more air into our lungs on a strong inhale, and Vitality makes oxygen use more efficient.

"Anyway, don't fall in, yes. I could come save you, but it would be annoying and I might not find you before you get fish-slapped to death. If you *do* fall in, make sure to swim for the surface as fast as you can, if you can figure out what direction that is without being able to see anyway." I winced as I imagined being sucked in upside down and swimming for the bottom by mistake. That would be bad.

The next hour passed without much drama. I'd expected this place to be crazy even outside the Riot Tide. Riot Bay didn't exactly sound like a scenic getaway, but to my surprise, it was pretty much exactly that. Off in the distance, the swirling blue lake water was like a glowing pane of opaque crystal, flat and smooth for as far out as I could see. Despite that, the swirl of the glowing substance created a sort of shifting effect that varied the glow from spot to spot. It was mesmerizing to watch.

Still, despite the beauty, we were about to be literally pelted with fish. I wasn't sure what that would be like, but it was bound to be unpleasant. It was impossible not to constantly brace for an attack from all sides, which made the faux serenity of our surroundings even worse. This was the calm before the storm, and we all damn well knew it. I could see Wren and Sloane's boats nearby, scything through the lake water, leaving barely any distortion in the surface.

My first clue that something was coming was Abel. He'd been sitting back looking bored for most of the time we'd been out here. Between one breath and the next, though, his eyes snapped open, focusing sharply on the surface of the water. He crossed the distance to the railing of the ship in a blink and looked down into the water as if to confirm something, then nodded. Turning back, he went to open a hatch, pulling out a series of heavy-looking braided metal baskets. He dropped one next to each of us, then walked to the other side of the ship and dropped the third next to himself.

"Alright," he said solemnly. "We're about to get hit. Plant your feet, try not to move around too much. I put your baskets close enough together to let you cover each others' backs. No weapons and no poison fire or any of that shit. If you ruin the fish, it defeats the purpose. Stun them and toss them in the basket, it's Enchanted to keep them in stasis. Any questions?"

We both indicated we had none, and his solemn expression melted into his usual anticipatory grin. "Good." He pointed off into the distance, where the shape of a cresting wave could be seen rolling across the surface of the lake. "Because it's about to start."

Chapter Forty-Five

THE MASSIVE TIDE of blue liquid hit the ship like... well, a tidal wave. Our feet were planted on the deck firmly as the wall of water rushed at us, and I could easily see the dark forms of writhing fish riding the wave like some nightmarish parody of birds on the wing. I could vaguely make out the shapes of Callie and Abel at other points on the ship, the hunched form of a heavy basket near each of them. Callie was especially close by, since we were working together.

I could see the fish wriggling as they approached, all G-ranked monsters of various levels. Still, there was no reason to freak out about it. I stopped, took a deep breath, and braced myself as the lake water slammed into me. My mask made it simple to breathe, though I suspected my Impact would have helped even if I hadn't been wearing it, since Callie and Abel didn't have the same protection. Still, even without suffocating, being hit with a wall of water was disorienting as hell.

Drifting into my combat trance, I let my senses unfocus, taking in every- thing and nothing all at once, straining to pay attention to my instincts. I felt a slight twinge and stepped out to take up position at Callie's back, then lashed out with a quick punch and immobilized a fish headed for my girl- friend. I grabbed its tail in the same motion, turning to hurl it into my basket with a triumphant grin... until I realized the damn thing was red.

Sadly it was too late to intercept the fish, and it dropped into my basket, subtracting two points from my already-negative value. I shook off the unhappiness, drifting back out of focus, and started countering more of the fish attacking Callie, even as she did the same for me. I knocked out a flat dozen of the things, but they kept being swept away by the water before I could grab them because I was pausing to note what color they were.

I tried to sense some fundamental difference about them beyond color, but despite how much I focused, I was completely unable to distinguish between one fish and another. So I switched to knocking them out and grabbing them, then checking them before I threw them in, and had moderate success with that. I ended up using one of the fish as a bludgeon as I reached for the next, not being able to leave Callie undefended long enough to check each one.

That worked a bit, but not fast or practically enough. This was a test from Abel, and that lunatic wasn't one to give a task without some ulterior motive. There was a trick to this fucking exercise, there had to be. He'd said it was to sense the power of incoming attacks so we could react more efficiently, or something like that. I could see the logic. Blocking low-level attacks would waste energy when they would be incapable of hurting Callie anyway. I needed some way to tell.

I closed my eyes, letting most of my senses fade, and focusing on one that I rarely had a chance to use: the sense that stemmed from Fantasy. This one picked up on odd or interesting things and subconsciously steered Ascendants toward them. Despite not needing any more craziness, I was at a loss for how to do this, so I figured some mysterious sense I didn't understand might work better.

It didn't. I was slapped in the face by the next fish I tried to catch. At the very least, it didn't get to Callie.

I was starting to get frustrated. I could use Seek Hidden, but there'd be no point. Abel didn't have that Skill, which meant that it wasn't the answer I needed to find.

Suddenly I felt a slight twinge coming from a sense I hadn't really thought to use: the sense that let me measure Impact. I wasn't sure what that sense actually *was,* but at the very least, I knew how it worked. I could feel the weight of a person or artifact's soul. However, paying closer attention right now, I could pick up that despite all being G-ranked, not all these fish felt the same.

Maybe it was the increased soul strength from all the training, maybe it was the crazy environment, but I could feel *differences* in those fish. They all had twelve Impact, sure. But the soul weight of them varied infinitesimally. This one was heavier, that one was lighter. It seemed soul weight varied based on more factors than just Impact if you knew how to look for it. I was sure that this was the key to working out how to do this little exercise.

Keeping my eyes closed, I tried to reach out with that same ineffable muscle I used to change a Skill: my soul, or at least the part of it I was able to use. I pushed my sense of Impact further, harder. I needed to go deeper into these impressions. I could feel the fish coming, just like before, but with my focus on sensing the variations, I could also discern that the strength of each fish differed slightly.

I lashed out at a fish with a punch, ignoring a weaker one right next to it as it bounced off Callie's coat. The one I punched, I grabbed by the tail and tossed into the basket, seeing a flash of green as it dropped in.

I almost cheered. Green was good, much better than red. It meant I had been able to sense the difference. I tried another fish, then another, carefully picking each one based on my feeling of how heavy they seemed versus the ones around them.

Some were losers, oranges, yellows. Some were greens, and I even got a purple. But as I went on, I consistently improved at picking them, getting better and better results as I fine-tuned this new sense.

I could see why I hadn't improved this before, too. This environment was perfect for this kind of training. Many hostile monsters that weren't too strong but were still variable levels within our own rank could be compared to each other. In the past, even when we'd been in fights with G-ranked people or monsters, there hadn't been this many coming this quickly.

Feeling my pulse pounding, I lashed out faster and faster, losing myself in the process as I slowly honed this new sense. Sadly, while I appeared to be doing well, Callie wasn't picking this up. Possibly because of her lack of experience with exercising her soul. In fact, this detection method acted like a very mild form of soul strengthening exercise itself. I was feeling that telltale strain in my head, though it was *much* weaker than when using a Skill.

That made this even more valuable for her to learn because it would give her a way to work her soul without devolving into a gibbering pain-blind mess or passing out, like sometimes happened when I went too far. In order for that to happen, I had to actually let her know what to do.

While Abel's whole "learn by doing" teaching method did work most of the time, Abel wasn't perfect. I didn't think telling her how it worked would sabotage anything. Plus, he hadn't told me not to mention it.

Hoping we were close enough for her to hear me through the waterfall-esque blast of liquid force, I waited until there was an opening and bellowed, "*Callie!*" There was no response so I waited a minute before trying again, screaming her name at the top of my lungs.

When she finally noticed, she was smart enough not to turn to me completely and ignore the fish. She just stepped back and cocked her head so her ear was facing me.

Knowing she would be straining all that Perception to hear me, and all her Focus to filter out the water sounds, I scaled back my screaming to a dull roar. "Try sensing their Impact! You can kind of feel a difference in their weight even without any of them being higher than twelve!"

I tried to think of a better way to describe it, but I came up short. I trusted that she would be able to detect what I meant once she had an idea where to look.

With that done, I went back to fighting. I got hit a bunch more by the fish, but my armor tanked pretty much all of it, and after a few minutes Callie got a better feel for at least the extremes of the weight scale, mostly letting reds and oranges through to tag me.

My own basket had been slowly filling with greens and blues since I started detecting everything, and even the odd purple. They *were* rare, but over the course of the next few hours we got attacked by *thousands* of fish, and I managed to identify and catch six purples. When the water finally receded, it took me a second to process. We'd been in there for so long I couldn't keep track of time.

Being soaking wet and sore didn't help. While my armor was F-rank and more than up to protecting me from random fish, as I'd noted before, blunt force tended to transfer through a bit. With G-rank fish, that wasn't much, but tens of thousands of hits over hours added up, even with my Vitality offsetting it.

I groaned, slumping back onto the deck with a thump. "Ow. Why is it that every single time we train with you, we end the day in pain and nearly unable to move?"

The comment was aimed at Abel, though I couldn't turn my head to look at him. My Vitality would repair the injuries eventually, but they were made by G-rank opponents, so the conceptual weight of the attacks impeded the process somewhat.

I heard Callie groan weakly from off to the side. "Yeah, and you couldn't have given us a hint or something? I'm starting to think you're just a sadistic asshole."

Abel stepped into view, standing between us so I could see him without turning my neck. He had a hand to his chest and was looking mortified. "*Just* a sadistic asshole? I'll have you know my sadism and assholishness are merely two of my many endearing qualities. But seriously, stop whining. That was a nice workout, but nothing too bad. I'll let you both recover back at the inn, though. You've certainly earned it."

I groaned at the cheer in his voice. "How much money did you just make off our suffering? Also, you know you're sharing that, right? Because no way in hell did we go through that for nothing." Come to think of it, Abel looked like he was in much better shape than we were. "How many fish did you even catch? Or did you just hide behind something and let us do all the work?" I doubted it, that wasn't his style, but I was annoyed and venting a bit.

Abel just snickered. "Hide? Kid, I was rerouting about half of your incoming tide with spatial lubrication. Between that and my increased skill, I caught easily three times as many fish as you did, and most of them were higher-end ones, too. I actually got fifteen purples this time. It was a pretty good day." Ignoring my shocked silence, he reached down and picked me up easily, throwing an arm over his shoulder before heading to grab Callie.

He carried us over to the mast to let us lean against the post. "Now. While I *will* be letting you take home a portion of the money, it won't be more than a quarter each," he said casually. "So sit back and enjoy the ride. I'll be handling the ship as we head back. Think of it as payment."

If I could have moved, I'd have attacked him as he turned and walked away laughing. Since I couldn't, I just glared at him really hard. What a bastard.

Chapter Forty-Six

By the time we got back to the shore, I was at least able to stand. I was still sore as hell, but my Vitality had patched me up enough that my muscles worked, at least. Callie appeared just as bruised and uncomfortable, but she also looked as ecstatic as I felt. Despite the annoyance at Abel and the physical discomfort and pain, it felt *good* to get stronger. To learn to be better and improve in a measurable way.

And measure we did. After we got back to shore, Abel carried the big metal baskets off the ship for us and we emptied them out on the black rocky beach, counting our haul and the number of points. I'd managed fifty total, while Callie had gotten forty-eight. Abel, though he wasn't competing, made sure to assure us he had broken triple digits, and that both of us together had failed to even approach his number. The asshole.

Still, as I stared down at the fish, I could see why these things were so sought-after. They were beautiful. The scales were vivid and every bit as breathtaking as the colors of a rainbow. They were also all motionless, apparently immobilized by the stasis field long enough to suffocate. I had thought it kept them alive, but apparently I'd mistaken the point of the baskets, the devices being more to keep them fresh than anything else.

As I stared down at them, I heard a crunch nearby and turned to see a bedraggled Wren and Vector jumping down and trekking over. They had obviously heard the little introductory speech Abel had given us, not a surprise on such an open expanse of water with two G-rankers. They still looked annoyed as hell as they glared at my mentor. "You know," Wren snarled, "you could have *warned* us."

Abel gave a derisive snort. "I didn't warn my own disciples. Why would I warn you two? Besides, it's good training. Don't tell me a pair of Ascendants from cluster-level forces can't handle a little light rain and some relaxing fishing."

We all turned and stared at him in mute horror as he described the... watery apocalypse we had just gone through as "some relaxing fishing." That took a serious amount of talent in bullshit to say with a straight face. Or at least what we could see of it.

Sloane, who had walked up in squelching wet boots, was glaring too. "Well, that's certainly kind of you. Be assured that I will return that kindness at the first possible opportunity. With interest." With that, she stomped past us, storming over to presumably get a change of clothes from her underlings. The effect was ruined by the watery squelch of her feet as she trudged across the beach.

"Alright." I drew attention back to the matter at hand. "What do we do with these fish? Where do we sell them, and for how much?"

Before Abel could answer, a new voice piped up. "Hey, dudes." We all turned to see the guy from the boat rental shack standing off to one side. "Bodacious catch, bros. That's a tubular multiplicity of aquatic lifeforms. Might you be interested in parting with your superfluence of fishy findings?"

I blinked at him. So did everyone else. None of us had a fucking clue what he'd just said. The man's scruffy brown hair and goatee, combined with his blank stare, made him seem like kind of a lazy, sleepy person. His speech, on the other hand, was confusing and in some places, I was pretty sure, made up. I wasn't a dictionary, but "superfluence" didn't seem like a real word to me.

Looking at him more closely, I tried to take in his outfit. Baggy tan shorts with too many pockets, a T-shirt with an open short sleeve button-up, and a surplus of metallic jewelry on his fingers and hanging from a black chord around his neck. He also wore a ton of varied leather bracelets with metal buckles and pins on them.

Abel grinned at him. "Dale! You're just in time. We were just talking about what to do with the fish. You willing to pay full rate for them? They're pretty fresh, and it'll save me some time."

Dale guffawed. "Most obviously, my compatriot. I have an abundance of most radical funds to disperse for the purpose of acquiring such a delectable piscine assortment. To my eternal sorrow, though, the monetary equivalency you speak of has mutated in the time since your previous embarkment. One credit of H-rank as a base for a red is a more efficacious offering to begin our fiscal negotiations."

The big dopey smile hadn't changed, but I caught a gleam of craftiness in his eye, and Abel's smile turned into a scowl. "The fuck you say. Don't pull that wasted philosopher bullshit on me, you money-grubbing layabout. I haven't been gone *that* long. Two and a half per red as a base. I'm not a moron, I did check prices before coming here. I'm not one of those stupid tourists you fleece."

Putting up both hands, Dale's eyebrows rose in alarm without his eyes actually opening from their lazy half-lidded state. "Whoa! Your accusations of malfeasance are farcical. But alas, I am no match for such a puissant practitioner of the pugilistic arts. Spare me your erupting wrath, your monetary offer is most acceptable for such a close personal friend. Our historical dealings are more than enough to justify such an expenditure."

Abel rolled his eyes. "Oh, stop it, Dale. I forgot how quickly that gets old. Just talk like a normal person, there's no one around to hear anyway."

Dale's relaxed smile twisted into an annoyed scowl. "Hey, man, why you gotta fuck up my aesthetic? If the tourists hear me talking like this, they'll be way more on guard. I've spent years cultivating my image. The combination of dazed moron and confusing linguistic savant really puts people at ease. If you fuck this up for me, I'm gonna be pissed, I have a business to run."

Mel snorted. "I can't believe it still works after all this time," she said wryly. "You'd have thought after all the people you've ripped off, someone would have warned the others."

The dopey grin returned. "I'm not sure as to the bamboozling you might be referencing, lady fair. I am simply a harmless and hapless proprietor of seafaring wares who chooses to invest in the local community through the occasional acquisition of delicious carp-tacular treats."

"Those are salmon," Mel said dryly. "But point taken. That really is convincing. No clue how you keep it up all the time. Though it explains why you haven't ranked up. People pretty much dismiss you out of hand."

Dale just shrugged, resuming a normal speech pattern instead of his lazy far-off drawl. "I do good business here. No reason to rock the boat, so to speak." He looked at us. "You guys keep this quiet, will you? I'd normally stay in character even after being caught out, but annoying Abel is never a healthy thing to do." He glared at the silver-masked man. "Not to mention there's no point, since he's decided to screw me on pricing."

That got an eye roll from my teacher. "Oh, please. You've been ripping off tourists for too long. Two point five is a solid baseline. The multipliers for color variants aren't even that high, except the purple at six, but there's less than twenty of those. Gods know you'll sell the damn things at a markup anyway. What do you charge after prep, like five?"

"They're paying for labor," Dale said self-righteously. "It costs to keep my chef on retainer. Not to mention I have to pay for processing to make sure the scales are treated right. They sell for a decent amount in bulk, not to mention the organs and bones can be crushed up to make a pretty high-end plant fertilizer."

Abel looked over to us. "This. This is why I call him a money-grubber. Despite his laid-back appearance, this miser can't let a single chit slip through his fingers." He waved away the line of thought, literally swatting the air like the whole conversation was an annoying fly. "Whatever." He pointed at Sloane and Wren. "You two, dump your catch. This is as close to market value as you'll get, and he won't pay nearly this much after I'm gone."

They both did so quickly, ignoring the annoyed scowl from Dale.

Abel looked back at the shack owner. "Well? What are you waiting for, an engraved invitation? Count them up. The longer they're out of stasis, the worse condition they're in, and I'm not taking a pay cut because you're a slow starter."

Dale muttered something vaguely insulting that even I couldn't hear and walked over to start counting up the fish as Wren and Sloane dumped theirs on the beach.

Abel turned to us. "This was a decent haul. Two point five as a base for the reds is a solid payout. It means twenty-five for each purple. That alone is going to be a pretty serious bump. I think people have been too distracted to come fish lately, because looking at the full haul laid out like this, it's easy to see it's denser than normal. I was only expecting pocket money, but this is going to come out to about fifteen F-ranked chits."

"Why H-ranked chits as a base, though, if they're G-ranked monsters?" I asked. If we got paid in E-ranked chits instead, it would obviously be much more lucrative. I hadn't been expecting that to happen, but I might as well find out why not.

He waved that question off too. "H-rank tends to be base currency here, even for higher-level Ascendants. The economy on a backwater planet like this is pretty limited as a whole. There's only so many chits floating around. I doubt anyone on Callus has any D-ranked chits, even if they have enough E-ranked chits to trade for them. Once you get past a certain point, scarcity plays a role. Not to mention these fish are pretty common. Nobody would make any money paying out G-ranked chits for catching them. Just like no one is paying G-ranked chits to eat them. Five H's, probably."

That was an economic wrinkle I hadn't considered. The whole money thing scaled kind of hard after the first few ranks, but if H-ranked chits were the standard of currency, that would definitely drag it down a bit. Sort of like the equivalent of a credit for local Ascendants.

Abel's tone was dry. "Ponder economics later, kid. If I know Dale, he's going to want us to carry them over as part of the fee."

Sure enough, Dale returned and insisted we help move everything. It wasn't much work, but it was wet and annoying. Eventually, though, we got them all transported and he handed over fifteen F-ranked chits, three of which went to Wren and Sloane, who hadn't had nearly the haul we had even if their catches had looked impressive. Lots of reds.

With that done, we headed off the beach, walking back toward the city proper. Wren checked a scan ring for the time and looked over at us. "Well, that was time-consuming. We're doing dinner with the rest of the legion, if you want to tag along? I'm sure Lament would be happy to meet some challengers, even if our escorts won't let her fight you. She has problems holding back when she gets excited, so we want to save some mystery for the tournament."

Callie answered for us, immediately accepting, and I just grinned in anticipation. Seemed like I was finally going to meet the Spear Legion's ringer.

Chapter Forty-Seven

In the end, we got six of the twelve remaining F-ranked chits to split between us, and everyone left Dale's for dinner with Wren and Vector. They had arranged a meal with the rest of the Spear Legion, but I was confused about where.

"So wait," I said, perplexed, "they aren't staying at the Blue Robin with you? I figured they were in their rooms or just not around. Why aren't they sharing accommodations with you guys?"

I said "they," but it was more like "she," since Lament was the one we were all most interested in.

Wren just shrugged. "The Robin is one of the safest places in Doomtown, but Lament doesn't really care about that. Our handler is E-ranked, and got special dispensation to come down here, though he can't act except in self-defense. The two of them decided to stay in one of the more… exciting areas. Some of the Doomtown hotels run by the local forces have interesting games and activities, if you're willing to accept the possibility of death every time you turn around."

Mel groaned. "She's staying at the Chaotic Wombat, isn't she?" I turned my eyes to her, confused by the statement. She shrugged. "The Wombat is infamous. Abel went once, though I never bothered. It has a gimmick where every person who enters is stamped with a marking. Once every twenty-four hours, at a random time, the markings all light up green. One person has a red marking and everyone else is supposed to attack them. The person who kills them gets ten F-ranked chits, and if they survive, they get ten E-ranked chits, though to my knowledge, it's only happened three times."

Abel grinned. "Oh yeah, the Wombat is a blast. Since the rooms are all in various wings and levels, the whole mess turns into kind of a scavenger hunt. I was kind of hoping to get picked as sacrifice when I went, but it ended up being this annoying F-ranker named Kamahl. His ability was changing the size of things after touching them. He did it on a delay so he would throw like, rocks at you and they would turn into boulders. He was only early F-rank, or he wouldn't have been down here, but he still didn't last too long. I think one of Silent Dagger's people got him."

"That's horrible," Callie said, appalled. "Who would even go somewhere like that? Does everyone die when they get picked?" She looked disturbed by the casual nature of the violence, and I didn't blame her. It was awful that there were places where you could die just for going. Hell, even knowing how lawless and awful Doomtown was supposed to be, the whole macabre nature of the game was just unconscionable.

Sensing how upset she was, Mel put both hands up placatingly. "Not at all. Plenty of people escape. Usually the ones who get killed are unlikable. Your friends are free to intervene even if you get picked, and most people's do. You just don't get the payout if you leave the premises. The sacrifice lasts for three hours, and if you leave, it's considered a forfeit." She patted Callie's shoulder to console her. "It's really not that bad."

It was easy to forget Mel and Abel weren't Unity. The WCP seemed like a quirky but stable place most of the time, but there was a reason it was considered a black-market underground force. Then again, based on what Zeke had said, it was probable that other factions weren't much better. The Black Sorrow Cult seemed like a pretty horrible environment based on their ruthless use of sleepers.

Maybe the universe was just kind of a shithole. It was something to think about when we finally got off this planet. Being an Ascendant wasn't all wine and roses. Monsters weren't necessarily the biggest dangers.

With the knowledge that we could have friends step in though, I wasn't *quite* as opposed to going. Abel chuckled at our indecision. "It's fine, kid," he told Callie. "It's still early for dinner, and while it *is* random when they do the sacrifice, it's usually when there are plenty of people around. It's, what…" He checked his scan ring. "Five p.m.? Most people won't be eating for a few more hours. We'll be gone before they start the festivities."

I was sort of ambivalent here. With Abel and Mel, not to mention Wren, we should be fine even if one of us got picked, and if it wasn't likely to even happen, it might be safe enough. The sacrifice could happen at any time during a twenty-four-hour period, and it could happen to only one person. That made the chances of being there and being picked vanishingly small if we were only there for a short time. I just left the decision up to Callie, cocking my head at her so she knew it was her call.

She bit her lip. In the end, though, we came here for the danger, so we could improve. If we avoided dangerous situations, we might as well have stayed up in G district.

That same realization showed up on her face. She nodded grudgingly. "Okay. Fine. But I want to make it clear that if the sacrifice *does* happen while we're there, even if we aren't picked, we're not participating. I'm not hunting and killing another person for fun. That's awful. If possible, I even want to help them. Is that okay with all of you? If not, we'll skip it."

I beamed at her. I was so proud of her for coming to that conclusion. I don't think I would have thought to specify that everyone help whoever got picked.

To my surprise, Abel shrugged. "Sure. Sounds like a party. I prefer odds to be against me anyway. Still don't think it's likely to happen, but if it does, I'm down to play defense."

We all rolled our eyes, because that was the most Abel answer possible and we probably should have expected it.

Mel also nodded. "That's doable. I'll be honest, it's been a long time since I worried about that kind of thing. It's so common down here there doesn't seem to be a point most days. Still, if that's what you feel you have to do, kid, we're behind you."

Callie looked poleaxed. "But… you're teaching us. Shouldn't you demand we toughen up and do what you think is best? Don't you think I'm being naive?" She sounded so confused at the concept of her teachers not forcing her to follow their example that it broke my heart. I was pretty sure I could guess why.

Either Mel didn't figure it out or she was too nice to bring it up, because she just laughed. "No. We're not trying to turn you into us. You kids are talented and you've helped us out, so we're giving you some lessons and a hand with this. Plus we might benefit. But we aren't you. Trying to brainwash someone into doing what you would do isn't teaching. You're ultimately Unity members, and doing things their way isn't always wrong. Sure, it might seem a little naive to us sometimes, but being naive is fine as long as you're smart about it."

Based on the shine in her eyes, Callie looked ready to cry for a second, but she shook it off. "Thanks." She gave a steady nod. "Yeah. Like I said. If someone gets picked, we help them. Even if it isn't to our benefit. I won't stand by while someone gets hurt for no reason." Her voice strengthened as she repeated her decision, steel in her tone.

Wren cleared his throat. "So... we *are* going? As for the sacrifice, you won't need to worry about us if you get picked. Lament isn't one to gang up on others. It's beneath her dignity, and she wouldn't let any of the rest of us pile on either. Though if she does get selected, probably don't try to help. She would be more annoyed at you for getting in her way than anything else."

With that decided, we headed back into the city, following Abel to the Chaotic Wombat. He was the only one of us who had been there, so he took the lead. Once again we walked through Doomtown, and as we moved, the streets around us subtly changed. Unlike Sunshine Avenue, the red light in this new area didn't fade, it just deepened to a darker color. Not just dimmer, but more scarlet somehow.

Abel took in a deep, happy breath. "Ah, Damnation Row. Been years since I've even thought about this place. If Doomtown could be said to have a 'bad part of town,' it would be here. Most of the city is anarchy, but the Row is always just a little worse. Don't you just love the smell of complete mayhem in the afternoon?"

As we walked, the stone facades of the buildings became more dilapidated and worn down. I wondered in passing what all the other buildings were. We passed dozens of them everywhere we went, and they couldn't all be casinos and fighting clubs or whatever. On second thought though, I kind of didn't want to know. Considering how messed up the stuff we had already seen was, I had a feeling random back-alley businesses might be even worse.

When we finally came to a stop, I was a bit underwhelmed. All the other places we'd been had stood out from the outside, been taller or more ostentatious. This was just one of a parade of squat stone buildings.

I looked over at Abel, my tone disbelieving as I said, "Really? This is the Chaotic Wombat? How can you even tell? It looks so… average. You'd think they would put up a sign around here or something, at least. We could've walked right past this place and never noticed."

It was hard not to be disappointed at the lackluster exterior. I wasn't exactly looking forward to our visit, but this place seemed significant if nothing else. Abel just shrugged. "The Wombat isn't really a standout kind of place. Most of the places we took you were important or well-known. The Wombat is the kind of place that only desperate or stupid people go." He paused, receiving strange looks. "Or… you know. Really confident warriors who aren't afraid of death."

Mel choked back a snicker at her boyfriend calling himself an idiot by mistake and cut in. "Yeah, plenty of places don't bother to make their location easily noticeable. Damnation Row is the kind of place where successful businesses get raided. Of course, the Wombat *still* gets raided by neighbors and customers sometimes, but keeping the outside nondescript stops random tourists from paying attention and joining in."

We all approached the door, but Abel stepped up ahead to pound on the dark metal. A hatch on the door at eye level slid aside.

"What?" snapped a hostile voice. I was starting to feel like no one in the WCP knew how to hire someone to watch their fucking door. Was a hello too much to ask for?

Abel glared. "Let me the fuck in, that's what. You think anyone would come stand outside this shithole for no reason? Like I picked this one building to ask to use the bathroom out of this whole gods-forsaken street? We're here to ride the Wombat, now let us in."

I had to stifle a chuckle at the ridiculous password, but it seemed to work, because after a few clicks, the door swung open and the man let us in. As we entered, he took out a stamp pad and placed a tiny mark that looked like an animal head on each of our hands. I *really* hoped we weren't here when they changed color.

Chapter Forty-Eight

THE INSIDE of the Chaotic Wombat was weird. I'd seen a lot of places, and even lived in a pretty unusual location myself. The orange-dyed house we had up in Rajak proper was strange to look at the first time. Still, the Wombat took the cake, or rather... it was made of it.

Which is to say, the whole place was covered in what looked like candy. The chairs were made of peppermint sticks, the tables were slabs of chocolate, the chandeliers were rock candy, and the various doorknobs and decorations were all types of sweets. Despite her worry over an attack, Callie went ramrod stiff when we walked inside, her wide eyes raking over the bounty of delicious treats.

Abel, noticing her expression, snickered slightly. "Yeah, I was wondering how you would all react. The *owner* of the Wombat has an Intermediate Candy Making Skill. Most of this stuff is higher-ranked food, like H-rank, maybe. Even two points of Impact can make a serious durability difference, and it makes candy décor more viable. Of course, any of us could smash through this with zero difficulty, but then again, we'd be just as able to smash through normal mortal wood or even some metals. Plus, I'm sure you can figure out the other benefit."

"Renown," I said without blinking. "This would definitely generate plenty of buzz. It's kind of weird, but in an interesting way..." I looked over at my drooling girlfriend with a worried frown. "If we eat any of this, will we get attacked or something?" This place was clearly crazy. The last thing we needed was for Callie to break off a piece of rock candy from a wall sconce and get us mobbed or something.

Hearing my question, Callie snapped out of her stupor and looked at me sheepishly. "What?" She said with an unconvincing laugh. "That's crazy. What kind of moron would just randomly start taking bites out of furniture." Her eyes locked on a nearby chocolate fountain made of what looked like waffle cone. "No matter how delicious it looks."

With an amused snort, Mel patted her on the shoulder. "Best to avoid that stuff. This is the *Chaotic* Wombat, remember. They lace the candy with psychedelics and other strange things. You never know what eating it will do. The food you buy is fine, or else no one would come here, but the rest of this stuff is eater beware. It's not a bad gimmick, all things considered. But since we're here for a dinner, there's no need to invite trouble."

Callie looked much less interested after hearing that, shying away from one of the nearby chairs.

As we walked further in, Wren noticed something off in the corner of his eye and turned to wave over at a table. "Oh, hey, Lestri! Vec, there they are, come on." He hurried off toward the table, leaving the rest of us to follow. Sloane, Beric, and Croll were all sticking close to Abel and Mel, which seemed wise, so I followed after.

We'd decided not to bring the others, having them head back to the Robin, because if things did get crazy, mediocre combatants would be most likely to be picked off around the edges. Keeping our group to only real elites would help us all remain safe.

As we reached the table, Wren clasped hands with a short, red-haired man with the sides of his head shaved. He waved us over. "Hey guys, come meet my brother Lestri. He's on our team too."

It was easy to see the similarities, from the olive skin tone to the red hair, and looking closer, I could see the same amber eyes, but the most shocking difference was their size. Wren was a massive towering man, but Lestri was only a few inches taller than Callie. Five five foot nine or ten, maybe? Still, he was corded with muscle in a sinuous way that made me think of a coiled snake. I had a feeling he would be pretty damn fast.

One thing I had picked up over time was that being small wasn't necessarily a disadvantage for Ascendants. One point of Might translated into a thousand pounds of lifting force, but that was a static value. Someone with a hand the size of a coaster would be able to concentrate that force more effectively than someone with a hand the size of a dinner plate. With the same physical parameters, smaller people tended to hit harder. Of course, they had to sacrifice range to do it, so it wasn't like bigger combatants didn't have their advantages, but it just went to show not to underestimate anyone.

Lestri raised an eyebrow. "Oh, these are the locals that kicked your ass earlier, huh? Interesting to see you met up with them again." He scrunched his nose. "Also, why in the gods' names do you smell like fish? It's faint, but pretty unpleasant." He sniffed a bit and then, realizing that Wren's hands were the culprit, pulled out some sort of sanitizing hand rub from the pouch at his waist and handed it to his much larger brother.

Rolling his eyes, Wren took the bottle and rubbed the contents on his hands, holding them up so his brother could smell them. The smaller man nodded with a modest grin. "Sorry, my brother can get a bit focused and forget things, so I tend to mother him a bit. Would you believe he's the younger one?" He shot Wren an annoyed glare. "I have no clue what our mother fed him to make him get so big, or why it didn't work on me. Anyway, do all of you want any?" He held out the bottle.

Seeing as Wren had just used it in front of us, none of us were worried about poison or anything, and our hands *did* smell bad (the impact spots on our armor had been washed clean by the water pressure, but our hands had soaked in small amounts of fish blood and viscera for hours) so we decided to take him up on it. There was a pleasant tingle from the liquid, and it smelled sort of pine fresh. I liked it. It also cleaned our hands *incredibly* quickly.

Once that was done we handed the mostly empty bottle back, and turned back to the table. There were two more people there: a small, quiet-looking girl with platinum blonde hair, dark eyes, and pale skin, and a tall man with bulging biceps wearing a carved wooden mask that looked like a grinning skull. Wren gestured to them. "That's Lament, and that's our handler Master Saiten. Lament is our top contender for the tournament."

The E-ranked handler was as intimidating as I'd expected. He reminded me a bit of Abel, but his aura of violence was much more condensed. Every move he made was dangerous, as if he was constantly resonating with his Spear Mastery Skill.

243

I swallowed hard at the realization the title Wren had just used might not be a formal political title. It might be literal.

Abel, of course, just outright asked. "Wait, when you say Master..."

Saiten chuckled, a deep, rumbling sound from behind his mask. "Indeed. I have achieved the Master rank with my spear Skill. Or course, the Skill is now simply Master of the Spear. Master Spear Mastery would be nonsense."

I was awestruck. Master level. I had no clue what that would require, but it was damn impressive. It also implied that Saiten might be close to D-rank if his spear Skill was the only one synergized with his ability. The sole requirement for an ability to rank up, aside from stats, was for all component Skills to reach that rank first.

Of course, whether he was a peak E-ranker or not was mostly irrelevant to us. Any level of E-ranker could swat all of us like a fly. We all gave him our most formal greetings, and he nodded courteously before summarily ignoring us completely to focus on eating. The wooden skull mask lacked a jaw, so he wasn't impeded by it as he dug into the food. Judging by the gusto he ate with, it must be good.

A waiter approached the table, wearing a crazy candy hat and suit, and passed out menus. I winced at the prices, but Wren just told us to order whatever we wanted within reason. They had a discretionary fund from the Legion for the tournament, and anything they didn't spend would be confiscated on their return.

Since Mel had mentioned that they held the purchased food to a standard (probably how they justified the absurd prices on the menus), I wasn't too worried about poison or that kind of thing. I scanned the menu before picking out a delicious-looking sausage gumbo. Callie ordered a pot pie, Abel a steak, Mel lasagna, and Sloane and her two friends all ordered clam chowder, for some reason. I mean, I liked clam chowder, but it seemed weird for them to get it as a group. Maybe it was some kind of solidarity thing?

As they left, Lament finally focused her gaze on one of us. Specifically, Abel. She raised an eyebrow in challenge. "So, you're one of the local elites. The rest of them don't give off much pressure, but I can tell you and red mask there are different." She chucked her chin at Mel, but never took her eyes off our mentor. "I take it I'll be facing you in the big tournament?"

Lament's hand clenched around the edge of the table reflexively, like she was gripping a spear haft.

Abel grinned back. "I'm happy to oblige you any time. Tournament or not. Feel free to attack me right where we sit." His tone was relaxed, almost bored, but I could see a manic glint in his eye that mirrored that frenzy I'd seen from him when he smashed the F-ranker from Sanctuary Hall.

Lament started to stand, but a crushing weight smashed down on all of us, driving her back down into her seat and the rest of us harder into ours.

With a lackadaisical smile, Saiten, who hadn't been moved, clicked his tongue. "Now children. No need to get so excited. We'll have plenty of time to battle when the tournament begins. For the moment, I think we should all just relax and enjoy our dinners. Don't you?"

I'd felt worse, of course. The metaphysical weight Zeke had dropped on us the one time he decided to show off still made me shudder in remembered helplessness. This weight, in contrast, was much more... condensed. It wasn't nearly as strong, even in a much smaller area (the waiters and nearby diners seemed unaffected), but there was intent here. Saiten was *trying* to restrain us, while Zeke had just been... existing nearby. I was pretty sure based on this that Zeke hadn't even fully unleashed his Impact, because a concentrated effort like this from him would probably have killed us.

Saiten eased up and we all just sat there, panting slightly. We could have moved, but it would have been a massive effort.

Callie smiled. "Th-thank you, Master Saiten. No need for us to let things become unpleasant. This is just a nice, relaxing dinner among friends."

Which, of course, was when all the lights went out at the same time.

In the darkness, points of green light flared up all around the room as stamps began to glow. Well... almost all the stamps were green. I followed the red glow to the illuminated and frightened face of a young-looking girl wearing a pair of rabbit ears at the next table.

The sacrifice had begun, and it wasn't one of us, but we would still need to help. Damn it. This was going to suck.

Chapter Forty-Nine

WITH ALL THE glows from the hand stamps and the Perception we all had, it was effortless to see in the darkened restaurant. It was sort of surreal, with the shifting glows moving along with the hands of the people nearby. Still, despite the minor confusion, we were all well-trained and ready to act.

Even as several dozen customers tried to mob the rabbit-eared girl, they were met with a fist the size of a train car that managed to appear between them and their target without damaging the intervening space at all.

As the first responders were sent flying, Abel stood happily from the table, cracking his neck as he started walking slowly toward the girl and her companions. Mel rolled her eyes, rising and flooding the room with light as a nimbus of golden flame blazed into existence around her arms. Despite being older and stronger, the two of them hadn't even hesitated to listen to Callie's declaration about protecting the sacrifice.

Of course, Abel was just a battle-crazy lunatic, but Mel was a rational human being most of the time, which meant she really took Callie's words as leader to heart.

I, of course, stood up and slipped my cane from its sheath under my coat. I activated my Touch of Tears and Consecration of Flame as I trailed behind my mentors, while Callie, Sloane, Beric, and Croll followed me. The Spear Legion members stayed sitting for the moment, which was better than having to fight them all.

Abel made it to the girl with the rabbit ears without much trouble. After his first attack everyone was waiting and watching. They weren't sure what had just happened, and no one here was stupid enough to risk their lives for some F-ranked chits.

When he got within range, Abel grinned at the girl. "Young lady! You have an excellent sense of style! Your ears are adorable. I don't suppose you'd be interested in doing a little business?"

The pale, tiny girl with blood-red hair and wide, stormcloud-grey eyes, swallowed hard. "I... I-I don't know what you mean, sir. Thank you for the help, though. What kind of business did you mean?" She glanced nervously at her friends, who all wore rabbit-themed accessories. To my surprise, *they* did not look worried. Most of them looked confident and ready to fight.

Wren, who had somehow appeared behind us when I'd been distracted, leaned in to murmur. "They're with the Wave Warren. Not the strongest group in the system, but definitely impressive. That's Sydney Whispervale. She's one of their ringers for the tournament. Don't underestimate her."

Due to everyone's high Perception, every person in the room heard him, and Abel cocked his head in interest. "I was going to offer to protect you for a cut, but it sounds like you might not need it, and my team leader said we have to help anyway. How about if we can escort you out of this place, you buy me and my friends a drink and we call it even?" His big, innocent smile made me want to roll my eyes. He was still trying to scam someone into buying that brandy.

Sydney bit her lip. "Well... I guess that doesn't sound too bad. If you really help us, then there's no reason not to say thank you." She twisted a lock of hair around her finger nervously. "Oh, I should never have come here. I never should have listened to Megan. She said there was no way I would get picked, and everyone was so excited to try the food." She'd stopped looking at Abel and begun to mutter to herself under her breath, seemingly castigating herself for every decision that had led her to this point.

"Hey!" Callie said after a minute. "It's okay." She looked almost panicked at how badly the girl was spiraling in what was possibly the literal worst place for it. "We're here to help you. We can all just leave. I'm assuming you don't want to stay to try and win the money?"

With wide eyes, Sydney shook her head rapidly, her red hair whipping back and forth and her rabbit ears coming loose. She reached up and had to fix them, looking embarrassed. I was pretty much dumbstruck. How was this girl the secret weapon of a system-level force? How was this girl allowed to come *down* here? She was so… meek and harmless.

"Of course not," she said anxiously. "I just want to leave." She looked at the others. "Can we just leave?"

One of the men, wearing a black coat with a rabbit's paw pinned to the lapel, sighed heavily. "Of course, Miss Sydney. Miss Megan wouldn't have sent us to accompany you if we weren't supposed to offer our protection. We can leave immediately." He turned to us. "We appreciate your help, though if you attempt to backstab us, I'm afraid you're going to suffer for it extensively." There was no threat in his voice, just a calm statement of fact.

A nearby patron of the Wombat, finally fed up with us ignoring them, piped up. "Hey! We aren't just going to let you take her and leave." A chorus of agreements rang out. His eyes pinned Sydney gleefully. "Sorry, girly." He stepped menacingly forward. "But in your next life, you should be more careful exactly where you g—" Without warning, the man's eyes flashed steel grey, and he rolled his ankle, stumbling into the man next to him, who had drawn a wicked-looking knife.

The knife drove into the man's side, and he growled, turning his now-brown eyes on the person he'd bumped into, fury written on his face. He hauled back and punched the other man, fist shifting in magma as it crashed into the hapless knife wielder. Knife Guy's friends decided to join in, and Magma Guy apparently had a group of his own. Within seconds, a miniature gang war had erupted inside the Wombat.

I blinked at the wilting form of Sydney. The grey flash in his eyes had looked just like hers. Ascendants didn't trip often, as a rule. Sydney clearly had some sort of ability that could affect enemies. Based on how spectacularly everything went wrong, I was guessing it was bad luck.

Now wasn't the time to think about that though, because when the two groups started fighting, their agitation set off the rest of the people in the Wombat, who all surged forward. Some attacked directly, some circled looking for an opening, but they still came at us all the same.

Letting myself shift into my combat trance, I slipped up next to Callie and neatly deflected a blow from some kind of fleshy tentacle. Callie slammed a hand into the ground, putting up a dome of condensed darkness to intercept a wave of icicles even as what looked like a swarm of purple energy bats tried to swarm us. Mel turned the things to ash without a second glance, freeing us up, and Callie dropped the shield just as I swept out a Mercy Kill-infused strike at the kneecap of one of the attackers clashing against a member of the Wave Warren.

The man, a guy in red with a winged cap and aviator goggles, howled in pain as he whirled his hands, conjuring a pair of whirling tornadoes to push us back. I used Sucking Mud, shaping the attack with my soul to hold us less deeply in exchange for speed, and the wind broke over our armor as the scarf-wearing Warren cultivator snapped out a kick. His leg had suddenly become a bladed hook, opening the red-clad man's throat from the side.

More power to him, he didn't pass out or drop from blood loss, only smashing his coat against the wound to staunch the bleeding and using his wind to hurl himself away. I really needed to put some time into coming up with proper counters to the elements. The vast majority of Ascendants had an element-based power, especially after getting the chance to synergize.

I didn't have a chance to get lost in thought, as usual. I was forced to burn a triple-stacked density-shifted attack, along with a Mercy Kill, to smash aside some kind of weird dog-headed construct on a chain with huge jagged teeth that tried to bite into Callie from behind. The blade-legged Warren cultivator bounded up into the air in a low arc, lashing out with a kick that took off the summoner's arm at the elbow and forced him to jerk the ball construct back to defend himself.

There wasn't time to do more than nod gratefully at the cultivator before the crowd surged between us. We backed up to try to group tighter with Abel and Mel, who had surrounded Sydney along with a pair of her guards and were beating back the crowd, Abel whooping with joy in the rush of battle. With our mentors at our back, we were *slightly* more secure, but not nearly as much as expected. This was fucking lunacy, people weren't just attacking Sydney and her guards, I could see several Ascendants backstabbing and attacking random people in the chaos, using the action as cover for murder.

Trying to give myself a bit of room, I reached for my power, triggering a clone and a density-shifted triple-stacked attack at the same time. I felt my head go slightly fuzzy as more soul weight than I could handle slammed down on me, but I managed to hold up under the strain until it passed. Of course, the clones were much weaker and more fragile than I was to begin with, but with the addition of the triple strength and density shifting, the one I managed to construct was about half as durable and strong as I was.

The clone dove forward into a crowd of G-rankers, lashing out with the most brutal attacks he could manage, bringing all the Skills and stats he had to bear. He broke a few limbs and managed to tie up several of them long enough for Callie to come in. While they were off-balance, she smashed them with a bulldozer made of shadow, sending them flying, though not doing much to hurt them. The cloud of gelatinous acid crawling across the floor took care of that when they landed in it, and though they didn't die, they were in *far* too much pain for it to matter at the moment, at least based on the searing skin.

Unfortunately, while we were holding the line for the moment, we were also being worn down. Abel and Mel were guarding Sydney as instructed, but that meant they weren't clearing a path out of here. We were getting penned in.

Despite the mess, it had only been about a minute since this all started, and I was already almost dead on my feet. We needed some sort of backup. Wren was helping, decimating anyone who came close with his spear, and Vector was doing the same. I saw Lestri flash between a pair of combatants, taking a limb from each in one swirl of his own long spear. Right when I glanced over to the table to check what Lament was doing, the Spear Legion's ace finally acted.

A spear, the size of a fucking bus, flashed through the air, parting the crowd with a brutal cleave, taking limbs and even heads off multiple enemies and opening up a path to the door.

I was in shock. That spear move had reminded me so much of Abel's fist attack, and I'd always thought that was just his ability. Thinking back, though, Abel had mentioned being peak Intermediate in his own combat Skill. Something to look into later.

Lament looked almost bored as she strolled away from the table, casting a derisive glare at the gathered enemies. "Noisy," she sneered.

From the huge bloody hole in the crowd stepped another figure, one I hadn't seen before: a man in bright yellow clothes and a top hat, with a sad face painted across his features. He shot her a grin, an incredibly odd thing to see on someone with a painted-on sad face. "Well, now. That was certainly dramatic." He flicked his hand and a shining golden whip unfurled in the air beside him. "Want to try it again?"

Apparently this mess wasn't over. Based on the figures stepping up behind him, it was just beginning.

Chapter Fifty

As soon as the man with the painted-on smile came out, I immediately turned to Abel. "Wow, that guy seems tough," I said excitedly. "Who is he?" Lament was supposed to be on Abel's level, or close to it, so this guy must be some local big shot, or maybe one of the outsiders I hadn't heard about yet. If it was the former, Abel probably knew who he was.

My mentor gave me an irritated look. "How the hell should I know?" Then he shook his head. "I'm not a population directory. Looks decent, not sure if he's local or not, but if he is, he's not someone I recognize. You can't expect me to know everything and everyone." He sounded genuinely annoyed by the assumption, but I didn't take it to heart. I had no way of knowing what he did and didn't know.

Luckily, while he might have been ignorant, Sloane wasn't. "Laughing Jack. His dad is Pierrot. Luckily he didn't inherit his dad's creepy puppet-making ability. He uses some kind of sunlight power, and that whip is magic. He has a Skill for it, too. All in all, he's pretty scary, though I'm surprised to see him down here. I've met him at a few social functions Melinda took me to, and he's not really one for slumming it."

That sounded interesting, but if Abel hadn't heard of him, I doubted he was on the same level as Lament. Abel made it sound like a peak-Intermediate combat Skill was pretty much unheard-of somewhere like Callus.

Speaking of which. "Hey, what did she just do, by the way?" I asked Abel. "That spear thing? It looked like what you do, but I thought that was your ability?"

To my surprise, rather than blowing it off or snapping off an easy answer, Abel ruminated for a bit. Finally he held up a hand and waggled it back and forth. "It is and isn't. My ability is definitely powerful and often used in conjunction with my combat Skill, but the effect you're talking about is called a manifestation." He spoke carefully, which was fair. This conversation was happening in public. "A lot of weapon masteries gain the ability when they hit Intermediate. My combat style is a combination of those two factors, with my spatial lubrication ability providing flexibility and options to a powerful Skill."

"Oh," I said blankly. "So that wasn't even her ability? Just the Skill part of her combat style? Because that's terrifying, she tore through that whole line of people like they weren't even there. Could you do that without using your ability?"

If he could, he'd been holding back against us more than I'd thought in training. No wonder he crushed us so thoroughly even without Skills. Reaching peak Intermediate must mean his martial arts were at an absurd level of competence.

For the first time since I'd met him, Abel seemed... uncomfortable. "Probably," he answered at last. "But I avoid displays like that. Being terrifying and competent is great, but you can push it too far. If I start demonstrating Skills at that level without consideration, some E-rank might decide to take offense and come deal with me." He looked annoyed by the idea, and I could definitely understand. I hadn't come into contact with that kind of suppression yet, mostly because of a combination of my background, Zeke, and the utility of my ability.

For someone like Abel, though, being able to reach the peak of an Intermediate Skill was a big deal. It meant he was most likely going to become an Expert as soon as he hit F-rank, and could potentially become a Master at E-rank like Master Saiten. I wasn't sure how rare that was, but chances were good it wasn't common. None of the other E-rankers would want a Master martial artist around at their rank.

It seemed like leaving for the dungeon was the best possible outcome for Abel, because once he hit F-rank, people were going to start taking note of him. At G-rank, the Impact suppression would make him basically a non-issue for them, but that wouldn't be the case forever.

I didn't have time to worry about that though. As we'd been talking, Lament had exchanged a few words with Laughing Jack, whose minions had fanned out behind him to block her path. The spearwoman didn't seem particularly bothered. Wren, however, looked upset, and stepped up to murmur something in her ear that I couldn't hear. Probably used a stealth Skill.

She grimaced but nodded, then stepped forward and vanished in a blur, appearing right in front of Laughing Jack to smash down with her spear. Wren exhaled in relief. "Okay. Good. She knows not to reveal too much. She could swat him like a fly with her Spear Mastery, but it would give away too much before the tournament. I asked her to keep it low-key."

"Low-key" was apparently fast and violent, but not super fancy. Instead of using the fluid, snakelike spearmanship I'd seen from Wren, Lament's moves didn't appear to suit a spear at all. From what I could tell, she was planning on beating the other man like her spear was a bat.

Unfortunately, holding back so much meant she wasn't able to one-sidedly crush him. As she lashed out, Jack flicked his whip up, coiling it into a sort of tunnel. The blow landed, and the whirling whip dispersed the impact of the blow down its length, bleeding off the damage.

Abel hissed. "Ouch. Whips are always a pain in the ass. She could demolish him, but if she's not using her Spear Mastery Skill, that's going to be annoying. I wonder what her ability is?"

Despite his words, he didn't seem concerned. He just took up a position in front of Sydney to make sure none of the onlookers tried to start some shit. As we watched, Lament probed Laughing Jack a few times. Despite not using her Skill or martial arts, she was clearly incredibly experienced handling a spear. Her grasp on controlling its force was extreme, even when she was just waving it around sloppily.

Laughing Jack looked serious now under his sad-face makeup. His whip spun up in concentric circles, each one bleeding off the force of a strike, but despite the swirling endless river of golden metal that was his whip rotating quickly, each blow was forceful enough to offset his rhythm and he was slowly shifting to the back foot. "What are you idiots waiting for?" he shouted in panic. "Attack her!"

His minions, who had grouped up behind him, seemed surprised by the plea for help, but not afraid. A ghostly skeletal energy hand smashed down on Lament as a pair of snakes made of stone leapt from the ground. The third member of his group summoned a series of tiny, fluffy white clouds that tried to get in close to wrap around Lament's spear, spewing lightning bolts.

Lament barely noticed. Even as she sidestepped the smash from the skeletal hand, she flicked out her spear in a slash, spinning it through the motion without even slowing down and cleaving through one of the clouds as she brought the spear up and over to bisect a snake. Two quick flicks destroyed the second snake and another cloud, and she speared the last cloud with a single thrust aimed at Laughing Jack's throat.

The yellow-clothed man eeped and flicked up his whip, and even as he did, the thing roared to life with golden sunfire. I felt a slight stir from Lament as she briefly engaged the slightest hint of her Intermediate Skill, and as her spear hit the whip, there was a colossal crash as Laughing Jack was sent soaring through the front of the Wombat, smashing through the stone in a way that couldn't possibly be comfortable.

I just... gaped. I'd been in sieges and battles, but those had mostly been lower-rank. The Bone Wyvern aside, the abilities I was seeing down here were far above what I was used to. I'd known that as people ranked up and could synergize more Skills, powers would become more unique and varied, but there were some seriously scary attacks being thrown around in this fight.

Still, I wasn't a rookie. I was hardly going to just gape. I stepped back to fall into position closer to Callie, Abel, and Mel.

Lament gave everyone else a hard look, but no one was stupid enough to pick a fight after what she'd just done. Not when a huge chunk of them were trying to reattach limbs from that spear manifestation.

She turned to us. "Seems like this isn't a great place to eat after all. Oh well, the pre-dinner warmup was nice. You guys know anywhere near here I can get a steak?"

Her glare pinned the surrounding crowd. "Unless someone else wants to give it a try? I'd be happy to give you the same treatment as your little friends over there." She whirled her spear in a lazy, ponderous circle, slow enough that the light really had a chance to glint off the edge of the spearhead, highlighting how sharp it was in an extremely threatening fashion. None of them chose to do so, most stepping back to get further out of her range.

We all looked to Abel, who didn't look offended at being the go-to choice this time. "Nah. Not near here," he said apologetically. "Not a ton of high-end restaurants down here. Doomtown isn't conducive to fine dining. The Raving Baby is pretty much the best eatery I know of down here. There are some pretty decent places in G district if you're up for a long walk, but I don't think it's worth it."

Neither did I, considering how delicious those enchiladas were. "Do you guys like enchiladas?" I asked, hopeful. "Because we know where to get the best you've ever had." Aside from being free, their taste had been haunting my dreams since we went yesterday. I was already drooling at the thought of wolfing down some more, and Callie looked just as excited. Even Sloane and her minions looked ravenous at the idea of going back to Owen's place for another all-we-could-eat buffet.

Lament just shrugged. "Sure, why not. I can always get a decent steak somewhere else." Wren likewise shrugged in acceptance when she looked at him, and Lestri and Saiten seemed ambivalent.

Lament seemed much more relaxed and laid-back than I had expected, at least once she got past her little threat display with Abel… and the whole "stabbing a dozen people with a single spear thrust" thing.

Maybe my standards for laid-back people had become a bit lax.

Sydney, the last person we checked with, was excited to try the enchiladas, and asked if she could invite her sister Megan. Since we were trying to learn more about the external forces in the star system anyway, we agreed, of course. Then we all made our way through the crowd to the exit, ignoring the dozens of dissatisfied G-rankers glaring after us.

I half expected them to attack us, but they didn't. The situation here was much more complex than it looked. Rather than all of them versus us, this was more like a team free-for-all. If they attacked, their enemies might attack them while they were distracted, not to mention Lament and Abel had both demonstrated terrifying levels of finesse and power, so some of them would probably die. No one wanted to be first on the chopping block if that happened, which lead to a sort of universal hesitation.

As we finally exited, the stamps on our hands winked out, and I heard a collective groan from outside. Hah. Served those bastards right.

Chapter Fifty-One

OWEN WAS NOT happy to see us again. He didn't bitch too much, though. We introduced him to Sydney, Lestri, and Lament, and given he was still gathering information on outsiders for the tournament, he seemed at least partially mollified. I briefly felt bad for not telling Sydney about it, but then realized anyone with any common sense would be aware that the locals were gathering intel, as evidenced by how much Lament had held back during her fight.

After we sat down, we were joined by Sydney's sister, Megan. Who was... much different. Where Sydney was tiny and shy with red hair, Megan was a tall blonde who looked like she could do some serious fighting. She wasn't as muscular as Lament, who was built like a seasoned warrior despite being slim, but still, she was in better shape than I was. With bright blue eyes and a big cheerful grin, Megan was as outgoing as her sister was hesitant to engage.

She had her own cadre of attendants, and had them sit at a second table with all of Sydney's guards and most of Sloane's crew, though Owen refused to feed all of them for free. Lament covered their meal, since the dinner thing had been her idea, and Megan jumped right into conversation.

"So, I heard you helped Syd out of a jam. I really appreciate that." She laughed wryly, scratching the back of her head in embarrassment. "I...

might have been wrong about the Chaotic Wombat. But come on, what are the chances of her getting picked?"

I was pretty sure that was what everyone thought, but Sydney just shook her head. "It's fine, sis. I'm just glad to make some new friends." She took a bite of her enchilada with a delighted moan. "Also, the food there couldn't possibly have been as good as this. What is in this rice?" She chewed for a minute with her eyes closed, savoring the food, before swallowing. "Sorry. Anyway, Miss Lament, was it? Thank you for the meal, and that was some impressive fighting. That spear manifestation was so amazing. Are you a Master Candidate?"

At the rest of our blank looks (from those of us whose faces were visible), Wren chimed in. "Mastery is a qualitative jump in Skill requirement, especially for weapon Skills. D-rank is considered a watershed for the higher ranks. People who reach the peak of the level above their own in a weapon Skill are considered prodigies who are much more likely to rank up to Master. Like Lament will be able to step into Expert pretty much the second she ranks up to F-rank. That gives her the whole rank to prepare for the jump to Master at E-rank. Master Candidates are considered elite in star system forces, though in the wider cluster, it's less uncommon."

"But wait," I said, "don't you need to reach Master to reach D-rank at all?" Abilities ranked up when people did, so Master being a dividing line was kind of odd. If that was really the case, then D-rank would be much less common, wouldn't it?

Though thinking about it, I'd never met a D-ranker, so maybe it *was* less common. Pseudo D-ranked planets (which couldn't support D-rankers, as far as I knew, just a multitude of E-rankers) were treated as pretty low-ranked planets, after all.

Wren didn't look surprised by my confusion. "Most people synergize some kind of Skill into their ability. People who use only their inborn power are rare. Hitting Master, or any higher rank, in a Skill is much different than hitting it with an ability.

"An ability is part of you, and grows as you do. It doesn't require any conditions or knowledge to rank up. Skills get more difficult as you go on. Weapon and martial Skills in general tend to be tough to reach Master in. Crafting Skills too. Of course, you have people born with a weapon Skill who can do it easily. Those are Naturals, and like people born with one of the three major crafting Skills, they're extremely valuable."

I hadn't even considered that. My own Wish ability didn't have any requirements aside from stats to rank up. Benny and the others had synergized, and needed Skill ranks to break through. But if someone had something like Inventing or Enchanting as their natural ability, then they would rank up easily like me, and I could only assume those ranks would come with the knowledge and talent necessary to put them to use. Considering how tough it was to rank up Enchanting, that was a scary thought. It also made me a lot more wary of Mad Scientists in general.

Callie seemed enthralled. "So if someone was born with a Spear Mastery ability, they would just grow in technique as they ranked up, without needing to learn or upgrade any Skills? That sounds amazing. But doesn't that mean that they can't do what Lament did and rank their weapon Skill up past their current rank? Like someone with an inborn Spear Mastery could get to Master easily, but only at D-rank, right?"

"Exactly," cut in Lament. "Naturals are tied to their rank. In the early ranks, that's a huge disadvantage, because ranking up a Skill to Lesser or Beginner is substantially easier than reaching a higher Ascendant rank. Being a natural comes with downsides too." She gave a self-satisfied smirk, her tone smug. "I much prefer the way I do it. I won't have any problems reaching Master, will I, Master Saiten?"

The spear master just chuckled. "No, Lament. I don't suppose you will. But don't get a big head. There are people out there stronger than Master Candidates. Especially in the main systems of the five factions. Some of the larger clans and faction leadership have specialized soul strength training regimens so extraordinary their descendants can breach the one-rank barrier safely. There are F-ranked Masters your age in some parts of the universe."

Even Abel seemed taken aback by that. "That's insane. What kind of soul strength would you need in order to survive being two full ranks ahead in a Skill? That's not a temporary thing, you would have to live with that for years, probably." He shuddered. "Even the thought of trying to breach Intermediate right now makes me want to vomit. My soul is already pressured just maintaining peak Intermediate. Is it even possible to beat someone like that?"

Saiten just shrugged. "Sure. There are all kinds of terrifying abilities out there. Some racial traits have absurd benefits, and there are Jobs that give access to power far outside the norm. Early Mastery is terrifying, but the right stat modifiers and Skills can make up for it. Not to mention just being higher rank. Still, those kinds of people are considered treasures even in big families and sects. You aren't likely to meet one all the way out here. Even things like Moonglow Dew aren't necessarily enough to rouse their interest."

At least that meant we wouldn't be fighting a monster like that. A Master Candidate like Abel or Lament was scary enough.

Speaking of which, Megan seemed to have picked up on my mentor's slip. "Wait, back up. You're a Master Candidate too? Aren't you local? That's *way* more impressive. I've never seen a Master Candidate on a pseudo D-ranked planet before." She paused. "Which, okay, I haven't been to many pseudo D-ranked planets. But still. That's pretty badass." She turned to Mel quizzically. "How about you? Are you a Master Candidate too?"

Our red-masked teacher shrugged. "My Fire Manipulation Skill is at Intermediate, but it just broke through a while ago. Plus, manipulation Skills are a huge pain in the ass to rank up. I'm not too worried about it, though. We mostly focus on combat standards and integration. Apollyon just ranked his martial arts Skill up because he had a few years with nothing to do but train."

She glared sharply at him, and he pretended not to notice as he dug into his enchiladas with gusto.

I tried to save my mentor. "What about you guys? Tell us more about the Wave Warren. We won't ask about combat specifics, given we might be fighting you in the tournament, but we love hearing about the forces in the star system. You mentioned not having been to D-rank planets before, does that mean you've mostly been on C-ranked planets?"

Megan nodded happily. "Oh yeah. Wave Warren's home base is on a C-ranked planet. Granted, we aren't a C-ranked force or anything, the Warren Master is a D-ranker. But we do okay. We're not the only people from Gralter that are here, either. Slime Hall managed to get invited too." She grimaced. "Damn summoners. Dealing with them is so gross. It's just the two of us from our planet, though. We found out about this through back channels, and managed to keep it *mostly* quiet."

"Slime Hall?" Callie asked with a grimace. "That sounds unpleasant. I don't know much about summoners, they aren't super common here.

Before today, I had only seen one or two. It's a pretty Fantasy-heavy ability, isn't it? You don't see many of those at G-rank."

That explained it. I'd been wondering where the summoners I'd seen came from. If they formed the ability through synergy at a higher level, or if they needed lots of Fantasy to be viable, they might not be in combat much up to this point. I knew that some stats could be more easily gained through alternative routes rather than fights and patrols. Granted, Might was an important stat especially at low ranks, and we could still gain other stats by making an impression, but other careers like artists and pop singers provided good returns on some of the more elusive stats.

Callie had mentioned that her dad actually tried to convince her to be a pop star when she was younger. She and her mom had both put their foot down about it, and her ballet lessons had been a compromise. He figured some more artistry in her combat would help generate Fantasy, which, to be fair, it might have done, especially in combination with all the crazy shadow antics.

"Yeah. They summon slimes," said Megan flatly. "Usually elemental ones, though some of them have weird trick slimes. The Slime Creation Skill is surprisingly easy to pick up at the Minor level, from what I'm told. And synergy with a few other Skills makes Slime Summoning. Most of them synergize *that* with other inborn abilities to summon unique and more powerful slimes. They're a giant pain in the ass. Sometimes literally. One of their team members summons giant slimes."

This was the first time I'd heard about someone making a Skill as interesting as summoning from scratch. I knew you could learn Skills like that. Some people could teach them because they were born with an ability and took on a Job, which turned that ability into a Skill. I assumed you had to be able to teach those, but this seemed like a completely different thing. Kind of like a heritage a clan would have, albeit on a much smaller scale.

She went on to describe more about Slime Hall, how Wave Warren had been neighbors and competitors with them for years, and how the two groups had found out about the Moonsong Glade opening from the same source and agreed to keep it secret. If some of the C-ranked forces on their planet had shown up, it would have made this whole tournament infinitely harder, so I couldn't disagree with the logic on that one.

We all traded stories and ate enchiladas together, learning about the visiting forces, and it was actually pretty nice. Sydney was shy, but extremely bubbly once you got her to open up, and Megan was essentially a wrecking ball in terms of personality, which meant she got on well with Lament, Abel, and Callie, who were all pretty outspoken.

When we finished eating, we offered to show Sydney and Megan to the Blue Robin, where they could get better sleep. All in all, it wasn't a bad night.

I hoped the next day could be as peaceful—I wanted to get as much relaxing as possible done before that damn auction. Sadly, I didn't think that was in the cards. Abel was bound to have something crazy planned.

Chapter Fifty-Two

BEFORE WE WENT TO SLEEP, I did all five wishes. I traded fifteen points of various stats for fifteen points of Fantasy. The summoners today had made a big impression, and I was interested in gaining the ability to do that kind of thing.

I'd been saving my wishes for the end of the day lately, just to make sure I didn't need them for some emergency. Doomtown wasn't exactly safe most of the time, so it seemed prudent not to waste them.

At 897, I was only three points shy of nine hundred, and I decided it was time to finally ask Abel and the others about ranking up. Or rather, about *not* ranking up.

I cornered my mentor at the pool table, playing a game with Wren. "Hey, boss man, was hoping we could talk. I'm coming up on a thousand points, and I wanted to know if I need to do anything specific to not rank up. Like… do I just not accept? Will that hurt me? I'm guessing you've been denying a rank up for a while. Is there some secret to it?"

He scratched his shot. "Fuck! Damn it, hold on." Wren snickered something under his breath, but Abel caught it. "Fuck you, that counts. I was distracted. Put the ball back where it was. I need to go have a discussion with my disciple. I have perfect spatial awareness, by the way, even with my stats suppressed, so I'll know if you move it." He turned back to me, aggravation in his eyes. "Come on, let's go talk somewhere less crowded.

None of this is really earthshaking info, but it's better shared in private."

Leading me back down the hall to me and Callie's room, he kicked the door shut. "First of all." He said as he turned around. "Good on you for bothering to ask ahead of time. Short answer is no. There is no penalty for suppressing rank, with the exception of being unable to gain more stats. All the stats you *could* have gotten are lost, which is why most people avoid it, but it doesn't hurt you or anything. I have been suppressing my rank, as has Mel. I did it partly for training and partly not to get attention, and she did it partly for training and partly for me."

He gave a wry snort. "Silly girl. I'd never have asked for that. But she did it anyway." He sounded distant and almost sad for a second, but then shook it off. "Never you mind, it worked out in the end. Point is no, you won't be hurt by suppressing your rank. People do it all the time. Not just Mel and I, there are more than a few E-rankers who engage in the practice. How the hell do you think Moravian isn't at D-rank despite being over three millennia old? Do you know how famous he is?"

"Wait." I held up a hand. "The Moravian is suppressing his rank? I thought he was just stuck because this planet can't support a D-ranker? Like there isn't enough renown for one to rank up, right?" That clashed with what I had been told badly, though to be fair, Cark had much less of a reason to know details about this kind of thing than Abel.

"No," Abel said slowly. "As in, it *physically* can't support a D-ranker. This is theoretically a D-ranked planet, but that's only because of the number of E-rankers here. It's more accurately a pseudo D-rank planet. As in, it hasn't reached D-rank yet. If one of the E-rankers tried to break through to D-rank, it would trigger the planet to attempt a rank up to compensate for the Impact increase. You know, I assume, what happens when someone ranks up without a proper foundation?"

I winced at the image. "Their soul collapses. I didn't know the whole rank thing was literal. Does that mean the planet is a dungeon, then? Callie told me that places with Impact are dungeons." This conversation was a lot more complicated than I had been expecting.

"No!" he snapped. Then he groaned. "Just... no. Dungeons are more concentrated. A planet's Impact is spread over a massive surface area, so it barely has an effect. Most higher-ranked planets actually get bigger to compensate. There are Dungeon Worlds, small planets with high ranks, but they're incredibly valuable and are usually used as training grounds or heartworlds for big factions and clans."

I held up both hands placatingly. "Sorry, I don't mean to get so off track. Just one more question?" He sighed but nodded. "So why don't the E-rankers just go somewhere else to rank up and then come back? Then they would be in charge of the planet, right? None of the ones who stayed would be strong enough. Or does the planet literally not support D-rankers on its surface?" I knew that wasn't the case, because Zeke was B-ranked, so it had to be something else.

Shaking his head, Abel confirmed my theory. "No. Higher-ranked people go where they want. It's complicated. D-rank is a watershed, like we mentioned earlier. The rank up to D is supposed to be... dramatic. I don't know the details, I've never seen one. Besides that, the Unity runs this planet. If people were leaving to rank up and coming back, it would fuck up the distribution of power, so it isn't allowed. The WCP discourages that kind of thing too. It robs higher-ranked planets of power concentration. When you leave a planet, you aren't banned from coming back or anything, but it's expected you won't be returning to live there."

Considering what I knew about renown being exponentially weighted as you ranked up, that made sense. Higher-ranked planets were renown farms, so they would definitely want powerful people there in droves. The important thing was, I'd gotten my answer, even if it came with about a dozen more questions.

I nodded. "Alright, I'll suppress my rank up, then, at least until after the tournament. If we do the rank up right after, we shouldn't lose out on the points from the tournament itself, right?"

"Right," he agreed. "No way any of the other entrants would have agreed to participate if they had to miss out on a big windfall like that. They'll probably have some kind of ceremony for the winners and let the ones who can rank up do it on the spot for the prestige bump. Most people joining up will be peak of G-rank about to Ascend. That's why there are a relatively low number of forces here. They needed a team that fit the conditions and was also strong enough to be a contender. Of course, not *all* of them are peak of G-rank. The prestige from the tournament will help some get there, which is why there's a wait time between the tournament and the glade opening."

That was something I'd been worried about up to this point, so it was good to have assurances. The whole planet thing was also way more complicated than expected. I'd known about the size differences, since supermassive planets had much stronger gravity to offset Might. But the Impact thing was interesting, and I wondered exactly how that affected Ascendants on the surface of that world. I also wondered if it meant Zeke was stronger here, or if he was just so much more powerful than this place that he barely noticed.

Abel chuckled at my silence, clapping me on the shoulder. "Don't worry so much about it, kid. We're a long way from having to worry about things like ascending to D-rank or how powerful people are on other planets. Take care of the problems you have before you start new ones. We have to get through the next two weeks, as well as the tournament itself, and *then* we're going to be competing with the winners of the tournaments from all the other systems in the cluster for the resources in the Moonsong Glade."

That set me to snickering. "Yeah, I guess I'm just borrowing trouble at this point, huh? We have so much more to focus on." I shot him a suspicious glare, not that he saw it behind my mask. "Speaking of trouble, what exactly are we doing tomorrow? I get the feeling Sydney and Megan will be coming along, plus their entourage, and probably Wren. We've picked up quite a few passengers in our time here. I'm assuming you have something suitably awful planned that we can all do together?"

Aside from spending time with new friends, which was nice, we'd also be seeing them in whatever situation Abel put us all in, and presumably learning more about their abilities before the tournament. "Awful?" said Abel innocently. "I'd never force you all to do something awful. All of my activities are fun team-building exercises. Like tomorrow we're going white water rafting! It's going to be a blast!"

"Hold on," I said, "there's a *river* down here?" The lake I... kind of got? I guess? Just Ascendant nonsense, but a river seemed weirder to me somehow. "But where does it come from? Like, I know Ascendants do crazy things and it's stupid to question how there can be a river but not freak out about forests and oceans and pocket dimensions that can implode. But... rapids need power? What fuels them?"

Instead of mocking me, Abel just burst out laughing. "Yeah. Everyone has those moments where they go 'how the fuck?' even with all the crazy things they've seen. The rapids aren't some crazy spell or anything, though. The water pressure comes from Riot Bay, actually."

"Wait." My blood ran cold. "Like… giant-hate-fish-attacking-us Riot Bay? Are there *fish* in the river? Because I don't want to worry about getting smashed by carp or something again. The Bay was stressful and awful." I shuddered. "Also, the smell was terrible. Plus, that was just an exercise in differentiating levels of Impact on the same rank. Money aside, how would doing it again even help us?"

Abel rolled his eyes. "Don't freak out about it. There's no fish in the river. The rapids are just where all that force and energy ends up when the lake settles down again. Since there are tons of parts of the Bay that are getting those waves even when you can't see them, the rapids are always going. But don't worry. I promise there are no fish in the rapids. Hell, I can promise you nothing lives in those rapids at all."

Something about the way he said that made me worry even more, but I recognized the smug glint in his eyes. My teacher wouldn't tell us any more about this trip, because he wanted it to be an unpleasant surprise.

"Alright. Fine. Well, if we're going to be doing something crazy tomorrow, I'd better get some sleep." I turned and started to head out, but stopped, looking back over my shoulder. "Also, just saying up front that if there's a fee for this insane trip, you can cover it. We made plenty of money for you last time."

As I opened the door to leave, I suddenly stopped again. "Wait… why the fuck am I leaving." I turned back to my now-smirking mentor. "This is my room. Get out." I had to bite back a scowl as he cackled at my stupid mistake and slapped me on the shoulder on his way out.

"I gotta admit, kid," he said as he walked away, "you can be a bit serious sometimes. But you're always good for a laugh."

I just sighed and rolled my eyes as I closed my door. I could do without being his comedic relief, but hey, at least the job came with combat training. I doubted I'd be where I was without Abel. Still… I was totally going to push his ass in the water tomorrow once I made sure it wasn't like a murder river or something. If only that wasn't such a strong possibility.

Chapter Fifty-Three

DESPITE THE NEWS of some dangerous river stunt the next day, I actually slept okay. I may have been adjusting to living in a state of perpetual peril. Not that I would ever say that to Abel. He would probably use it as an excuse to double my training intensity or something. Still, it was hard to be worried or upset curled up with my girlfriend after a day meeting new people and protecting strangers from crowds of Ascendants trying to kill them.

Yesterday's entire ordeal had been... fun. No one had actually died that I had seen, though I hadn't exactly stuck around to check on the people Lament cut up. It had all just been one big adventure. And Callie was right, it felt *good* to be on the right side and know it. The WCP was so murky most of the time I'd kind of lost the feeling of just helping people. Hell, maybe I never had it. Even at the Unity, I'd been running from crisis to crisis rather than taking time to just do some good.

Not that I was planning to devote myself to helping the helpless full time or anything. But Callie had reminded me that being an effective Wishmaster Candidate and being a good person didn't have to be mutually exclusive. And I'd probably *made* some alliances helping Sydney out. It was a model I could keep in mind going forward. Just because the WCP existed in a grey area didn't mean I had to. Not all the time.

So it was with a weirdly cheerful demeanor that I hopped out of bed the next morning, ignoring my girlfriend's enraged hiss as she was exposed to sunlight. After an obligatory vampire joke and a quick kiss, I was off to get ready, meeting up with everyone in the dining room off the front entrance.

While at night the room seemed to be some kind of gathering hall, with the pool tables in use and some darts games, during the day it was used to serve meals buffet-style. They had a whole breakfast laid out in chafing dishes. To my surprise, Sydney and Megan had managed to get a room. I'd thought the Robin was full, but maybe they paid to get someone bumped or something.

They waved enthusiastically when they saw us, while Wren just sat at the table, eating waffles and sipping orange juice with a stoic expression. Lament, Lestri, and Saiten had already shown up and were enjoying some eggs with Sydney and Megan.

I fixed myself a plate of steak and eggs and plopped down across from them. "Hey guys. Morning. How's the food?" Despite asking, I didn't wait and dug right in. It wasn't bad. The steak was a bit overdone, but not like shoe leather or anything, just more pink than red.

Sydney, who was clearly a morning person, took a long sip of coffee and chirped. "Oh, we don't have any plans. Megan was probably going to go out looking for trouble again, and I wanted to check out the Unceasing Stairs. They sounded pretty cool, if a bit confusing." She shot a pout at the black-coated man I only now realized was sitting next to her. Five other attendants sat nearby, but he was the same one who had threatened us back at the Wombat. "Unfortunately Riley says that the place is dangerous, and that the rumors I heard were probably meant to lure gullible tourists on so people could attack them."

The dark-haired man with the scruffy cheeks gave a long-suffering sigh. "Yes, well, it is traditionally a poor decision to announce how much you have to spend in areas such as these before asking for directions. If those young men had been any more obviously drooling over the potential windfall you represented, their eyes would have been replaced with chits." He glanced to me with a frown. "I suspect your new friend may have another potential location to visit, in any case."

I just shrugged. "You got me. Nightstrike and I had so much fun hanging out with your guys we figured we would invite everyone along on the trip we have planned today. Be warned, Apollyon planned it, so there's about an eighty percent chance that it involves potential dismemberment. He says we're going white water rafting, and that sounds like fun to me, at least." I glanced at Wren. "You guys are invited too, of course, though after the fish incident, I wouldn't take it to heart if you declined."

Lament cut in with a laugh. "He told us about that. It sounds fun. Your teacher seems like an interesting guy. I'll accept on Wren's behalf. Boy needs to toughen his spine a bit, and Lestri was complaining about missing out on the fun anyway." She asked Saiten, "Am I to assume you won't be participating, Master?"

The big man shook his head. "Not on your life. I doubt anything your pugilist could arrange would be any significant threat to my person, but I don't particularly enjoy being wet. I'll most likely follow along on land, just in case you run across someone too high-ranked to be reliably countered."

Ah, so he really was like her version of Zeke. Considering Doomtown was closed to E-rankers, I doubted he had reason to worry, but they weren't from around here, so being a bit wary was the smart call.

That made me wonder exactly what Zeke would *do* if I was ever attacked. I knew that despite not being nearby, Zeke could keep track of me easily. If nothing else, stats in the B-ranks were potentially in the tens of millions. He probably had enough Perception to be listening to this conversation from the literal polar opposite spot on the planet. I also suspected my mask might have some kind of Perception or conditional defensive Enchantment on it.

Part of me hoped I'd never have to find out, but a deeper part really hoped I got to at least witness him cutting lose someday. Seeing what a B-ranker could do would be eye-opening at the very least.

I was jarred from my thoughts as a plate smacked down next to me, a rumpled and glowering Callie sitting down to my right. "Coffee," she growled. I smirked slightly as I stood up to go get her some.

I made it like she preferred, then dropped it on the table in front of her with a thud. She took a long pull, closed her eyes, and let it seep into her bloodstream. Callie's morning demeanor, as usual, relied heavily on how she woke up. Being roused early tended to make her grumpy. Coffee helped. After a few seconds to get her head straight, she was fine, though. The extra morning sulk was partially a factor of her trying to do things for herself and be a bit selfish like I asked, even if she never said it.

"So," she said, after polishing off the whole mug, "what were we talking about? My brain just switched on a minute ago and it had to boot first."

I snickered at that, grabbing her plate and heading to the buffet to fill it up with things I knew she would like while she talked to the others. I didn't feel like rehashing, so this seemed faster. Speaking of hash, there was some corned beef hash I hadn't noticed, as well as biscuits and gravy and I added some eggs before bringing the plate back and setting it in front of her.

She almost swooned at the smell. "Thanks, honey, you're the best." She never took her eyes from the plate, but gave me a perfunctory peck on the mask before she assaulted her breakfast like it had sworn vengeance on her family line. Since everyone had already seen Callie eat yesterday, they understood that as long as you kept your appendages away from her mouth, she was safe enough to eat with, and didn't stare at her devouring her food with relish (not literally, thank the gods, I'd have left the table).

"Anyway," said Sydney. "I was just telling Nightstrike that rafting sounds like a lot of fun! I doubt even Riley would complain about it, the big worrier." She stuck her tongue out at the somber, formal man, and he gave a small smile. Sydney had warmed up to us all immensely over last night's bonding, and it was jarring to see what a big difference that made in terms of our interactions. She reminded me a lot of Jessie now, actually, though still less outspoken and a bit more timid.

Megan nodded. "Rafting sounds like more fun than trolling for a fight. At least in this town. Half the idiots I met yesterday were garbage in combat anyway. If I was included in the invite, I'm in. We can pay our way, and pay for our people too." She nodded to Riley and the five rabbit-themed attendants. "We brought two teams for this. Kind of like your friends over there brought three." She nodded over at Sloane, who had just come into the room with her own posse.

I almost literally smacked myself in the face with my palm. Of *course* Sloane brought twelve people to form three teams. Why not triple your odds. Hell, Melinda was an E-ranker. She probably knew about the tournament before I did. I wouldn't be surprised if she'd sent along the twelve of them specifically so I could get them ready for the tournament in the first place. I felt like an idiot for not considering it before.

The only thing that made me feel a bit better was that Callie looked as shocked as I did. It was a little petty, but it was nice to know I wasn't the only one thrown in the deep end with all this. She was way more suited to political maneuvering than I was, but she was still learning, same as me.

Picking up on my amusement, she rolled her eyes, then mimicked Sydney's earlier gesture and stuck her tongue out at me.

We all finished up breakfast, with Mel and Abel being the last to arrive and eat, and then Abel hopped to his feet excitedly. "Alright," he said with gusto, "since we're all finished, which of you are planning to come along on our little excursion? I'm assuming the kid told you all about it and invited you. He prefers to share the pain." That drew an uneasy chuckle from a few of the minions, and a middle finger from me, which my teacher just laughed off without acknowledging it verbally.

Everyone who was interested held up a hand, letting him know who was in. He nodded in satisfaction. "Oh, good. None of you are trying to weasel out of it. I knew I liked you for a reason." He clapped his hands together. "Well, then, let's get going. It's a bit of a walk to the river, and we want to get there early before all the boats are gone. They run out sometimes, and we'd need to wait for the next day for them to get new ones."

With that, he turned on his heel and strolled out of the room without another word. I had another ominous feeling from that last statement, but once again, it mostly just confirmed what I knew. This would be dangerous or life-threatening in some way, that wasn't news.

The others gave me exasperated smiles, for the most part, but we all stood up and followed after him once we paid for our meals. As we left, I couldn't help but look forward to the coming day. This had been a lot of fun so far, even the dangerous parts. I had no reason to believe this next activity wouldn't be the same.

Chapter Fifty-Four

We avoided Dale's place on the beach as we approached the lake, taking the long way around the shore and circling along the edges in a direction I hadn't even realized we could go. The whole of Riot Bay was absolutely huge, but it wasn't a perfect circle.

After walking for a bit, we came to a place where the lake let out into a river about five hundred feet across, and as we approached, one very important thing became clear.

"We're all going to fucking die," I said matter-of-factly. I glared over at Abel, who was now grinning in satisfaction. "Like, I know you've had us do some crazy things, but that's a meat grinder. It's going to kill all of us."

He let out a happy sigh. "There it is. Your reactions have been getting so banal and sedate. I find the whole 'I've seen it all' demeanor tiresome. I love the fear and anxiety." He gave a melodramatic cackle. Hands clenched into claws in the air as he really hammered it up. "Tell me more how scared you are for your lives, worms!"

Without any hesitation, Mel reached out and smacked her lunatic boyfriend upside the back of his head. "Enough of that, you moron." She turned to us, her tone softening. "Don't listen to him, kids. It's not as bad as it looks. I know it seems scary, but don't forget how much Impact you all have. This is just water. Sure, it's being whipped around pretty crazily, but you're more than up to it. You got hit with spray almost as strong out on

274

the bay when fishing. You're not going to die from getting tossed around in the river."

"Unless they get dashed on the rocks!" Abel crowed gleefully, clearly enjoying this entire performance way too much. I made a mental note never to let Abel get bored. I hadn't seen this side of him, and while it was probably meant in part to put some fear into our competitors, I suspected this was also just how he dealt with boredom.

Mel, contrary to my expectations, didn't immediately refute him this time. "Well, yes. Unless you get dashed on the rocks. Don't do that."

We stood waiting for her to continue, but she just gave an apologetic shrug.

"That's it?" I yelped. "'Don't do that'? Gee, thanks, Auntie. I've been wondering how to improve my dodging skills too. Do you think not getting hit would work? Or maybe I can improve my accuracy by hitting the spot I'm aiming at. Sweet revenant, you can't give us better advice than 'don't do that'? You're supposed to be the sane one!" Then I paused, glancing back and forth between them. "Comparatively."

She snickered a bit. "Okay, first of all, that hurts. Second of all, this isn't really that kind of exercise. I guess I can tell you the point, but it'll be obvious once you get out there. Each of you will be in a two-person canoe. All you have to do is manage your oars properly so you keep upright and straight. It requires good teamwork and reaction time." She shrugged. "Not everything is a mysterious lesson you have to puzzle out. Don't flip over. It's not that complicated."

"And the rocks?" Callie asked desperately. Her voice was almost as high and worried as mine had been. It wasn't that this was *actually* any more reckless than the other things we'd done either as a group or individually, but it was so... scary. Standing this close, I could see the glowing blue water crashing against itself. Hear the roar of the river even from dozens of feet away, so loud I doubted I'd have been able to hear anyone speak if not for my Perception, and even feel the bullet-like snap of droplets of water peppering my face as they were thrown free by the collisions.

Intellectually I realized that the water wouldn't be a huge danger (though apparently the fucking rocks would be), but as someone who had been mortal not too long ago, this was terrifying to me on a visceral level. Which... was probably the point.

Sensing my hesitation, Mel decided to actually say something comforting. "Hey, don't get so worried. It's extremely rare for people to die here. Especially with your armor, as long as you stick together, you'll be fine. The chances of *both* of you having your heads dashed against the rocks and being knocked out are vanishingly small."

Well… she *tried* to say something comforting. I could see her point, though. Even on the off chance one of us got knocked out (which was incredibly unlikely for me, at least, considering my armor) and stayed unconscious, the other could rescue them. The buddy system was pretty safe here.

Still. I turned to the others. "Okay. Well, when I told you guys we would be risking life and limb, I kind of assumed I was being alarmist. You can always wait here if you want, instead of wading into… that."

I gestured at the water. It was moving fast and rough enough that I was pretty sure it would at least hurt getting battered by it, even if it couldn't actually damage me. I was deeply uncomfortable with going out there, but I was also here to train, so I would suck it up now that I knew we almost definitely wouldn't die. I'd done riskier training… probably. The others had no reason to stick around, though, and were free to avoid this lunacy.

"Not a chance in hell." Lament cackled. "This sounds like a blast. I'm just sad Falken couldn't make it yet. He's showing up later, and it's a shame I won't have my proper partner. Lestri, you can sit in for him, if you want."

I blinked. I'd thought Vector was their fourth, but it sounded like he was just along for the ride. Guessed that was my bad for assuming. Come to think of it, I hadn't seen Vector in a while. I guessed he wasn't one for this kind of craziness. At least one of us was sane.

"Alright." I turned to my smirking mentor. "So how do we do this?" I glanced around, finally spotting another small shack. It was harder to see this one because it was squat and made of stone, almost lost in the spray of the rapids. "We getting the canoes over there?" Everyone else turned to see me pointing at the hut.

Gesturing us forward, Abel headed for the shack. "Yup. No one in their right mind wants to sit in that place all day and either get pelted with rough water bullets or listen to them drum the walls. They have it set up so that you can insert chits into a series of locks that hold the canoes in. You add the chits, the locks open, you take the canoe. There are a limited number per day, and they honestly overcharge because the damn things nearly always break. They just go with disposable ones and then refill them every day."

Remembering him mention that they could run out, I understood the situation. Luckily, if they were disposable, at least they shouldn't be too pricey. As we approached, it made even more sense. The low roar of the water and the occasional snap of water droplets had become what was basically a permanent hurricane as we got close. I was glad I was wearing armor and a mask, because even the constant drumming on the skin of my wrists and neck was driving me crazy. I stepped sideways, putting my body in front of Callie. Whether it was her legs or most of her face, wasn't as covered as I was.

She gave a sigh of relief and reached out to grip my hand tightly, and I squeezed back. Most of the others seemed fine in the spray, though Sloane and Sydney looked bedraggled as they were pelted with droplets.

When we reached the hut, Abel grabbed the door, twisted the knob, and kicked it sharply, popping it open and leading us inside. As he'd mentioned, the droplets stopped, but we could hear them constantly pattering on the stone outside.

The inside of the hut was much bigger than the outside, and while it was kind of damp and I could feel stray bits of sand under my boots, it was orderly, for the most part. A large, metallic floor led to walls lined with a series of sort of metal clawlike devices. The claws themselves were each wrapped firmly around a canoe, holding it in place securely, and next to each device was a metal waist-high pillar with a coin slot and a sign.

A canoe cost a single H-ranked coin, and I gave a long whistle, which won a chuckle from Abel. "Yeah, they buy these in bulk," my mentor said. "They're flimsy as hell. They're only made to last a single day and they start breaking down as soon as you get out there, so be careful how much you trust them on the water." He gestured for us to put in the coins, but I just sat there and stared at him.

When he didn't make any move to insert coins, I cleared my throat. "We had a deal, old man. I'm not paying for your murder attempts. I'll do your exercises, but after how much you made on our work last time, I refuse to foot the bill. Pay up or we bail."

Abel looked aghast at the statement, but Mel rolled her eyes. "Oh, just cover them. They have a point, you made some decent change at the bay, and I did pretty well betting on them at the Bone Arena."

As Abel sighed and walked sulkily over to start depositing coins to open up the claws, Mel turned back to us. "Oh, and just a bit of friendly advice, since jackass over there is unlikely to mention it. Balance is key here. Not just staying upright, but making sure to exert the right amount of force on each side. It's too easy to flip out there, or even end up going in circles because one of you is paddling too hard."

That actually seemed helpful, and we thanked her as we lifted the canoe up to carry it out to the river.

Abel shouted one last bit of advice to us. "By the way! Make sure to go into the water with plenty of space between you. If you're too close, you'll smash into each other and both pairs will go under. And remember, *have fun!*"

As we approached the shore, we all split off, Callie and I carrying our canoe. Well… I was carrying it because Callie was a foot shorter than I was and doing it at an angle would have been annoying, but still. It was easy enough, considering my Might. As we drew closer I shouted down to her, "So you think they were doing a 'good cop bad cop' thing to convince us to accept the challenge?"

Callie laughed. "A really obvious one, yeah! But still, I trust them. I doubt they would go through all this trouble just to kill us. If they wanted us dead, Abel could have beat us to death a hundred times in training. It's not like he wouldn't be just as culpable if we died in the river after he led us here. We have a ton of witnesses that this was his idea. No, I think this will just be another painful training opportunity."

Shifting the canoe to one shoulder, I scooped her up onto my other one, earning a squeal as she was pelted with water once I wasn't acting as a blocker anymore. As she shrieked, I laughed and shouted up to her. "Well, in that case, we should listen to our teacher and do the assignment correctly. Like he said, we should have some fun!" Then I jogged off toward the nearby shore, Callie cackling in glee as I went. I just hoped I wouldn't come out of this one smelling like fish.

Chapter Fifty-Five

As THE CANOE hit the water, the two of us slipped inside without too much trouble. We had a running start, so it wasn't too tough. We just had to be sure to land in the canoe before the water swept it away. Once we did, we each took up one of the paddles, slamming them into the water quickly to prevent capsizing as we were swept up into the rapids and yanked out into the riot of water.

My eyes widened a bit as the canoe jerked around and we barely managed to stabilize, having to adjust on the fly as the angles and pressure changed. It took a minute to get the hang of it, but luckily my mask kept me from being splashed in the face. Callie had covered her own face with a veil of shadows, and despite how confusing the helter-skelter waterway was, we finally got the hang of it after a few minutes.

I realized quickly that rowing wasn't exactly the right move here, but rather, I needed to use my oar to angle the water in a way that pushed the canoe in the right direction. Callie was doing the same, and we definitely needed our combat trance to properly adjust the oars as the water changed constantly, with each of our attempts altering the course of the canoe.

Still, once I adjusted, I couldn't help but grin in delight. This was wild and crazy, but it was also fun. Aside from the crush of water making it harder to see, being thrown around was actually really entertaining.

I was so caught up in it that I barely noticed the dark shape forming in the water in time to plant my oar and jerk us out of the way, just missing a *huge* G-ranked rock rising out of the rapids and concealed by the spray. Swinging a hard left had taken us down a fork in the rapids, but I didn't have time to pay attention to that aside from noting the others had followed us as the river changed.

Callie shouted something that I couldn't really hear, but it turned out to be a warning as we suddenly dropped and began plummeting straight at yet another huge rock. The rapids were descending, and we had to steer with all our might as we were essentially thrown into free fall, hurled back and forth with barely enough time touching the water to steer. I considered using Leaf on the Wind on the canoe, but I was genuinely worried we would be flung off the river entirely by the water pressure.

As we were tossed around, I could see the other canoes being thrown into the same part of the rapids, and we had to adjust to those too. Our friends were having just as tough a time, but also seemed to be enjoying themselves just as much. As we came within a foot of Sloane, we could hear her howling with joy, and couldn't help but laugh at how crazy all of this was.

Of course, right now this was far too tame for a training session Abel had come up with. While this was all fun and difficult, it wasn't enough to really push us. The rocks were stationary even if the water wasn't, and I suspected that we hadn't figured out the real purpose of this test, or at least, hadn't noticed its real form. Sure, Mel told us what to do, but Abel loved nasty surprises. I couldn't imagine what exactly he'd come up with, though. Rapids were all the same. Just crazy waterslides with dangerous rocks and... waterfalls... at the bottom.

My eyes snapped up, focusing through the spray as hard as they could, and sure enough, when I looked hard enough I could see a cloud of more diffuse spray down the river about a mile or two from us.

I nudged Callie, who turned around in confusion, barely reacting to a rock in time because of the distraction. I leaned in and bellowed. *"Waterfall!"* Right into her ear.

Even our Perception wasn't suited for picking sounds out of this kind of tumult, and it took me a few tries to shout it through—along with a couple seconds and a few hundred feet. She looked where I pointed and screamed. "Oh fuck! Waterfall!"

I'd probably have laughed if we weren't about to plummet over a cliff on a death stream. Focusing hard, I leaned even closer, my mask pressed almost to her ear. "What do we do?" I bellowed.

I had no idea how to avoid this. It wasn't like we could just make a turn. We were pretty fucking stuck on this path. I doubted Abel would give us a test that would definitely kill us, but I was pretty sure it would come close if we didn't figure out how to deal with it.

Based on the speed and force of the river and how fucking big it was, this drop would be a doozy, too. The spray down there was being flung up pretty high into the air. If not for the steep downward drop along the way it would have been way more noticeable.

Unfortunately there wasn't really time for a plan. We'd have to just take it as we went, making sure not to get dashed on the rocks. Hell, we were still trying to control our forward momentum to avoid the ones in the rapids themselves. But there were several along the top edge of the waterfall we would need to slip between to escape. I planted my oar in the river, curving the water as best I could to force it to push the back of the canoe.

As I made sure my end was in line, Callie was desperately doing the same on her side, making sure we had force acting in the opposite direction to keep us straight, not to mention adjusting that force to account for all the rapid changes in pressure. It was like walking on the edge of a knife blade.

Shockingly, I noticed Lament's canoe slide up next to us, scything through the water with seeming ease. As she came within reach, she looked over casually. "Hey," she shouted, "you guys know there's a waterfall coming up? This place is great!" For probably the first time, she looked genuinely excited outside battle. I wasn't surprised. She and Abel were similar in a lot of ways, and apparently this was easy for her, so she was probably treating this like a vacation.

I was confused as to *how* she was doing that, until I took a closer look at her oar. Or rather, the oar she should have been using. Which turned out not to be an oar at all. She was steering with a fucking spear. That... how did that even work? The oars were large and flat, easily able to shape the water, but that spear wasn't a giant-ass blade like Wren's was. Lament's spear was much slimmer and more deadly, but she was managing to somehow cut the water currents in a way the altered her trajectory.

Lestri, who was in the boat with her, wasn't even doing anything, just sitting back and enjoying the ride. I could only assume that this was more Spear Mastery bullshit. It seemed like having a high-level martial art or weapons Skill really could offer a lot of utility. She might have been using her ability in conjunction with it like Abel did, but still, this was just blatant cheating. I really needed to start grinding up my Balam Skill. I was betting it could do some amazing things in conjunction with my DS Mastery.

Shaking off my jealousy, I shouted back, "We noticed! Have you seen the others?" I couldn't see Sydney or Megan anywhere, and Sloane had vanished after we almost ran into her earlier. The only reason we could even have this conversation was because of Lament's craziness. Since the others would still be pinballing around, it would be dangerous as hell for them if they didn't see the waterfall coming.

Luckily Lament nodded. "Yeah! They all know. I think they're aiming for the gaps closer to the banks, though! The splashback from the edges of the river neutralize some of the force! Not much, but a little. Anyway, I'm heading through, catch you on the other side!" She turned back to the waterfall and struck out with her spear at the front of the canoe, apparently cutting through the water and somehow speeding up her advancement.

I hoped I didn't have to fight her in the tournament. She would fucking destroy me. My only real chance was if Abel ran into her first or we took her out in the team matches. I didn't have time to dwell on that, because we were drawing closer and closer to the waterfall, and it was taking all we had to thread the needle between those huge rocks before we went over.

Seeing the rocks flash past my eyes as we began to tip, I paled slightly. I'd come within inches of being smashed flat. While the water itself wasn't enough to hurt any of us with our current Impact, Abel had been right to warn about the rocks. They were G-ranked too, and hitting stone with the same Impact as we had at whatever absurd speeds this maelstrom was flinging us about would absolutely have done extreme damage. We might not have died, but getting knocked out as mentioned was a strong possibility.

As we went over, I let out an involuntary scream as we were grabbed by the mightily descending torrent of blue glowing liquid and shoved downward easily three times faster than the most extreme speed on the rapids. I lashed out with my oar as I shifted my weight, trying to angle the canoe sideways to break some of the momentum and create drag. I saw the shapes of other canoes as dark blots across the waterfall, each at different altitudes. Sharp rocks poked out of the water along the length of the several-hundred-foot drop.

Unlike before, when my worry was being thrown clear, this was a place where being lighter would actually help. I used Leaf on the Wind, straining to cover the whole boat, and our descent slowed noticeably. It was still a rapid drop, but we were managing to resist the push of the water some-what. The resistance gave us the chance to put our oars to work and steer ourselves as best we could to avoid hitting protruding rocks on the way down. Not that we could see the situation at the bottom.

The spray from the water smashing into whatever was at the base of this cliff (we really should have done a complete lap around the Bay before agreeing to any of Abel's ideas) was obscuring whatever was down there. I was *pretty* sure it had to be a lake or something. No way Mel would have let Abel hurl us at flat ground to be crushed to death. Though I didn't think he would. Even my teacher wasn't quite that much of a dick.

As we wove our way past several jutting spurs of stone, we came close enough that I could see the water *was* collecting in a basin. There were more rocks, but maneuvering along this waterway was easier than doing the rapids in some ways. We skidded along the length of the waterfall, and I had to strain hard to resist the pressure as we smashed into the water.

Luckily, since it was the bottom of a waterfall, the constant disruption of the new water broke the plane of the pool's surface. We smashed through it, the canoe below us taking all the damage and basically dissolving into scrap as we were submerged. We swam up quickly to get out of the way as another canoe made contact, and crawled out onto the shore.

As I slumped over onto my side, shaken and gasping, I looked up to see something interesting. At the bottom of a massive cliff was a cave. Huh, those were usually fun.

Chapter Fifty-Six

THE CAVE in front of us was actually kind of inviting. The subtle blue glow that emanated from the hole in the rock made it seem like it had been designed just for us. The dark stone was worn mostly smooth, probably by the splashback of water. Regardless, I could see small spikes of crystalline material the same shade and luminosity as the water from the river lighting our way down the tunnel.

Focusing on what was important, I shook Callie slightly. "Hey, Cal, you alright?"

She groaned and rolled over. "Ow."

I nodded sympathetically. She had much less armor coverage than I did. I knew it was partly for mobility, but I also figured she just liked the style. Fashion hurts, I guessed.

She sat up slowly, reaching up to wring out her soaking hair, which was dripping with luminous water. "Shit. This isn't good. My hair is glowing, which means I can't use it as a vessel. My coat should still work because of the material."

I reached up to touch a bruise on her forehead with a scowl, and she yelped a bit and pulled back. "Damn it," I snapped. "What the hell is Abel playing at? This is too far, even for him. We could have died. The others might have been injured—I saw at least one of them hit the pool. Lament should be fine, but if that was Wren, Sloane, Sydney or Megan, it could be bad."

Wren had ended up going with Beric while Croll had partnered up with Sloane, since there were only three of the Spear Legion here. I hadn't seen him near us, though. Either way, I was seriously pissed we'd been sent here.

To my surprise, Callie just shook her head. "I don't think so." When I cocked my head, she sighed. "We turned during our trip down the rapids. I barely even noticed it, but right after we started to descend, I think we might have gone off track."

That… was a good point. Fuck. I hadn't considered this might not be within Abel's calculations. Thinking about it though, if he'd been aiming for us to come to a place like this, he'd have tagged along.

I heard noises from behind us and whirled, putting myself in front of Callie. Lament stepped forward from the shore, followed by Sloane, Croll, Lestri, Beric, and Wren. "Oh, good. You all survived," she said sunnily, in a better mood than I'd ever seen her.

Sloane sighed. "Ignore the lunatic with the pointy stick. Have you two seen Megan and Sydney? Also, where the actual fuck are we? I don't know anything about Doomtown, but I feel like they should mention to people that there's a big fuck-off waterfall when they rent canoes. Maybe put up a sign."

"I mean… could we have even read it in that mist and splashback?" I said. "Hell, maybe there actually *was* a sign, and we just missed it."

She seemed flummoxed by that thought for a second, but before I could continue, we heard another sound not far from where we were standing. I turned and noted with relief that it was Sydney and Megan, both of whom looked a bit bedraggled but still fine.

We hurried over to meet them. "Hey, glad you guys are okay!" said Callie. "We were worried there for a second. Pretty sure we took a wrong turn there. Though I'm surprised we all ended up going the same way."

Megan snickered at that. "You guys were out front at one point, we followed you. If everybody's fine, it's no big deal, though. I guess we need to climb back up, then?"

"We could..." said Lament slowly. "But don't you kind of want to know what's in that cave? My Fantasy sense is pushing me toward that thing. Plus, it's a secret *cave* behind a waterfall. What kind of Ascendants would we be if we didn't at least check it out?"

I sighed internally as I saw Callie's eyes snap to the entrance. My girlfriend was a rational and logical person most of the time, but when she picked up even the slightest hint of loot, she essentially turned into a ravenous beast. Not that I didn't love loot. But Callie took the same sort of primal joy in finding treasure that I did in finding a good fight. I was betting there was absolutely zero chance of leaving here without exploring, now that it had been phrased that way.

On second thought, Lament was right. This *was* a pretty limited place. G-ranked and low F-ranked Ascendants were the only ones allowed. No way the WCP hadn't swept this whole place for anything over the threshold. There might be some monsters down there, sure, but we were a pretty badass group. We should be able to handle anything we came across.

Still, I put a hand on Callie's shoulder as she started forward. "Wait."

She stopped, confused, and I slipped off a glove, spinning up my scan ring. A few seconds, and Abel's face appeared on a screen above my open hand.

"Oh, hey!" he said cheerfully. "We were waiting down where the rapids calm, but you guys never showed. What's the deal?"

I panned the call around, showing off where we were. "We're... somewhere? We took a turn off the main rapids and went over a waterfall. There's some kind of cave down here we were going to check out. Figured I'd see if you guys wanted to come check it out too." Whatever was down here, I'd feel better with Abel on board. Our mentor was a Master Candidate like Lament, and we knew him a lot better.

To my surprise, he perked up. "Wait, really? That's awesome! I didn't even know that was there. I've only done this a few times. Maybe your Fantasy senses pushed you to turn? Either way, I'd love to come, but I have no clue where you are. I'll try to figure out where the waterfall is. You guys go ahead and we'll catch up if we can." He sounded ecstatic about the possibility, and I smiled ruefully under my mask as I hung up. Fucking Ascendants, man.

"Okay," I said, turning back to the others. "Apollyon and Starbreaker are going to catch up, they said to go ahead. I guess… let's check this place out."

I doubted we were the first to find it. Even if it had been a Fantasy thing, I couldn't have a Fantasy that much higher than everyone else given how I distributed my stats (even distribution allowed for better wishes). The only possibility I could think of was that only Might-focused people had tried the rapids, but even so, there was no way *someone* hadn't been down here.

Callie squealed with joy, bouncing up and down before grabbing my hand and dragging me toward the cave. I snorted at that and eased out my cane, preparing to deal with anything we came across. The others trailed behind as we stepped inside. The crystallized lake water (I assumed) cast a glow that let us see but still left patches of shadows along the walls, and our feet echoed across the eerily smooth surface of the tunnel.

Small rocks and gravel soon appeared, crunching underfoot, the density of the fragments increasing as we followed the tunnel further in. We all tried our best to be quiet, Callie and I shifting into stealth, but Lament seemed unworried, strolling through the cave tunnel with her spear over a shoulder, looking around with interest.

The small spider that dropped from the ceiling was dead almost before I noticed it. Her spear lanced out lazily to perforate it multiple times before she stepped smoothly out of the way and let it smack wetly into the floor. I jumped. "Huh," she said. "That's interesting. I wonder if there are any more?"

Sloane stepped forward, kneeling down next to the corpse. "Rockjacker. Nasty variant. Venom turns body parts to stone." She poked it a few times. "This one seems to be a baby. So… yes, probably a few more." She slipped out a knife and jammed it into the spider's mouth, levering it open before cursing. "Shit. You nicked the venom sac. They're actually worth some money. Still, let me…" She cut into the body casually, with no hesitation at all, until she shouted. "Jackpot!"

She reached into the wound and yanked out a small lump of red that I realized was a half-digested ruby. "Rockjackers refine their venom by eating precious stones, usually ones with some amount of stats." She held up the ruby, looking closely at it. "Damn. I think this had a naturally occurring fire rune… looks like the stomach acid ruined it, though. Still… should have a few points of Might left."

Reaching out for the stone, I weighed it in my hand. It *did* have Might in it. Not a lot, but enough that it could be used in crafting. She was right about the corroded rune, but it would be worth a decent chunk of cash. "So... why did the spider attack Lament? I thought they eat rocks?"

She shrugged. "Bones are rocklike. Plus, they have super high stats, when you're talking people our level. Still, it's surprising that it jumped out at a group of us. Rockjackers are usually pretty timid. Granted, it's just a little thing, but that should make it more wary, not less." She frowned pensively. "Who knows though. We'll have to take a closer look. It'll be valuable, though. Breeding Rockjackers collect tons of stones for their young to feast on when they hatch so they can grow to adulthood and strike out on their own. As young as this one is, there's no way they've finished the stockpile yet."

Callie's head snapped around. "Are you telling me," she said slowly, "that somewhere in this cave, there is a giant spiderweb containing a huge pile of valuable Ascendant gems that we can just *find* and take?" She was starting to breathe heavier, and I could swear I saw her hands twitch.

"A spiderweb," I reminded her. "Presumably containing a spider. Which, considering how big this thing is as a baby, is probably fucking *huge* and might be F-rank." Not that I expected that to stop her. Besides, we were all approaching peak G. We could take some stupid spider, especially with Lament here helping with her cheat-level spear Skill.

Callie had the same thought, apparently, because she turned to the spear wielder. "Can you kill a Beginner F-rank spider? Not alone or anything, we'll be right there helping, but we need to make sure we have a finishing blow that can put it down. You're the best shot at that."

Lament looked positively gleeful. "Hell yes I can! I've killed worse. Especially if you can pin it down for me. I'll pincushion the eight-legged bastard." She whirled her staff around, spinning it dexterously between her hands. She struck out a few times to demonstrate her point, the air cracking from the speed and force of the stabs. I could see everyone was getting into this idea already.

I didn't mind doing it, but I wasn't going to let Callie die because she was treasure-hungry. Her head wasn't in this.

"Okay," I said, hesitant. "But if we do this, we aren't doing it with just us.

We need to wait for Apollyon and Starbreaker. They'll want to be involved anyway. You know how much Apollyon loves money."

Callie looked a bit impatient, but at my intense stare, she nodded and I sighed in relief. Normally I liked seeing Callie make dumb decisions for her own happiness, but facing an F-rank monster without Abel and Mel's backup gave me a bad feeling. I was glad she'd come around.

Chapter Fifty-Seven

Luckily for me, I didn't have to wait long for Mel and Abel. The two of them were fast, and when they were told to look for a giant-ass cliff, it wasn't exactly tough to find the right spot. Of course, they didn't come down the waterfall. As we watched from outside the tunnel entrance, they slowly descended from the sky, held aloft by Mel's flames as they blazed up from underneath them like some kind of rocket booster.

"I didn't know she could do that," I said to Callie. "Did you know she could do that?" Seeing the two of them come down on a cloud of fire was breathtaking… and also extremely aggravating. We'd had to fall down a fucking waterfall. I wasn't ashamed to admit watching them leisurely floating to the ground was pissing me off.

Abel grinned cheekily as he touched the ground, looking us all over critically. "Wow, you all look like shit. No wonder you decided to wait, everyone looks like a drowned rat." He paused. "Well, not Lament, she seems fine. But the rest of you look like something that was clogging my sink."

"First of all," said Callie, "shut up. Second of all, what took you so long? We found a nest of some kind of gem-eating spiders down here that is supposed to have a stockpile of valuable Ascendant materials." She grinned over at our Beast Lord Garden friends. "We're just lucky Sloane is a huge animal nerd, or we might have just decided the creepy spider cave was more trouble than it was worth and left." I hadn't mentioned the details on the call. There were far too many valuable things in this cave for me to trust bringing it up on a scan ring.

That got a nod from Mel. "Understandable. Spiders are gross." She looked around with interest. "Seriously surprised nobody found this place before. Even if it's pretty out-of-the-way and flight at our rank isn't common. How did someone not find this before you guys?"

Lament laughed lazily. "They probably did. That spider was sneaky as hell. If I wasn't so well-trained, it would have completely blindsided me. Sloane said the venom turns people to stone, too. They've probably killed dozens of G-rankers down here. I'm guessing other than the bones, which apparently they wanted, the rest of the body gets petrified and destroyed."

My face paled. "There... was a lot of gravel in that cave. Not at the entrance itself, but further in. It might have been bodies." My stomach turned a bit at that. Fuck, every time I forgot how dangerous it was down here, someone reminded me. "Plus, there's a potentially F-rank adult spider down there too. Even before the babies were born, I have no doubt it would have been able to easily kill the few stragglers who showed up."

Now I was even more glad that I'd waited for Abel and Mel. Who knew how many G-rankers had died in that shitty cave. Thinking about it, if we hadn't had Lament with us, we might have been bitten, and even if the venom hadn't killed us, there were bound to be more of those things in there. If we'd been swarmed, we would have been fucked.

I didn't know if Fantasy was the reason we'd found this place, but if so, I'd need to be way more careful of that sense. Sure, it would guide you toward things that would grow your renown and help you ascend, but things that helped you advance could also kill you. I wasn't afraid of a good fight, but it might be prudent to be a bit more cautious about that kind of thing.

After we discussed what to do next, we settled on having Lament as the advance guard, with Abel following behind. Mel would bring up the rear for a wider view of the field. Her fire abilities made for great crowd control. I was pleased to see her carrying the orb we'd picked up for her.

Finally we began our trek inside. Along with having my cane up and ready to swing, I also kept a close eye on the area around us with Seek Hidden. Granted, it worked better on larger things, but I could still see the spiders if they came close, and pointed several of them out for Lament and Abel to kill.

More than once I had to act directly when one of them dropped from the ceiling toward Callie, or was saved by her quick thinking when they tried that on me. Not every part of the cave ceiling was close enough for the Skill to work perfectly, and some of the rooms with higher ceilings had multiple nasty surprises. This pattern went on for about twenty minutes, until we came to a new room with a fairly low ceiling, and I froze in place at what my Skill was picking up.

The others all came to a stop when I did, the ones in front turning to look at me in confusion. I swallowed and set my feet. "Twenty. On the ceiling. They seem like they might be sleeping, but there's no way they won't notice us walking below them. Starbreaker, can you fry them?" Avoiding combat sounded boring, but fighting almost two dozen venomous spiders sounded like a huge pain.

Sadly, it wasn't to be. Mel shook her head. "Not in here. They're G-rank, and the amount of power I'd need to use would be enough to fry most of the people here. Your armor might protect you, since you're pretty much entirely covered, but not the others."

I cursed, but wasn't surprised. That had definitely been too convenient to work.

But I was far from the person I'd been months ago. Not just in terms of stats, but my Skills and combat standards were both much higher.

Reaching into my stores, I triggered a shadow attack along with Sucking Mud, forcefully synergizing the two and pushing them to activate as fast as possible. Just like the last time I'd used that combo, tendrils of dark mud lashed out from the ceiling the spiders were crouched on.

Five of the damn things were actually caught, the rest squealing with distress and hurling themselves off the rock before they had a chance to get grabbed. With fifteen spiders in free fall, their overwhelming advantage of having a bunch of legs and being skittery fucks was pretty much neutralized.

Wren, Lestri, and Lament picked six of them out of the air, two stabs each finishing them off before they even hit the ground, while Abel smashed three with a series of massive punches. Mel couldn't carpet bomb the place, but she was free to shoot condensed darts of flame. The blossom-shaped attacks landed on the spiders as closed buds and then consumed three of them in flames as they opened.

Callie was focused on the ones on the ceiling, targeting the five I was holding with ease thanks to the abundant shadow energy already condensed into the area. She shredded them easily as Sloane, Beric, and Croll lashed out at the last three, each taking one and reducing them to ribbons within moments.

All in all, the whole fight took about thirty seconds tops, and we were all left staring at the absolutely decimated cavern in shock. Well, not all. Abel, Lament, and Mel seemed to be pretty calm. The rest of us though, were in shock at how dangerous our combined assault had been. My head was a bit sore from the soul weight of launching that attack so quickly, but still, this had been almost no effort.

Megan, instead of looking shocked, just looked annoyed. "Damn it!" yelled the tall blonde. "I wanted to kill some of them! Did you guys have to hog all the kills?" Turning to Sloane, she demanded, "Are there going to be more of these things? That's like thirty, counting all the ones we killed on the way here. If I don't get to fight anything, I'm going to be pissed."

The dark chuckle Sloane let out was anything but comforting. "Minimum egg-laying size for Rockjackers is a hundred. Some of them can lay twice that many. You don't need to worry about having targets. Still, this was a good thing. Killing the bastards before they could bite us was important." She brandished her knife. "Of course, not as important as scavenging their venom sacs and checking their stomachs for gems. Anyone care to help a girl out?"

To the surprise of literally no one, Callie gleefully volunteered to help disembowel dead spiders looking for magic jewels. She and Sloane made excellent time tearing into the bodies, and managed to dig up a whole bunch of half-digested gems. Some of them had apparently been swallowed recently enough that they hadn't degraded much, and even more amazingly, one of the intact ones had a functional lightning rune on it.

Since this trip was turning out so lucrative, we decided to sell off the proceeds and then split the credits after, so everyone was just passing their stock to Sydney, who apparently had an honest-to-gods spatial ring on her. Even for the heir to a powerful sect, that was pretty impressive, and it made the whole trip way more convenient.

Once we finished with that, we moved forward again, taking out the odd spider here or there as we swept through the cave, until finally we came to one absolutely massive chamber that was much different than the others.

The inside of this cavern was brightly lit. The rest of the cave hadn't had more than a few of the crystals on the ground, so the ceiling had been cast in heavy shadow. In this room, though, the ceiling was festooned with huge spikes of blue glowing crystal.

More than that, though, between the crystals hung strands of glittering crystalline material, spun into delicate patterns and traceries that it only took a minute for me to recognize. "That's web," I said in awe. "The lake water dripped down the web and crystallized it. I don't know how it isn't breaking, but it looks like it retains its flexibility. Maybe it's the spider? I don't see it—" I stopped talking as Seek Hidden finally picked up the adult spider in its spot off in the back corner.

Callie looked at me with concern. "Solomon? Everything alright?"

I didn't have any words to respond. I was too busy pointing up at the monstrous arachnid crouched away from the crystals in the darkness.

Well, there should have been darkness. In reality, the spider was glowing too, its monstrously huge form coated in thick chitinous armor shot through with veins of the same glowing crystal as the web. Eight abominable eyes blazed blue as they fixed on our group, the creature not advancing or attacking, but waiting.

"Step into my parlor," murmured Abel, before grunting at an elbow from Mel. I appreciated that. I'd have done it if I was close enough. Like this shit wasn't horrifying enough.

Of course, that wasn't what caught Callie's attention. When I pointed, her eyes fixed on a much denser weave of web directly under the spider, which was covered with multicolored gems of varying sizes suspended on the same crystalline strands. The light from the spider shone down through the gems, creating dancing auroras on the cave wall behind it.

I recognized the frenzied look in my girlfriend's eyes as she looked at it and sighed, drawing my cane. "Alright. Who has a battle plan?"

Chapter Fifty-Eight

As IT TURNED OUT, most of the suggestions for a plan amounted to "group up and hit it 'til it dies." Callie, even nearly apoplectic with treasure madness, did not approve of anything that sloppy, and visibly forced herself to snap out of her trance and come up with something better.

I wasn't entirely sure if Abel really couldn't think of a better plan or was testing us, but with his bloodlust, I wouldn't put it past him to really just decide to try to overpower it. Since that would probably be dangerous, and there would *definitely* be other spiders hiding around here (though I couldn't see them, since they were much smaller and this cavern was too big), we couldn't just attack. We'd get swarmed from behind, and I doubted even Lament or Abel could take on an F-rank spider monster solo while under siege.

Once I explained that, Sydney suggested a possible solution. "Well... I might be able to help. My ability is luck manipulation. I can curse people or animals. Things will go wrong for them if they can." (I'd totally called that.) "For an F-rank... well, it'll be difficult to do much," she added, grimacing. "Impact can resist most powers, but intangible things like luck are the hardest hit in terms of defense. If I go all out, I can maybe prime it for something bad, but you'll need to provide some impetus."

At our blank stares, she sighed. "Do something dramatic to create opportunities for things to go wrong. Stab it or burn it or throw a huge rock at it or something. The more it has to try to defend, the more openings for things to go wrong. It probably won't be anything big, even with all my effort, but it should put us in a good position. Especially if Megan helps me out."

Her sister nodded. "I can bless people with good luck. Same basic idea, but backwards. Syd is the bad rabbit, and I'm the lucky rabbit. Our abilities are stupidly rare, so we're considered kind of like the star disciples of the Wave Warren despite not being too strong. People like Riley are way stronger in direct combat, but it's almost impossible to get luck abilities through Skill synergy unless you buy some crazy expensive Skill from one of the factions with the Job system."

Thinking about it, I wasn't sure how the hell I'd make a Skill like that either. In any case, it gave us some options. "So you can use your good luck aura on the person who attacks while Sydney uses hers on the spider?" I might be able to help a bit with this. When she nodded, I grinned. "Okay, then. I think I might have a plan." I leaned in to whisper it to Callie, using my Stealth Skill to make sure I wasn't overheard.

She was delighted. "That might just work. Can you manage it from here? I'm not sure what your range is, but if you missed, it would just set the thing off." She looked nervously at the gems in the web, and I rolled my eyes. She was worried about them getting damaged in my attack.

"It's fine," I said firmly. "I'm not aiming for them, and the worst that could happen is they get a bit dinged up. They're Ascendant materials." A bit of a drop wasn't going to destroy them. Stomach acid from a G-rank spider was a whole different level of harm than a few hundred feet down to a stone cave floor, if they even fell. Though on second thought, I made a mental note to use Sucking Mud on the ground below them just in case. The rocks here were tough enough to hurt *us*, after all.

Seemingly reassured, Callie turned back to the others. "Okay, when you see the opening Solomon is about to make, Lament, I want you to attack. Apollyon and Starbreaker will stick with the group to counter the spider horde with us. If you see an opening, you can help Lament from range. Wren and Lestri, your martial arts should be very compatible, so you'll follow her to attack once the opportunity presents." She nodded to the Wave Warren girls. "You two go ahead and do your thing."

No one asked what the plan was for me, because there was no way to announce it to everyone at once without the spider hearing. It would be fine though.

Once the two girls focused, their eyes both glowing, I grinned and leveled my stare at the spider. Or more specifically, at its web, where the strands were most concentrated in their connection to the wall. Then I triggered a flame attack from Cark along with Touch of Tears, shaping the blast into a long, thin area near the wall.

The corrosive green flame snapped into being with a lance of pain through my skull, and the spider reared back reflexively. This chamber was much bigger than the last one, so we didn't need to worry about it cooking us, but the spider screamed in an undulating multi-tonal howl that made me want to cover my ears.

As the acidic poison fire ate away at the strands, I felt the ineffable strings of fate pulling in both directions. My flame seemed to hit all the right spots connecting the web, and the spider made the exact wrong moves as it jerked back. There was a crackling, ripping sound, and strands on the other side started to fracture and fall away. The spider scrambled across the web toward the ceiling, but the rock was superheated from the flames, and on contact it screamed again and jerked away.

Which was the absolute last bit of strain the web could take as the section it had perched on gave way. I used Sucking Mud, both to save the gems and to trap the spider when it hit, and managed to get the Skill in place before the giant beast impacted the cave floor. The wet crash seemed to have set off a tidal wave though, as smaller spiders poured from every crack and crevice of the room and converged on us.

"Fuck!" I spat. I had plenty of attack options, but I was dangerously low on defense. I might be able to manage a combo with Callie, but my head was already ringing. I didn't want to rely on soul strength too much at the beginning of a battle like this. It would be far too easy to overdo it and become a liability. This was going to be a marathon, not a sprint.

I pressed my back to Callie's, doing my best to eliminate openings for both of us, and slipped into the combat trance. At the same time, I tried something new (a calculated risk) and triggered my DS Mastery overlay... then extended it to Callie.

The ability never cost any charges, and adjusting it to work through the trance and allow Callie access just brought a tiny bit of pain. It didn't tax me overly much so I wasn't worried about burning myself out.

As soon as it happened I felt everything... shift. The arrows I knew appeared, but not just for me. I heard Callie gasp as the tapestry of red and green arrows covered the world. Our Balam Skills were incredibly synergized already, since she was my teacher, and the combat trance made us almost a single entity in battle. Adding on the overlay just made everything click into place. It was that last push we needed for our cooperation to become perfect.

My cane came up without thinking, following an arrow on instinct to smash past Callie and knock away a spider leaping for her. A blade of shadows shredded the one trying to drop on me. I was a bit worried about the others, but they were strong. We had to pay attention to ourselves. I used my poison fire on the cane, and the world turned into a tapestry of blood and death as the spiders poured over us like meat into a grinder. I smashed and burned and crushed them as Callie tore them apart.

At one point I saw Lament's spear manifestation out of the corner of my eye, the spear user targeting the giant spider and creating a path with her weapon. But I didn't watch long. I had enemies to kill, and this whole battle was calling to me, showing me how to move, how to react, in the most perfect possible way. It wasn't just the overlay, or Balam. It was all of it. All the disparate elements. Callie taught me my Skill, and we trained together constantly.

Between one breath and the next, I felt things click into place I had to fight back a grin. A Skill. This was all I needed to create a Skill. I wondered if even Mel and Abel had this one. I knew it was going to be wildly useful in the tournament. I might not know what it was called, but I could tell what it was for. Teamwork.

But within seconds, I knew they definitely did. This Skill wasn't unique, sadly. In fact, based on the way it worked, I was pretty sure this had been the point of all the training up to this point. So many things we'd been told, some of them almost contradictory at times, finally came together into one whole package.

It was a strange feeling. The combat trance wasn't really necessary now. It wasn't like it was gone, but like it had become part of us, just another sense like touch or hearing. This wasn't just because of what we already had, either. Now I could see where the building blocks of our training were leading even as I felt it twinge and lashed out for an attack. First step

298

predicting the other person's moves, second step sensing their peril as your own, third step abandoning defense to protect them.

I didn't need to abandon my defense to protect Callie anymore, and she didn't need to abandon hers to protect me. We protected each other, and ourselves. Under this new sense, our cooperation was seamless. No longer a give-and-take, no longer a circle, but more like two hands attached to the same mind. I could sense not just her movements and weaknesses, but her intentions for her next attack.

This was how Mel and Abel were so damn good at fighting together. I could feel the name of the Skill, too. Minor Paired Dueling Mastery. True seamless teamwork. I had no idea what this Skill would even look like at higher ranks, but for the moment, it had completely upgraded our combat efficiency.

Before, I'd felt almost lopsided, hanging by a thread and hoping Callie would come through, but now that feeling was gone. I knew when she was moving to defend, when she wasn't going to make it, and she knew when she didn't have to try because I could intercept an attack myself. My blows and her shadow blades chained together like a whirling storm of crushing, slicing death.

I felt a few of her clones form and could perfectly take advantage of the shell game she was playing with them, her armor covering her in a way that made it impossible to tell what was shadow and what wasn't, unless of course you were me. I smashed my cane down on one spider, and turned my back on another to unleash the stored force in my cane on a third, not even needing to look as shadows bisected the one flying at my back.

After almost fifteen minutes of pitched battle, I smashed the last of the small spiders. It took me a second to realize they were gone because I could still hear the sound of battle. Mel and Abel had finished their section earlier, and were even now helping out with the powerful F-rank spider. It was injured in several places, legs damaged and armor cracked, but its blue eyes blazed with rage and hate.

I looked at Callie and she returned my unasked question with a nod. We still had one more monster to kill.

Chapter Fifty-Nine

I WAS SHOCKED that the spider seemed to be handling all three of our best fighters so easily, even with the rest of our group as support. Megan and Sydney were off to one side, eyes glowing as they doubled up on their abilities. Sydney was using hers on the spider, obviously, and combined with Megan's good luck aura (on top of the Master Candidate's technique and Skill) Lament was able to counter the limbs of the spider as it tried to skewer the others.

Sloane had her wings out and was flashing around the massive beast, striking with wing attacks, while Beric and Croll defended the Wave Warren sisters. Wren and Lestri backed up Lament, or rather, used opportunities she gave them to take cheap shots, while Mel hosed the monster down with fire and used her flames to maneuver away when the spider inevitably attacked. Abel helped Lament counter the limbs, mostly focusing on one or two specific legs as they went for Mel.

The spider was also much deeper in the Sucking Mud than expected, probably due to its weight, and was having trouble pulling free for attacks. The combination was keeping it from smashing anyone into meat paste, but even with that pretty fantastic strategy, the cracks spreading along the spider's armor were slow to form and already healing.

I grimaced. High Impact kept the wounds from being too severe, which meant Vitality was taking care of them. Given this thing could spawn a hundred kids, I was guessing its Vitality was high.

"We need to handle the regen," I murmured to Callie. "At this rate, we won't be able to wear it down. You up for another try with the overlay to get past its defenses? I only need to land hits on the cracks that are still healing."

My cane was still crackling with poison fire from the last fight. The ability, especially combined with augmentations from some of Benny's attacks, should at least counter the healing factor. That would help our heavies wear the thing down. I was pretty sure with enough attacks stacked, I could do one massive blow that would at least hurt it, but then I would be out of commission and the spider would still be around.

Spreading the poison fire through it and making sure Lament and Abel's moves really stuck was a much better use of my limited soul strength. And Callie seemed interested. With the new Skill, the two of us essentially had two perspectives to use for Perception. It wasn't anything crazy like doubling our senses, but we could Perceive things through each other and the Skill could process that.

It made it infinitely harder to sneak up on us, and theoretically should have exponential benefits to Stealth Skills once we had some time to train with it. Since Stealth relied on our own ability to find and eliminate traces of our presence, the Minor Paired Dueling Mastery Skill would have compounding effects.

That was a matter for later, though; for now, between the two of us and the overlay resonating with the Paired Dueling Skill, we should be able to get past the spider's attacks.

As soon as she agreed, I triggered Leaf on the Wind. I felt like I could use the bond from Paired Dueling as a connection to cast Skills on Callie, rather than needing touch. It still strained my soul, but minimally, and I could handle it easily enough for now. With that taken care of, the two of us blitzed in toward our allies, bypassing them to attack.

I whirled my cane up in a circle, triggering a triple stacked tranq blow with my cane as a medium. Since I wasn't combining Skills or overclocking anything, it didn't really strain me at all, and I knew I could use all ten of these hits without much trouble. The spider, sensing an attack, smashed down with one of its legs. Abel and Lament hadn't known I was going to attack, so they weren't able to counter the spider, but Leaf on the Wind and the overlay were a fantastic combination.

Throwing myself up over the blow, I felt the shadows beneath me push me up like a trampoline, right along the path of the arrow I was aiming for. The overlay allowed Callie to see what moves I might make, and Paired Dueling let her sense what I would do and when through our new strange bond. The combination meant she could support me perfectly from behind even without directly interfering.

With such a powerful monster, we couldn't risk a head-on attack, but augmenting my dodging was just right. I brought my cane down hard where Abel's most recent blow had cracked the spider's armor. The triple-strength mixture of poison fire and tranquilizer didn't seem to have much effect, but that wasn't a shock. This thing had a ton of Impact.

"Apollyon," I bellowed as I flipped away. Lament caught the leg as it came around and deflected it with a spear manifestation. "Hit the green spots!"

Then I darted around, Callie creating an aisle of shadows for me to slide on in a move I hadn't ever seen her use before. I could sense it before she did it though, so I didn't slip as I flashed over the ground.

We came in for a second attack from the other side and scored another hit, a glowing green fracture stark on the already-glowing blue armor. The third time we went in I followed the overlay as best I could, but I wasn't able to avoid the retaliation of the spider.

The monster noticed me coming and tried to spear me with a viciously sharp attack. The only things that saved me were my F-ranked armor and the type of blow. Piercing attacks were up there with energy in terms of my ability to tank them. If the thing had laid a solid smashing hit on me, my bones would have been powder. Instead, the F-ranked spider only managed to do some nasty pressure damage in a very limited spot.

Still, the force sent me skidding back across the floor, cracking at least one of my ribs. I hit the hard surface of the cavern floor and bounced a few times, skipping like a stone. My teeth rattled multiple times as I hit, and in the end, I was left on my back, staring up at the glittering ceiling gasping for air. My entire chest was on fire and I could barely move. I heard Callie scream my name, and within seconds, she was crouched over me.

"Shane!" She shook me, making sure I stopped staring into space. I groaned as her shaking jarred my injured rib. That spider blow had caught me in the side. It hadn't penetrated my armor, thankfully, or I'd have been impaled and probably killed, but it had seriously fucked me up.

Forcing myself to focus, I triggered a scan heal and then a healing surge, making the two abilities cooperate to maximize the recovery speed.

I expected to be flooded with energy and immediately knitted back together like usual, but the damage only slowly began to recover. The attack had been F-ranked, and the Impact difference was mitigating the effectiveness of the heal. At this rate it would take fifteen or twenty minutes for me to recover.

I groaned up at my worried girlfriend. "Ow. Careful." I tried to get up, but found myself unable to right my body. "Here, help me sit up without messing up my ribs?"

"Right!" Her voice was frantic, and I could feel her distress through the Paired Dueling Skill. An echo of her intent allowed me to pick up the strong emotion. It was... kind of sweet. Knowing for sure someone cared like that. Most people never get to feel for sure what someone else thinks of them. I knew Callie loved me enough to be afraid for me.

She helped me sit up and waved a hand in front of my face. "Are you okay? Do you have a concussion?"

I laughed, grimacing at the pain of the motion, and slowly reached up to stop her waving hand. "That isn't how you check a concussion, Cal. But no, I'm fine. The scan heal says a few broken bones and torn muscles, and they're mending. It's just slow because of the Impact difference. Did the hits we got in help out at all? I was planning to stack a few of those to make sure it was countering the regen properly."

She looked over her shoulder, then back with worry. "Maybe? The thing looks a bit slower. We might have overestimated ourselves here. Abel taking out a shitty F-ranked random is *not* the same as trying to kill a spider the size of a small house covered in plated armor. We kind of forgot that materials vary in strength even within a specific rank. Armored spider beats human in terms of durability."

Fuck. She was right. We'd been cocky after seeing a bit of success with our training. Fighting up a rank against a single person who was freshly

Ascended wasn't the same as a battle of this level. I'd blame Abel, but my mentor wasn't the type of person who considered limitations. Hell, he might be able to finish this fight alone over a long enough timeline. But we didn't have that.

Luckily, I had an idea of how to finish this. It was just going to suck a lot.

I looked up at Callie's worried frown. "Get Abel over here. I have a plan, but I need him for it. If this works like I expect, I might be able to help him put this thing down for good."

Sensing my seriousness, Callie didn't bother to argue, running over to grab our teacher. Mel came with him, since he wasn't there to provide fire support.

"Hey there, kid," he said. "Nasty smack you took there. This isn't a 'last words' thing, is it? Because those are always a bummer." I glared at him, managing to muster the strength to flip him off. Then I explained my plan.

After I went over the details, he blinked at me. "That... that could work. You sure you can manage something like that in your condition?" I nodded grimly and he shrugged. "Well, why the hell not. Let's give it a go. I should be able to aim it well enough to avoid the damage. I assume this will knock you the fuck out?"

"Yeah." I winced. "This is going to suck. A lot. Kneel down and put your hand on the ground. The G-ranked cave material should help with power, but it's going to take even more effort from me." He followed my instructions, and I put a hand on his arm, preparing myself to not only use a series of powerful combo moves, but to twist them to fit someone else. This was going to be the biggest soul weight I'd ever shouldered.

Stone Limb. Consecration of Flame. Touch of Tears. Mercy Kill. Flurry of Blows. A fire blast from Cark, a triple-stacked density-shifted attack. I layered on every Skill and move I could stand, my vision swimming and my head in so much pain I thought I would black out from it, as I created a poisonous blazing magma limb of such destructive power I was sure I'd never done anything close to as strong. Abel stared in awe at the limb, which was blazing with such bright green fire that it was hard to look at.

He grinned manically at me. "Thanks, kid. I'll take it from here." I had Callie help me stand up so I could watch. Without any hesitation, my teacher turned and threw out a punch. Space warped, and a massive green and black magma fist appeared over the distracted spider, smashing down into it with more force than I could ever remember seeing. The thing was flattened into the Sucking Mud, which I dispersed, trapping the spider in rock as Abel hammered it over and over with the Enchanted limb.

As the armor cracked under the repeated blows, I felt my sight dissolve into darkness. Yeah, I'd been afraid that would happen. Worth it.

Chapter Sixty

LAMENT WAS NOT PLEASED at that big flashy death of the giant spider. "I *had* it," she groused. "I was having fun, and then you had to go be a big show-off."

Which, to be fair, might have been true, even if that wasn't really the point. While Lament *could* have probably killed the spider, it would have taken much longer and the rest of us would have been in way more danger.

Wren, who obviously understood that, cleared his throat. "Yeah… I'm with them. We were wearing it down, but that thing was dangerous. You can scratch your battle itch in the tournament."

She glared at him, but he seemed unperturbed. While he might have been scared of her, she was also a teammate. He wasn't worried about her attacking him for no reason, and he was right about this.

To my surprise, Callie stepped up next to the spear wielder and patted her on the shoulder. "It's okay. We still have all the loot to gather. You can help me with that. Collecting treasure always makes me feel better." Her voice was almost bouncy as she started forward to once again gut tiny spiders and check their stomachs for valuable materials. Lament, not having anything better to do, helped, while I went to check on Abel.

My mentor was flexing his hand, grimacing at the motion. "You okay?" I asked as I approached. I'd never used any abilities like that on another person. Maybe one ability, but not a massive stack of powerful attacks. My head was still pounding from the strain of manifesting all of them.

Abel looked almost grim. "I'm fine," he said tightly, still flexing his hand. "There are downsides to that kind of attack. It was exceptionally powerful, but using it the way I did increased the strain on my body. My hand is a little raw. It'll heal, it's just going to suck for a while." I wasn't sure what that meant, given his hand was in a glove, but to make Abel, one of the toughest people I had ever met, react like this, it must have been agony.

That was kind of a scary thought. It was easy to think of my teacher as some invincible badass, but knowing he was mortal under all that terrifying combat prowess wasn't comforting. If anything, not being able to take his invincibility for granted was going to make this tournament more of a worry, not less. I reached out and put a hand on his shoulder, activating another scan heal/heal burst combo.

Scan heal on its own wasn't incredibly useful for someone our rank, but Jessie's heal bursts were incredibly effective, if unfocused. The combination let the powerful healing energy of the life force target injuries and mend them directly instead of wasting the extra power supercharging the body with extra energy. Abel blinked at me as the green life force swarmed his hand and began repairing it, though the damage didn't go away immediately.

My own injuries from earlier were still mending, though most had faded after a few minutes and another scan heal/ heal burst combo. The stored attacks were extremely useful, but at this rate wouldn't last long.

To be fair, we normally wouldn't be hunting down an F-ranked creature. Being able to finish it off was pretty impressive, even as a team.

I glanced over at the cracked and damaged armored spider, which Wren and Lestri were trying to pry out of its protection.

"That was damn impressive, though." I gestured to the spider. "Even with the augmentation from my Skills. Being able to kill that thing so easily is no joke." We'd set the fight up perfectly (if we hadn't, I wasn't sure we'd have won) but Abel's contribution was by far the biggest. Granted, having so much hard stone to act as an anvil to that blow had certainly helped.

Abel didn't look happy though. He just shook his head. "Yes and no. We got really lucky. That thing wasn't made to fight on flat ground, and your Skill restrained it. Even so, there were several times it could have killed us. I got overconfident. I've killed F-rank humans before who got in my way, and it made me confident in fighting up ranks. Seeing Lament fight, though... it reminded me that I was fighting useless trash when I did that. There are other powerful people like me, and even at my own rank, they might pose a challenge."

I glanced at the spear wielder helping Callie. "Are you saying you don't think you can beat her?" Lament was scary, but Abel was Abel. I couldn't get my head around him being afraid of someone. Sure, I felt that kind of fear, but Abel seemed so unshakeable. He was a force of nature.

He shook his head. "No." Then he paused. "It's more that I don't *know* if I can beat her. Which on one hand is exciting. I love a good challenge. On the other hand, though, if she's here, someone else at the same level may be as well. The team match will be fine, but what if one of you or Mel run into someone like her. Not all of them will be as affable as she is. I'm starting to worry about how our team will do in this tournament."

I had my own ideas for dealing with that. "Don't worry too much about us. I have ways of keeping us safe." We'd already tested wishes for retreating, and a tournament would make that kind of thing even easier to arrange. A single breach of the rules and we could be spirited off to the waiting room. I wanted to win this, but not at the cost of one of my friends. Worst case, we would give up on the Moonsong Glade. It wasn't worth losing anyone I cared about in this competition.

Escape wishes were the best possible safety net, and with four of us, it was entirely possible without compromising my contract with the Beast Lord Garden for even a day. I couldn't wish for a safety net myself, so that only left three, and Abel didn't seem to feel he needed one. I had two spare wishes a day, and that meant I could ensure the safety of our teammates without letting anyone know those two wishes had been used.

This was all a matter for later though. I clapped Abel on the shoulder, eliciting a small wince, since it was his still-healing arm. "Anyway," I said, "don't sweat the small stuff. Just make sure you're at your best. In the meantime, we should head over and move that spider. It's on top of a fortune in Ascendant materials."

He grinned at me then, a quick flash of gratitude and amusement that settled into his usual mocking smirk, and we headed over to where the shattered spider lay.

As we closed in, I couldn't help but whistle. The sheer size of the thing was awe-inspiring up close. Seeing it on the web or from a distance hadn't done it justice. A thrill of fear clenched my stomach and weakened my knees as I imagine frontlining something this big and terrifying like Lament had. No running or dodging, just me against the enemy head-on.

At the very least, I knew that wouldn't be a problem here. This thing was dead as a doornail. Half-submerged in stone, the top of the monster was cracked and broken, but more than that, the armor and meat inside were damaged and corroded. Touch of Tears, under the magnification of all my Skills and Abel's own tremendous power, had been carried along with the force and truly destroyed the spider. Even with that corrosive effect gone after I dispersed it, the remains had been seriously damaged.

Which we gave no fucks about. We weren't here for spider meat. We'd strip the armor for sale just in case, and probably the legs and mandibles in case they could be made into weapons, but at the moment, it was what lay under the beast that we wanted.

I activated Sucking Mud, wincing slightly. My soul was extremely strained right now, to the point even normal Skills hurt, but they were usable, at least.

Luckily my body was fine, and Abel and I had no trouble lifting the bulk of the spider and hurling it off to one side. A quick use of Seek Hidden left me seeing all of the materials, and Callie's timely arrival (she'd seen us move it and come running) supplied me with a shadow-forged net, letting me fish up all the gems and leave them in a substantial pile.

Most of them were G-rank, since they needed to be digestible for the baby spiders. A few large pieces of stone were apparently F-rank materials the spider had been saving to consume itself, but they were few and far between. With the base currency in H-ranked chits, it was estimated most of the smaller ones would go for a few dozen. Materials could only be worked by crafters, and unless we held onto them to sell piecemeal, we were going to need to give a bulk price to unload them all.

The F-ranked stuff we would keep for the big auction. We were going anyway, so we figured we might as well. We'd unload the spider armor and claws at the same time.

Callie took great relish in totaling up the gains, figuring out exactly what we were going to get, and when she finally reported the total, even I was pretty gobsmacked by exactly how much money this trip had netted us.

Three E-ranked chits. Three thousand H-ranked coins. It was... a *lot* of money. Even someone like me with almost no grasp on how the Ascendant economy worked was blown away. Abel looked like he might pass out.

In the end, we decided on the obvious even split. Sydney and Megan got one, the Spear Legion got one, and we got one to keep for the Pavilion.

Sloane and the others felt like they hadn't done much, and I was a guest elder anyway, so my force growing was a net benefit to them. They abstained from taking a share. Which left us with a single E-ranked chit to invest in the Pavilion. Deciding that growing our new faction was the most important thing, we handed it over to Mel.

Resources were strength too, and there were so many ways spending money could help increase the power of our faction. Improved training equipment, alchemical pills and elixirs, even Skill Crystals. Those were extremely rare here on Callus. You could find useless ones in some of the Unity branches, but nothing impressive or worth the price. The reason was that the production of the Skill Crystal itself was a closely guarded secret. The blanks had to be specially prepared to be imprinted with Skills. Buying blanks was much pricier and much more useful to forces like ours.

I'd even considered having Callie imprint Balam on a blank for our people to learn. Not that it was a direct transfer. More like a way to watch memories and get a feel for the Skill. I figured I could try to learn enough to push my Balam Skill up to Beginner and end the geass, at least. Paying for a wish with a Skill Crystal of a Skill I made probably wouldn't work, but since we hadn't considered it beforehand, it should be a solution at the moment.

I dismissed the idea, though, for the moment. We'd need to see if we could even get any. It wasn't like blanks grew on trees. One more reason to look forward to the auction.

Chapter Sixty-One

IT DIDN'T TAKE TOO long to get back up to the top of the cliff, where the others waited. I noticed Master Saiten had stuck around up at the shore rather than come down. Knowing what E-rankers could do, I wasn't sure that actually mattered, but I made a note anyway.

Once we got back to shore we all split up to head back to our relative hotels. That gave me a chance to grant the wishes for the Beast Lord Garden, giving them all five again, and putting another fifteen into my Fantasy stat.

Once we got back to the hotel, Abel pulled Mel, Callie, and I aside to talk. He led us back to one of the rooms, closing the door.

"So," I said once it had been shut. "We got the Skill for Paired Dueling. Does this mean we don't need to finish the training down here?" I wasn't sure if that was an intriguing or disappointing prospect. Doomtown was a dangerous mess, but it had been interesting so far.

Abel shook his head. "The Skill is still at Minor, I assume?" We both nodded. "Then we can still get plenty out of this. Minor Skills are the easiest to rank up, and a Lesser version of that Skill will serve you much better. Plus, you're getting a better idea of the kinds of things you'll be dealing with in the tournament. Hell, *I'm* getting a better idea. Despite being experienced, Mel and I are still locals. Our view of things is ultimately still too shallow."

Seeing Lament fight seemed to have excited and scared him in equal measure. I knew for his own sake he was more than enthused for a fight between them, but it had put the potential danger to the rest of us into perspective. He wasn't the only one, either. I was planning to focus on raising my DS Mastery Skill to Intermediate. Knowing what Abel and Lament could do with theirs, I was interested to see if I'd notice any changes. Even if I didn't, it would be worth it. I'd be getting another finishing move next rank.

But I had a bad feeling in the pit of my stomach. I wasn't sure why or from what. It wasn't about the tournament or Lament or anyone from the rafting trip. My Fantasy stat was higher now, and I was getting a better feel for that ineffable sense it brought. My best guess was that this had some-thing to do with the auction, and I didn't intend to keep that to myself.

"So..." I said, trying to figure out how to put it into words. "This auction. I get a not-so-great feeling about it. Does anyone else feel that, or am I just letting my imagination run wild?"

To my surprise, Abel's eyes snapped up to mine. "Really? How long has this happening?" At my shrug, he bit his lip. "I don't sense anything. But there's more than a few possible reasons for that. For one, my Fantasy probably isn't as high as yours at this point. For another, fate sense isn't really one-size-fits-all. It tends to point you toward things that will be inter-esting or dramatic for *you*. Just because you'll be running into something that will get you attention doesn't mean I will."

I'd never heard it called "fate sense" before, but that was a pretty spot-on description, and I decided I liked it.

Still, it left the obvious question. "Does that mean we shouldn't go? We can always give it a miss if it'll be too dangerous. I'm sure they have some way to sell our items and pick up the money later."

I wasn't one to run away, but I also wasn't one to risk my friends pointlessly. If the others decided we shouldn't go, I was fine with that. Callie was the one who would ultimately make the decision, but I knew she'd be just as interested to hear their take on it as I was.

A quick glance told me I'd been right, as she nodded her interest in hearing the answer.

Mel fielded this. "No. We can't afford that. Not just because of the auction itself, though there are bound to be expensive materials we can't get elsewhere, but also because if we back down, the others will smell blood in the water. They'll swarm us and we won't survive. Ascendant confrontations are a matter of reputation as much as combat, as you probably know. If we get a rep for being weak, we'll be buried in half-assed challengers until we get taken down by numbers alone."

That didn't sound pleasant. I could kind of see her point, too. An impressive team would scare off a lot of low-level challengers. I doubted we'd have many teams just giving up when we faced them in the prelims, but we'd probably see *some*. We were pretty scary, and we could continue making an impression. A bit of danger now would save us work in the future.

Plus, we needed some Skill Crystals. Balam was a dangerous and useful martial art, and Callie's foundation would bring our fighters right to the edge of making their own strides in it for Intermediate. Prior to that, Skills were a bit more standardized, so learning Callie's version of it wouldn't hurt anyone's potential advancement.

"Alright," Callie said with a nod. "Then we go. We have the spider armor and some of the F-rank gems to sell off, and that should give us some money to play with, even on top of what we have. I'm sure there'll be plenty of interesting items to pick up. That just means we have a few more days to kill before it's time to attend. Once that's done, we can reassess. Do you have any ideas by the way? On how to get our Paired Dueling to Lesser?"

I was curious about that too. The mild situational empathy and predictive ability was useful, but I didn't know where it would go from there. We basically fought like two halves of the same whole. There was room to improve that, of course, but I wasn't sure how. Then again, Minor Skills were usually pretty weak, being only mortal level. It was highly possible the main benefit of Lesser was just a more complete version of what we had, though that made me wonder what Beginner Paired Dueling might entail.

Sadly, there didn't seem to be some special method. Abel's shrug made that clear. "Not really," he said apologetically. "Just more of the same. Minor to Lesser is just a matter of polishing. You usually see extra utility in Beginner, which somewhat prepares you for finding your own path to Intermediate. Not always, though, really just depends on the Skill."

That did make me a bit confused about something. "If Intermediate is where people usually start to do their own thing, how come you and

Lament have such similar manifestations?" I'd been wondering why it seemed like Intermediate, which was so personalized, seemed to manifest the same way for them. He'd mentioned that manifestation was common with Intermediate martial arts too, so it wasn't just them.

"Utility," he said calmly. "While it's true Intermediate is mostly self-determined, two of the main weaknesses of close combat and weapons Skills are range and scope. Addressing this is one of the most common steps down the path to Mastery. It's not universal, but it's compatible with a shockingly large number of combat styles. Expert-level martial arts start to branch more, though there are still some themes that a majority of them follow."

Mel broke in. "What he's not saying is the similarities are only superficial. Intermediate isn't just adding a new aspect, it's about personalizing a Skill to be something more attuned to you. Perfectly adapting your martial art to your combat style and your other Skills and ability. It's why he's so far ahead. He spent years doing that. Of course, soul strength plays a big part as well, since as you know, a strong soul is needed to modify Skills, which is an integral part of stepping into Intermediate and beyond."

I knew what she meant. "Is that why Mastery is such a stumbling block? Because people don't work their souls enough and get stuck relying on the native soul strength from rank ups?" I asked. Rank ups would increase your soul strength naturally as you Ascended, I knew, but it never occurred to me when they mentioned Mastery being difficult that the two things could be related. It made sense, though. It also reminded me of something else. "And is soul strength what lets you resist recursion?"

Abel shook his head. "No to the second, yes to the first. Lack of soul strength is one of several reasons Mastery poses a challenge to most people, but no, soul strength isn't the same quality that allows someone to resist recursion. It's... related? But not the same. There are people who manage to reach the higher ranks warped by their recursion. They aren't common, but they exist.

"We're getting off topic, anyway. We were talking about training. We'll be doing more generalized combat going forward. Some sparring, maybe some days at the Bone Arena for the last day or two."

Mel cut in. "That will be later, though. For the moment, our biggest windfall down here is interacting with and learning about the external factions before the tournament. The Wave Warren and the Spear Legion are mostly on good terms with us, but we have one other faction we don't know too well yet. We have an in with the Darkling Institute but haven't exploited it. Our best move here would be to learn more about them before the auction."

I was torn on that, actually. I also had a bad feeling about the Darkling Institute. On the one hand, that meant I should be looking into them more deeply to head off any backstabbing, but it also meant I didn't want to be near them. I wasn't sure what was tipping me off about them, since it didn't feel quite like fate sense.

The only other source I could think of was some kind of bleedover from my diviner class. Still, that felt nebulous and ridiculous. As much as I trusted my instincts on some things, I couldn't justify depriving my team of powerful allies because of a bad feeling I couldn't even put into words.

I decided to keep quiet about my concerns for now. If we hung out with the Darkling Institute's fighters, I'd have a chance to observe them up close. Maybe then I would be able to put my finger on what bothered me about them. It was possible it was just necromancy that I had a problem with.

"Well," I said cautiously, "where should we meet them, then? Assuming we can get in touch. Maybe we could avoid any activities that involve water. I don't really think there's anything more to gain from Riot Bay after all the time we already spent there. Unless there's a secret water park that you forgot to mention? Because that actually kind of sounds like fun."

Abel's mouth was stretched into a grin. "No water park, I'm afraid. But I do have a slight inkling of something fun to do. There are plenty of interesting games to play down here that don't involve water." He looked to Mel. "What about the Shatter Lanes?"

Her eyes widened, and she started to chuckle, before bursting into a full-on laugh.

Abel looked back over at us. "Yeah, I have an idea. Just out of curiosity, how do you feel about giant birds? Specifically, how do feel about the idea of racing on them?"

Chapter Sixty-Two

SADLY, being that he was a sadist who lived to torment us, Abel refused to say another word about the Shatter Lanes until the next morning when we were just about to leave. He did invite the others, but Sloane and her posse had gotten an offer to spend the day with some of the low F-rankers in the Beast Lord Garden. Apparently they were planning to take their seniors down to Riot Bay to do some fishing, hoping to make more money.

I wished them luck. That left us with Sydney, Megan, Wren, Lestri, and Lament, which would be nice. We also had the wolves with us. They weren't fans of water, so we hadn't brought them to the bay, but the Shatter Lanes weren't water-based, and Abel insisted they would have a blast there. We'd had them wait in the rooms before, and I felt kind of bad about cooping them up inside, so it would be nice to let them run a bit.

Sydney was absolutely enthralled by Jin and Rellia as soon as she met them, and spent the entire morning at breakfast sandwiched between the big fur balls, cuddling them mercilessly. When it was finally time for us to head out, Abel filled us in.

"Alright, fine," he said after the twentieth time I asked. "Racing. It's not a complicated thing. The Shatter Lanes are a huge dirt track. When you show up, you can pay to race on the backs of giant wingless birds called Ralkors. They have scales instead of feathers, and their beaks and claws are metal. Scary little fuckers if you piss them off, but they're trained not to attack their riders."

I was beginning to sense a pattern here. "Let me guess. During the race, the Ralkors attack anyone besides their rider who gets close, and to win, you need to battle your way through the pack of them to reach the front?" I should have known Abel wouldn't suggest any activity that didn't have a chance to kill us all, training or not. Still, it definitely sounded like fun, especially since Callie and I had our F-rank armor to fall back on even if we did get attacked.

Abel gasped in feigned shock, putting a hand to his chest. "What? Me? Put you in danger? Preposterous! Lies and slander! Absolutely... Okay, yeah. They'll try to kill anyone who gets too close, but you have to kind of nudge them. Riders can team up too, and attacks take away from running, so it's not like every single Ralkor will be attacking. Some riders choose to go all out on speed, or set traps. It's fun trying to figure out exactly what people will do.

"I'm actually going to be taking part in this one. Personal strength is much less of a factor here because the Ralkors are all about the same, though admittedly my spatial perception might help a tad."

He sounded genuinely excited to take part, and it occurred to me that Abel had mostly been forced to stay out of most of the activities we'd been doing. With the exception of the fishing, this had been more of a supervisory thing for him. For someone who obviously loved Doomtown and all the things he was showing us down here, it must have been hard to just sit back and watch, but he'd never complained. I felt kind of bad for only noticing that now.

It was easy to forget that while he was a bit older than us, Abel was still a G-ranker too. We'd been treating him more like a mentor than a friend, and during training that was fine, but he wasn't the formal type. I was pretty sure he'd prefer we treat him like one of the gang when we weren't mid-training session. Now I felt stupid for not considering that before, but it wasn't too late.

I chuckled lightly. "I guess that means we finally have a chance to take you down, huh? Get ready to taste defeat."

"Taste the feet?" he said archly, wrinkling his nose. "Whatever weird stuff you and your girlfriend get up to isn't my business, man, just keep me out of it."

Megan choked down a snicker even as Callie squeaked in embarrassment. I grimaced. I'd kind of set him up for that one, but I would have my revenge eventually.

Luckily the conversation was cut off by our arrival at the Shatter Lanes, a fact I was alerted to by the growls and yips of Jin, who it seemed did *not* like the smell of Ralkor.

"By the way, you mentioned Jin and Rellia would have fun here?" I asked Abel as we got in line. "Are they able to race with us or something?" That sounded like it might be dangerous, but the puppies did need some exercise, and chasing scaly hate birds would probably be a blast for them.

Abel laughed. "Sadly not. But the adolescent Ralkors are much less dangerous, and they train them on a smaller track. The wolves should be allowed to race with them, and since they haven't developed the metal claws and beak, they should be much safer."

He turned to the man behind the counter we'd just arrived at. "Nine for the noon race. Plus two tickets for the training lanes." Then he paused for a second, checking his scan ring. "Actually, we'll rent one of the novice pens for the next half hour, if there's one open."

The man, a lanky fellow with dark skin and hair and bright blue eyes, just grinned at him. "Sure are. Anyone with any sense has already done all the training they need. You're free to use one. Just go around back and receive your Ralkor assignments."

We turned to do just that, but Callie called us to a stop as her scan ring buzzed. "One second. I think that's Mordaunt. She decided to meet us here."

Sure enough, within a minute or two, Mordaunt made her way over, the hulking form of Rahm lumbering behind her silently. Well, that wasn't fair. Rahm didn't lumber. He was a pretty graceful guy. But the whole dead person thing combined with his total silence creeped me out.

After stopping to pick up her own tickets, she came around to meet us so we could walk over to our assigned Ralkors together. As we walked, I had to ask Abel. "So... Ralkors. Is there a lot of variation? Because being assigned a bird makes it seem like some of them might be... recalcitrant." (Which was a polite way to say "crazy rage beasts that tried to rip apart their owners.")

He just shrugged. "There are good birds and bad birds. Some of them don't like riders much, but we'll see what we end up with. They don't give the best ones to the early attendees or anything, that would just make it a matter of who showed up first. It's random."

Mordaunt looked fascinated. "This sounds like a blast. I'm glad you invited me. No hard feelings if I maim some of you." Her teasing grin made it clear she wasn't planning to actually maim us... or that she was? I didn't have enough of a read on her to be sure.

It didn't really matter. With our armor, Callie and I would be fine, and anyone else who got hurt had the Vitality not to bleed out before I could fix them with heal bursts.

When we came to the spot at the edge of a fenced-off area, a bored-looking woman with blonde hair in a ponytail yawned at us. "Welcome to the Shatter Lanes," she droned. "Please be aware that any mutilation or untimely deaths caused by the Ralkors or your competitors during the course of your visit is not our responsibility. A stipulation you will agree to before being given your Ralkor."

Since this was Doomtown, that seemed to be pretty much par for the course. We all agreed, and the woman nodded, leading us through the fence to where a series of massive bipedal birds waited in their pens.

The scales of a Ralkor were much more delicate than expected, the dense coating of small plates retaining flexibility and durability regardless of thickness by virtue of overlap. The beaks and talons, as mentioned, were metal, and gleamed imposingly in the low light.

Abel nodded in satisfaction as he took them all in. "Just as scary as I remember. The Ralkor is actually a pretty cool animal. They feed them scrap metal as youngsters, letting the metal build up in their bones. When they get old enough to go through puberty, the metal is vented into their beak and claws, creating the effect you see here."

There were about a dozen Ralkor left and eleven of us, so I knew I would be riding one of these.

Jin and Rellia just growled at them menacingly as they tried to back away. Sydney knelt down next to them, pulling them against her and cooing softly. I rolled my eyes at them. Big babies. What kind of wolf is afraid of a giant chicken? Still, I reached down to scratch Jin behind the ears. Even if he was a scaredy wolf, he was still a good boy. Besides, those metal beaks actually did look kind of scary, so I couldn't blame him too much.

The woman from the entrance gestured to the Ralkors scattered around in the pens. "Alright, now each of you take out your tickets, one by one, and tear them up."

I'd been handed a ticket when I showed up, but hadn't paid it any mind. Still, it was her show. I took the ticket out and ripped it apart, and the scraps of paper burst into green flame. The flames floated as a ball in the air before zipping over to be snapped up by a green-scaled Ralkor.

When the woman made a shooing gesture, I shrugged and walked over to the Ralkor. Its eyes were glowing green like the fire when I arrived, and as that faded, I felt a small link form between us. Nothing as permanent or strong as my link with Callie, but similar. Some kind of empathy, maybe?

I turned to Abel, cocking my head, and he grinned at me. "Beast bonds," he said with amusement. "Only temporary, but they're good for learning to interact with bonded partners. Bonding Skills can be pretty similar sometimes."

I burst out laughing. "You lying ass, you said you didn't have any special training in mind. This whole thing was one big game to get us here." He'd been planning this from the start, or at least as soon as he'd confirmed we'd gotten the Paired Dueling Skill. He just winked at me, and I rolled my eyes. Then I narrowed them suspiciously. "Wait, this doesn't give you an advantage in the race, does it?"

He chuckled. "Not much. I'll adapt faster because of experience, but the beast bond isn't a Skill I actually have. It's just as temporary for me. The training pen should give you plenty of time to get adapted before the race, so we'll be on even footing when I absolutely demolish you all with no real effort."

He said that last part with casual confidence that made me want to punch him a little, but I just rolled my eyes again.

Once we all got our Ralkors, we headed for the training pen he'd reserved to get used to our bonds and learn to control our temporary mounts. It didn't take long to pick it up, like he'd said, so we were ready to go by the time the race started.

As we all stood at the starting line, I realized that though we were the last twelve, there were about fifty people here. This was going to be much more chaotic than expected. I couldn't wait.

Chapter Sixty-Three

By the time the starting horn sounded, I was pretty used to my bond with the bird. Thus, I immediately leaned on it to push the Ralkor into a full-on sprint. Though I couldn't use any active Skills, my passive connection to Callie through Paired Dueling was still there, and I had enough of a sense of her to match our speeds as we took off down the track, bringing my Ralkor close to hers as we raced ahead.

Unfortunately, as mentioned, the Ralkor distribution was random. Callie's was a bit slower than mine, and several of the enemies were much faster. Not only that, several started to drift in toward me as if preparing to attack. Ahead of me, I saw Abel, sprinting along on his own red Ralkor, and as a blue and a green drifted in from both sides, it leaped into the air and kicked out with both feet, attempting to gouge each of them in succession.

The first rider, the one on a green ralkor a lighter shade than mine, was coming in too fast. When Abel's bird attacked, he had to put his arm up to block and got laid open to the bone, falling back with a howl of pain. The blue rider, however, flipped up into a picture-perfect counter, claws clashing against claws in a shower of sparks as they were thrown away from each other.

The two trying to close on us made their own move while we were distracted by the attack, but unfortunately for them, I was within arm's reach of Callie. I leaned over and grabbed her hand. Her Ralkor leapt into the air, and with a heave I swung her, along with her purple Ralkor, entirely around my head. Her legs kept her Ralkor under her, and her mount kicked out with a series of dangerous bicycle kicks to attack both of them.

One of the attackers got driven back, but the other dipped under the kicks and managed to slip in to slash at my leg. Sadly for the tall man on the back of the red Ralkor, I was wearing strong armor, which soaked the blow easily, even if it hurt like crazy.

I urged my Ralkor in closer and leveled a heavy punch at his head. He dipped back and took it on the shoulder, but Callie came up around on the other side of him and executed a spinning taloned kick at his head with her own purple Ralkor.

The man tried to counter the attack, leaving him open for a hard kick from me, his Ralkor turning to dart after him as he flew off into the pack behind us. I winced as I saw him get trampled, though from the brief glance I got he didn't die or anything, and his Ralkor managed to snatch him up.

Callie pulled up even with me and shot me a grin. The two of us had a huge advantage here even without active Skill use, the training we'd done over the last few months giving us a passive awareness of each other and what the other would do. Of course, that meant Mel and Abel had an advantage too. It was easy to see the two of them had joined up. They were in the center of a crowd of Ralkors, seamlessly fighting them off.

After giving a nod to them, Callie made a gesture that we'd worked out in training and I flashed her a thumbs-up. We split up and closed in on the crowd from either side, flashing a few hand signs at Abel and Mel as we came in, pincering the group of five enemies in between us. I saw Mel's orange Ralkor leap straight up about ten feet into the air as Abel smashed sideways to drive one of the five out of formation at me. I kicked low as the rider swung partly off his Ralkor, my leg striking out at the head of the one between us, the racing bird unbalanced and thrown behind by the dual attack.

Mel, meanwhile, came plummeting from the sky like the stars she was named for breaking, and when two of the others tried to move aside, Callie body-slammed one into another and shoved them both into the path of our descending mentor. Ralkor claws flashed even before the heavy bird

323

smashed into them, opening long slashes across arms and back and forcing them to retreat.

For the last two, Mel and Abel converged to pull the same swing move we had used earlier, taking them out. I saw our mentors consider attacking us directly, but they evidently decided to leave that for the end of the race. The winners would get half the entry money, but we'd use it for the Pavilion anyway, not that it would stop Abel from competing if we ended up being that last ones left.

As we belted forward at top speed, I saw the other riders avoid us completely and nodded with smugness. Sadly, this wasn't a brawl, it was a race, and we weren't winning. I didn't want to leave Callie, knowing not only would she be more vulnerable without me, but I'd also have to worry about watching my back much more thoroughly. Taking a lesson from Mel's huge jump, I noted the faster speed of my Ralkor and shot Callie a few hand signs. She responded quickly before closing in.

Taking her hand, I did the same swing maneuver, but instead of in a circle, I hurled her up and around, then let go, shooting her forward through the air alongside her squawking Ralkor. I sent her hurtling into the near distance as I kicked my own bird into high gear, sprinting full out to catch up before she landed among a large group.

I managed to beat her there and smashed into them like a scaly wrecking ball. Mostly I cleared them out so she could land delicately. The long tough legs of her Ralkor absorbed the impact as she crashed down, only for me to grab her again and throw the two of them a second time, before sprinting all out with my much faster Ralkor to catch up to her. We were essentially leapfrogging to close with the lead elements of the pack.

The furthest ahead were in a state of near-constant combat even as they ran. Coming to grips with the bond was simple and martial arts experience helped maneuvering, but the most advanced riders were racing specialists, old hands at this kind of racing. While their actual capabilities weren't any more impressive, their grasp on the movements that the Ralkors excelled at was much more refined. I took a moment to study, learning more about the bodies of the animals we were riding as I watched the dizzying arrays of kicks and slashes from these veteran racers.

Abel, of course, managed to pull ahead just fine without any of those considerations, his spatial awareness monstrous even without using Skills. Mel was doing surprisingly well too, probably from her perception of Abel through a bond similar to what Callie and I shared. As we watched the attacks, Callie and I refined our own techniques, noting certain kinds of explosive movement that Ralkors seemed built for.

For instance, Ralkors were front-heavy, a fact they countered with extremely solid traction, but relied on to sprint faster. A forward flipping motion that whipped the legs up over the heads and down on the enemy was extremely suitable for their physiology. After a glance at Callie, we decided to try a variation of that. I grabbed her hand, and she pushed her Ralkor to flip up over me. I swung her as she traveled along the arc of my extended arm, ramping up the speed to deliver a brutal overhead slash to the pair of Ralkor riders in front of us.

The two were so distracted trying to outdo each other that they missed the attack until it was too late, and both of their backs were slashed open. With cries of pain, the two split, falling back to treat their wounds and being overtaken and passed by the pack within seconds.

It was notable that no one in this little race actually attacked the Ralkors. I personally avoided it because they were just racing animals and didn't deserve to be hurt, but I somehow doubted the people of Doomtown were nice enough to keep that in mind. If I had to guess, the Lanes had a rule about it. That gave us a distinct advantage, because due to our armor, the Ralkors couldn't do much harm to us.

With those two dealt with, we picked up the pace, pushing Callie's mount for just that little bit of extra speed. I was able to keep pace, but she'd managed to eke out a little more momentum, and we slowly closed on the mad scramble of battling Ralkors at the front. I'd lost track of how many laps remained on this long track, but I knew one thing: we were catching up.

Despite our advancing, we still needed to break through the line of battling Ralkors with advanced riders. Even Abel and Mel seemed to be stuck, as they'd run into a pack of five riders who worked with shocking coordination to repel them. I supposed Abel wasn't invincible after all. I was jarred from that realization by a feeling of alarm from my bond with Callie, and barely managed to weave to the side to barely avoid a vicious slash aimed at my throat.

Mordaunt laughed happily as her Ralkor pirouetted through the air, claws flashing right by me and actually scraping across my mask as I leaned back, though not doing any damage. I felt more than saw Callie lunge for her in

325

retaliation, only for her to be intercepted by the hulking form of Rahm on a massive black-scaled Ralkor, interposing himself between my girlfriend and his mistress. I cursed as the two of them broke past us to surge into the midst of the pack of frontrunners.

Slowing down to meet up with Callie, we exchanged a few hand gestures, and got a few in response, glad once again that we'd decided to refine our communication during all that practice. Honestly I suspected the hand signals were much less effective than they seemed, and at least some of the understanding we developed of each other was just intuition that came as a precursor to developing the Paired Dueling Skill.

Looking ahead, I glared at the crowd of Ralkors. I had no idea how to get past them, or if we even could. If we leapfrogged as far ahead as we could, those frontrunners would just catch up and pick us off. Skills were not an option right now. Abel had mentioned they had ways of detecting that. I scoured my brain for something, *anything* that would let me break through the line.

At this point, I didn't even care about winning. I just wanted to beat Mordaunt. That attack had pissed me off. Armor or not, it had been way too dangerous for a friendly race. Something was seriously wrong with that girl. She could've put my eye out, not to mention slitting my throat.

Finally, I had an idea. I had no chance at winning this. There was, however, a gap between the pack of frontrunners and the very best who were leading the charge.

I shot Callie a look and a few gestures, and she grinned back at me. She drifted out in front as I slowed down, and with no hesitation, I steered my Ralkor to jump onto her shoulders. With a single powerful leap, her Ralkor hurled itself up about twenty feet, and I had my own Ralkor jump as hard as it could using her shoulders as a platform. As I sailed over the battling crowd to land between them and the frontrunners, I had a good laugh. Mordaunt didn't seem nearly as amused now.

Chapter Sixty-Four

As EXPECTED, I didn't win the race, but I did beat Mordaunt. Her glare when the big leap happened was incredibly brief, so quick I almost missed it, but she was definitely pissed.

By the time she met up with us past the finish line, though, she was all smiles. "Wow, that was an interesting race. Wasn't it, Rahm?"

Rahm, who, as far as I'd heard, didn't ever really speak, just grunted. I didn't think the big zombie was stupid. He moved like someone with a brain, careful and deliberate. Even so, he wasn't exactly a stellar conversationalist, and Mordaunt seemed to use him as more of a set piece for her own chattering than anything else.

As we all made our way over to the pens near the smaller track to check on the wolves, I said, "So, only two more days or so until the auction. Anything special you plan to pick up there?"

Her eyes danced with amusement as she glanced at me slyly. "Actually, I'm more interested in selling. I stumbled on a great find here that one of our regular trading partners will be pretty excited about. I couldn't believe my luck. How about you? Anything specific you plan to look for there?" Once again I got bad vibes from the woman for no provable reason, and it mostly seemed to be just me.

With an internal sigh, I ceded the conversation to Callie while I moved to put some space between me and the Darkling Institute ringer. To take my mind off things, I took up a position next to the pen where the wolves were playing, and I had to admit, watching them definitely helped.

Jin and Rellia were having a blast. Ralkors were dangerous, scary beasties, but the younger ones hadn't grown into their claws and beaks yet. If I had to guess, the teen Ralkors were more like H-rank than G. Despite that, there were dozens of them, and they definitely exhibited herdlike behavior. The wolves were happy being chased down by the smaller birds that were unable to hurt them at all.

The mocking chuffs of the big wolves as they darted past and the enraged squawks of the Ralkors made for an amusing picture as they led the things on a merry chase. Abel chuckled as he stepped up beside me, drawing away from where the rest of the group was chatting with Mordaunt. "They certainly seem to be having a blast. I admit, I didn't expect them to enjoy it quite so much. I figured the birds wouldn't be able to do much damage to the pack with their numbers, but leading them around like this… They're stronger now than when you first got them, aren't they?"

I shrugged. "Probably? Honestly I don't know. It's not like we can check their stats. Jessie tops them up with her life force when she has any to spare, and her ability mentioned long-term effects, so I think so? They certainly seem to be getting smarter. To be fair, though, they've also been following us around, so it's possible they got some renown rollover. I wonder if they'll hit F-rank soon?"

Abel laughed. "Not that soon. Did you forget my lesson at the Bay? There's variation in the feel of Impact at the same level. I'd put them at maybe three-quarters of the way to F-rank, but then again, they were already probably halfway there when you got them. It'll be a while, I bet." He stood beside me, watching with amusement, until eventually he said, "Something going on, kid? You seem off."

It surprised me that he'd picked up on it, honestly. Callie hadn't even noticed. Granted, our bond wasn't really empathy so much as intention, and usually worked better during combat, but I'd assumed that meant I was keeping my discomfort to myself pretty well.

I focused on my stealth Skill, resonating with it as I spoke to hide my words from prying ears. With my current Perception, it was easy enough to wipe all traces of the sound once it reached him. "Mordaunt. She gives me a weird feeling. Like she's laughing at us. Is that just me?"

That got a shrug. "I don't really trust anyone I work with except Mel, kid. You and Nightstrike are exceptions, I suppose. But this is the WCP. People being suspicious or willing to fuck you over is par for the course. I think the Unity has you all spoiled. There are no eternal friendships, only eternal benefits." He paused. "Though… maybe I'm just a cynic. Your little gang seems pretty close. I could just be jaded after so long."

Snorting out a laugh, I turned to him with amusement. "That's it? That's your advice? 'Don't worry if she's out to get you because everyone is out to get you'? Thanks, man, that's real fucking helpful."

Despite my sarcasm, it actually *did* help. Knowing that Abel didn't trust her made me feel better. Pulling one over on me wasn't that big an accomplishment, but pulling one over on him would be.

Besides, Doomtown was limited admission. Low F-rank and G-rank only. As long as that was the case, I wasn't worried about us being overwhelmed. I could figure something out as long as we didn't get killed instantly. With our armor, we would be fine for a bit, and with Abel and Mel backing us up, not to mention our new Paired Dueling Skill, I was genuinely confident we could take on anyone.

With a chuckle, Abel clapped me on the shoulder. "Come on, kid, let's get out of here. Now that that auction's coming up, I think we should head back up topside for this last day of the week. We need to gather resources anyway, and we can pick up those two friends of yours and bring them with us. We can bring Alden with to help watch out for them, but they can probably pick up some useful items that'll help with their growth."

I nodded, whistling for the puppies. They seemed hesitant, but broke from the pack of young Ralkors easily enough, loping over to easily hop the fence. As for bringing Benny and Jessie, I agreed. I missed my friends, and I wanted them to see Doomtown. Escape wishes could be prepared for them just in case, and that should prevent anything bad from happening (not to mention Jessie's giant-ass F-ranked bear). This would be an opportunity for them to gain some rep, too. I was curious to see how they'd grown when we were away. They weren't the types to just loaf around while we were training.

Callie, meanwhile, had been talking to Mordaunt for a bit, and when I came back, she shot me a questioning look. I snagged her up in a hug and spun her around, drawing a surprised giggle, and then set her down, leaving an arm around her shoulders. "What's the occasion?" she said in amusement. Despite the lightness and happiness in her tone, I could see some concern in her eyes. I was affectionate most of the time, but this hug had been kind of out of nowhere.

I snickered, making sure my voice was as light and happy as hers. "Oh, nothing big, I was just talking to Apollyon about how much I was missing home. Figured we might take a break from the trip and go up for a visit." Mordaunt being around made me wary to say we needed to stockpile our cash and pick up our friends. It might have been stupid, but I felt like I needed a pretense to stop the necromancer from paying attention.

Amusingly, it actually seemed to work. Though her polite smile didn't waver, I could see a look of disdain in her eyes.

Once I'd started really looking, my Perception made finding evidence of her bad intentions a bit easier. I was pretty sure this was an aspect of my diviner class. Part of that particular powerset was a passive sense for intention, but I'd never seen any evidence I had that sense in real life. Now it seemed that my Perception just hadn't been high enough.

It was nice to see. My diviner class hadn't done much for me in a while, with Monk and Rogue doing the heavy lifting. Seek Hidden was extremely useful, but the diviner was fundamentally a support class, and most of its functions were geared towards Doom Sovereign itself. I didn't have a subskill for this yet, so there was nothing I could do to improve, but I should pick up Sense Intention as a codified active subskill once I ranked up DS Mastery.

Saying our goodbyes, we headed off to the Blue Robin to pick up the others. Sloane and the Beast Lord Garden initiates had come down with us, and it would be pretty rude to leave them alone. They weren't there when we arrived, so we decided to wait, and while we did, Callie dragged me into our room to question me.

"Okay," she said plainly. "What's up? That wasn't really like you, and you were twitchy most of today. Is everything alright?"

I didn't really have an explanation, but after figuring out my bad feeling was my diviner sense at work, I felt much better about talking it out. I told her about what I'd noticed, the bad impression I'd had, and Abel's unhelpful advice. Then I told her about his idea to have Benny and Jessie come down, and why I thought we should allow it. In the end, Callie would make the call on this, but she took my advice into account, and once I explained myself, she seemed open to it.

More than that, she seemed sympathetic. She reached up to pull off my mask, going up on her toes and pulling me down for a quick kiss. "Hey. You always support me when I feel like doing something. If she gives you the creeps, I'll keep an eye out. I trust your judgement. It's not like I have some big attachment to her anyway. She's interesting, but she isn't exactly a close friend. If you want, I can talk to Uncle Alex, see if maybe he can spare a few low F-rankers from his faction to tag along to the auction just in case? I agree we can't miss it and it'll be good for Benny and Jessie, but some more firepower couldn't hurt. Plus, I'm sure he'll want to snag some of that stuff for himself."

I let out a breath I'd been unconsciously holding. Knowing she believed me without blinking and came up with a solution nearly instantly made me feel better right away. It was a good solution too, but I wasn't sure we could manage it.

"Is that an option? I said. "I mean, it's pretty last-minute, and F-rankers don't exactly grow on trees. Does he even have any that are allowed in Doomtown?"

She said, "I don't know. Can't hurt to ask. Plus, I think that we've only seen the tip of the iceberg when it comes to the E-ranked factions. Considering what we know about the dark districts, not to mention we've never even been to F district, I have to assume we haven't seen most of their forces. Not everyone can be hanging out in the headquarters, otherwise how could the factions operate."

That was fair. Beast Lord Garden was the busiest of the E-ranked factions we'd visited, but I knew they'd been able to pull a bunch of elite G-rank youngsters out of nowhere to follow Sloane and join the tournament.

With that decided, Callie spun up her scan ring and shot her uncle a message. Sure enough, he'd heard about the auction and was already planning to send some people along. He agreed for them to follow us in disguise in case we needed an ace in the hole. Knowing that made me feel so much better.

Once Sloane and the others got back, we were officially on our way back up to G district. It would be nice to see everyone again. I had so much I wanted to tell them.

Chapter Sixty-Five

BEING BACK in the Pavilion was like walking out of the heat into a cool familiar house. I hadn't even noticed the shift in tension brought by Doomtown. Even when I was enjoying myself, I'd been actively on the lookout for traps or murder attempts. Up here in G-district, I could finally let down my guard and relax.

The first thing I did when I returned was see my best friend. Callie came along, and to my shock, Benny was actually at the Pavilion instead of at the Academy with Celine. To my even bigger shock, he was currently running the obstacle course, or at least about to finish it. I'd missed most of the actual run. Judging by his combat standards against the golems, he had been putting in a ton of work, too.

Callie and I came over to stand next to Alden and Jessie as they watched, letting out a low whistle. "Wow," I said, "someone made some big leaps."

Despite not having gained many stats in the week we were gone, Benny's integration of the abilities that his artifacts gave him was exponentially more polished. His density shifting, both lower and higher, had been trained diligently. He appeared to be able to extend the effects of his enhancements to his whole body now, using them as comprehensive Skills. He had to concentrate hard to do it, and it was clearly taxing, but it allowed him to contend with much stronger opponents.

Alden chuckled. "Aye. Been putting him through his paces. He still sneaks off to see that lass of his now and then, thinks I don't notice, but a bit of downtime isn't doing any harm. Still, he's been training like the devil is on his tail." He shot a fond look at Jessie. "And this little miss hasn't been far short of that, though I admit I see less of it, since she trains so much up at the fancy E-ranked faction building. Us lowly G-rankers aren't good enough, I suppose."

Our perky blonde-haired teammate didn't even bother to respond to him. She got so excited when she saw us she launched herself off the bench, catching Callie mid-stomach in a tackle hug. I suspect she picked Callie because she was closest, and because trying to tackle both of us would be nigh impossible given the height difference. "You're back!" She squealed so loudly I thought she might shatter glass. "I'm so glad to see you!"

I laughed and reached down to ruffle her hair, since she was already engaged in a hug. She huffed at me, blowing some of it out of her eyes so she could fix me with an emerald glare. "Stop that. Jerk." She climbed off Callie, gave me a light shove, and then plopped back down next to Alden. "Also, shut up, I so didn't do that. Randall just doesn't like training here. Can you blame him?"

He shrugged, conceding the point. "You lot are back early. You finish that training so soon?" His tone was casual, but I saw a hint of shock on his face. Considering the Paired Dueling training was passed down to Abel and Mel by Alden, he would know how it worked. What I wondered was where he'd learned about it. Though obviously adapted for the local environment, this whole training regimen had the feeling of a systematic teaching tool. Things like that were supposed to be important assets to bigger forces.

Had Alden been a member of some big sect or group? Had *he* had a partner at one point? I was deathly curious, but that all seemed like personal stuff that might be painful to talk about.

So instead of saying all that, I just smirked and said, "Yeah, we got the Skill a few days ago. But we're not really done. We came to pick up some things. There's a big auction, and we're going to try to buy up some training resources. We want to make sure the Pavilion can keep pumping out strong elites."

This time it was his turn to whistle. "Not bad, you two. That's damn fast.

Still, fits with the two of you. Always been a bit quick on the uptake, least since I've known you."

I smiled and nodded my thanks at the compliment. Alden had trained Abel, so him being impressed was an honor.

"So, how much has he improved?" Callie asked, flopping onto the bench next to Jessie. "I can tell he's a lot smoother with his ability. I assume that's a result of building soul strength? Using those abilities as Skills must be tough for him. How did he manage to grow so fast?" That was a good point. Soul strength training was slow and incredibly difficult to manage. It was basically just "work until your head hurts, then stop and recover."

Alden grinned. "He's been working on some new inventions since you left. Threw everything but the kitchen sink together, and finally came out with something useful. He built a spiritual calming belt. They help the soul recover faster. They're extremely rare, even lower-tier versions. Once he integrated that, he increased his Skill training tenfold. He's been progressing quite quickly. Sadly the belt is too low-tier to be effective long-term. Once he catches up with Solomon, I'm guessing he'll slow down."

Still, though. It had given him a terrifying new ability. And I knew how much it sucked recovering from excessive soul weight. Even a bit of recovery would help in the future, no matter what tier it was. Benny's refined integration had absurd potential. Even items of limited use would be helpful if used like a part of you. He'd catch up much faster with that power, and I was glad to hear he'd found something so useful. We'd need to help Jessie learn to train her soul too. Based on what I'd been told, it seemed like it was almost necessary to advance past E-rank.

We waited a bit for Benny to finish his fight before he headed over to where we were sitting. He had originally been jogging, but when he noticed Callie and I, he bolted over. "You're back! How was the dark district? See any cool stuff? Bring me any souvenirs? I accept tribute in the form of food, clothes, and expensive inventing materials." He paused. "Though not necessarily in that order."

I snorted. "Amateur. Why bring you souvenirs when we can bring you to the dark district? We came back to drag you down there in person." Also, I hadn't considered buying souvenirs, which I kind of felt bad about now. Not that I would admit that even on pain of death.

Benny was momentarily derailed from our banter. "Wait... really? I thought it was super dangerous down there and all that? Aren't you worried about us getting killed down there? Because I was joking about needing new stuff. I can definitely wait on inventing materials if it means I don't have to die."

Callie cut in. "No. I have a plan for that. We both do, actually." She bumped me with her shoulder. "Solomon has an idea for keeping us all safe, and on top of that... well, I won't talk about my plan here. The walls have ears and all that. Suffice to say there's a big event down there we don't want either of you to miss. On the upside, Agria, you can take Randall for a walk, finally."

I had to smother a laugh at the idea of the giant F-ranked bear coming with us. Still, he would give Jessie plenty of security, especially with the F-rankers we were going to request from Alexander.

That actually gave me an idea. "Agria, do you have a beast bonding Skill?" I'd never heard Jessie mention anything like the bonds with the Ralkors, but if there was a permanent version of that, something like to our Paired Dueling Skill, it would make Jessie infinitely safer.

She seemed surprised I'd even heard of it. "Not even close. Those Skills take forever to develop. I'm pretty sure the Beast Queen has one, and a fairly high-level one too. I know you can synergize them with your ability to make some interesting powers, though I won't be doing that." She didn't say why, and didn't need to. Everyone here was well aware of her long-term goals in regards to her healing ability.

Still, that seemed odd to me. "It takes that long? I'd figure with how taming works, it would be pretty easy for you to form a bond." Even easier than for Callie and I, though I was starting to think I'd cheated with the overlay somehow, based on how everyone was reacting.

"The opposite," Jessie said firmly. "Bonds require a deep understanding and connection. Animals don't think like people, so it's harder to make that connection to begin with. Beast Taming just teaches you how to train an animal and teach them certain behaviors. It doesn't turn them into part-ners. Bonding is also usually permanent. Tamers often find new beasts, but a bonded companion is rarely tossed aside."

That was an interesting thing to note. I also saw Callie blushing furiously under her mask at that last bit, which made me grin. Not that we couldn't feel how closely we were connected, but hearing it out loud like that was kind of intense.

Benny, to my delight, seemed to catch on to what I'd been insinuating, and pulled Jessie aside to talk to her about wishing for a bond with Randall. Since I hadn't told her to do it myself, my own bias wouldn't mess with the pricing so much. Plus, I could always use more heals.

While Callie caught up with Jessie, I pulled Benny aside to check on him. "Hey, you okay, man? Heard you've been working yourself pretty hard. Impressive you managed to rig up a spiritual calming belt, but don't run yourself into the ground, okay? We're planning to help you two catch up before the end of the tournament so we can bring you with us into the Moonsong Glade. You've got plenty of time to train."

Benny shook his head. "You don't get it. You and Callie are pulling farther and farther ahead. I've been making sure to spend time with Cel so she doesn't feel ignored, but other than that… we're in this together, man. I can't let you leave me behind. We might be able to use wishes to get our stats filled out, but the Pavilion has shown us there's way more to combat than that. It's not just me either, Jessie has been training harder than she lets on."

That was… touching? Worrying? I didn't know. But it wasn't my place to tell them what to do. It wasn't even really Callie's, group leader or not.

"Alright, but just remember that you don't need to overdo it. You both bring other things to the team. That spiritual calming belt proves your Inventing must be getting better, right? No way that thing is less than G-rank. Did you get Inventing to Intermediate?"

He grinned at me widely. "Yup. I haven't been slacking as much as you thought the past few months. Even when I was at the Academy I was usually working. The hardest part was keeping financially solvent while I worked."

Which reminded me. "Speaking of finances, we're also here to stock up on chits. Not sure how much we have in the coffers, but I know Abel and Mel are planning to toss their own cash into the pot. With all of us, we should be able to afford some pretty good stuff."

Eager to see what exactly we had to work with, Benny and I headed over to talk to Abel and Mel. After we finalized that, we just needed to wait for the reinforcements Alexander was sending (hopefully), and then we would be ready to head back down. Though we might be able to take the evening off too. Would be nice to have some downtime before the big show.

Chapter Sixty-Six

WE DIDN'T HEAR BACK from Alexander until the next day. Since we had one more day before the auction, I let the Beast Lord Initiates do another full five wishes to preload some more days for later. I'd have to work out some kind of arrangement for after I left. I managed to get the points in Might this time, which was nice, and put me at 919 points total.

When the F-rankers arrived in the morning, I left the five wishes for that day unused, ready for the emergency escape wishes my friends would need, and went to greet them with the others. I'd been curious what Alexander would manage to put together for his niece, if anything, but I was shocked to see four fresh F-rank elites waiting for us at the Pavilion when we woke up (we slept in the spare rooms that Mel used when she worked overnight), all looking ready for a fight.

The four people that Alexander sent were... weird. They all wore black robes and masks, and seemed pretty much indistinguishable from each other. Not just at a surface level, either. Their actual conceptual weight was basically identical. Only one of them ever spoke at a time, but which one it was changed sentence to sentence, with seemingly no communication among themselves to decide whose turn it was.

When we arrived, all four of the figures bowed to Callie. "Young mistress," said one. "The Nothing sends his greetings," said another. "We are the four as one. Though only recently having reached F-rank, we are powerful for our tier. We will be your guardians on this mission," a third said. It was functionally impossible to tell their voices apart.

Abel whistled. "Quadruplets, I'm guessing. And they probably cultivate as a group. It's tricky to pull that off. Makes it much harder to accumulate individual stat points. Still, I bet they have some variation of the Paired Dueling Skill that works for all four of them. Sucks for them they're already F-ranked. They would have been a hell of a team in the tournament. Still, I see why they were available to take us down there. They're going to be at early F-rank for quite a while, having to share all the renown like that."

One of the four nodded. "You are correct." Another spoke up. "Still, we do not feel displeased. We can be of use to the Nothing—this is our honor." I raised an eyebrow at that, but didn't comment. I imagined training quadruplet Ascendants would be extremely taxing. Alexander must have invested a ton into their development, in time if not resources. It made sense they would be grateful.

Mel cleared her throat. "As... nice... as this all is, we still have to discuss our resource allocation for this. We've cobbled together a total of three E-ranked chits for this auction, with a few F-ranked left over. That's not a small amount by any means, but some of the visiting factions will have just as much if not more. We should expect that we'll end up using all of our money on two or three big-ticket items. We might be able to afford some smaller stuff like armor and weapons too, but we need to decide what we're aiming for, at least in general terms."

I looked over to Callie, who nodded. "I've been considering that. We know we want a blank Skill Crystal. G-ranked if possible so I can imprint a Beginner Skill on it. If we can get our hands on something that can increase soul restoration like Clockwork's belt, that would be good too. Hopefully something that works on an area rather than an individual. Other than those priorities, we should just pick up anything we can find that can help multiple people improve. Maybe a few useful Skills, if they pop up."

We'd been looking into faction building since we took over the Pavilion, but at our rank, there really wasn't much you could do to improve the foundation of so many people at once. Soul strength, as we had learned recently, was important, so having a way to replenish that for training would be huge, but other than that and buying Skills like Callie said, pills were the only real option, and those were of course limited by the elixir limit at each tier.

The only bright spot was that while there weren't too many options right now, any results we saw would bring prestige to the Pavilion itself, and as members, our people would benefit. Once more people heard about the Pavilion, wearing its symbol and being a known member would add reputation to those who worked under us. It would turn into a feedback loop.

That was why factions were so ubiquitous on Callus, and pretty much everywhere else. Any possible way to squeeze out a bit of extra rep was necessary. Honestly I'd been surprised by the way the cultivation worked when I'd first heard of it. I'd expected more politics and PR. But the fact was, people cultivated for power, and *showing* that power was what they did to prove the results of that cultivation.

Directly demonstrating power was the easiest way to cut through the bullshit. Branding and PR were important, as we saw from the Academy, but when there were people blowing up cars and hurling fireballs in the streets, it was much less impressive to *hear* about someone doing that. Stories and rumors still influenced growth of course, but not as much as getting out and showing tangible evidence of what you could do. Especially since those feats spawned stories and rumors of their own anyway.

After Callie finished her list, Mel took a minute to think before nodding. "We might be able to get a bulk price on some pills, too. Our people haven't hit their limits on elixirs, for the most part. The way we used to run things, we prioritized combat strength over everything. I still think that's the way to go, but if we're pushing for active expansion, a marked improvement in a large number of people in a short time would be best. With the Beast Lord Garden backing us, we won't have to worry about standing out and getting smacked down."

I hadn't considered before why the Pavilion wasn't more well-known. Granted, Abel had been away, but Alden had trained both him and Mel, so logically he should have been able to train more powerful Ascendants. Even if they didn't reach the same level, they should have been pretty strong. Instead, it had been a small regional force in the Cavalcade that no one outside the circus had heard of.

Thinking about the whole mess with the deed and the attack from Sanctuary Hall, though, it was pretty dangerous to stick out in the WCP without some kind of background, even in G district. That was easy to see when you took into account how quickly things escalated once Burning Fist and the Peace Lord became involved.

"Alright," I said. "Agria, Nightstrike, Clockwork, I had some things I wanted to talk to you about if you have a second." I'd expected to wait longer before we left, but if we were heading back down soon, we should go ahead and deal with the escape wishes.

When they followed me over, I didn't need to say anything to them. They already knew about the escape wishes from before, so the three of them naturally didn't need to be reminded.

Each of them made a wish to be able to escape from Doomtown if they were put in mortal danger, and I granted them all. Given how much power was needed, I had to take five of each attack before I could grant the wishes. Since I was at my full ten after only two attacks from Callie and Benny and three from Jessie, we settled on a geas that they would let me store attacks as I used them up. I felt better having topped up my heal bursts, and those density-shifted triple-strength attacks were damn useful, so it wasn't a bad deal for me.

Once that was done, Benny and Callie headed back over to join the others, but when I moved to follow them, Jessie grabbed my arm. "Hey Shane, hang on a second." I turned to cock my head at my tiny blonde teammate. "I was hoping we could try a wish. Specifically I was hoping to wish for a Beginner-Level Beast Bonding Skill with Randall as my bonded beast. I can pay with another... let's say twenty-five heal bursts added onto my tab."

Wish detected. Grant wish?

I confirmed, interested to see the cost.

Stat points sufficient. Requirements: 36 Impact, 450 Perception, 444 Focus, 540 Fantasy.

I blinked. Fantasy wasn't what I'd have expected, but Perception and Focus both made sense. Actually, now that I considered it Fantasy did too. Given the way the fate sense worked, Fantasy clearly had a sensory component.

Since the message didn't mention requiring compensation, I supposed the payment was enough.

"I can do it," I said slowly. "But are you sure? Wishes scale in difficulty, and not just to grant. Beginner Skills are *extremely* painful to receive. I'm not

342

saying you can't survive it or something like that, but it's going to be agonizing. You sure you don't want to wish for a lower level of this Skill and work your way up?" I knew it was unfair to Jessie to worry like that, but I couldn't help it. Callie was tough as nails, and despite that, she'd been devastated by receiving her Beginner Shadow Manipulation Mastery Skill.

Jessie just stared at me, eyes hard and stance firm.

I sighed and nodded. "Alright. Go get Randall. Having him here for this will be necessary. He should be waiting outside for the trip, right?"

She nodded and lit up, racing off to fetch her companion. I was pretty sure if he was here, he could take some of the pain. Truth be told, though, that wasn't the main reason he had to be present. He actually did need to give permission at least, since he'd be gaining a Skill too.

It also occurred to me that this was the first time someone had wished for a paired Skill, and she'd paid for it all by herself. No wonder the damn Skill had been so expensive.

I also knew that Beginner Skills from my wish power gave a better foundation for advancement. While Intermediate Skills weren't viable to wish for without fucking up your advancement, my teammates could still wish for Beginner versions of new Skills they wanted to acquire later in our journey.

When she came back with the bear, I led them both off where the four wouldn't see me granting this wish. A big electrified giant bear was bound to be eye-catching. Once there, Jessie explained what was going to happen to Randall, using her vital energy to convey the messages more easily. Randall didn't mind, and actually seemed excited, despite being warned of the pain.

I briefly considered Jessie's lifeweaver ability, and how consistent infusion of life energy could alter an animal. I wondered how this bond would work out for them? Regardless, I'd been paid and the excuses were out of the way. As I let the electricity build across my skin, I reached out and placed either hand on Jessie and Randall, closing my eyes as I allowed the wish to wash over them both, infusing the Skill into their brains. As they choked back screams, I winced, but forced myself to persevere. This would definitely make them much safer in Doomtown.

Chapter Sixty-Seven

WITH ONE WISH remaining for the day, I was still feeling pretty secure as we headed back down to Doomtown. Benny spoke as we walked. "Tell me about this place. What did you all do for the last week? I hope this wasn't some excuse for a second vacation, because if I was training my ass off while you were lounging on a beach somewhere, I'm going to be pretty pissed."

I cracked up at the beach remark, because we'd gone to the beach twice, and could have died both times. "Yes to the beach, no to the lounging. We spent most of the time down here either fighting or doing crazy training exercises that would have probably killed anyone else. Still, we've gotten a lot stronger. You'll see when we take part in the tournament. Speaking of stronger, Agria, how you doing over there?" I shouted over to Jessie. She was seated on Randall's back, swaying slightly as he walked.

She shook her head hard, noticing us seemingly for the first time. "Huh? Oh, sorry... this is... intense. I felt some level of connection with my ravens during the scavenger hunt, but this feels like... more. I feel stronger now, or at least able to draw on more strength. I think my Might will increase over time. Plus, my life energy is pouring through the link. It feels like Randall is constantly being infused and growing too, though *very* slowly."

I'd considered that possibility, but she made it sound more impressive than I expected. Having a way to get stronger like that was amazing. "You think he'll get to E-rank eventually?" That would be astounding. This Skill was only at the Beginner level, and being able to make her companion rank up passively as it improved would be *huge*.

Jessie just giggled. "Gods, no. At least not anytime soon. There's a huge gap between ranks. Randall's Vitality will slowly rise over time, but unless I break through to F-rank and rank up the bond, there's no way it'll get that far. Still, the effects will get more impressive as I get stronger. This is amazing—it'll definitely cover for my specializing in healing."

"How is it so strong? Gradual growth without training is crazy." I couldn't hide the shock and slight envy in my voice. She'd gotten insanely lucky. "I mean, I'm glad you're getting so much out of it, but still, I can't believe a Beginner Skill gives so much benefit."

She laughed again. "It's resonance between the bond and my ability. They're extremely compatible. I could probably synergize them at my next rank up if I wanted, but I'm staying focused on healing, personally. Randall will handle the attack and defense stuff. Plus, it's less impressive than it sounds. Randall will grow *so* slowly, probably slower than he would with just regular exposure to people, and my Might won't ever get higher than his, and probably won't even catch up."

Knowing there were limits helped a bit, but still, Jessie was going to benefit from this a ton. Her lifeweaver ability offered amazing utility. It was shockingly powerful for our rank. I knew if her Vitality hadn't been so overwhelmingly high, she never would have gotten such an overpowered ability, but it was still staggering. Surely someone had studied what combinations of Skills and stats unlocked what, but I doubted anyone had managed to synergize Jessie's exact Skills with such a high percentage of Vitality.

It made some sense that the Skill would be so strong, though. The combined effects of her having frightening amounts of Vitality to fuel it and her ability being almost exclusively based on that one stat harmonized to create a limited but monstrous power. With Randall to cover for her one weakness in the form of low battle potential, there was no telling how far Jessie could go, especially with me here to keep funneling Vitality points to her. If she wanted to resurrect her brother, I suspected she was definitely headed in the right direction.

Benny, meanwhile, looked exasperated. "I should have waited before I wished for my ability. Oh well, doesn't matter. With my Inventing at Intermediate, I can begin to steer the basic direction I want my created objects to go in. Not by much, but I can at least decide on a general vibe. I might not have Agria's overpowered ability, but my own is only limited by the fantastic items I can make. I won't let the rest of you leave me in the dust."

Personally, I was pretty sure that strengthening his soul would be far more important than the raw stats Jessie was accruing, but he'd figure that out on his own eventually. I'd seen huge dividends from my soul strengthening over time, and definitely planned to get a belt like Benny's if I could find one. It would be insanely useful for me, even if not quite as useful as it was for my friend.

We kept talking about subjects like that as we walked, discussing how they might improve, how we had already improved, and where we might go as a group in the future. The Moonsong Glade would be a huge opportunity for all of us, especially Jessie, considering some of the animals we were bound to come across there.

Randall being her bonded companion didn't mean she couldn't still tame beasts. Lily was still trailing behind her mistress, and Rolf was playing with Rellia and Jin as we walked. The wolves had been incredibly happy to see each other, though not as happy as they'd been to see Jessie, with her magical life force infused ear scritches. It was sweet to see all the puppies playing together.

In general, I was just happy to have the team back together. I loved spending time alone with Callie, but being in combat and going on adventures without the whole gang just felt kind of wrong. Being down here with everyone was much more fun.

Sadly we had to stop talking about the bond pretty quickly, since Sloane came over to chat with Jessie. My Stealth Skill had a huge workout when I discussed almost anything, given all my secrets, I had to constantly make sure not to be overheard.

Still, Sloane was very excited to see Jessie. The two of them were close, having trained together often in the Beast Lord Garden, especially while Callie and I had been doing our months of training with Abel and Mel.

We headed back to the Blue Robin when we reached Doomtown. We hadn't actually checked out, just missed a night sleeping there, so we still had our rooms, and Sydney, Megan, Wren, and Vector were all there when we arrived to say hello. Wren was the first to notice us as we came into the main room. "Hey, there you are! Didn't see you all yesterday. Looks like you picked up some strays."

I shrugged. "They followed us home. We were going to tell them to beat it, but she has a giant bear, which is pretty cool, so we figured we'd be nice."

Benny rolled his eyes and smacked me upside the back of the head, not that I even felt it through my hood.

I plopped down at the table with them, gesturing for the others to pull up some chairs. "So, where's Lament? She and Master Saiten getting ready for the big auction?"

Wren snorted. "They're meeting with Falken, he finally showed up. We've been waiting for that lazy moron for months now. He's almost as strong as Lament, though, so he does what he wants, which admittedly is usually sleep. As for Master Saiten, sadly he can't come. The local forces made an exception for him to come down here and guard Lament out of respect for her status as a Master Candidate, but even that won't convince them to let an E-ranker attend an auction."

I grimaced, but nodded. I could see it. It would be impossible for that to happen fairly. Granted, there would be external factors in any auction, but since everyone in the auction house would be low F-rank max, Master Saiten could literally do whatever he wanted. Even if he was too honorable to actually do that (which I had no way of confirming), the other people at the auction would take a step back to avoid pissing him off just in case.

Wren seemed to know what I was thinking. "Yeah, he would compromise the proceedings. Still, he's pretty pissed about having to miss it, and he would probably have forbidden the two of them from going if the others attending were capable of harming them. Plus, neither of them listens particularly well, even to him." He snickered at the older Ascendant's misfortune. "You know how Lament is."

I'd known Lament for like a couple of days and yes, I knew how Lament was. I didn't even need to question if she would ignore someone because she felt like it.

Jessie, who had been forced to leave Randall outside, held out a hand to Wren. "Hi there, I'm Agria, since Solomon forgot to introduce me. That's

347

Clockwork over there. We're members of his team, though not for the tournament itself."

That startled a laugh out of the big spearman, who took her hand and shook it firmly. "You're the one with the bear? Or was that a joke? Because I would love to see a giant bear. I'm Wren, by the way, that's Vector." He nodded to his traveling companion.

"I do have a giant bear!" Jessie chirped excitedly. "His name is Randall! Do you want to meet him?" She turned her head to Vector. "Nice to meet you, by the way. You two as well." The last was aimed at Megan and Sydney, and the two rabbit-eared girls smiled back at her warmly.

They'd been staying out of our banter, but after being addressed directly, Megan spoke up. "You too. And I'm with big and stabby over there, I'd love to meet a giant bear." She tapped her sister in the ribs with her elbow. "How about you, Syd? You've always been a big fan of animals. Want to meet a giant teddy?"

Sydney blushed at the obvious dig at her being childish, but she didn't say no, which won a laugh from all of us.

Callie rolled her eyes at me. "See what you do? We're back ten minutes and you're introducing our secret weapons to the competition." Despite the criticism, her teasing tone made it clear she didn't really care. Jessie wasn't in the tournament anyway, so it hardly mattered.

Chatting happily, we all headed outside so the others could see Randall. The Blue Robin had a stable for mounts. They weren't incredibly common, but beast tamers *did* show up in the WCP from time to time and some of them rode on their beasts. Plus, they could repurpose the stable for other uses when there was no one in it, so it wasn't really a waste. It turned out that it was actually underground, which explained why I hadn't seen it when we first arrived.

Everyone fussed over Randall, who seemed much more docile after bonding, though he still had that same imperious air to him.

As we all talked about the upcoming auction, I considered again what might be coming. I still had a bad feeling about Mordaunt, who had invited us, but Callie had taken my worries seriously and we had four F-rankers who could probably fight twice their number, not to mention Abel, and probably Lament.

Whatever would happen tomorrow, I was confident we could handle it. All I could do now was enjoy a day of peace with my friends.

Chapter Sixty-Eight

THE REST of the day passed quickly, and at the end of the night, I gave my last wish to one of the Beast Lord Initiates. I got three points of Might, bringing me to an even 160. With that out of the way we set out to meet with the others and attend the auction. Lament was coming along with her partner Falken; Sydney and Megan were bringing Riley and the rest of their people; and we had the quadruplets with us, along with Benny and Jessie, Abel and Mel, Sloane, Beric, Croll, and the wolves. Even Randall was able to come, since apparently the auction house was fucking huge.

The auction house was a towering structure of black stone, standing out from its short and squat neighbors. Looking up at the massive facade of the building, with its dark columns and a pair of black stone lions perched out front, it was hard not to be impressed. I had to keep pushing my definition of "impressive" up a notch every time I saw something new down here.

Lament met us out front, and standing next to her was a tired looking guy with messy dark hair and dark circles around his brown eyes. He looked pale and kind of thin, but not in an unhealthy way, more in the way of someone who never goes out or does anything. He had a spear that he was leaning against like a staff, and his eyes were heavy-lidded like he was about to fall asleep. I could see what Wren meant about him usually being asleep. His demeanor just screamed laziness.

Mordaunt appeared beside us, Rahm at her heels, so quickly I almost didn't notice that she hadn't been there all along. "You're here!" She smiled broadly. "Oh, good, I was worried my guests wouldn't show up and that I would end up looking stupid. Wasn't I, Rahm?" The massive bandaged man didn't respond in any appreciable way, but Mordaunt nodded like he had. "Oh, and you brought more friends? Oh well, the more the merrier."

That set off alarm bells. I'd been pretty sure that this was a trap before, but that made me positive. Callie had explained to me when I told her my suspicions that an easy test would be bringing more people. Mordaunt had mentioned spots for the auction, and we'd clearly gone over what she'd implied she was allotted. The fact that she didn't even blink at that made it clear the slots had just been an excuse.

I could have brought the others in anyway, I was pretty sure, given my ties to the WCP, but this had been a good test. Now we knew for sure she was up to something, and to be on guard. Luckily, the four followers of the Nothing came with us, and they could be a huge asset in any fight. As I shot Callie a look, we followed Mordaunt as she led us in.

The inside of the place was even bigger, of course, and I was impressed by how fancy it was. Wall-to-wall black marble, with luxurious thick rugs and several large marble counters, behind which sat people in black-and-gold clothing that looked way nicer than pretty much anything else in Doom-town. "So." I scanned the workers. "How exactly is this place not constantly robbed? Because this looks like the kind of place where someone would break in and steal everything that isn't nailed down. And then steal the nails. Especially in a lawless shithole like a dark district."

Granted, we were near the Robin, and I knew this part of town was nicer and safer, but still, this whole thing seemed to rely on a preponderance of force.

Abel, of course, answered with a chuckle. "Because the WCP says not to. Don't forget where we are. This entire lawless area exists at the sufferance of the WCP leadership. If the bosses decided to clean this out, they could do it in an instant. The E-rankers have enough power to raze this whole district. It's happened before. Places like this are declared neutral areas and people listen, because they don't want to die."

That... hadn't occurred to me. I still had trouble viewing the WCP in the way that he was talking about, but it made sense. They were a powerful and terrifying organization, not just at a local level, but in general. The fact that they were strong enough to force the Unity to allow them to have a presence like this in the Conglomerate, when he was a literal god and this was his territory, was evidence enough of that.

My mentor stopped talking as he noticed someone nearby, and his eyes narrowed as he tensed up. I was shocked to see that. He wasn't the type to be worried about other people, especially not down here, but as his eyes focused on a tall, tanned man in worn clothing with a thick beard, his body seemed to shift unconsciously into a defensive stance.

"Shit," he said, heatedly. "Helix is here."

Helix was an Ascendant Owen had mentioned, one of the old Titan Twenty from Abel's day who'd gone slightly crazy in one of Mad Madigan's maze. I remembered that clearly because Abel had described him as "scary," which wasn't a description I'd heard him use for many things.

Megan cleared her throat. "Slime Hall is in attendance too." The Wave Warren ringer grimaced.

One by one, powerful people were noted. Some local, some not, some we'd heard of, some we hadn't. Rayka Vale, another of Abel and Mel's old competitors; Dread's daughter; an early F-ranker named Abomina; and the child of Screaming Stevie, who called himself the Wailing Win. As well as a few people we knew like Cold Snap and Macgregor. The place gradually filled with powerful Ascendants, and the combined weight of their Impact gave it a strange and worrying feel.

One of the workers, a man in a black-and-gold suit, stepped out from behind a counter. "Ladies and gentlemen. We will begin the auction in a few hours, once all the parties have arrived. Feel free to chat amongst yourselves, out here, or in the main auction room. There's also a side area where you may sell some of your less exotic wares to raise funds for the main event, should you feel it worthwhile. Please remember that the Walking Silence Auction is a peaceful affair, and any attempts to disrupt it will be met with harsh reprisals."

No one looked even remotely interested in trying anything like that, given the people guaranteeing the safety of this place. You'd need to be a member of the five-faction alliance to be willing to mess with the WCP, and none of them had a reason to try. Not for something this small and out of the way.

As he finished talking, he retreated behind the counter again, letting everyone mingle. Which is how we were approached by someone I hadn't expected to see.

Fisher, who had actually ridden his motorcycle into the auction house (which I guessed was fair, since Jessie had ridden a bear), rolled up to us. "You," he said faintly. "Members of the Academy. Wasn't expecting to see any others at this thing. We aren't exactly at the right level. Most of the Unity members here are the children of E-rankers."

He didn't say it like an accusation, or like he even cared that much. Just like a statement of fact, like he was telling us what the weather was like. Despite being fairly scary for a G-ranker, he struck me as kind of dull in some ways.

Callie, ever the politician, smiled and held out a hand. "We remember you too. I'm Nightstrike. This is Agria, Clockwork, and my boyfriend Solomon. It's nice to see a classmate here. Will you be taking part in the tournament?"

Because he seemed a *lot* stronger than he had during the scavenger hunt. It was frankly worrying how quickly he'd managed to advance. To be fair, he did have a hundred points of elixir potential to use, so that probably helped.

He gave a single sharp nod as an answer, and I had to fight a smile. This guy was not talkative. Seeming to have found what he wanted, he stared at us for a few seconds, then turned around and rode off without another word.

"Cool bike," said Abel conversationally. "Weird kid. But cool bike. You guys want to go and check out the market before the auction? I know we had certain things we needed to buy, but there are a few odds and ends we could probably pick up there. If nothing else, Clockwork may be able to find some more powerful items to use as materials." He sounded... guarded. In a way I hadn't ever heard from him before.

Still, it was a good idea, so we agreed, and headed off to the side area where the suited man had pointed us all when announcing things. We could see people setting up tables and stalls, some with furniture supplied by the auction and some with items they seemed to have brought with them.

I saw Mordaunt slip away, and resisted the urge to follow her. It was better to stay in a group, and trailing the Darkling Institute member en masse would draw attention I didn't want or need.

We looked around for a while, and didn't see too much. I managed to find an honest-to-gods space ring, but I couldn't justify buying it because it would have cost a chunk of our funds for this whole trip. Though I did manage to get a physically larger and much less spacious spatial belt pouch for the three F-ranked chits we had outside the auction funds. I suspected it would be well worth it when we got to the Moonsong Glade.

Other than that, we mostly just looked around, taking note of who was doing the best business and how much they were making, so we could see who we would be betting against. The whole affair had a feeling of tense unease to it. Nothing overt, everyone tried to play relaxed, but there was discomfort and worry bubbling under the surface. The puppies were the only ones who seemed not to care about the tension, with Jin and Rolf playing tag around the tables.

Surprisingly, Celine even showed up, though unlike Martin and Sarah, she had a dangerous-looking elf in leather armor at her side, a female F-ranker with purple hair and intense glacial blue eyes she introduced as Shana. They joined up with the group, with Shana shooting suspicious looks at the quadruplets and at Abel, obviously competent enough to tell that they were threats.

Finally, after a few hours, the man in the suit stepped back out, clearing his throat. "Attention! May I have your attention!" Everyone turned to look at him. "It is now time for the auction to begin. We expect everyone to take their seats in an orderly fashion. Once all the guests have been seated, we will begin the proceedings. Thank you." He turned and headed into the seat-filled auction room.

We all followed, slowly and deliberately, but trying our best to seem at ease. Despite that, I felt my stomach clench.

I didn't see Mordaunt anywhere.

I wasn't sure what was going on, but I suspected I wouldn't like it. At the very least, I hoped we'd get through the auction first. Once that was done, we could worry about the rest of this.

The question was, what *was* the rest of this? What could she do in a place like this? And why was I so worried, despite knowing how safe we should be?

Chapter Sixty-Nine

THE MAN IN THE SUIT, whose name we still hadn't been told, headed up onto the stage to wait patiently while everyone was seated. Then he cleared his throat, his voice somehow covering the entire room without going above a normal speaking tone. It cut through all the chatter, silencing everyone still talking. With a wide smile, the man said, "Welcome... to the Walking Silence Auction! I am your host and auctioneer, Selwyn Carridan."

He gestured to one side, where a pair of heavyset men in black and gold carried out a chest, setting it on a pedestal that had just risen from the stage. "Tonight, you will see many items. Some will be amazing, some macabre, some simply strange. Please remember to keep your seats, as well as your wits about you. And remember that the protection the auction house affords buyers will last until you leave this district, or for three hours after the auction. Whichever comes first. Past that point, the fate of your purchases lies only on your own shoulders."

That was actually much kinder than I had expected from the WCP. Then again, their reputation for business had always been sterling.

"Now," said Selwyn, moving on, "I will begin the auction with something enticing, but perhaps not nearly so intriguing as some of you may hope." He snapped his fingers, and the chest fell open, revealing a single, blue metal glove.

It was easy to feel that the glove was G-ranked, and on the higher end of that scale. "This is our first item up for bid: the hand of a Frost Knight. A powerful but slow-acting chill pervades this gauntlet. It isn't much use in combat, but is, happily enough, a perfect seal or container for powerful flame-based materials. providing excellent restraint for such energies when the artifact is wrapped in the fist."

He reached over and picked it up, slipping one hand into it, and snapped with the other one. One of the heavyset men stepped up and pulled out a bag, dumping a black and red stone that looked like a hot coal into his gloved hand. The stone, shockingly, was F-ranked, but when he closed his hand around it, there was only a long, low hiss as steam wafted up, before even that faded. All traces of the F-ranked stone vanished, and all I could see was a closed blue fist.

"We begin the bidding at one F-ranked chit. Proceed." He waved a hand and a dozen people began to bid. They'd clearly found some use for the thing.

To my surprise, I saw Cark stand up. Sage next to him. "Five F-ranked chits!" Apparently Burning Fist was bankrolling this trip, because I knew for a fact that was already nearing the limit of Cark's savings, and he seemed willing to keep going. With H-ranked chits being the primary currency standard here, each F-ranked chit was the equivalent of a hundred. For someone at Cark's level (or ours, honestly), it would have taken ages to gather that up in Rajak proper.

People started bidding in earnest, but Cark didn't back down, and eventually won the gauntlet for four E-ranked chits. I blanched a bit. I wasn't sure we were going to have enough to afford any of the things we wanted. Callie shot me a worried look.

At the very least, we had a chance. It was clear Cark had some important use for that glove, and a blank Skill Crystal at G-rank should be much less pressing, though many more people would want it. We could only hope that it came later in the program when people had wasted more of their money.

I wanted to go over and talk to Cark, but we were all stuck sitting down until the halfway point on the program. So I leaned in to whisper to Callie, using my Stealth Skill to erase the sound so no one eavesdropped. "Do you know what they wanted that thing for? I assume it was some item an inventor made, but Cark seemed pretty focused on it. Do they have some kind of artifact to suppress?"

She said, "No idea. Probably, though. Maybe something with a backlash? Anyway, the money they're spending is insane. I hope that hasn't set the standard for pricing. It's still so early."

I reached out to take her hand in mine and squeeze. I felt the same, but I doubted that last point. They'd bid high because they'd needed that for something. No one was going to overpay for an item they didn't need because someone else had bought something pricey earlier.

And I was vindicated in that assumption about twenty minutes later when the next item sold, a gourd that could apparently refine and concentrate poison. There were a fair few bids, especially from Slime Hall, but in the end, the thing sold for two F-ranked chits. The starting point seemed much more important to the final price than what had gone before, and we were relieved.

After the gourd was a pair of bracers that could create powerful shields, and an arm in a box that made me extremely wary to look at. The arm was, as far as I could tell, F-ranked, but it had some sort of additional aspect that made it scary, because I'd seen F-rankers before but never felt that particular vibe. The bracers sold for eight F-ranked chits, and the arm for a whopping five E-ranked chits to someone I was positive was from a necromantic force, though possibly not the Darkling Institute.

When the next item was brought out, it stirred up quite a bit of interest. The small black box was woven from metal and densely Enchanted, and when Selwyn opened it, every person in the auction hall went silent. "Now, this," said Selwyn gleefully, "is one of the most valuable items we have available. A runic core. Made from a specially treated, naturally forming ice rune. By ingesting the core, you can mutate your natural ability to contain an ice attribute. Much like that gauntlet, this was donated by our friends at Final Frost Heaven."

Sydney and Megan both flinched at the name, and I leaned over to ask as the bidding started. None of my crew needed ice powers, besides which the bidding had started at an E-ranked chit, so we had no fucking possibility of winning it.

"Who or what is Final Frost Heaven?" I asked. They sounded kind of scary, and if they had someone here we'd have to fight, I wanted to know more about them.

Megan looked around warily. "C-rank force. Not just one C-ranker, either. They have six Frost Lords, all in the C-rank. They're one of the top forces in the system, and even at the cluster level they aren't pushovers. There's no way at least one of their competitors isn't a Master Candidate. I hope I don't run into them in the tournament. We don't have any counters for things like that."

I tried to imagine how powerful someone would have to be for that kind of reaction, but couldn't really place it. They were clearly on a level I couldn't even hope to see on Callus.

Still, people were excited about the runic core. I could understand why, too. If I had a normal ability, I might have been tempted. "Ice wishes" probably wouldn't be useful, though. And even if they were, I didn't want to risk losing my three times modifier by changing my power.

Callie probably could have benefited from the core, but I didn't have nearly enough to compete for it. Which was why I couldn't fight back a grin as one of the quadruplets placidly bid eight E-ranked chits for the thing. Apparently Alexander was looking out for his niece even when he wasn't around. He must have given them a decent nest egg.

The bidding kept increasing, but despite passing ten E-ranked chits, they didn't jump to D-ranked. Abel had mentioned D-ranked chits were qualitatively different, much like D-ranked people, and said there probably wasn't even one on the whole planet. I wondered if it had a one hundred- or even one thousand-to-one conversion rate from E-ranked, and resolved to ask.

The core didn't go to the quadruplets, sadly. They ran out of money. It sold for eighty E-ranked chits, an absolutely monstrous amount, to someone from the Twilight Order.

"Alright, my friends," said Selwyn. "This last lot marks the halfway point of the auction, and its conclusion will see us enter a brief intermission where you might move around and speak to other participants."

Everyone seemed happy about that, but Selwyn paid them no mind. "Now," he said, raising his voice, "may I introduce our next item for bid: a summoning whistle, capable of calling an F-ranked Nether Butterfly that can be ridden by the summoner!" He flipped open the box to reveal an intricate purple crystal whistle sitting delicately on a black silk bed and nearly glowing in the soft light of the auction hall.

A hush fell across the crowd, and I couldn't help but stare myself. This thing was definitely F-ranked, and high in the F-ranks too. I wondered how the hell it even worked. Was there a spatial Enchantment on it that brought the mount from somewhere else? Did it create the thing through Fantasy? Did an Enchantment somehow store it inside the whistle? However it functioned, it was apparently just as interesting to everyone else as it was to me, because not a single person could take their eyes off of it.

Not that it mattered. Selwyn's continued, his voice quiet. "We begin the auction at a dozen E-ranked chits."

Before he even finished talking, there was an offer for fifteen, then another for twenty. The number passed a hundred quickly enough, and amazingly rose into D-ranked chits. I guessed that answered one question. I could only assume chits at the Master level had some other requirement making them harder to produce, since they were a hundred-to-one instead of ten.

Sure enough, just like Abel said, none of the local forces could place a bet once it passed that point. Slime Hall, Spear Legion, the Twilight Order— they all offered multiple D-ranked chits before the thing finally sold at a price of twelve. Which was more money than I had ever seen in my entire life so far. Considering how much effort it took us to scrape together a single E-ranked chit, I could only hope a blank Skill Crystal would be too small-potatoes for these monsters to bid on, or else we might not get anything.

As the winners of the whistle, Final Frost Heaven, sent a low F-ranker up to retrieve it, we stood up and rushed over to talk to Cark. He saw us coming and grinned, waving us over. "Hey, guys," he said as we got within range. "Fancy meeting you here. Didn't realize you were coming to this thing."

"Yeah," I said guiltily. "Guess we didn't actually check in during our little trip. We could have coordinated or something. Seems like you're doing okay, though. Congrats on your… cold glove." I said that last bit with a slightly teasing tone.

"Oh, bite me. I have my uses for it. But it's good to see you guys. Cass has been missing you like crazy, especially Agria and the wolves. She spends time with Zeke, but he isn't exactly the most social person."

We joked around for a minute, and I let myself relax a bit as I considered that I might have been silly about this whole thing. There was nothing to worry about. This auction had gone perfectly fine...

Until I realized something. The Darkling Institute hadn't placed a single bid. Not even on the arm. Where the hell were they? They were supposed to be heavily involved in this auction.

Which was, of course, when the lights went out. And the screaming started.

Chapter Seventy

THE FIRST THING that went through my head as I tried to catch sight of *anything* in the darkness around us was "why are there no *windows* in this building?" It was pitch black in the auction house, and not even my Perception was helping. Which... on second thought, seemed wrong. How was it possible nothing in here was giving off the slightest bit of light? Considering how much random Ascendant shit tended to glow, there was no feasible way someone managed to shut off *all* the lights through normal means.

Which meant someone had used abnormal means. Probably some kind of darkness artifact or ability.

"Everybody *shut up!*" Bellowed a powerful voice. Specifically, a powerful voice nearby. Abel. Shockingly, everyone did. "Alright, now, I am almost positive we are currently under attack. So why doesn't whatever wiseass did this speak up and turn the damn lights back on, since you probably have us all surrounded at this point anyway."

There was a soft click, which took me a second to place as someone clicking their tongue, before the lights came back on to reveal... corpses. Kind of.

Some of them were pure meat, some had metal parts, and interspersed in between them were figures in dark clothes holding wicked-looking weapons. From among the corpses stepped, of course, Mordaunt.

"Did you have to ruin my fun?" She pouted. "I was enjoying the panic. Oh well, pleasure is over, time for business, I suppose. Oh, Solomon?" she singsonged, eyes scanning over the crowd. "Where are you?"

Apparently she'd momentarily lost track of me when I moved to talk to Cark. I didn't know why that made me feel better, but it really did.

When her eyes landed on me her smug grin grew even wider. "There you are!" Without looking away, she turned her head slightly and called out. "I found him, Your Excellency." As she spoke, she stepped obsequiously to the side, then took a sweeping wide bow as literally the smarmiest looking human being I had ever seen walked out of the crowd.

I'd seen people with faces I'd wanted to punch before. In fact, it was becoming increasingly common as I went higher up the ranks. This guy, though, this guy took obnoxious to an almost conceptual level. Just standing there I wanted to punch him. I wouldn't have been shocked if he was a Master Candidate in the Pissing People Off Skill. When his amethyst eyes stopped on me, his thin lips quirked into a sneer and I realized that somehow, the effect got *worse*.

The pale, almost emaciated teenager with the greasy black hair strode out among the corpses with the air of someone who was positive he was better than everyone in the room. Now clear of the crowd, he stopped about halfway to me. "Well," he said in an oily voice. "If it isn't the little pissant who killed one of my Heartrippers."

I froze. That was... actually not bad. If he was here about that, he didn't know about my mom. Apparently Aiden really had died before reporting in. Still, he said "*my* Heartrippers," which meant not only was this guy from the Black Sorrow Cult, he was high up in their pecking order. I wasn't sure if the cult had some kind of royal family, but I suspected there were descendants of Black Sorrow herself among the upper echelons, with an inherited ability every bit as broken as mine. I just really hoped this guy wasn't one of those.

On the upside, if he had been I doubted he would be here. As far as I knew, the Cult wasn't like the WCP, which dispersed its upper-echelon kids to grind up their power on their own. The five factions were much more insular, and chances were good any real descendant of Black Sorrow with the corresponding power wouldn't touch a shitty backwater like Callus with a ten-million-foot pole.

Still, judging by how cocky this guy was, he was probably someone important, and I wasn't thrilled at having to deal with him. Which didn't affect how I responded at all.

"Nah, that guy isn't here. I heard he went home to hide in his shower because he heard you were coming. I assume based on how greasy your hair is that you don't know what one of those looks like?"

The smarmy dick's mouth fell open, and his teeth clicked shut as he growled. "Peasant, what did you just say to me?"

He was thankfully only G-ranked, so I wasn't too worried about him crushing me, but then again, I'd already seen proof that there were many different levels of G-ranker. It was probably better to shut up at this point.

My mouth, unfortunately, did not get that memo. "Oh, I'm sorry, are your ears clogged with grease? I said you look like an oily dirtball who never bathes. Is your ability some kind of filth embodiment? Maybe you wrap yourself in a protective layer of grime? Or are you just trying to make yourself so disgusting your enemies won't hit you?"

Smarmy started laughing, but based on his eyes, he wasn't amused, he was so fucking furious he didn't know how to process it. "Wow, so some jumped-up little space peasant thinks he can talk down to me? Do you know who I am, boy?"

I could see his hands clenching and unclenching, but he didn't actually attack. He probably suspected I was baiting him into launching an attack on me so I could counter. Joke was on him, I didn't have a plan. I just really didn't like him and wanted to piss him off.

On the upside, I was now ninety percent sure he wasn't a descendant of a god. There was no way anyone with a power on the level of mine that wasn't support-based would have hesitated to attack me. Still, that left plenty of room for other inherited powers. There was no way a force on the level of the Black Sorrow Cult didn't have more than a few S-rankers, and probably not just those that were descended from their goddess.

"Let me guess," I said scathingly. "Your mommy or daddy told you that you were a very special boy, way more special than all the other kids." I wasn't scared of anyone who wasn't another member of a god clan, or possibly one of those freaks able to reach mastery at G-rank. Considering I'd have been swatted like a fly if that had been the case, there was no reason to worry, army or not.

The sneer grew more pronounced. "My name," he said with derision, "is Pietro Verralan. My father is Sellfren Verralan, a High Priest of the Black Sorrow Cult."

I blinked. That actually was kind of impressive. If the Cult used the same Job rankings as the church, that meant his dad was a D-ranker, and had already reached Mastery, possibly even Grandmastery.

But I still didn't care. My parents were A-rankers, and my uncle was at B-rank. Not to mention my S-ranked grandpa, and my ancestor the god. If we were having a "whose family members are scariest" competition I was going to win. It also made me aware that this guy definitely didn't know who I was, or he wouldn't have bothered with the flex.

"So, what, you found out I killed Aiden and decided to come to this backwater to kill me?"

Pietro laughed derisively (I wasn't entirely sure he could do things any other way, he seemed to just be naturally dickish). "Fool. I came for the tournament. I'm simply taking care of some business while I'm here. If you're waiting for reinforcements, by the way, don't. My own entourage of E-rankers are holding back the others, and all these corpses are G-ranked, just to prevent the detection Enchantments from picking them up."

"You... you're doing all this because I killed some random-ass cult member? That's insane. You're declaring war on the WCP, literally invading sovereign territory. You'll drag the whole Cult into it." There was no way anyone was actually this petty.

"Hardly." He snorted. "As long as things don't escalate beyond the level of this planet, the Unity and the Wish Curse Palace won't make trouble. These kinds of squabbles on a D-ranked planet are far beneath the notice of the true powers of the universe. At worst, the Unity will demand I kill some of the E-rankers who participated, and they're expendable anyway."

I suspected he was underestimating how much he was biting off, but I had zero hope of convincing him of that. At least he hadn't brought any F-rankers. Or many of them. I could only assume whatever means the WCP had of detecting them were too nebulous for him to be sure he wouldn't trip the security. Oh well. I slid out my cane, spinning it up between my fingers as I imbued it with poison fire.

"I'll teach you that the Black Sorrow Cult's prestige is not to be challenged." Pietro grinned, his eyes beginning to fill with black mist. His allies moved into place.

I was annoyed. This asshole just stumbled on me by accident, and I was probably going to have to kill him. If the Cult wasn't after me hard before, they would be this time, and all because some smarmy stuck-up prick wanted to get bragging rights while he was out on a trip.

Despite his old man only being D-rank, he might still have an inherited ability from an S-rank grandpa or something. No one would be this cocky based on nothing but rep. Still, D-ranker or not, I had the protection of the WCP when it came to anyone E-rank or above. At G-rank, I was confident not even these weird science experiments could stop Callie and I, so what was there to be afraid of?

It was weird that I was so easily considering killing this guy. I'd killed people before, of course, but it had been a hard thing to come to terms with. I wasn't some bloodthirsty psycho who just murdered anyone who pissed me off.

It took me a bit to pin down why the idea didn't bother me, but I finally landed on the fact that this guy was an embodiment of the Black Sorrow Cult itself to me. I'd seen them do terrible things to people for no reason. Sacrifice innocents for power just because. And I'd subconsciously started to hate them for it.

You could tell me that cultivation was brutal, that people trying to gain power was normal, that recursion was partly to blame, but I didn't care about any of that. I didn't even care right now about trying to be more heroic. I just hated them. Maybe not all of them, there were trillions of people in the Cult. But this guy personified the worst traits of that place, and thinking back to poor little Cass, who was still recovering from the things they did to her head, I wanted him to die.

I looked over at Callie. "I want to kill him." I didn't mince words or beat around the bush. I just came out and said it. She would agree or not, and if she didn't, I'd let it go. She was the leader, and her morality was more developed than mine anyway. I wasn't willing to fuck up my relationship for this idiot no matter how much of an asshole he was.

To my surprise, she just grinned. "Better get to work, then."

She looked at Abel and Lament. "He has a pair of early F-rank guards with him. Can the two of you take them on?"

That wasn't a shock. Since his old man doted on him enough to arrange for him to cross to another star cluster and fight for a chance to get into this dungeon, he was probably under serious protection. Not just F-rankers, the E-rankers he mentioned were probably his guards too. Luckily we didn't have to deal with them.

Sure enough, two guys stepped out from behind him, emerging from the crowd. F-rank. Callie had noticed then before I had. Her Perception was better. Scary or not, I had to admit, this was definitely going to be an exciting fight.

Chapter Seventy-One

I'D EXPECTED anger when I announced that I wanted to kill Pietro, but oddly, he just seemed shocked. "You... you dare?"

It was like the idea that I was willing to kill him was some kind of alien concept to him.

I was suddenly really glad my old man had sent me off to grow up a normal person instead of raising me in the clan. This was obviously what happened when you gave someone an unlimited amount of leeway and protection.

"Yeah," I said bluntly. "I literally just said that." I looked around at all the people attending the auction. "Anyone else down for a battle? I somehow doubt that Petey here is going to let everyone spectate from the side. Might as well join up with our side so you can get some support."

This was mostly aimed at Macgregor and the other outsiders. They were the ones likely to make the most difference. Sydney and Megan both looked ready to fight, as did the Spear Legion group, so that was hardly an issue. The quadruplets wouldn't let Callie be hurt, but if we could get support from the other factions, like Slime Hall and the Twilight Order, we would certainly come out of this ahead, even if we had to bleed for it.

Looking closer, I saw several F-rankers among the enemy. Not corpses, since they had to bring those in all at once and didn't want trip the restrictions, but a few people who had most likely come as guests to hide themselves among the attendees and wait for this exact moment.

Glaring around at our side, Pietro snapped, "Trash, can your forces even withstand the anger of the Black Sorrow Cult? Don't get involved beyond your means. I could see all of your factions razed to the ground, so just shut up and sit there while I deal with this peasant."

Mordaunt was looking almost embarrassed to be working with someone this stupid, which was fair because I would be too. Our allies didn't seem to notice how dumb he was, though, because they actually looked nervous.

Callie spoke up to reassure them. "Friends, there's no need to worry. This is an isolated attack by a moron. If the Black Sorrow Cult could just charge into other people's territory and slaughter whoever they wanted, they would own the whole universe."

I nodded. "Honestly I doubt this is going to be ignored as completely as he thinks it is. I wouldn't be surprised if Petey's daddy ends up having to pay off some price on his head to keep the Unity from hiring professional killers to take him out." Of course, the fact that the Cult were the ones people usually paid for that would probably help. Still, Pietro looked flabbergasted at the idea.

"You all should die!" he roared. "This is unacceptable! To think I would be forced to endure such disrespect. Kill them all!"

Well, that solved the whole "convincing everyone to help" dilemma. Revenant, keeping this idiot alive must be a full-time job.

Regardless, he *was* in charge of the enemy forces, as evidenced by the tide of the bastards that rushed toward us at his howl. Guess the battle was on.

Callie appeared at my side without either of us needing to say anything, and we both swept forward to meet the oncoming tide. Despite his arrogance and stupidity, Pietro *did* attack personally, though I didn't get to fight him as soon as I'd have liked because he wasn't very fast and one of the corpses got to me first.

I decided to test out their defenses and see what the Darkling Institute could do, so Callie and I engaged with a pair of the things directly. I kind of expected the quadruplets to stop us, but they just fanned out nearby, taking care to keep any F-rankers off us as we fought. Probably instructed not to hinder our growth too much.

The first two monsters we came up against were strange, and very different from each other. One was short and fat, with orange flesh shot through with thick streaks of metal. The metal bits had spikes on them, and each spike gleamed with a toxic-looking green substance. I took that one because my armor had more coverage, while Callie took the tall pale-blue one with the beefy frame and the glowing sharp fingernails.

I noticed as I engaged Orangey that the corpses weren't *exactly* a combination of science and necromancy. More like zombies with scientific parts added in. Some of the parts looked more integrated than others, but they struck me as being more like Benny than anything else. That didn't stop them from being dangerous, and as my poison fire enhanced cane landed on the Orangey, I grimaced at the lack of obvious effect.

My first blow smashed into the zombie's side, driving it back a few steps, but not damaging the orange flesh much. It triggered a berserk charge from the monster, who planted his hands and kicked up his feet in a sort of failed handstand that let him back-flop on the ground in my direction. I activated Double Trouble, appearing behind him and attacking his exposed face as his body passed through my illusionary double.

Which didn't have as much effect as I'd have liked. I used Mercy Kill on the strike, and even dumped in a triple-strength density-shifted blow, and while I felt a crack as the facial bones shattered and saw the poison fire seep into the broken flesh, it didn't do much to actually slow the monster down.

Unfortunately I didn't have time to worry about that as I got a sense of impending danger and rolled to the side as laser nails flashed forward to carve me up. As they did, Orangey rolled the other way in a whirling spin that was much more graceful than I'd expected him to manage and attacked Callie, the two of them seamlessly switching targets… or trying to, at least.

Sadly for them, they were showing off in front of an expert. Callie took the short reprieve as an opportunity to create a few clones, and I grinned under my mask as I felt her slip away. The orange one attacked a clone, only to crash right through it as Callie appeared behind Laser-Nails, condensing a drill of shadows aimed right at his spine. I triggered the triple-stack density-shift attack combined with a spider leg attack to intercept the thing's claws.

The pair of golden spider legs smashed into the wrists of the monster as Callie speared him through the back of the neck, where the brain stem would be. Heart blows weren't much good on undead, so she aimed for the spot where the spine met the brain to do the most damage.

Laser-Nails dropped like a rock, and we both turned in time for Callie to intercept Orangey, who wasn't doing great, as his head was slowly being consumed by venomous flame. The damage from the initial strike hadn't been much, but over time, it had seeped in and seemed to be driving the thing crazy. As the monster's blow was swatted off by Callie, I triggered a Sucking Mud and a shadow attack, creating mud tentacles that snagged the rabid monster and dragged it under.

With that out of the way, I turned to look for the next target, only to get a feeling of danger just in time to dive out of the path of a bandaged fist that would have easily crushed my skull if it had landed.

Looking up, I saw Rahm staring down at me coldly, the silent behemoth positioned right next to his mistress. Mordaunt looked annoyed. "Damn. I thought that would get you. You're much more annoying than a G-ranker from a backwater like this should be. Your freak of a teammate I get, he's a Master Candidate, but can you just hurry up and die already so I can get paid?"

Looking back, I saw that fully six of the damn F-rankers had engaged the quadruplets, drawing them off and away from us, leaving us free to attack. The only saving grace was that Pietro appeared to have been waylaid by Megan and Sydney, with Riley playing support as Lament and Abel took on the guards. Mel was showering the corpses with fire, to minimal success, so we were on our own here.

That was fine. I didn't believe we couldn't beat the Darkling Institute monster maker. She wasn't Lament or Abel. Just a crafter with a scary bodyguard.

I climbed to my feet, taking up a spot next to Callie. "Well," I said pleasantly. "That answers the 'why' question. Thanks, that saves me an annoying conversation. Also a lot of wondering after we crush you both."

Mordaunt snickered. "Confident, aren't you? No idea why. Rahm could take you both alone. With me here, you have no chance." With a snap of her fingers, she materialized a pair of wicked looking black daggers. The metallic portions were straight and thin like needles, and the hilts were clear glass, full of a sickly glowing green liquid. Along the length of them were measurement lines, like they were a pair of really dramatic syringes.

In the distance, I heard a roar, and then a crash, as Randall the bear came plowing through a wall of corpses and slapped Rahm away like a wrecking ball. Jessie was sitting on his back, with Benny following behind her and carrying a huge hammer that I was pretty sure he had just randomly stolen from one of the auction lots. There was a lot of sickly green blood on the head, though, showing that he'd been crushing corpses with it.

Mordaunt glared as she walked over to kick at Rahm. "Oh, get up!" she hissed. "You'll be fine."

The man groaned, rising to his feet. Some of the bandages fell away from his face, revealing a pale blue visage covered in stitches and traceries of circuits. She reached up to check him over, not in concern, but more like she was checking her car engine to make sure it still worked.

Jessie cheered. "Whoo!" she bellowed. "Did you see that? He just went flying. Bear to the face! Hey Clockwork, did you see what Randall just did? You can only crush their heads with that stupid hammer, my big buddy is a corpse-killing machine!"

I grinned at her. Jessie was a sweet girl, but she could be scary when she considered you an enemy. Zombies and kidnappers weren't people she would worry too much about. Especially zombies. We'd killed tons of undead.

Benny sighed loudly. "Yes, Agria, I know. Still, this thing is pretty useful. F-ranked Mass Impact Hammer. I wonder if they'll let me keep this when we're done? Probably not, I guess. Shame. No wonder Beat and Sever were so overpowered. Seriously, using an F-ranked weapon is like playing on easy mode." Despite his cheerful tone, he was talking more softly than usual. I was guessing the soul weight of an item like that wasn't light, though the belt was probably helping. Especially if he was using his triple-strength density-shifted attack pretty often.

Mordaunt glared up at them. "Oh, what fresh hell is this? Can't a girl commit murder in peace anymore? You know what, *fine.*" She whistled, and another five or six corpses surrounded us, as well as a single F-ranker who had come from opposite of where the quadruplets were holding down the fort. "No more messing around. Every single one of you is going to die if that's what it takes. I'm *getting* paid."

Rahm began to unwind his bandages, and as he did, I felt his power spiking. Not just his power. His conceptual weight.

As we watched, the big zombie officially broke through to F-rank.

Huh. Well, that was one way to hide from detection. I hadn't considered that. This... could be a problem.

Chapter Seventy-Two

IT WAS HARD NOT to panic as the pair of F-rankers rushed us. Rahm was only newly ranked up, but he was already clearly powerful. I doubted he could now counter Randall, who was a veteran F-ranked beast, but the newcomer would probably end up doing the heavy lifting there.

Which left engaging with the new F-ranker to me and Callie. There was no way we could leave him to Benny, even with that hammer on hand. He could probably help us out as support, but my best friend was still early in the G-ranks, and there was no way I'd let him engage someone like Rahm head-on.

I didn't even need to gesture to bring Callie on board. Our bond made it much easier for us to communicate mid-battle. As the other F-ranker (a tall, thin man with blue skin and three red eyes) was attacked by Randall, the two of us flashed forward to launch simultaneous attacks at Rahm. Having just advanced, the big man was still unsteady. I knew how much rank ups took out of you from experience, but he hadn't made a sound during the process.

Still, as I flicked out a blow at his exposed face, Callie spun out and attacked his ankles with a pair of bladed snowflakes large enough to slide her fingers into the gaps like handholds. Despite not being able to make anything near strong enough to hurt an F-ranker with her shadows, Callie wasn't a rookie. She'd honed the edges of those things so sharp that they could cut through G-ranked steel.

As my blow landed on Rahm's head, hers hit his ankles and shattered, though I saw a small hint of greenish blood ooze from the wound. With those attacks opening his defenses, we switched, our Paired Dueling and Balam Skills both allowing us to move flawlessly as I swung at the same ankle while she attacked his face. My poison fire had done a bit of damage but nothing spectacular, having barely moved past the single point of impact due to his newfound conceptual weight.

Poison fire was meant to be a debuff that I stacked until it began whittling away at a person. I could overpower it for a quick drop, but against an F-ranker, it would barely even stick… normally.

As Rahm snarled, reaching up to bat away the black snowflake blades reforming in Callie's hands before they could cut his face, I drove my cane's head into the ankle Callie had cut.

The open wound let me drive the poison flame deeper than I could have managed, and the stacking of Mercy Kill and the triple-strength density-shifting attack, despite a bit of strain, let me land the blow hard enough to stagger the big bastard. There was a sharp crack, not a particularly large one, but one that told me I'd at least cracked the bone, which meant the poison fire would be seeping into it.

Which was enough to put him off-balance as Benny smashed that giant fucking hammer into the back of his skull, his blow layered with a triple-strength density-shifted attack.

A loud bang echoed as Rahm stumbled forward, his damaged ankle rolling and his skull cracking under the impact of the hammer as he was thrown sprawling. I would have celebrated, but this whole exchange had taken several seconds, and Mordaunt had circled around to try to backstab Callie, not even noting her companions' troubles as she waited for the moment to attack.

Unfortunately for her, trying to sneak-attack someone with a Stealth Skill like Callie's wouldn't be easy, especially not when we were in proximity and could alert each other to the danger. I lashed out with my own cane to counter the daggers, Callie moving seamlessly from the path of the strike without me needing to actually warn her it was coming. The pair of daggers sparked a sickly green light as I deflected, and I saw flares of power as whatever was in them burned up on contact with my poison fire.

The daggers would be dangerous. I wasn't worried though. Callie and I were perfectly in sync, and despite Mordaunt easily dodging the heavy swing from Benny, she was forced to back off as the two of us launched a flurry of attacks. I could feel my bond with Callie becoming stronger, our experience in live battle helping us hone this Skill in a way training never could have.

We had the foundation. Every exercise, every bit of training, all to prepare us for this. It was why we'd done everything as we had. Not just to let us unlock the Skill fast, but to prepare us to rush it up to Lesser. I could feel things clicking, little aspects of our training becoming more understandable. It wasn't enough to break through yet, but it would be. We could get there.

Sadly, we didn't have the luxury of time. Rahm was rising now, unsteady but clearly enraged. I wasn't sure what the fuck that hammer was, but I absolutely did not ever want to get hit by it. Any blow that scrambled the brain of an F-ranked abomination made from undead flesh and science with one blow, augmented or not, wasn't the kind of thing a normal person could shrug off. I didn't think my armor would even protect me, though my mask might do the job.

We rushed at the big undead, not wanting to give him time to recover, and I activated Double Trouble. Appearing behind him, I doubled up Mercy Kill and another triple density stack on the back of his cracked skull, the poison fire seeping through into his head. He roared and whirled on me, but luckily Impact makes you tougher and not faster, so I could dodge the attack.

I cursed as I looked around. We had no help incoming, Mordaunt was waiting to pounce and cut us down, and we were probably going to lose this if I kept going as I was. I had a Skill that would help me bridge the gap, but I couldn't use it. Afterburner wasn't a smart choice in a battle this size. I'd need to stack my magma leg and hope it would be enough, because I couldn't be weakened with this many enemies still coming for us.

Slipping back, I readied my cane, letting Callie clash with Rahm as I deterred Mordaunt. Seeing me waiting, she didn't seem willing to put herself in danger, opting to hang back and wait for the right time to strike.

I pressed my foot to the ground, the contact enough for me to trigger Stone Limb after all the training I'd been doing. My soul strength could handle pushing the Skill that much, allowing me to use the touch of my boots instead of bare skin.

Then I felt my leg toughen, my boot and armor doing the same with a bit of soul strain, and triggered my other Skills in succession. Mercy Kill, Touch of Tears, triple-strength density shift, I even shoved a fire attack into the limb to enhance the magma's power, and almost fell over from all the pain. Almost. I could force my way past it after a moment of clearing my head.

Before Rahm and Mordaunt could react, I activated Double Trouble. I'd had Callie position Rahm so he was blocking my new location from Mordaunt as I appeared, and since Double Trouble left an illusion, it gave me time to use Balam to its fullest and strike out with a brutal spinning kick to the back of his head, the most damaged area on his body.

The F-ranked hammer had seriously hurt him, cracking his skull and tearing open flesh, and since it was the same rank as he was, he wasn't healing very quickly. Keeping my leg close to my body as I spun, I let it whip out along the axis of my rotation as it came around, putting every ounce of Might and Precision behind the blow as I smashed it into the injured back of Rahm's head.

At the peak of G-rank, and with every possible stacked modifier on my leg to boost it, the blow, combined with his injured state, drove an explosion of poison flames directly into his head like a fucking mortar shell. Adding the fire attack made it burst out on contact, and the combined power of every bit of extra energy I had lit Rahm's head up like a fucking green torch. F-rank or not, the brain is the most delicate part of the body, and a toxic frag grenade going off inside your skull after something cracks it open should overwhelm just about anyone.

Rahm threw his head back and *roared*, his F-rank body so strong that even that hadn't been enough to finish him instantly. I saw the metal from the chains climbing up his limbs under the damaged bandages, his ability activating, but too late.

Rahm's eyes and mouth poured out green fire as he screamed, his body shaking before he fell over with a crash. Fucking miraculously, he *still* wasn't dead. Which I honestly wasn't super upset about. Rahm hadn't been as actively malicious as Mordaunt. I grimaced at how terrifying Abel was. Granted my stats were all pretty low because they were so diffuse, but the difference was pretty clear.

Turning from the not dead, but definitely unconscious for a while enemy (his brain was currently poisoned and on fire, for the gods' sake), I spun on Mordaunt, whose eyes were gaping. Sadly, the shock wasn't enough to distract her from Callie's attack behind her. She dodged sideways, lashing out with her daggers at my shadow-covered girlfriend, who looked just like the clone she'd left to keep the monster maker's attention.

The daggers were scary, but Callie was no amateur, and we were wearing F-ranked armor. I suspected my sneak attack on Rahm had worked partly because of that. But I couldn't manage another attack on that level, and actually needed to let the magma leg go so my pounding head could recover. The soul weight I'd used so far was almost too much for me to bear and still be mobile.

I nearly jumped as I felt a hand on my shoulder, and then a wash of soothing coolness flooded my head. I turned to see Benny, eyes closed in concentration, somehow managing to push the energy from his spiritual calming belt into me to help me recover. Considering it was a part of him after integration and he'd learned to spread his other abilities around his body, it was feasible, but I could tell from the grunt of pain as he steadied himself it wasn't easy.

I let the coolness flood me and calm down as Callie kicked the living shit out of Mordaunt. While the other woman had clearly been trained and possibly even augmented herself based on the battle, Callie had nearly two hundred Might, and Mordaunt was a crafter. Focus had to be her main stat, so she wasn't equipped for direct confrontation.

She tried to escape, eyes wide with terror as she glanced down at her bodyguard, who was obviously still out of commission, even as his vitality and undead nature battled the poison fire. Even after that faded, I was betting it would take a while to recover.

Sadly for Mordaunt, there was no escape, and Callie beat her into submission with brutal efficiency, smashing every limb to make sure she didn't escape. Once that was done, she created a braided rope of shadows and tied the woman up, then turned to come check on me.

My soul was *way* overstressed, and I wouldn't be able to modify any Skills or anything, but Benny's calming belt had cleared my head enough that normal attacks and movements were fine. I gave him a grateful nod and stepped forward to meet Callie. She smiled at me, and as Randall and the other F-ranker battled in the background, we turned to meet Pietro as he finally made it to us.

Chapter Seventy-Three

PIETRO'S FACE still *really* pissed me off. Sadly, I was also still incredibly drained, and without access to my soul strength, my options for dealing with him were limited. Still, I'd just beaten my first F-ranker, having successfully fought up ranks like a true elite, and I was riding high on the confidence.

Glancing dismissively down at the tied-up Mordaunt and the still form of Rahm, Pietro sneered. "Trash. Oh, well, I suppose this means I don't have to pay them." He looked around for the quadruplets, who were still occupied, and Randall, who was fighting his own F-ranker, and chuckled. "Seems like you don't have anyone to save you this time. You were impressive taking down the zombie, I'll give you that, but there's no way you have much in you after a battle like that."

I stared at him for a second. "How are you not dead?" He looked at me in surprise. "No, seriously, I've known you for all of five minutes and I want to kill you. Granted, I have a bias against the Black Sorrow Cult, but still. Do you have a Skill for pissing people off? I'm not sure how your guards have managed to keep you alive, but they're fucking miracle workers, because I have a hard time believing no one has tried to push you down a flight of stairs. Or into a volcano."

Rather than get offended, Pietro laughed. "Do they dare? My father is the strongest D-ranker on Ranton. A genuine High Priest of the Black Sorrow

Cult. I hold the life and death of everyone I meet in my hands. Killing me would result in the complete extermination of everyone they know and love." He grinned at Callie. "How about you, boy? Are you willing to see everyone you love killed? Not just the girl, either. Even if you manage to successfully kill me, your whole family will die."

I couldn't help it, I laughed. He looked confused, and I choked down the giggles. "I'm sorry, I'm sorry, that was rude. You're doing this whole spoiled-brat villain monologue and I'm interrupting. I shouldn't be so insensitive. It's just... you have no clue how stupid you sound."

Honestly I could have interrupted him, but Benny had posted up behind me and placed a subtle hand on my back, letting the spiritual calming flow into me again.

This wouldn't fix the soul strain, not enough to let me use my soul more, but it *would* let me partially recover and ease my headache, which would help.

I wanted to draw the asshole in, make him babble more and delay the fight so I could get back into fighting shape. Callie and I could take him, I was sure, and just in case, I was preparing my Afterburner Skill to make sure I could keep up with her and put my best foot forward.

Without stacking stored attacks or altering techniques, I would be way less deadly, but Afterburner should make up for that somewhat. I also still had a full charge of stored force in the cane, and I could use Mercy Kill, even if I couldn't stack anything on it.

Sadly, Pietro, while stupid, wasn't *that* stupid, and didn't have any interest in monologuing for ten minutes in the middle of a pitched battle.

As he concentrated dark power onto his hands, I had a sudden and very unfortunate realization. I'd been thinking about what ability he had, and how to counter it. But I'd forgotten that fucking Black Sorrow Cultists didn't *use* the ability system. He'd have one for sure, but it would be treated like a Skill. They used the Job system, or something like it, and this asshole would have a whole host of weird powers like Aiden had, though not exactly the same, since Aiden had been using a Job from the Red Revenant Church somehow.

That meant it didn't matter if he wasn't a descendant of Black Sorrow— he'd have crazy overpowered bullshit tricks anyway. Annoying but still manageable.

I spun my cane up, stepping away from Benny's hand begrudgingly, because if this guy was about to attack, I didn't want my friend dragged into it. I gestured for Benny to back off and go help Jessie and Randall with their fight. The bear was having trouble, and a sucker punch with that hammer would help. He left without complaint, most likely planning to slip in a shot on Pietro when he had the chance to hit him without being noticed.

Pietro, for his part, didn't seem to care about my best friend as he slowly advanced on me, gathering dark power into his palms. "You seemed so impressive earlier," he said gleefully. "That'll make putting you down so much sweeter. I'll show you that the Black Sorrow Cult aren't people you can easily offend." Without a second of hesitation, he hurled his hands forward, unleashing a wave of darkness at us.

Or rather, "darkness" might have been the wrong word. Rot, corruption, desolation. None of these was right, exactly. Rot affected living things, as did corruption. Desolation was closer, but still wrong. This wasn't a destructive force exactly. Destruction unmade things, this just changed them. It was like some conceptual blight on the world, altering things to more effectively suit its vision. Sorrow.

As if the world itself was grieving, as if all hope had been lost. Hope of continuance ceased to exist within the wave of darkness. It was, in a word, terrifying.

Callie snarled and flicked a hand, and a wall of shadows flashed out to block the progress of the wave. To my surprise, it actually stopped. You couldn't steal the hope of continuance from darkness, because it was already the absence of light.

Pietro cursed. "Shadow touched. I hate dealing with you. No one told me you had a shadow touched." I sensed that even if they had, he'd have ignored it. I was pretty sure he just did whatever he wanted and let the consequences sort themselves out later.

"Thanks," I said to Callie emphatically. As I stood, I shivered at the thought of that... stuff touching me. "I doubt that would have been pleasant." We were insanely lucky that she could block the attack. I doubted a G-ranked ability would instakill us, and it might not even get through my armor, but the idea of letting it touch me made me want to gag. No wonder the Cult were so unpleasant, if that was the force their Jobs gave them access to.

Still, it did make some sense that even powerful Jobs would have counters. Callie's shadows didn't do so well against the Red Revenant Church's light abilities, but she had a natural advantage against the Cult. That was useful to know. Of course, she wasn't some kind of perfect counter, just at an advantage. That wave had been fairly spread out, and being able to block it was more a factor of Pietro making stupid-ass decisions in battle than Callie having some perfect immunity.

I wasn't letting this chance go either way. I activated Double Trouble, appearing behind him as I triggered Mercy Kill on my weapon, then unleashed the force stored in my cane at the base of his skull, hoping to put him down like I had Stricture all those months ago.

That wasn't to be. There was a dark burst of smoke and a shield appeared behind him, clearly the activation of some defensive item. My blow smashed into it hard, but sadly wasn't enough to even crack the shield. I activated Leaf on the Wind and danced away from the retaliation. His dark fist swept harmlessly through the space I'd just been in. That wide-range attack had taken time to charge up and I wasn't giving him more.

Neither was Callie, as evidenced by the field of dark blades springing up under his feet. The attacks drove him in exactly the right direction to open him up to another blow from my cane at full extension, Balam-style swings allowing me to build up a truly frightening amount of momentum for the attack.

His coat-like robes took the blow easily, and I cursed as I realized they were F-rank defensive items. Rich asshole. I conveniently overlooked that I also had those, because now wasn't the time for rational introspection.

With a grimace, I triggered Afterburner. Technically using my normal Skills did use soul strength, but unmodified and without stacking, they were only mildly annoying. Unfortunately, when spamming multiple Skills one after another, that still added up. I was glad Benny had helped me recover because I wasn't sure I could have managed this in the state I'd been in after beating Rahm.

I had enough in me to use a few normal Skills, and triggered healing burst after a slight delay, followed by Mercy Kill, and then, painfully, Flurry of Blows. My head was screaming again, but it was enough to make me a serious threat as I lashed out with my still-poison fire-imbued cane at the vulnerable face of the wildly dodging Pietro, trying to score a hit with the speed Flurry of Blows granted me. I landed a glancing blow on his jaw and temple, which, since the armor wasn't there, meant the poison fire started to spread.

He got his arms up in front of his face to block the other attacks, not paying enough attention to his surroundings and completely missing that Benny had already sneak-attacked the F-ranker and provided an opening for Randall to start really laying into the man. The hammer smashed hard into the back of the Pietro's robes. While clearly heavily Enchanted for defense, they weren't up to a hit from a weapon at the same rank enhanced with extra density and triple strength, even driven by the power of a G-ranker early in his Ascension.

Pietro stumbled, face slashed open by my shadow blades, and his eyes widened in panic. "Malachai, help!" he shrieked at the top of his lungs. Throwing his arms over his head in fear, he tried to mitigate the damage. Unfortunately that was more than enough as every single person in the auction hall was smashed to the ground by the forcefully exerted Impact of an E-rank Ascendant bearing down on us.

I cursed. "I thought you said your E-rankers were holding off the others," I gritted out through the pressure. I was not at all qualified to fight this asshole, considering he wasn't a cloud of red mist right now. Pressuring me with his aura didn't count as an attack either. If he made a move on Callie or Benny or Jessie I'd have to throw myself in front of the attack or something.

Snarling in rage, Pietro pointed at me mockingly. "Fool! As if I would ever walk about unguarded. While the others were detained, Malachai is my personal guard. He was specially trained to be able to conceal himself even from those of his own rank! Now that you've forced me to make him reveal himself, I'll have to take it out of your hide." He began charging his power again, getting ready.

My eyes widened in alarm. I wasn't sure whether or not this counted. Holding me down like this while his boss killed me. This had to be an attack, right?

Before I could question further, the pressure suddenly vanished, the aura completely cut off. A man appeared behind Pietro in a white half-mask and a hooded black robe. He was looking at me intently, as if curious what had just happened, but he didn't do anything else.

Pietro turned angrily on the man. "Why did you do that? I was about to kill him! Pin him down again!"

Despite his ranting, though, Malachai just stared at me. Seemed like Zeke was already on the move. Something told me I wasn't out of the woods quite yet, though.

Chapter Seventy-Four

MALACHAI HAD me pinned with his gaze, but he looked wary. He also ignored Pietro's whining completely, stepping around the guy to block him from my line of sight. "Might I ask your name?" he said cautiously. His tone confirmed what I'd suspected. Someone had forcibly stopped that pressure earlier. He probably thought it was one of the other E-rankers, but he had to know that whoever it was, they were stronger than him. Of course it could have been a D-ranker who retired here or something, but regardless, he was pretty sure I had some power in my corner.

I just shrugged and said shortly, "Solomon." I wasn't going to say anything. My mother and the Cult were bitter enemies, and if he found out I was a Candidate, he might figure that out. The less I said, the better. Worst case, he flipped and tried to murder me, and Zeke turned him into meat paste.

He seemed frustrated by the answer, which was valid. It wasn't a great one. He also seemed torn. Pietro came here to kill me for killing Aiden. This whole fucking farce was a power trip of his own making. There was no easy out. No option to say "hey man, bygones okay?" because the whole purpose of coming here was for me to die. So if I didn't, then he failed, and Pietro didn't strike me as the kind of person who handled being told no particularly well.

So without the option to bail, it was clear that Malachai wanted a new angle. He took in my condition, which wasn't fucking great because this asshole had me pinned down and I was stuck in my Afterburner state. I'd managed to finally get this one altered, a big step in my path to upgrading DS Mastery. It now multiplied my attacks by only three times instead of five, but worked for ten attacks instead of one. I'd used up one blow just not trying to crush him with Mercy Kill, but I still had nine. Staying in this state wasn't comfortable at all.

The E-ranker gave a mischievous humph, as if just figuring something out, and my stomach sank. "Since we seniors are so much more powerful, it's naturally wrong for us to get involved with your fights. I'm simply worried that Pietro is being ganged up on. That bear and the boy with the hammer, not to mention the girl with the shadow abilities… this is clearly a lopsided fight. Since it's come to a battle to the death, naturally we need to make sure it's fair. One-on-one is how battles between warriors should be handled."

Shit. He'd noticed that Zeke hadn't attacked when he backed off. Figuring out the conditions for my uncle's intervention wasn't hard, but it *was* annoying.

I was impressed he was enough of a brazen asshole to make it sound like I'd been cheating in a fair challenge when his dickhead charge had jumped us with a crowd of fucking zombies. Everyone had stopped fighting now, and were all watching as the guy basically strong-armed me into a one-on-one fight.

But I didn't actually mind that. I didn't like this guy, and Zeke's protection was supposed to ensure I had to fight my own battles without being overwhelmed anyway. This was within the bounds of that.

"Fine," I said curtly. "A one-on-one match, Pietro and I with no interference. But if I win, will you really just let things play out?"

Pietro sneered at the question, and even Malachai looked smug.

"Of course," said the bodyguard in the least convincing voice I'd ever heard. He was clearly convinced I was at the end of my rope and wouldn't be able to win, which wasn't far from true, but I still had tricks. I was buzzing with a healing burst from earlier, and I had nine power attacks with Afterburner.

As a finisher, Afterburner enhanced the complete move, stacks and powerups included. Granted, that wasn't useful to me right now, but was definitely an important trump card. Benny's triple-strength powerups for density shifting and tranq blows worked on those aspects of the attacks rather than the whole attacks and all of their components. Afterburner would, in fact, even triple the power output of one of those triple-strength attacks, resulting in a massive boost on stacked blows like my magma leg. Sadly I was incapable of using any of those yet, but I was sure I could manage something.

Everyone backed off as I faced Pietro, who was grinning from ear to ear. He clearly had an idea of how he'd beat me, and was sure it would work.

Malachai looked at me mockingly. "Well, are you two both ready for this battle?" He must have thought Zeke didn't care about what happened to me as long as Malachai didn't attack personally. He'd blatantly bullied me into this fight with no reaction, so he figured he was safe. Which he was, because of the geass, but still, I was annoyed about it.

I just nodded, and he gave the signal to begin.

My soul had recovered enough that I could probably trigger one or two stored attacks if I pushed it. I would need to be *very* careful, though. I couldn't stack or modify them or I might damage my soul too much for it to heal. That would be bad. Really bad.

Pietro was casually gathering his power again, giving me a cocky smirk. "Well. Now you're alone. You don't look so good. Little unsteady on your feet. Bringing down that corpse take it out of you?" His mocking tone was sugary sweet, as if he was concerned, making it all the more obnoxious. I didn't think his face could get more punchable, but it definitely had. Like... three times more punchable at least.

I started to move, circled around. His attack was wide-range, but it did have a radius. I only needed to dodge it. But he didn't release the damn thing. Just saved it up, waiting for me to slip. It was more patience than I'd have credited him with. I didn't really want to give this asshole any credit for anything, actually, so I decided to just chalk the waiting up to sadism and consider it a bad thing.

After a minute or two (good for me, since it let my head clear a bit more), I figured that too much of a good thing wouldn't help and decided to lure him into using up his attack. I wanted to use Double Trouble, but I knew he'd seen it before. If I used it now, he'd just expect me to pop up behind him. I didn't know if he could deploy that attack close-range, but I didn't want to find out by feeling it go off in my damn face.

So, to hurry it along, I tripped. Not really tripped. I rolled my ankle on purpose and started to fall, letting out a pained cry, and he, of course, pounced like the asshole he was. He hurled the vortex of dark energy right at the spot where I was going to land, clearly planning to detonate it right in my face and kill me outright, at least if that stuff could get through my armor.

Or he would have done that. If I'd been there. It was kind of interesting to see the blast consume the illusion of me as I triggered Double Trouble right before the blast arrived. He clearly couldn't control or turn the thing, and had assumed that since I was vulnerable, I'd be easy pickings. See. Sadism and not patience.

As I appeared behind him, I considered briefly what to do, and then decided I needed a way to deliver fast, brutal attacks. I used the spider legs, feeling them sprout from my back.

My head swam, but it was only one attack without alteration or stacking, so I could handle it. I attacked immediately, using my cane and both spider legs to slash out at the asshole's head with enough force to do serious damage. The black shield appeared again, but as my cane hit, it lit up, and as the two spider legs struck, it began to crack. The Afterburner-enhanced blows were much less effective without my stacking, but they were also completely free of soul weight and could be used multiple times. Six left.

I struck twice more before the shield shattered, and that left his head open as I swung the cane at his temple. I triggered Mercy Kill, still able to use regular Skills easily enough. Pietro shrieked again, pulling his arms in front of him to shield himself.

"Stop!" a voice roared. Malachai dashed out to grab me, not hurting me but restraining me.

Cursing, I glared at him. "You really gonna do this? You know what happens if you interfere, right?" I was fucking incensed. I'd been about to end this, my head was killing me, and I wanted this whole mess to be over. This asshole's cheating bullshit was keeping me from making my friends and girlfriend safer, and I was pretty much fucking done with it. "Do you want to die, asshole? Because if you don't let me go and let me finish this fight, you're going to die. It won't be quick, either."

That was a lie. I had no clue if it would be quick, but I wanted to scare him. I was too angry to be rightfully afraid of being in the hands of a powerful E-ranker who could squish me like a bug.

Malachai snorted in disdain. "If you could do that, you would. I don't think your protector cares what I do as long as I don't interfere too directly. But I don't need to hold you down for Pietro to kill you. After all, you just threatened me. I'm sure your guardian won't mind if I teach you a little lesson. I wonder how you'll protect yourself with both arms broken?"

I wasn't sure if that was legit. Like, I doubted I could just attack any E-ranker and expect Zeke to kill them when they defended themselves. Was threatening him enough to allow him to injure but not kill me? I didn't know. Zeke never talked about the terms of my protection, probably to keep me from abusing them.

As Malachai reached for me slowly, a malicious gleam in his eye, I started to worry that I might have really fucked up.

Which was when my mask jumped off my face and fucking ate him.

Not, like… in one bite, either. It streaked over and latched onto his head, the wood expanding to encase his entire skull.

"What the fuck?" he screamed. "What is this? Boy, get this off of me. I'll kill you!" He reached up to try to tear it off and his hands sunk into the wood, submerging in the grain and being swallowed. His screams grew louder as his arms were pulled in deeper. Then the wood expanded over his shoulders, swallowing and compacting his body at the same time.

We all watched in horrified fascination as his whole body was consumed by the wood, which then fell to the ground with a thunk. By the time it hit the floor, it was back in its normal shape, just a simple wooden mask with no adornments or eyeholes. There was no sound as we all stared at the spot where a fucking E-ranked Ascendant had just died within seconds.

I'd… been wearing that on my face. For months. And apparently it could murder people who tried to hurt me. Which on the one hand was reassuring, since it meant I was safe without Zeke having to interfere directly, and it would probably help keep my identity from being blown, but on the other hand… creepy.

I shook that thought off, turning to Pietro, who suddenly looked very afraid, and shot him a grin. "So… Petey. Where were we? I believe we were in the middle of a duel to the death." I should probably be worried about my face being exposed, but I didn't really have a secret identity anyway, and the mask was freaking me out right now. Besides, I wanted him to see how smug I was. This was going to be fun.

Chapter Seventy-Five

PIETRO DIDN'T APPEAR to have any idea how to handle watching his E-rank bodyguard get eaten by a mask. Which... I mean, that was fair. I wasn't really sure how to process that either. It had been horrifying. Still, I was much more interested in putting down this arrogant little pissant who had brought a whole crew of zombies to wipe out me and my friends just because I put down his child-stealing psycho of an underling.

"Y-you... what do you want to do?" he said shakily as I approached. I admit I was pretty gratified seeing him pale and back up. He cried, "I'm here for the tournament! You can't kill a member of a five-faction alliance team, the Black Sorrow Cult won't let you off!" His words had the ring of something he desperately wanted to believe. An old truth that had turned against him and that he was trying hard to hold onto.

I had a feeling he did this sort of thing often. He was used to throwing his weight around (as if that wasn't obvious), but more than that, he was used to his background saving him when he fucked things up. Now his body-guard was dead, killed seemingly by someone at the same level as him, and the only people he had close enough to help were being obstructed by our forces.

It had taken me a minute to understand how he could possibly be dumb enough to do this. To bring these people down here to try to kill us in a place as dangerous as this one. But then I considered it from another angle.

Given how strong someone pathetic like Pietro could be with a good Job, that E-rank guard had probably been substantially more dangerous than any random fighter from a backwater like Callus. He might have even had some gear at D-rank as an emergency measure.

In the face of a mask created by a B-ranker, it had all been for nothing, and that in itself showed how easily deeper foundations could let someone do whatever they wanted. Without backing from Zeke, I'd have been fucked, and Pietro really could have gotten away with this without even a slap on the wrist. Unfortunately for him, he'd run into someone even more connected than him.

Clicking my tongue, I shook my head. "Sorry to tell you this." I stopped about five or ten feet from him. "But no one cares. This is the WCP, and more importantly, a dark district. Where you came from doesn't matter here. 'Fuck around and find out' is the only rule in this place." I gestured around to all the now uncertain looking zombies, of which there were far fewer than there had been to start. "You got that first part down, now it's time to find out. Tell me, what do you think that's going to be like?"

Pietro was shaking as he stared at me, eyes desperately scanning around for an escape. He was actually strong enough that if he went all out, he might be able to beat me in my current condition, but he was so paralyzed by fear he couldn't seem to even conceptualize fighting back. He wanted to run, but there was nowhere to go. The forces arrayed against his own army of corpses were keeping him penned in.

Before I could mockingly comment on that, I was interrupted by a loud explosion of flames and lightning nearby. I was preparing to be attacked when a muffled voice I didn't recognize called out, "Sorry."

Another voice, this one easily identifiable as Cark's, bellowed, "Gods damn it, which one of your dipshits let Quentin use the Thunderfire Cannon?" I turned to glare at him, and he cleared his throat. "Sorry, Sol!"

He started muttering to Sage. "When I said to give one of them the Thunderfire Cannon, I obviously didn't mean Quentin. He has absolutely no ability to aim at all." He paused, obviously listening to a response I somehow couldn't hear. "I don't know, Lyle? Brent? Allison? Fucking *Wendell?* Literally anyone else."

Turning forcefully and ignoring my friend, I took a deep breath and focused back on Pietro. "Sorry about that," I said with a blank expression.

"Ignore them. You were about to beg for your life. Probably offer me tons of money or some treasures that would be useful for my growth?" I gestured leadingly, letting him pick up where I was going, and his eyes widened with hopeful excitement.

"Y-yes! Of course." His old arrogance started to come back. "Naturally any conditions can be talked about. You're in the better position, so getting some benefits is natural. What kind of resources were you hoping for? Gems? Elixirs? I could just pay you in chits? I'm sure I can find something to satisfy you."

He chattered on for about ten minutes, listing off all the valuable things he could take out and growing more and more agitated by my seeming ambivalence. Honestly some of the stuff sounded pretty good, but I didn't make a sound, didn't even smile. I just waited, and let him go on and on until finally, he couldn't take it anymore.

"*What?*" he screamed frantically. "What do you want? I can get you anything. I'll call my father right away, I'll have him find whatever you need. Just *tell me!*"

I finally smiled at him, but it wasn't reassuring or pleasant. It was cold and brutal. I didn't even need to see myself in a mirror to know how terrible it was. I hadn't thought I had that kind of expression in me. His face went even paler, and he started to back up.

"What do I want?" I asked calmly. "I want lots of things, Pietro. I want those kids to have their childhoods back. I want the headless bodies of the 'puppets' Aiden killed resurrected. I want my friend's sister to be able to sleep without a nightlight on because she's so scared someone will sneak into her room at night and take her away again. Can your father give me any of those things?"

This wasn't a game. This wasn't even cultivation. I enjoyed struggling for resources, fighting, I didn't even take being screwed over to heart most of the time. That was just business. That was life as an Ascendant.

But this? The Heartrippers, Cass, the other kids? That was wrong. It was disgusting, and I'd forced myself to ignore how angry it made me for far too long. If he'd stayed away, I might have kept on burying it. Kept on living in denial. But Pietro had to come out and poke the bear, to pardon a slightly on-the-nose metaphor.

Based on the expression on his face, that was when he finally figured out I was going to kill him. There was nothing he could possibly do to stop it.

He turned and tried to run then, not even looking for a way out, just trying to force his way past everyone, throwing out his hands and releasing explosions of dark power to drive back anyone in his way.

He slammed headfirst into a pitch-black wall of shadow courtesy of Callie. It would have been sad watching him scratching uselessly at it, trying to get away, if I didn't hate him so damn much. As it was, I just found it pathetic.

I walked up to him slowly, and I marveled at the way I felt right now. I'd been pissed before. I'd even been enraged. But this wasn't like that. I was murderous. Literally. I wondered how much of this was recursion, because I was sure this would have terrified me a few months ago. Now it only left me cold.

I raised my cane, with multiple blows still left in Afterburner. I focused, and with soul strength I didn't even know I had, bolstered by the cold fury burning in my gut, I forced the Skill to condense. I layered all those blows together forcing them into a single strike, I used Mercy Kill, I used another of my triple-strength density-shifted attacks, and I *wanted* to use a gravity burst too, but I knew it would be too much.

It was fine though. I had enough power. I whirled the cane around between my fingers, using Balam to build up speed, and then brought it smashing down on the back of Pietro's head like a hammer with every ounce of Might in my body. The dark shield flared, but the blaze of my poison fire and the strength of the attack cracked and then shattered it, the blow continuing down to crash into his head.

Much like my own armor, the robe was F-ranked, but also like mine, it specialized in dispersing cutting and energy attacks. Cloth, even super durable cloth, doesn't do much to stop blunt force. I felt his head cave in under the blow and he slumped to the ground. Maybe not dead yet, but getting there.

The last time I'd killed someone like this, I'd been in battle, and the time before, I'd blacked out right after. I'd never just... murdered someone. Not even someone who deserved it. I felt strange. Empty.

Callie sidled up next to me, slipping under my arm and pulling me against her. I heard the corpses being forced to surrender. The Darkling Institute members who were controlling them weren't idiots. They had no backing and no support. Continuing the fight would just be asking to get got.

As for me, I was just… tired. My head hurt, I felt cold and hollow. I just wanted this to be over. I'd had enough of Doomtown. I wanted to go back up to the Pavilion and spend the next week with my friends. Granting them wishes and doing stupid shit at the circus and spending time with my girlfriend and going on dates and checking on Cass and literally anything except be *here* for even another minute.

Sadly that wasn't an option. We were here for the auction and I wanted to make sure we got something out of it.

We kept Mordaunt and Rahm. I was planning to ransom them for something good. They'd tried to kill us for money, so it was only fair we got paid for kicking their ass. Unfortunately we did *not* get to keep the hammer, and we couldn't justify buying the damn thing, considering it was only useful to one person at a time, so Benny got all sulky about it.

We did manage to get our hands on a blank G-rank Skill Crystal, which was what we'd come here for. I suspected some of the other bidders might have cut us a break as thanks for dealing with Pietro, or else we might not have even won that, but it pretty much cleaned us out.

Once we had it, we unanimously decided to leave. No one was in the mood for the auction anymore. Even Abel and Lament were unhappy, since their opponents had surrendered along with the corpses.

The walk back up to G district was silent as we mulled over everything that had happened in Doomtown. It had been… a lot. We'd fought, bled, thankfully none of us had died, but despite the fact that we had an overwhelming victory, it didn't feel like a win.

I forced myself to snap out of it. We hadn't lost anything. Had gained plenty. We'd made friends, formed alliances, grown stronger.

We were ready.

We would win the tournament, get to the Moonsong Glade, become even stronger and leave Callus to explore the rest of the system, then the cluster, then the whole damn galaxy. Nothing was over. This was only the beginning, and it could have gone a lot worse. So why did I still have this gnawing sensation of dread in my stomach?

About the Author

Malcolm Tent is, in fact, smarter than a fifth grader. He enjoys reading, writing, and spending time with his dogs. He's lycanthrophobic and addicted to Cajun food.

Author website:

About Timeless Wind Publishing

Founded in late 2020 by Lorne Ryburn and Silas Sontag, Timeless Wind Publishing is an up-and-coming indie publishing house. We love sci-fi and fantasy—progression fantasy, power fantasy, LitRPG, time loops, cultivation, system apocalypse—genre fiction of all kinds! We're prolific readers within these genres and endeavor to bring awesome books into the limelight.

We look forward to helping authors (aspiring and published alike) develop and expand an audience of readers who believe in their vision.

Our logo is an exotic cat from a Palmyrene ruin. The word along its back roughly translates to, "Alas!" or "What a shame!" This word is present on all gravestones in Palmyra. It's a recognition that all things come to an end… even the best people and stories. Alas!

We hope our readers will have "alas" moments when they finish our books.

Connect with Timeless Wind Publishing
TimelessWind.com
Facebook.com/timelesswind
Twitter.com/timeless_wind
Instagram.com/timelesswindpub